Desert Shield

Crisis in the Desert Series, Book Two

By

Matt Jackson

&

James Rosone

Copyright Notice

Table of Contents

Chapter 1
Last Call

29 August 1990
Kremlin, Moscow

The Soviet President was not pleased with the outcome of the latest vote at the United Nations. Once again, the Americans and their lackeys on the Security Council and in the General Assembly had managed to outmaneuver them. This latest move was going to make it incredibly difficult for them to continue to support Iraqis' war and the Iranians closure of the Strait as they had.

"So let me get this straight, Eduard. We were able to stop the Americans from getting a binding resolution passed in the Security Council; however, the Americans were able to get a handful of nations to put forward a resolution in the General Assembly condemning the Iraqi military actions on the Arabian Peninsula?"

"Yes, Comrade President," replied Eduard Shevardnadze, the Soviet Foreign Minister. "They are trying to get around our Security Council veto by taking the case directly to the General Assembly."

"Then, in practical terms, what does this mean for us?" asked the President.

"I believe it's a signal from the Americans that they intend to proceed in building what they are calling a 'Coalition of the Willing,'" replied Shevardnadze. "If they cannot get the UN to authorize it, they will simply act of their own accord in conjunction with other sovereign nations. They'll then use this multinational force to fight on behalf of Saudi Arabia and the other Gulf States."

The controversial vote required a two-thirds majority and had been approved by a tight margin, signaling that not everyone at the UN agreed with action—something the Soviets planned on fully using to cause fissures within the global body.

"Yes, Comrade President. The resolution signals America's willingness to commit their forces to military action. It will probably lead to other nations moving forward to join them as well, further complicating the Iraqis' ability to maintain control over the Middle East."

Vladimir Kryuchkov, the head of the KGB, felt he should say something. He cleared his throat. "Comrade President, this is an unfortunate setback. But we can still work around it. It's just going to complicate things."

Mikhail Gorbachev had known the Soviet spymaster long enough to know that when he used the term *unfortunate setback*, it usually meant whatever plan they had concocted was going to fail or need to be concluded sooner than they had planned.

"When the vote was concluded, the American Secretary of State, James Baker, asked to speak with me privately," Shevardnadze interjected. "When we were alone, he told me they knew we had provided Saddam with substantial military aid prior to the war and that we are even now providing them with military aid—aid that is currently being used against their forces in Saudi and Oman." He paused for a moment to pull a folder out of his briefcase and show everyone a series of images likely taken from a high-altitude reconnaissance aircraft.

"He showed me these. They are images of the As Sultan Qaboos Port in Tartus, Syria. These are images of our naval base, as you can see. They have also annotated the cargo vessels being offloaded and their contents being placed on trains and nearby trucks. This image is of several ships waiting to be offloaded."

"What's your point?" Dmitry Yazov, the Minister of Defense, asked.

"This arming and supplying of the Iraqi Army was supposed to have been done in a more secretive manner, not out in the open for everyone to see. It's hard for me to deny what's taking place when they can point to pictures like this," Shevardnadze retorted angrily.

"Then don't deny it. The Soviet Union has had a long-standing relationship with the government of Iraq. As allies, we are providing them requested support. This is no different from the Americans intervening in Saudi. As a matter of fact, we are doing substantially less than the Americans," Yazov countered.

"Listen to me," growled Gorbachev as he stood and glowered at his senior advisors. "I said from the very outset of this operation that our nation was not looking for a direct confrontation with the West. We would provide the Iraqis with state-of-the-art front-line equipment, intelligence, and advisors to help them achieve a swift victory over their neighbors, and by and large they have achieved that. They have a singular pocket of Saudi resistance and American soldiers holed up near Jeddah and Mecca that need to be defeated and then they will have achieved their goals. We," he said, pointing to everyone in the room, "cannot wage an open war against the Americans. As it stands, the Warsaw Pact members are in the process of self-implosion and revolution. The last thing we can afford to have happen is a direct confrontation with the Americans. They have just demonstrated their willingness to wage an all-out war in the Middle East. At this point, we need to figure out what support we can continue to provide the Iraqis without forcing ourselves into a direct military conflict with the Americans."

No one said anything for a moment as they watched Gorbachev angrily pace the room. They knew he was under an immense amount of pressure right now to hold together not just the Soviet Union but also the satellite nations that made up the Warsaw Pact, which were slowly disintegrating in front of them. Many of the hardliners were pushing for him to intervene militarily, but thus far he'd been able to stave off those calls by pointing to their ongoing operations in the Middle East.

Bristling at what he felt was a capitulation of their multiyear plan. General Valentin Varennikov, the head of the Russian Army, shook his head in disagreement at the assessment. "This changes nothing. Our plan is still working. The Iraqis have nearly captured all of Saudi Arabia. They have gone on to add the United Arab Emirates and isolated the Gulf States of Bahrain and Qatar, so it is just a matter of time before they join with Iraq. That encompasses nearly all the Middle Eastern oil-producing states, and they've done it in forty-five days. Now is not the time to cut and run."

"What more would you have me do, Valentin? I have authorized nearly an entire Soviet army's worth of tanks, infantry fighting vehicles, air-defense systems, and fighters, along with tens of thousands of technical advisors to aid them. We have done what we can. It is now incumbent on the Iraqis to do their part," Gorbachev chided his Chief of the Army. He then turned to Shevardnadze. "You need to work the United Nations better. I need you to find a way to slow things down. It is obvious the Americans are going to move forward with their coalition, but you can still apply pressure to the nations joining it. You can still push for a negotiated peace that will hopefully buy the Iraqis time to consolidate their gains and reinforce their positions."

Kryuchkov nodded in approval. "I agree. We can spin this recent vote as another case of American interventionism in yet another country. We can point to the military intervention they waged against the people of Grenada. We can bring up their coup in Panama. Yes, we can and should look to make this a public relations nightmare for the Americans and the West. Paint them as the warmongering interventionist. Maybe we can even rally the Syrians to come to Iraq's aid and get the Iranians to do more than just blockade the Strait."

Gorbachev smiled as he nodded along. "Yes, this is something we can use to our advantage."

Holding a hand up, Varennikov offered, "While I still believe we should threaten to intervene if the Americans move forward with building a coalition to go after Saddam, another thing we could do that might prove just as useful is to allow more of our airmen and soldiers to leave the military to join one of the volunteer units. The pilots who have crossed over to the volunteer units have been instrumental in going after the American units. Plus, when this conflict does end, it's going to give our air force a lot of combat experience. Will you allow me to see how many more volunteer units I can raise?"

"He has a point, Mr. President," Kryuchkov agreed. The volunteer force was their brainchild, so to speak. "The Americans can balk all they want, but at the end of the day, if people want to volunteer to defend Iraq against American aggression, who are we to say no?"

Gorbachev thought about that for a moment as the others waited. Finally, he said, "You have my permission to increase this force. However, no front-line units. They can be advisors to some of the front-line units, but I do not want to hear about a volunteer tank battalion or something along those lines. You can increase the number of pilots and air-defense units, but do not place our own defense at risk. Is that understood?"

Everyone smiled and agreed. For the time being, the hardliners had won another concession. Now they needed to show some better results.

****

48 Hours Later
Al-Salam Palace
Baghdad, Iraq

Foreign Minister Eduard Shevardnadze hated visiting the Middle East between the months of May and October—the hottest time of the year for this region of the world. At this point, he just needed to get through the next forty-eight hours and then he'd be on his way back to New York. He'd try to work the angle of painting the Americans as the aggressor by picking and choosing sides in a regional dispute.

Tariq Aziz walking up to the car to greet him. "Minister Shevardnadze, it is always a pleasure to meet with our Soviet allies. But you have flown a long way unannounced and in secret to meet with us privately. Please, let us get down to the reason for your visit."

Shevardnadze smiled slightly at Aziz's bluntness. The man was likely the brains behind Saddam, though few would ever say such a thing. They walked inside the palace and made their way over to a room where Saddam and some of his senior officials waited. As Shevardnadze entered the room, they went through the normal customs and courtesies before they got down to the business at hand.

Saddam started the conversation. "I assume your short-notice visit is in regard to the recent vote at the UN?"

Sighing, Shevardnadze responded, "Yes, Mr. President. As you are aware, the Americans have been pushing for one resolution after another condemning your nation for your acts of aggressions towards your neighbors. Up until now, we have managed to stop these resolutions from moving forward. However, they have finally managed to push through a resolution we could not stop."

"I am aware of the resolution and what it will mean. Surely you didn't fly all this way to tell us this?" Aziz countered with a raised eyebrow.

"No, of course not. I flew here to meet with you in person to share a very sensitive piece of intelligence we recently acquired that I believe will have a direct impact on your current military operations." Shevardnadze motioned to Colonel Chekhov, the KGB station chief, to hand them some documents. They were in Russian with a translated copy attached.

As the Iraqis read over the papers, Major General Sokolov explained the significance of the information in their hands. "This report came to us from a highly placed source of ours in Washington. The American President is far more hawkish than Reagan when it comes to utilizing military force. He saw how quickly his military was able to overwhelm the Panamanian armed forces last year and he believes, wrongly, that they will be able to do the same thing here in Iraq."

Saddam snorted at that assessment. "Well, we've already disabused them of that notion in Medina."

"Yes, but the Americans are still in control of that area as well. They are now staging their army out of Oman," Major General Sokolov countered, to the chagrin of the Iraqis.

Saddam did a good job of keeping his poker face on while Sokolov kept speaking. "This summary is from a meeting President Bush had with his National Security Council eight days ago. The Americans are mobilizing for war and they are rallying their allies to join them. As a matter of fact, in seven days, the British Parliament is being called back for a special session to vote on some sort of resolution the Americans are crafting. We believe they are going to organize some international coalition sanctioned by the UN now that this resolution has passed."

Saddam bristled a bit at this last comment, realizing the implications of what an international coalition against him could end up looking like. Finally, he said, "Minister Shevardnadze, while I appreciate the information you are sharing with us, is there something more the Soviet Union might be able to help us out with short of your nation directly fighting with us?"

"Mr. President, as you know, our own nation is coming under direct economic and political attacks by the Americans and the West. We are finding ourselves in an ever more precarious situation at home and abroad. The Americans and their CIA are instigating civil unrest across our own country to cause a collapse. Your war, however, has more than doubled the price of oil, which has provided our government coffers with a much-needed infusion of cash. World nations are needing to turn to the Soviet Union to meet their oil demands in light of the situation here.

"Our government wants to aid you further by providing you with additional volunteer squadrons of aircraft and pilots to fly them. We are also going to provide you with another brigade of S-300 missile systems and 'contractors' to operate them. We will also look to provide additional intelligence support to your forces. As a matter of fact, as we speak, Colonel Chekhov has several aircraft worth of equipment and personnel on their way to Baghdad to assist you," Shevardnadze finished.

Not waiting for Saddam or anyone else to respond, Sultan Hashim Ahmed al-Tai, the Defense Minister, jumped in, asking, "When will these new weapons and contractors arrive?"

Saddam knew the importance of receiving this equipment hastily, so he let the interruption slide. "Minister Shevardnadze, my nation and I appreciate this latest offer of military assistance. I believe the additional intelligence assets and improved radar systems will be critical in knowing in advance where the Americans are likely to attack. I have a meeting with my commanders tomorrow and I will relay your information to them, but intelligence on the American movements and positions is something we could put to great use."

"The aircraft and S-300s I spoke of should start arriving tomorrow. As to the intelligence, that will be handled by Colonel Chekhov and his capable people. General Sokolov will know in the coming days how many additional squadrons of pilots and aircraft will likely join your cause. Once the notice is announced, we'll see how many pilots opt to join. We'll then get their aircraft painted and remarked to reflect an Iraqi squadron. Before I leave, Mr. President, I must urge you to finish this war quickly and consolidate your gains. We will assist you in suing for peace, but if the Americans are able to muster a large coalition against you, there may be little that can stop them."

The two parties talked a bit longer before Minister Shevardnadze returned to the airport. His jet was spun up and ready to go. He'd now fly back to New York and the UN.

Chapter 2
Duel in the Dark

2 September 1990
3rd Squadron
Western Saudi Arabia

The plan was simple. *But aren't they all?* The problem always comes down to execution. In this case, the plan called for a massive multipronged air strike against multiple Saudi and American positions in hopes that some of the strikes would slip through the American air cover. Major Vitaly Popkov and his squadron of sixteen MiG-29 Fulcrums would be flying cover for a squadron of Su-24s as they made a mad dash for the American buildup around the Jeddah International Airport and a squadron of Su-25s looking to carry out some CAS missions along the Iraqi-American lines.

The Americans were still reeling from the previous days' ground assaults, so the Iraqi Air Force wanted to keep the pressure on. For his part, Popkov had broken his squadron down into eight flights of two. His thinking was that this would force the Americans to divide their forces to try and go after his pilots. After the last month of aerial combat, he'd developed a handful of tactics and formations, all in hopes of gaining an advantage against the Americans. The last time Soviet pilots had flown against the Americans was during the Vietnam War. The number of Soviet pilots back home volunteering to be a part of this off-books expeditionary mission was through the roof. Still, it was dangerous work. The Americans had better support than they did.

Ten minutes into their flight, the Su-24s were now fifteen minutes from the target. As they got closer to the airport and the coast, their passive radars picked up an enemy E-3 Sentry. Its powerful search radars had found them. The only problem for Popkov was the damn things were flying a racetrack formation on the opposite side of the Red Sea with a carrier battle group between him and them. The damn Sentrys allowed the American aircraft to keep their active radars off longer, thus helping them get in much closer to the Iraqis before they knew they were even there.

Then his radio crackled to life. "Strela Leader, Strela Two. I'm being lit up by an E-2 Hawkeye near that American carrier. Requesting permission to go active with my radar." He'd put his best pilots in the lead element, knowing they'd be the first to make contact with the Americans. If they were being painted by the E-2s, then chances were some fighters were being vectored towards them.

Popkov depressed the talk button. "Strela Two, Strela Leader, understood. You are cleared to engage. Happy hunting, out." Switching his radio frequency, he transmitted, "Gonshchik Leader, Strela Leader. We're going active with our radars. Good hunting."

A moment later, Popkov heard two squawks on the radio, letting him know the Gonshchik teams were moving to engage. The Gonshchik teams consisted of eight MiG-25 Foxbats that would now rise up from fifty meters in altitude to around seventy-five hundred meters and go supersonic in their race out to sea. They were tasked with going after the E-2 and possibly even the E-3 if they could catch it. The threat to the American airborne early-warning aircraft would force them to divert some of their fighters to defend them, leaving fewer fighters to provide cover over the airport or the current front line. The Foxbats might even get lucky and get a few shots off with their long-range missiles and bag them. The supersonic interceptors were clumsy rockets, but they were damn fast and hard for the Americans to catch.

In the morning, hours after their duel in the dark, the ground forces would make another hard push to dislodge the American paratroopers and hopefully throw them into the sea.

Looking down at his own radar scope, Popkov saw that two pairs of F-14s flying near Medina were attempting to give chase and go after the Foxbats. Additional F-14s flying over the carrier were now being vectored after the Foxbats.

The two pairs of F-15s flying over the Jeddah international airport were going after his lead aircraft. Then, right on cue, Major Konstantin "Kostya" Ayushiyev's flight of four MiG-29s made their move to engage the F-14s as they diverted to chase the Foxbats.

The fight's on. It's time to earn our bonuses, Popkov thought ruefully as he gave his aircraft some thrust and headed towards the F-15s.

Flying just fifty meters above the ground, he hadn't been spotted by the F-15s yet. They were busy engaging Strela One and Strela Two—just as he had engineered to happen. When he got within eighteen kilometers of the first F-15, he pulled up on his stick and angled his aircraft towards the two trailing F-15s that were flying cover for the two currently chasing down Strela One and Strela Two. Popkov activated two of his R-73 infrared homing missiles, placing the targeting reticle on one of the F-15s just long enough for the missile tone to let him know it had a lock. Once it did, he pickled off the first missile, then the second at the same target.

In fractions of a second, the blackness of night around him momentarily lit up as the solid-fuel rocket engine ignited and took off after its intended target. The F-15 he'd just locked up and fired on immediately took evasive maneuvers, banking hard to the right as the pilot popped off some flares in an attempt to throw off Popkov's heat-seeker missiles.

Popkov felt incredibly proud when, moments later, he saw that his wingman, not hesitating in the least, had also pickled off two of his own missiles at the American's wingman. In seconds, they had four missiles racing after the American aircraft.

Giving his aircraft some additional power, Popkov dove to the right to give chase to the American he had just fired on. He saw his first missile get spoofed by the Yankee's countermeasures and blow up when it hit one of the flares. Not wanting to let this one get away, Popkov switched on his R-27 active-radar-homing missiles. He had to fight a little bit, but he kept the targeting reticle on it long enough for it to get a solid lock. He fired. Moments later, his second R-73 missed the F-15 and flew off harmlessly as a result of a brilliant maneuver the American pilot had pulled off. That miss only confirmed his earlier decision to fire a third missile at the F-15.

Then he saw a bright flash off to his eleven o'clock. Looking in that direction, he saw it had come from one of the fighters. Which one, he wasn't sure just yet. Then a handful of bright red objects zipped right past his canopy, forcing him to dive to the left to avoid whatever was shooting at him. Before he could react, his Beryoza radar-warning receiver blared in his ear, letting him know that some sort of missile was attempting to lock on to him.

Then his RWR shouted a new warning. A missile had been fired at him. Looking down at his scope, he saw the missile had originated from one of the F-15s. It was racing towards him quickly, almost too quickly.

Pulling back on his flight controls, Popkov attempted to gain some altitude, as he'd wandered a bit too close to the ground when he had chased after that other American fighter. A flash occurred somewhere to his right. It was in the direction of the fighter he had fired on earlier, but he wasn't sure if his missile had hit it or if another fighter had blown up.

Warning, warning, warning, kept blaring in his headset. *That damn missile is fast*, he thought as he banked his aircraft to the right while dispensing a couple of flares.

Another flash occurred somewhere behind him. His aircraft was momentarily buffeted by the concussion of the blast. *I'm alive, that's all that matters*, he thought briefly as he pulled up hard on his flight controls and nearly cut his throttle.

His Fulcrum flared up almost vertically in a Pugachev's Cobra maneuver as it practically hovered momentarily in the air. Moments later, the F-15 that had just fired at him zipped right past him, with both its engines lit up as the pilot tried to put as much distance between them as humanly possible.

Popkov pushed his throttle to the wall, sending a rush of fuel to his engines, reigniting them with an urgency and renewed fury. He activated one of his R-73 heat-seeker missiles, and while he tracked the large American fighter visually, the missile's seeker gained a lock on the aircraft. He depressed the firing button on the side of his flight stick, firing his fourth missile of the morning.

His missile leapt from its rail and raced ahead of him after the two red-hot glowing Pratt & Whitney F100 engines, which were still in full afterburner mode. Seconds later, the 7.4-kilogram warhead had gotten within its proximity range and detonated. It fired what was essentially an aerial shotgun blast of steel ball bearings right into the rear of the F-

15's tail, shredding its left engine, vertical tail stabilizers and wing. A trail of smoke and some flames followed in the aircraft's wake as the pilot clearly struggled to maintain control of the stricken plane.

The American had turned the plane to head towards the international airport, no doubt in hopes of getting closer to friendly lines before he had to eject. Then the fire around the engine of the plane winked out, likely from the aircraft's internal fire-suppression system. Popkov watched as the pilot deftly maneuvered his stricken plane towards the international airport to save his aircraft. That was when Popkov knew he needed to finish this guy off. He wasn't about to let him land the wounded plane, only to get it airborne again later to kill him or his buddies.

Dropping in behind the F-15, he switched his weapon systems over from missiles to his gun system. With his 30mm autocannon activated, he lined up his gun sights on the one operational engine on the Eagle and depressed the trigger just long enough to send a handful of his hundred and fifty rounds into the rear of the aircraft. His goal wasn't to kill the pilot—he'd fought gallantly. He just wanted to remove him as a threat.

When his handful of 30mm projectiles slammed into the plane, they ripped a couple pieces of metal from the aircraft, which then burst into flames and exploded. This sudden eruption of fire and bright flash momentarily stunned Popkov. He hadn't intended on killing the enemy flier, only forcing the pilot to eject.

Then his radio crackled. "Strela Leader, Strela Two. I think it's time for us to get out of here," came the voice of his second-in-command. "Congrats on the kill."

That makes eight…

"Agreed. We've done what we came here to do. Let's get out of here."

Turning to head back home, Popkov did a quick head count. He'd started the mission with sixteen fighters, and he was returning with nine. Talking briefly with his pilots, he learned they'd scored seven kills of their own. He'd check with the Foxbat commander when they returned to see how they'd fared. The E-2 Hawkeye wasn't lighting them up, which meant they'd likely taken it out. How many F-14s they'd managed to nail was a different story.

Coming up on the radio, he found out the Su-25s had only lost a single aircraft while the Su-24s had lost three over the airport. The battle of Jeddah would go down as one of the largest aerial battles in decades.

Chapter 3
Wartime Patrol

2 September 1990
SS *Ford* FFG-54
Indian Ocean

The USS *Ford* FFG-54, an Oliver Hazard Perry–class frigate, had been cruising in the Arabian Sea for the past two months, conducting routine maritime inspections and interdiction missions until hostilities had broken out with Iraq. Now they found themselves in a role they had actually been designed specifically for—convoy escort duty and antisubmarine warfare screening.

Their new orders had them shepherding the PrePo ships out of Diego Garcia to the waiting ports in Oman and the Saudi ports in the Red Sea. Thus far it'd been relatively smooth and quiet—just the way they hoped it'd stay. That seemed likely given that Iraq didn't have much of a navy to speak of and the Iranians were still licking their wounds from Operation Praying Mantis a few years back. During that single day's battle in April of 1988, the US Navy had sunk six Iranian Navy vessels while sustaining zero losses of their own.

While the crew of the *Ford* was maintaining a standard "five and dime" watch schedule—five hours on, ten hours off—Commander (promotable) Scott was lying in his bunk, attempting to sleep. After having been interrupted three times in the last two hours, Commander Scott was half-asleep when the phone next to his board rang yet again. *Christ, people, at least give me two hours of uninterrupted sleep*, he thought angrily to himself.

"Scott here. This better be good!" he said, the fog of sleep not fully removed from his brain or he might not have snapped so quickly.

"Sorry, sir, this is Lieutenant Harris. I'm in CIC and think you should come take a look at something our sonar is picking up."

"OK, I'll be right there," Scott said as he rolled out of his bunk and grabbed his pants. *Might as well get dressed. Not going to be getting back into that bunk anytime soon*, he thought as he put his shoes on. The damn merchant ship crews were skittish, sending him one report after another of a possible submarine sighting.

Looking down at his boots, he had to admit, he loved these new things. They were the most comfortable boots he'd ever worn. They were ankle boots, so they didn't look like a standard boot, and they were a hell of a lot more comfortable than what the Navy issued. He'd bought them as a promotion gift to himself. He'd been selected for captain; now he was just waiting on a new assignment after this current patrol ended.

Buttoning the last button on his khaki uniform, which was incredibly comfortable for this part of the world, he reached for his ship's baseball cap on the way out. Leaving his stateroom, he made his way to CIC, or the Combat Information Center. This was the nerve center of any ship and a place he was finding himself in more and more as he rose through the ranks of command.

Along the way, he stopped by the officer's wardroom, grabbing a fresh cup of coffee and a half sandwich. He'd try to find some time to eat more later.

Entering the CIC, he found the man he was looking for. "OK, Lieutenant Harris, whatcha got?" Commander Scott asked as he fought off a yawn.

Lieutenant Harris had been aboard the *Ford* for the past two years. He'd joined them right out of antisubmarine warfare school. Scott had found him to be a very solid officer. His quick promotion to full lieutenant was a testament to his proficiency as an officer.

"Sir, we've been picking up some strange sonar returns. At first, I thought it might just be a whale. Then we'd lose it, only to pick it up again. The water isn't very deep here, so it could be an underwater anomaly, but it keeps moving every time it's detected," the young officer said. The sonar operator for the AN/SQS-56 sonar kept watching his screen, saying nothing.

"What speed has it been moving at?"

"Only about two knots, sir. It's almost like it's just drifting with the currents."

"OK, let's run a track on it and watch it for a while. Once we have something solid, we'll launch the chopper and let him drop the phones," Commander Scott said. The *Ford* had two SH-60 helicopters on board that had a variety of capabilities perfectly suited for this kind of cat-and-mouse game.

******

PFC James Anderson
Indian Ocean

Their third day at sea, the PrePo ship M/V *PFC James Anderson Jr.* was steaming towards the coast of Oman. The *James Anderson* had originally been a commercial container ship in 1979 before being transferred to the Maritime Service in 1985. It was 755 feet in length with a ninety-foot beam and a draft of thirty-three feet. Average cruising speed was seventeen and a half knots. It had deck and hold space of 120,080 square feet for vehicles and a helicopter landing platform. She was part of Maritime Prepositioning Squadron Two out of Diego Garcia. Her sister ships steaming behind her included the M/V *1LT Alex Bonnyman* and the M/S *CPL Louis J. Hauge Jr.* They had departed Diego Garcia for Oman on August 15.

Between the three ships, they carried enough equipment and supplies to outfit a Marine Air-Ground Task Force of sixteen thousand Marines and sustain them for a thirty-day period. This load was earmarked for the 7th Marine Expeditionary Brigade, which would be flying its personnel to Oman. The seas were especially calm this morning, almost flat, with just a slight swell coming from the south. The morning sun reflected off the mirror finish, blinding anyone looking east.

Able-Bodied Seaman Alfred was on the helm and had just started his watch at 0800 hours. His heading was set on the auto helm, so basically, he sat and made sure the ship stayed on the assigned course. He liked this position. In the mornings, it was usually just him and the watch officer. At this time of day, the standard bridge crew would be in the wardroom stuffing their faces. As it was, the third mate, who was the watch officer for the moment, was sighting some navigation fixes in between reading a book. Global Positioning Satellite navigation systems had yet to be installed aboard ships. As Alfred sat, he scanned the horizon and marveled at the open flatness of the sea. It was awe-inspiring to look at, no matter what kind of weather they faced. Then a glint of something caught his eye.

"Sir, there was a flash on the surface at eleven o'clock. I think there's something out there," he said to the duty officer.

Picking up a pair of binoculars, the duty officer began scanning the surface. "I don't see…oh shit!" the officer said, still looking through his binoculars.

"What is it, sir?" Alfred jumped to his feet, ready to disconnect the auto helm and change the ship's course.

"Call the captain to the bridge," the duty officer instructed Alfred, not removing his binoculars. Alfred did as he was told, picking up the phone and punching in the numbers for the wardroom.

A mess steward answered, "Wardroom."

"This is Able-Bodied Seaman Alfred. The duty officer requests the captain to the bridge immediately," Alfred said and waited. He could hear the request being given to the captain.

"Cap'n says he'll be right up," the steward relayed.

"Sir, the captain is on his way up," Alfred relayed to the duty officer, who was now scanning the horizon.

Entering the bridge, the captain looked about, expecting to see another ship on a collision course or something urgent. When he didn't, he turned to the duty officer. "What's up?"

"Sir, Alfred saw a flash and told me. I grabbed binoculars and started looking. Sir, it was a periscope. We have a submarine on our course somewhere ahead of us, and I have no idea if it's friendly or not."

"Send a message to the *Ford* and tell them we've spotted a periscope and where it's approximately located," the captain ordered. "Maybe they can send a helo to investigate or figure out what's going on."

****

B-808 Yaroslavl

(IRIS Taregh)
Indian Ocean

Captain First Rank Aleksandr Nemits was uncomfortable with this entire plan. Two years ago, he'd been approached by headquarters with an offer of promotion if he'd take on the task of mentoring and training a partner nation on how to use and operate the Kilo-class diesel-electric attack submarine, which had been decommissioned from the Soviet Navy two years before. At first, he had been excited about the opportunity. Then he'd been told who the partner nation was, and his heart had sunk. Iran prohibited alcohol, and for a Soviet sailor, that was a tall order considering vodka rations were a true and actual legitimate part of their daily consumption.

Still, the opportunity to help a partner nation field one of his country's best submarines was one he couldn't turn down. It'd fast-track him to the admiralty. Luckily, he'd been allowed to recruit his own crew. He'd chosen men who'd previously served under him and men who knew the sub's workings inside and out.

When the training had first started, the Iranian crew they were to teach had been sent to the Black Sea fleet for their initial training. That had gone on for nearly a year, until the Iranian Navy had finished constructing a fully covered submarine pen in Bandar Abbas. This new facility could house up to four submarines at one time. It was also fully enclosed and cut off from outside observation, meaning no one from the West would have a clue what was there.

Once the facility had been completed, Nemits and his Iranian counterpart had carried out their first undersea cruise from the Black Sea to this new submarine base. When they'd had to surface in order to transit the Suez Canal, they'd made sure to fly the Soviet flag. The ruse was to keep everyone believing this was in fact a Soviet sub, which technically it was. Once they'd reached the new subbase, the boat had been officially handed over to the Iranian Navy, but their Soviet trainers would continue to work with them for another six months, then the war broke out and things changed.

With only a month left in their training and mentorship program, Iraq invaded Kuwait, Saudi Arabia and the UAE. Captain Nemits had been asked to pick a handful of sailors to stay on and help the Iranians as they looked to put their new submarine into action.

The Iranians were looking for payback for Operation Praying Mantis, an enormous black eye to the Iranian Navy that had cost them six ships. When the Soviets had made an offer to help the Iranians if they worked with their former enemy against the West and the puppet regime of Saudi Arabia, the Ayatollahs hadn't hesitated.

At first, Nemits hadn't been in favor of this. However, since he had started this training program with the Iranians, he had seen the Berlin Wall come down in Germany. He had seen Poland move in the direction of democracy, all but ending communist rule; the Baltic states had come next, then the Caucasus. Nemits was no fool. He could see the writing was on the wall. The Soviet Union as he knew it was coming to an end. That also meant his chances at becoming an admiral were likely coming to an end.

Part of him was glad the empire was crumbling, but part of him was upset at how it was happening. It wasn't because they had made a choice to end it—no, it was ending because of Western, and in particular American, intervention. Nemits knew that in the end, it was the Soviet people who would ultimately suffer if the entire system collapsed. The fact that it was the Americans who were deciding the fate of the Soviet people galled him. It galled him to the point of wanting to help the Iranians he had been training during this tumultuous time hurt the Americans. When the admiralty had asked if he would stay on, he had gleefully agreed.

Prior to leaving their sub pen in Bandar Abbas, Captain Nemits had been able to coordinate a strategy through the Soviet embassy and the admiralty back in Moscow. The goal was to help deliver a naval victory to the Iranians while at the same time helping the Iraqis in their current war. He'd developed a strategy, coordinating his movements with that of a *Shchuka*, one of the newer nuclear-powered submarines the Americans and NATO were truly concerned about. The *Shchuka* would play a game of cat and mouse with the Americans as they transited supply ships between the British territory of Diego Garcia and ports in Oman and the Red Sea. While they played their games, Nemits would lead his Iranian counterpart into a position to deliver a critical attack against the American supply vessels.

At this point, four days had now gone by. They'd gone up to snorkel depth when they needed to recharge their batteries, and only at night. Steadily, they had gotten themselves moved into the path of several supply ships being loosely protected by a single Oliver Hazard Perry frigate.

Looking at his watch, Captain First Rank Nemits noted it was nearly 0700 hours. The sun had risen nearly an hour ago, giving them perfect light to spot whatever might be on the horizon.

"Conn, Sonar," came the call over the internal communication system.

Captain Sayyari anxiously grabbed for the handset that'd connect him to his sonar room. "Sonar, Conn. What do you have?"

"Conn, Sonar, multiple contacts. It appears we found that supply convoy," the sonarman announced excitedly.

Captain Nemits walked next to his Iranian counterpart, whispering, "We need to stay calm, and remember your training. Find out how many contacts we have, their bearings, etcetera, and then let's develop a plan of attack."

Captain Sayyari nodded in agreement, his face turning deadly serious as the gravity of the situation set in. Grabbing the receiver again, he said, "Conn, Sonar. Call out your tracks and begin designating them as Sierra One on down the line."

"Sonar, Conn, that's a good copy. Stand by." A moment of silence passed as the sonar operator likely consulted with his Soviet counterpart, making sure he had everything annotated correctly before he replied to the captain.

"Sonar, Conn. Contacts are as follows: Sierra One, bearing two-two-seven degrees, speed fifteen knots, range nineteen kilometers. Sierra Two, bearing two-two-six degrees, speed fifteen knots, range nineteen kilometers. Sierra Three, bearing two-two-one degrees, speed fifteen knots, range eighteen kilometers. Sierra Four, bearing two-three-one degrees, speed sixteen knots, range twenty-four kilometers. Sierra Five, bearing two-one-eight degrees, speed fifteen knots, range twenty-six kilometers. Sierra Six, bearing two-two-zero degrees, speed fourteen knots, range twenty-seven kilometers. Final contact, Sierra Seven, bearing two-two-four degrees, speed fourteen knots, range twenty-nine kilometers. End of contacts. Sir, if I had to make an educated guess, I'd say Sierra Seven is most likely a frigate, and so is Sierra Two based on the screw noises. The others appear to be freighters or oilers, sir," the sonar operator explained.

"Conn, Sonar, thank you. Stand by for further orders and continue to track the targets for us."

Captain Sayyari turned to Nemits and in a hushed tone asked, "What should we do? There are seven of them, two escorts. If we attacked them… do you think we could get away?"

Captain Nemits could see the look of excitement, fear, and concern written on the face of the man he'd spent nearly two years training and mentoring. He knew the Iranian officer wanted to do what was in the best interests of his country, but he also felt he needed to weigh that against ensuring he didn't lose his nation's first real submarine on its maiden voyage.

Motioning for the two of them to walk to a more private place where they could talk, he explained, "Hossein, you are in a tough position right now. You have been given what every one of us submariners dream of: an opportunity to attack and sink a desperately needed supply convoy. While you are only facing two frigates, you have an inexperienced crew that lacks confidence in their own abilities. This is only your maiden cruise and that's to be expected. But our orders are clear—if we come across a target of opportunity, maiden voyage or not, we are to attack it."

If this pep talk was supposed to make Captain Sayyari feel better, it didn't. Nemits could see the tortured look in the man's face as he tried to figure out what to do. Sensing the man's hesitation and how this could prove deadly, he thought up an idea.

"Hossein, what if I issue orders and then you repeat them? Just like we did during training. This way you can gain one final understanding of how to fight your boat. Would that make you feel better?"

The Iranian captain's face suddenly lit up as though this was the best idea he'd ever heard. "Yes, that could work. You can 'advise me,' like a training exercise," he said, using air quotes, "and I will relay the orders to my crew. Only we'll know this isn't a training exercise."

With their plan set into motion, the two of them returned to the bridge. They brought the sub up to periscope level and took a quick look at the area, verifying that the contacts were in fact supply vessels being escorted by two frigates. One in the lead, one in the rear. Then, as if on cue, the escorts began their search for the *Shchuka* that had once again caught their attention.

For the next hour, they maneuvered their sub into position. They were only going to get one shot at this. They had to make it count. Once they were in position, they assigned two of their Type 53 torpedoes to go after each of the two supply ships they had settled on. Once they'd released their torpedoes and they had acquired their targets, the sub would look to escape and find another ambush point where they could try to sucker punch another convoy or perhaps go after the enemy warships themselves.

Leaning in, Captain Nemits calmly said to Sayyari, "This is it. Everything you've trained for up to this moment. Go ahead, the honor should be yours and your country's."

Smiling at the gesture, Captain Sayyari turned to his bridge crew and the few Russian advisors. "Today we make history. Today we exact our vengeance on the Americans for their cowardly attack on our fleet." He then grabbed for the hand receiver that would connect him with the weapons officers. "Weps, Conn. Fire torpedoes one and three at Sierra Three. Fire torpedoes two and four at Sierra Five. Cut your wires once they've acquired their targets, then close outer doors and get those tubes reloaded."

"Aye, Captain," was the only reply he got.

Nemits could tell by the tone on the other end that the men were excited to be attacking something. He just hoped the sinking of these two transports would make a difference in the ongoing war. If his country was going to fall apart from within, then he sure as hell as hoped their actions in the Middle East hurt the Americans.

Chapter 4
Logistical Nightmare

3 September 1990
XVIII Airborne Corps HQ
King Abdulaziz International Airport
Jeddah, Saudi Arabia

The past ten days had seen some of the fiercest fighting the 82nd and 101st had been in since World War II. At times, the battles along what was being called Wadi Reem and Medina Ridge would dissolve into hand-to-hand combat. Still, the American airborne soldiers and their Saudi counterparts just couldn't give an inch despite the nearly daily ground assaults being launched against them. If the 1st of the 101st attack helicopter battalion, along with the 1st of the 82nd and their Apache helicopters and the US Marine Corps's AH1-W Super Cobra helicopters, hadn't arrived when they had, the paratroopers likely would have been forced to withdraw or would have died in their foxholes.

As it was, the casualties from the daily battles were constant. At the large field hospital they'd set up near the Jeddah International Airport, wounded were brought in daily. Some would be treated at the hospital and sent back to the front line; others would be flown out to the carrier *Saratoga* and return once they were able to. The more seriously injured were sent out on the now-daily medical transports back to Germany and then to Walter Reed.

While this new war was only a few weeks old, the logistical support to keep it going was becoming a grave concern. Aside from the desperate need for replacement soldiers at the front line, they were in desperate need of provisions. The paratroopers at the front had now gone two weeks without a regular meal beyond an MRE, a shower, or any other basic creature comforts. While the XVIII Airborne Corps was the tip of the spear, it was only as strong as the shaft that supported it. In this case, the shaft was almost nonexistent.

Lieutenant General Luck, the commander of XVIII Airborne Corps, sat in his office with the Corps G-4, Colonel Jeff Dailey, the officer responsible for logistics and keeping the XVIII Corps supplied with beans and bullets.

"Dailey, what is the status of getting the COSCOM closed in here?" General Luck pressed. He'd been on Dailey about this for days, to no avail. They desperately needed the 3rd Sustainment Command to help them unscrew this entire mess.

Dailey sighed at the question. He knew this was a major concern, and he was practically pulling his hair out trying to get it taken care of. "Sir, right now logistical elements have a low priority compared to combat units. I spoke with a general on the CENTCOM staff and he's just as frustrated as we are. It appears that people in Washington are scrubbing the rapid redeployment of logistical and support units and moving shooters up in priority. This last week of fighting and then these constant air raids are scaring the hell out of Washington. They're afraid we're going to be overrun. They want to send us more combat power, not supporters."

General Luck was pissed. "I get it, and that policy might work on a REFORGER[1] exercise, where you have a host nation with infrastructure to support you, but this is a come-as-you-are knife fight. There's no doubt we need shooters, but I need supporters to keep them going. We're fortunate as hell to have the haji tent city and running water, but those kids out on the line have nothing, and I'm sure they're getting tired of eating MREs at this point. I need you to unscrew this situation and right now," an exasperated General Luck explained before adding, "I know you're trying your best, Colonel. But right now I need more. Those buses, trucks, and heavy equipment we managed to secure probably saved our asses at Medina Ridge. By the way, how did we get that stuff? And don't tell me we commandeered it."

Dailey sighed. He'd hardly slept since he'd arrived in-country, and he doubted the general had either. "No, General, we did not commandeer it. Seems a lieutenant colonel that's assigned to the US Army Military Advisor Group in Riyadh hightailed it over here when the first plane landed and started working with the local Emir to get things rolling for us. The King made a phone call and things started happening pretty fast. This Emir and the King have appointed someone to handle some of these logistical challenges for us. As a matter of fact, we should start seeing some fresh food in the coming weeks—and get this, the King is paying the tab. Their guy is over in Egypt and having the food shipped to us from across the Red Sea if you can believe it."

---

[1] REFORGER (Return of Forces to Germany) was a major annual deployment exercise conducted from 1969 to 1993 to practice moving a division to Germany rapidly.

General Luck almost laughed at the answer to his prayers before adding, "I hope we aren't talking camel steaks or burgers." He could just see his soldiers now looking at racks of camel or camel hamburger—not that beggars can be choosers, but still.

"Evidently the guy put in charge of this, his father is the grocer for the King. He has a worldwide organization and pretty much understands the tastes of Westerners. The lieutenant colonel from the advisor group is out contracting for someone to start cooking for us until our own mess facilities are set up. Unless you oppose, General, I'd like to have the priority for fresh food to be the front-line guys. Once we have a better handle on the supply chain, we can expand that to include the rear-echelon troops next if that meets your approval," the colonel explained.

"Damn straight it meets my approval, Colonel. If we're not careful, those rear-echelon types will try to get their share and then some before it ever gets to the line doggies," General Luck said. It wasn't that he didn't appreciate or like his rear-echelon soldiers, but the REMFs in the rear traditionally had a reputation for poaching the best equipment for themselves instead of making sure those that really needed it got it.

This had always been a problem since the dawn of the modern army. In the American Civil War, the REMFs, meaning Rear Echelon Mother Fuckers, had poached the boots earmarked for front-line soldiers, making sure they always had a nice new pair. In World War II, Eisenhower had wanted Paris to become an R&R center for the front-line troops. Instead, the REMFs running the show in the rear had made sure they and their buddies were given those limited slots over the front-line soldiers who truly needed the reprieve. In Vietnam, it was boots again. The Saigon REMF commandos in the air-conditioned offices had the newly designed jungle boots, leaving the line doggies with their defunct leather boots that rotted away in the jungle environment.

General Luck's eyes narrowed a bit. "You watch, Dailey, every REMF here will have new desert boots while the kids on the line are wearing leftover Vietnam jungle boots," he fumed before turning to another major topic of concern. "Water. What are we doing on this?"

"General, as you know, we have sufficient fresh water for our needs in and around the airport area. To get the water to the units in the field, we're leveraging some refrigerator trucks that'll keep the bottles cool until we can get them brought to the different unit distribution points. That lieutenant colonel I mentioned earlier was able to rent a myriad of trucks and SUVs for the battalions and brigades to help fill in for our vehicle shortage. When the distribution center is low, they send in another request for water or whatever else we're able to bring up."

"Excellent. At least some things are falling into place. Changing topics, did you hear what happened to the Navy this morning?"

Dailey looked at his watch. It was nearly noon. He hadn't heard anything about the Navy.

"It's OK, Jeff. I hadn't either until I talked with someone down at CENTCOM forward in Oman. Apparently either the Iraqis or the Iranians have acquired a sub. That or those damn Soviets sold them one prior to the war. In either case, the bastards sank two ships the other day in the Indian Ocean. I was told the ships lost were the USS *Sacramento* and the USS *Seattle*. I'll be frank, prior to talking with some Navy commander in the J-4, logistics, I had no idea what those kinds of ships did. Apparently they're the Navy's largest combat logistics ships. This commander told me they'd been designed to carry out three primary functions—to serve as an oiler, keeping the ships topped off with fuel and the carriers topped off with aviation fuel; to carry ammunition, and not just ammo for the five-inch guns but bombs, missiles, and ordnance for the carrier's air wings; and lastly, to function as a supply ship, keeping the battle groups supplied with food stores and other consumable parts needed to maintain the warships," Luck explained. He was a paratrooper through and through, so while he didn't fully understand the Navy, he knew enough to know that losing two ships like that in the middle of an air war wasn't good.

Colonel Dailey let out an audible sigh. He wasn't responsible for the Navy, but he knew this would likely only further compound his own supply problems.

"Jeff," General Luck started. He didn't often address his officers by their first names, but when he did, it was usually because he wanted to add a personal touch. "I'm sharing this with you not to stress you out but to let you know there are others who are in a far worse position than you. You've done an outstanding job given the circumstances we've had to face. I just wanted you to know that and to understand that it could always be worse."

"Thank you. I appreciate that, and you're right. The situation could always be worse."

"OK, Colonel, if I'm reading this correctly, between the 82nd, the 101st, the Air Force elements and that small group of Marines with us, we have somewhere around forty thousand personnel. Correct?"

The colonel looked at his own notes for a second before nodding in agreement. "That's about right, but keep in mind that number changes every hour. We're starting to get a steady gravy train of aircraft being flown in from Europe and the States. What are you thinking, sir?"

"If I'm not mistaken, the haji tent city here holds some eighty thousand people. I've been running some calculations in my head, and by the time we get the 101st fully deployed along with the Marines and their assets, which should start showing up shortly, we're going to be stacked up on each other pretty tight. After last night's air raid on the airport and then the tent city, I don't want our troops packed any tighter than they already are. We can't let the enemy savage us like that again."

Dailey rubbed his chin. "True, I think we got off lucky last night. They seem to have gone after some of our A-10s and helicopters at the airport itself more than they did the tents where the troops were sacked out."

Pausing for a moment, Dailey added, "Sir, right now with our limited logistic package, we can't disperse too much. The majority of the 82nd is up on Medina Ridge, so that makes things more tolerable, but that's taxing our logistic tail for right now. Class I, III and V is about all we can handle right now. It's also my understanding that Oman may end up being the primary location for any future land force buildups. If that ends up being the case, then I hate to say it, but we may soon become a backwater operation. If that happens, support may be even more difficult to come by."

"Yeah, I heard the same rumor. Let's keep that to ourselves for right now."

"Sir, north of here is Yanbu, with a major port as well as a major airport. We should look at putting part of the force at that location once we get the corps support group here. It's one hundred and seventy miles north of here," Dailey offered.

"Yeah, let's take a look at that once we get the corps support group on the ground.

******

CENTCOM Forward HQ
Military Technological College
Muscat, Oman

"Colonel, I am damn glad to see you," Major General Neil Pegasus, the CENTCOM logistics commander, exclaimed as he stood from behind his desk and extended his hand. "Welcome to Muscat, John. I can sure use you."

"Thank you for the warm welcome, sir. I'm here to help," said Colonel John Engels, a bit jet-lagged from the long flight. "My troops are at the airfield, waiting for orders. I understand there are some PrePos arriving in a couple of days and the 7th Transportation Group is ready to unload them."

General Pegasus nodded and then pressed, "How many troops did you bring?"

"I have three hundred with me… all stevedores," Engels replied. He'd brought as many dockworkers as he could, knowing they'd have a ton of ships to offload in the coming days and weeks.

"Good. I'll need to take about two hundred of them off your hands and unfortunately leave you with only a hundred," General Pegasus explained, getting right down to it.

Colonel Engels said the only thing you could to a two-star who had just taken two-thirds of your command from you: "Yes, sir."

Seeing the look of disappointment on his friend's face, General Pegasus explained, "Look, John. Here's the deal. I'm attempting to get this rear logistical mess straightened out ASAP because we're about to have a massive gravy train of supplies and personnel headed our way in the coming days and weeks. Until I get sufficient units in place to help me, I've got to make do with what arrives and plug the holes and fill the gaps where I have them. Everything is a bit fluid around here right now."

He paused for a moment to let some of what he had just said sink in before adding, "I know this isn't what you were expecting when you arrived, but these are the facts on the ground. The hundred you have left, put them to work with the locals and unload ships like our lives depend on it. The other two hundred I'm going to turn into MPs to help with convoy security and traffic control for the trucks moving the stuff from the port to where it needs to go ASAP. I'm not sure if you heard, but the Navy lost a couple of critical supply ships to what they're saying is a Soviet Kilo-class submarine—"

"Jesus, are the Soviets getting involved in this war too?" Engels interrupted.

General Pegasus shook his head, "Thankfully, no, at least not right now. What I heard during the commander's brief was this sub was likely sold to the Iraqis or the Iranians sometime prior to the war. That said, the last thing we want right now is to have the docks piled high with vehicles and munitions."

"No joke, sir. I get it, and thank you for explaining the big picture to me. It'll help me develop a plan to make sure the ships are offloaded as fast and best as we can and get the stuff out of the port faster. What I'm going to do is have my executive officer take charge of two companies I'll have for the docks and then we'll create a provisional MP battalion with the rest."

Just as they were about to discuss a few more details about the ships that would be showing up over the next couple of weeks, Major Whooley, General Pegasus's aide, stepped into their meeting.

"Excuse me, sir," he interrupted hesitantly.

"What's the matter?" Pegasus asked, seeing the look on Whooley's face.

"Seems we have a complaint from the Emir, sir. The female soldiers that are working over at the distribution center we're building have their blouses off and the local men are finding it offensive to see their naked arms and sweaty T-shirts. The females are also upset at all the catcalls they're getting from the nearby locals. It's hard to fault the women for working without blouses like the men—it's a hundred and twenty degrees out there," Whooley explained.

Pegasus looked at Engels. "See what we're dealing with, John. Besides the logistic nightmare, we have local customs and religious norms to consider as well. General Schwarzkopf made it clear he doesn't want to win the war and lose the peace. Keeping the locals happy is paramount in this operation. Please be sure your people are briefed on the customs of these people and what offends and what does not." He looked back at the major. "Have my car brought around and I'll go see the Emir and smooth this over. Tell whoever's in charge over there to take the females off the detail and get them inside until I sort this one out."

Before he left, he turned back to his friend. "Colonel, welcome to Oman."

****

Georgia Ports Authority
Garden City, Georgia

"Colonel, you can't load your vehicles with a double basic load of ammo," Brigadier General Smith, the commander of the eastern region of the Military Traffic Management Command, angrily explained.

"General, you don't understand. We may have to fight our way out of the port as we unload the ships by the time we get there. For all I know we won't have local ammo dumps we can draw more from— that's why we need to carry a double basic load," Colonel LeMay tried to explain.

"Have you looked at the inside of one of your vehicles?" General Smith barked before motioning for the colonel to follow him to the back of one.

The two of them walked over to one of his Bradley fighting vehicles. The tail ramp was down. The entire troop compartment was full of ammunition, stuffed in every possible nook and cranny they could find, none of it secured. They had TOW rounds stacked on boxes of small arms ammunition and hand grenades.

"First problem, you said you may need to fight your way out of the port. I call bullshit because these things are so full you can't fit any soldiers inside here to fight the vehicle. So that ain't happening. Second problem, Colonel, is none of this ammo is secured. It's just tossed in here. If the ship hits rough seas, this loose ammo is going to start rolling around inside the vehicles, which may cause some of the vehicles to slide around. That could cause the entire ship to capsize if all the weight rolls to one side during a storm because you thought you would get cute and load these things the way you saw fit. If the Coast Guard inspects this, they're going to hit the roof. I suspect that ship that you just finished loading is pretty much the same, isn't it?" General Smith growled.

The colonel said nothing. His facial expression said it all. As they talked about how to rectify the situation, General Smith noticed that the loaded ship had not left the dock despite all the mooring lines having been cast off. Several people were standing on the bridge and the dock, looking into the water. *What the hell is going on now?* Smith thought when the chief dockmaster started walking his way while talking on his Motorola radio.

"What's the problem?" General Smith asked when the man was close enough.

"We have a big problem, General. Seems the vehicles are weighing a lot more than we were expecting. The ship appears to be resting on the bottom in the mud and can't move. We're going to have to unload the vehicles until we can refloat the ship and figure out what the problem is," he explained, exasperated. They needed to get this ship moved out so they could bring the next one in to be loaded.

General Smith looked at Colonel LeMay. "Oh, I think we know what the problem is, don't we, Colonel?"

LeMay could feel the daggers being sent his way. "Yes, sir, I believe we do. I'll get it corrected as the vehicles come off," he mumbled.

"Colonel, your little antic just costs our guys in Oman at least one and possibly two full days without their equipment. You better hope like hell our guys don't lose the port because their equipment didn't arrive because you thought you'd pack a double basic load in each of your vehicles. I ought to have you brought up on charges. You best unfuck this situation, Colonel, or I'll have you busted down to lieutenant!" General Smith berated the colonel as he and the chief dockmaster walked back towards the grounded ship.

Chapter 5
Saddam Briefed

4 September 1990
Al-Salam Palace
Baghdad, Iraq

As Saddam entered the briefing room, everyone stood. Tension was thick in the air along with the cigarette smoke that clouded the ceiling. *The invasion of Saudi Arabia should have taken a week. It's now going on a month and the army still hadn't secured the country*, Saddam thought as he sat and surveyed the room. The conversation with the Soviet Foreign Minister five days ago replayed in his head. He knew they didn't have a lot of time left to finish their objectives.

Taking his seat, he nodded to the briefing officer to start the meeting; he needed to know where they stood.

A colonel from the Republican Guard walked up to the front of the room. He puffed his chest out a bit as he began. "Sir, the current situation is as follows," the man said as he pointed to a map of Kuwait, Saudi Arabia, the UAE, Oman, Qatar, and Yemen.

"The 1st Republican Guard Corps with the 1st Hammurabi Armoured Division, the 6th Nebuchadnezzar Mechanized Division, the 2nd al-Medinah Armoured Division, and the 3rd Tawakalna Mechanized Division are located in the UAE at these locations," he indicated, pointing at Abu Dhabi, Dubai, Ras Al-Khaimah, Al Ain and Al Wagan. "The 18th Armoured Brigade is in Salwa, Saudi Arabia, undergoing a refit of equipment as it was severely damaged in an air strike launched by the Americans."

Almost immediately, Air Marshal Hamid Raja Shalah al-Tikriti started to speak. "Sir…"

Saddam shot him a look and raised his hand to stop him. "Continue, Colonel," was all Saddam had to say.

"Yes, sir, the 9th Corps is in positions from Al Jubail to Al Khobar, to include Ras Tanura, Al Qatif, Dammam and Al Hofuf"—again he pointed to the respective cities—"with the 45th Infantry Division occupying Al Jubail, the 49th Infantry Division occupying Dammam, and the 1st Infantry Division in Al Hofuf. The 10th Armoured Division is in the north to respond to any attempt at an amphibious landing, and the 17th Armoured Division is in the south, prepared to do the same."

"Good," Saddam said, then motioned for him to continue.

"Sir, in the center of Saudi Arabia, the 4th Corps has seized Riyadh and positioned their divisions with the 16th Division remaining in King Khalid Military City, the 20th Infantry Division in Buraydah and the 30th Infantry occupying Unayzah. The 34th Infantry Division is in Riyadh and the 36th Infantry Division is in Al Majma'ah. The 1st Mechanized Division is in Al-Kharj and occupies Prince Sultan Air Base with security; the 6th Armoured Division is in Ad Dubaiyah, and the 21st Infantry is in Al-Muzahmiya to pacify any resistance." The colonel pointed to several locations around Riyadh as he spoke.

Saddam said nothing but stared at the map. Finally, he nodded for the colonel to continue.

The colonel seemed a bit uncomfortable with what he was about to say next; more than a few corps commanders shifted in their seats as well. "Sir, the 2nd Republican Guard Corps currently occupies Medina with the 7th Adnan Motorized Division and is in a defensive position with the 5th Baghdad Mechanized south of the city."

Saddam looked over at Lieutenant General Ra'ad al-Hamdani, the 2nd Republican Guard Corps commander, but did not ask anything and was not offered anything in return. "Please continue, Colonel."

"Sir, the 2nd Corps is moving south at this time with the 7th Infantry Division at Masader, the 37th Infantry Division at Al Jadid, and the 51st Infantry Division at Madain Saleh. The 2nd Infantry Division is occupying Tabuk. The 14th Mechanized Division attempted to attack and seize Dubai along the Red Sea but was hit by American jets and badly damaged in these mountains. They are currently at Shigry and are being refitted with new equipment and personnel," the colonel explained, almost hesitantly.

Saddam turned slowly in his chair, his frown so deep that his black eyebrows almost covered his eyes. "Tell me, Air Marshal Hamid Raja Shalah al-Tikriti, why my divisions are being bombed and by whom. You told me you had swept the Saudi Air Force from the sky. What seems to be the problem?" Saddam asked. He already knew the answer, of course, but he wanted to hear it from his air marshal. The others in the room knew that when Saddam used your entire name, you were typically in trouble.

Squirming in his seat, the air marshal responded, "Sir, the Americans have reinforced their single carrier in the Arabian Sea with two additional carriers in the Red Sea. They also have some Air Force F-15s flying out of Egypt. It also appears a single squadron of F-111 medium-range bombers that had been stationed in England have been relocated to that same Egyptian airfield."

"And you are not capable of dealing with these aircraft. Do you not have the latest in Soviet fighter planes?"

"Yes, sir, we do."

"Then why are you not able to defeat these aircraft? Are they a better aircraft? Or are they better pilots? Or is it the case that your pilots are afraid to tangle with the Americans? Are they not trained in the use of these latest aircraft?" Saddam was rapid-firing questions to the air marshal. "Get back to me later and explain the situation to me," Saddam said, letting him off the hook for now.

He turned to the briefing officer. "Colonel, what is the enemy situation at this time?" he asked, needing to know what else was going on.

"Currently we are facing off against a mix number of Saudi forces in and around Medina. The Americans rapidly deployed their 82nd Airborne Division along with elements of their 101st Airborne Division to Jeddah. From there they were able to reinforce the remaining Saudi units and currently have us held up in the mountains just south of Medina. It appears they intend to either delay the 2nd Corps or attempt to further delay the 2nd Republican Guard Corps from reaching the port city of Jeddah. There are also some Saudi National Guard forces operating around Medina as a guerrilla force raiding the supply convoys from Riyadh," the colonel explained.

"And the Americans—what are they doing beyond blocking us from taking the port?" Saddam inquired.

"It appears the Americans are in a defensive position just west of Medina. In addition, the Soviets have provided us with intelligence that indicates a new plane ferries supplies or reinforcements continuously every forty-five minutes around the clock. What has kept us from overrunning the American positions entirely has been their attack helicopters. The Soviets provided us with satellite images that show at least one and possibly two battalions of attack helicopters in the area."

Saddam pressed, "Explain to me why these attack helicopters have been able to stop our forces again?"

Looking uncomfortable with the question, the colonel tried to explain, "Sir, when we launch an offensive with our armored vehicles, the attack helicopters show up and shred them with their laser-guided and TOW antitank missiles. This has forced us to leverage more of our forces as light infantry, something the Americans are substantially better at than we are. Even then, when it looks like we might overrun one of their positions, their attack helicopters swoop in and save the day."

Saddam shook his head in frustration as he glared daggers at his air chief. "And in Oman?" he pressed as he turned his gaze back to the briefer. This was the one area he was most concerned about. If the Americans could build up a large enough presence there, they could push them out of Saudi Arabia.

"In Oman, it is reported that the Americans' Central Command headquarters is being established in Muscat. They appear to have a number of pre-positioned support ships from Diego Garcia arriving in Duqm, As Sultan Qaboos Port, and Masirah Island. These are the kinds of supply ships the Americans have in different regions of the world, pre-positioned with tanks, light armored vehicles, munitions, and other supplies for their military to fall in on at a port or airfield. Again, Soviet intelligence has shown us that a squadron of American aircraft have landed at Muscat International Airport and US Marines have been seen setting up a base camp outside of Muscat."

Saddam held a hand up to stop the colonel. "Tell me, those two American ships that were sunk. They obviously weren't sunk by us, so who sank them and what did they sink?"

The question caught the briefer off guard, but he quickly regained his composure. "We believe it was the Iranians. We've known for some time that they had been looking into purchasing some Soviet submarines. It would appear they have purchased at least one of them. As to the ships, our understanding is these are the types of ships that resupply the American carriers and other warships at sea. It is possible that their sinking may curtail some naval missions, maybe even some of their fighter operations."

"Huh, that is good to know. Back to Oman and Jeddah. Have we seen any American heavy armor forces arriving there yet?" asked Saddam.

"Only a company of light tanks from the cavalry squadron with the 82nd Airborne, but four tanks and four Bradley fighting vehicles from the 24th Mechanized division arrived also."

"What do the Americans consider a light tank?"

"The American light tank is a M-551 called a Sheridan after one of their famous generals from their civil war. It can be dropped by parachure and swim rivers. It shoots a 152 millimeter gun and the MGM-51missile with a range of 2000 meters.

"So, Colonel, what you are telling me is that the Americans and the Saudis have very little ground combat power in that region at this time? Is that assessment correct?" Saddam asked, slowly turning away from the briefing officer to look at Lieutenant General Ra'ad al-Hamdani, the 2nd Republican Guards Corps commander.

"That is correct, sir," the colonel replied, glad that he wasn't the one in charge of any of these divisions or corps.

"Lieutenant General Ra'ad al-Hamdani, can you please explain why your two divisions could not destroy an airborne division? A division that, I might add, is not fully deployed yet?" Saddam inquired, his eyes boring holes in his commander.

The others were relieved that the heat was off them now.

"Sir, the 7th Adnan Division was the lead division from Buraydah to Medina. They faced an intense delaying action with American jets engaging them at every wadi, combined with ambushes from the 45th Saudi Armoured Brigade. We believe there may even be American Special Forces soldiers fighting alongside them, advising them, and calling in air strikes. Once the 7th reached Medina, the fighting turned into a vicious street battle, which further depleted the division on top of being attacked from the air by the Americans and then American artillery guns being flown in," the general lamented as he recounted some of the battles the Adnan Division had been fighting.

"And the 5th Baghdad Division, what was his problem that he could not get through this 82nd Airborne Division and seize the international airport and cut off this spigot of American supplies pouring into the country?" Saddam casually asked, like this should have been a trivial thing for them to have accomplished.

"Sir, the mountains west of Medina have a limited number of routes through them, and the Americans concentrated their forces along those routes. While our forces had a three-to-one advantage in numbers, the Americans were able to concentrate their forces where it mattered most. Then they introduced their Apache attack helicopters, which utilized some kind of laser-guided missiles. When they fired on our tanks, they never missed," General al-Hamdani said, explaining as best he could how the battle had unfolded.

"If I am not mistaken, we have our own helicopters, yes?"

"We do, and they did participate in the attack. But our helicopters do not have this same kind of sophisticated weapon system. Our Soviet helicopters require our aircraft to be moving while attacking. The American Apaches were able to hide and hover, allowing them to pop out from behind a ridge or hill to carry out a devastating attack and then duck back down behind that same hill. This is not a capability our Soviet helicopters can replicate," al-Hamdani explained.

"Well, in that case, I suggest you change our tactics to fit the situations," Saddam pointed out. "What about close-air support? Did you not employ it?"

"We did, but the American interceptor jets were on them very quickly and effectively. We lost a number of jets before they were able to reach the front or carry out any serious damage," al-Hamdani said in a resigned voice.

"Tell me, Air Marshal, how did this happen? You tell me we have air superiority and yet our ground units are taking a beating," Saddam asked, looking directly at General Shalah al-Tikriti. Saddam was no longer smiling.

Al-Tikriti hung his head in frustration before replying, "As I mentioned previously, we did not expect the Americans to respond so quickly. They repositioned not one but two of their aircraft carriers into the Red Sea and then secured basing rights in Egypt, allowing them to relocate several of their fighter squadrons and now medium-range bomber squadrons. Utilizing their airborne, warning, and control aircraft, or E-3s, over the Red Sea, they were able to spot our ground-attack aircraft taking off and heading towards their objectives. It's the same with our helicopters. Once they saw our air and helicopters getting airborne, they guided their own interceptors in to engage ours before we knew anything was going on. We've tried to spoof the Americans by deliberately holding our interceptors back at a higher altitude, hoping they would go after them while our ground-attack planes went in low and fast, which is why they did not have fighter cover. But their E-3s saw through our deception and guided different groups of their own fighters to engage ours. It was a mistake that I will not allow in the future."

Staring at his air marshal, Saddam thought to himself, *You are right, Air Marshal, it is a mistake you will not make again.* Finally, Saddam told him, "See me after this meeting. We have much to talk about." It was obvious to everyone in the room that this would be a tough conversation.

Taking a sip of his tea, Saddam turned his attention to General Muzahim Sa'b Hassan al-Tikriti, commander of the country's air-defense forces, and asked, "General, what have our air-defense forces been doing? How many American aircraft have your forces shot down?"

"Yes, Mr. President. The air-defense forces have not been idle." The remark was meant to sting his air force counterpart. "We have engaged the American aircraft successfully on several occasions, forcing them to abandon several of their missions. The SA-9 and ZSU-23-4 systems our Soviet advisors provided are making a big impact. As our supply lines are being stabilized, we're deploying more of our surface-to-air missile systems in groupings and patterns designed to tear the American aircraft apart."

Saddam seemed to perk up a bit at the news, excited to hear about something going well.

General Muzahim continued, "During the battle of Medina, we positioned several of our SA-6 systems further back from our ground forces, and while they were not effective against these low-flying American Apache attack helicopters, they were able to engage the American medium-range bombers flying out of Egypt. Since these aircraft first appeared over the battlespace, we have successfully shot down five of them."

Saddam smiled at the news, so General Muzahim continued. "We have also engaged and shot down twelve American F-14 Tomcats, A-6 Intruders, F-4 Phantoms, and F-15 Eagles. I do want to point out that while we are scoring victories, when we turn our radars on, the American A-6 Intruders and F-4 Phantoms engage our radar sites with their antiradiation missiles. These are missiles designed to zero in on the radars being used to guide the missiles to their targets. This has resulted in us losing nineteen radar vehicles and half a dozen launchers. We have not deployed any of SA-2 or SA-3 systems near the front lines as of yet. I am having them emplaced around the east coast, covering Ras Tanura and Al Jubail. I would like to move two batteries and place them in the vicinity of Dubai to help cover the Strait."

"Do it. And, General, good job thus far. Gentlemen, I cannot stress enough that we must secure Saudi Arabia as quickly as possible." As Saddam spoke, his glare fell upon General Ra'ad al-Hamdani and General Ra'ad Rasjod, the II Corps commander. "If the Americans get a foothold, then it will be very difficult for us to continue our actions into Oman while our side is exposed. Do I make myself clear on this matter?" Both al-Hamdani and Rasjod avoided eye contact with him but nodded their heads.

"Before I return my attention to the Army," Saddam continued, "General Muzahim, prior to this war starting, our Russian friends provided us with a limited number of their advance SA-10 surface-to-air missile systems. When the Foreign Minister visited me a few days ago, he said they were leasing us an additional two brigades' worth of these systems. If I understand our current deployment, we have one of those systems deployed around Baghdad, and one around Imam Ali Air

Base in Nasiriyah, and two more in Kuwait. Now that we know the Americans are going to intervene and they are specifically going after our supply lines and armored units, perhaps we should look for other ways to implement this strategic surprise where it can cause the most damage."

General Muzahim thought about Saddam's question. Finally, he knew where they should place them. "Sir, I'd like to recommend we place one battalion in Al-Kharj, where our Russian contractors are currently staying. This will help protect our fighter squadrons and provide a wide umbrella of SAM coverage. To aid our efforts in the west, we should move one of these systems to the airport in Medina. This will greatly increase our aircraft's ability to be guided to the enemy without having to turn their own radars on until the last moment. The system's missiles also have a range of up to one hundred and fifty kilometers, with up to three hundred and thirty kilometers of detection and surveillance."

"Yes, this is what I want to hear. Ideas like this," Saddam said excitedly.

Smiling, General Muzahim continued, "I'd also like to propose another battalion in Salwa. This is a critical supply junction the Americans have already hit us on. By positioning the battalion in Salwa, we'll be able to better protect our supply lines and most of Qatar. Then I'd like to place two battalions around the King Khalid Military City and Dhahran. These last two positions will provide a wide interlocking bubble of air defense against future American attacks. Lastly, I want to move two of the remaining four battalions to the UAE in preparation for what will likely come next. The last two I'd like to station here in Iraq, further reinforcing our defenses at home. The Americans are likely to use their B-52 bombers or B-1 bombers at some point soon, and I'd like to have a special present waiting for them, one they'll never suspect."

Saddam laughed at that. He seldom laughed during these meetings, but the thought of how surprised the Americans would be when they discovered the S-300 system brought a true smile to his face.

Turning serious again, Saddam looked at his ground commanders in the west. "General al-Hamdani, do we need to commit the IV Corps to replace you at this time?"

"No, sir, with the refitting of the 7th and 5th Divisions and them joining up with the II Corps, we should be able to overwhelm the American positions around Jeddah by the end of next week, fourteen days, tops," al-Hamdani said. Ra'ad Rasjod nodded his head in agreement as well.

"Good, then see that it is done. Time may no longer be on our side. We need to complete our objectives and consolidate our gains before the Americans are able to marshal their forces. We need to make taking Saudi Arabia and the Gulf States too costly for the Americans to endure," Saddam explained. He then stood and turned to leave the room. As he left, he turned back again. "Gentlemen, no more mistakes." He then motioned the air marshal to follow him.

Chapter 6

101st Moves to Defend

8 September 1990

King Abdulaziz International Airport

Jeddah, Saudi Arabia

"Benny, I'm damn glad to see you finally arrived," Major General Ed Ford said, a broad smile spreading across his face. He and Major General Benny Peters had been classmates and friends at the Virginia Military Institute or VMI. Physically, both men were about the same size, but personality-wise they were complete opposites. Peters was the quiet one, whereas Ed was always talking and seldom listening.

General Gary Luck liked working with them. They were each other's yin and yang and he fully planned on exploiting that.

"Alright, if this lovefest is over, we can get down to business," General Luck said with a slight smile as he motioned for the two commanding generals to walk over to a table with a map spread out. "Benny, what's the status of the 101st now?" he asked.

"Well, sir, all of my Apache and Cobra gunships are in-country now, along with the 229th Apache helicopters from Fort Rucker. The 2nd Brigade closed this morning on Jeddah. Soldiers from the 1st and 3rd Brigades started flying in yesterday morning. Without any unforeseen shipping problems, I think we will have closed the entire division here by the end of the month, minus some equipment. Our first ship left Jacksonville on the nineteenth of August and the last ship sailed this morning," General Peters noted.

"That's great. Right now we need some fresh troops. Look here." General Luck pointed to the map. "Benny, Ed's division is occupying this ridge west of Medina and has the 7th and 5th Republican Guard divisions scratching their heads trying to figure out how to get past him.

"So we have a tough situation shaping up in the north around Medina. If I had to guess, I think the Iraqi commander is planning to wait until the three divisions of the 2nd Iraqi Army Corps move down from the north and attempt to take Ed's position from the side and behind," Luck explained as he dragged his finger from the top of the map down to Ed's position on Medina Ridge.

Peters nodded in agreement. "Hmm—well, sir, it sounds like I need to prevent that from happening." Laughing, he added, "Here I go again, covering Ed's ass just like I had to do at VMI."

Ed jabbed him in the ribs but didn't disagree with General Peters's assessment. His airborne units were in a very tough position along Medina Ridge, especially after this last battle. His division had taken an absolute beating but had dealt one too.

General Luck went on to explain, "My intelligence folks tell me there are three approaches they could use from where they are currently located. One division, the 7th Infantry Division, is located here at Masader, about one hundred miles to the north. Another is located at Al Jadid, about one hundred and twenty miles to the northeast, and we think that's the 51st Infantry Division. The 37th is following the 7th, so we suspect this will be the main effort or line of attack once they make their next move.

"I'd like to point out that the 7th Division got chewed up pretty good by a few air strikes when they got to Tabuk. I think they'll attempt to break through or at least try to punch a hole in our lines and allow the 37th to move through it. The 51st also has a good road but some difficult terrain. If he gets off that road and it brings him into play on the northeast face of Medina Ridge, we could be in trouble. The 7th has the worse approach over a two-lane road through some really nasty terrain if he gets off the road. My fear is the 37th will hit just as the 51st joins the 7th and 5th Republican Guard divisions and makes a push against the ridge.

"Benny, how soon will your division arrive?" Luck asked again.

"Sir, we only have some minor stuff left at Campbell. All the attack aircraft are here along with the Cobras in the Cav squadron. Black Hawks should be arriving in a week aboard the ships. We'll fly them off as soon as they're within range. Who's coming in after us?" Peters asked.

"The 3rd Herd is supposed to join us, but I doubt if we'll see them or the 24th. I think General Schwarzkopf wants them in Oman, and I can't blame him. This is pretty restricted terrain in this part of the country," General Luck explained. There was silence as all three general officers studied the map. Finally, the silence was broken by an air raid siren.

"What the—" General Peters didn't finish his sentence when the first bomb slammed into the parking ramp in front of the main terminal building. As the three generals found themselves on the floor, more explosions could be heard on the far end of the runway. General Peters just had to ask, "Does this happen very often, sir?"

"Not sure yet. This is only the second time since I arrived. I guess I'm going to need to look into getting us some air-defense units, aren't I?" he chuckled as another bomb went off.

****

XVIII Airborne HQ
Jeddah, Saudi Arabia

The various colonels representing the different G-directorates sat and listened to the G-2 intelligence officer give his initial brief. For many of them, this would be their first major overview of what was going on with the war in their particular sector of the war.

"General, looking at the terrain, I can see three avenues of approach into our sector," Lieutenant Colonel Mike Cordray said, pointing at the map. Lieutenant Colonel Cordray was the division intelligence officer. He'd been an infantry officer earlier in his career and transferred to military intelligence just prior to making major. It wasn't that he disliked the infantry, but he was more intrigued with the intelligence systems and the intelligence preparation of the battlefield. He was also damn good at what he did.

"The first and most dangerous avenue runs from Masader in the north to Abu Caramel to Shajwa and enters our sector at Al Dhalyiah. It's a one-hundred-and-six-mile run, with the widest point being thirteen miles at Huraymil and Sililah Anezah. In most places the route is less than a mile wide with high ridges overlooking it. It's also some pretty difficult terrain for wheel vehicles to negotiate," Colonel Cordray concluded.

General Peters acknowledged the information with a nod but said nothing. That was his style—say little until he had formulated an intelligent question.

"Sir, the second avenue of approach, and frankly far worse than the first, starts at Al Jadid over very open and easily negotiated terrain, following this highway to Al Eshash, to Khaybar, to Al Latin and coming in on the right front flank of our sector. Once the Iraqis reach the mountains, they're restricted to a two-lane road all the way through our sector. This area on the left side of his approach appears to be open ground, and it is, but it's flint rock, boulders, and deep crevasses and will be almost impossible for a wheel vehicle to cross. Even track vehicles will have a difficult time of it. The first forty-five miles are open ground with good mobility, but from then on for the next one hundred miles, it's follow-the-leader with no place to go if stopped," Cordray explained.

"So a solid air strike on them if they go that route pretty much bottles them up. Good to know. So tell me about this third avenue," Peters asked.

"The third avenue starts out like the first, but at Sulailah Juhainah, it breaks off and goes southwest through the mountains to the coast. It's also through some very rugged terrain and has few places that they can disperse and spread out," the colonel stated.

"Where does this third avenue terminate?"

"It terminates on the coastal plain in the vicinity of Yanbu. If the Iraqis were to get here, they'd have good mobility to roll into Jeddah one hundred and seventy-six miles to the south." Pausing for a moment, Colonel Cordray said, "I would think if he got to the coast in any kind of shape, the 10th Saudi Mechanized Brigade could take him, depending on how badly chewed up they were coming through the mountains."

"Well, we might see what we can do to help out the 10th," Peters said.

"One other point I would like to make, sir. It'd be very difficult for their heavier air-defense system to track our aircraft in this terrain. Their SA-7s and ZSU-23-4 will be effective, but anything that relies on radar guidance is going to have a tough time of it in these mountains," Cordray added.

"Good. That will make Cody and the chopper boys happy," Peters acknowledged.

"Sir, if there are no questions, I will be followed by the three," Colonel Cordray concluded. Peters nodded his head again.

Colonel Provost, the Operations officer, took the pointer as he and Cordray passed and stepped in front of the map. "Sir, I have reviewed the orders from XVIII Airborne Corps, and our mission and sector. We've been assigned a wide sector, but considering the terrain and the restrictive nature of this sector, I believe we can accomplish our mission. The first and second avenues of approach are the most dangerous to us. I told our air liaison at CENTCOM that we're going to need more air defense and offensive support if we're to hold our current positions. We're facing at least one and potentially two Iraqi corps. I believe I sufficiently made the case for an increased air presence, but we'll see in the coming days."

Peters said nothing.

"Sir, I propose two courses of action. First, we establish the forward edge of the battlefield from Shajwa to Al Latin with the forward limit of troops being established from here to Umm Hushim. This gives us a depth of about twenty-six thousand meters for the deep battle on the left flank and eighteen thousand meters on the right flank. I propose we put one brigade on the right avenue and one on the left. A third brigade would be positioned in depth around Al Mulaylih. This would provide sufficient depth for the attack birds to hit them and wear them down before they even got to the forward limit of troops well as the artillery and any tac air we get to engage them. There's also an opportunity for the attack birds to strike that third division as it approaches Al Faqa'ali," Colonel Provost said as General Peters moved forward in this seat to study the map.

"And the other?" Peters finally said.

"The second would have two brigades taking up positions, with one brigade defending from Abu Haramel to Tara'ah. Another brigade would defend from Huraymil to Shajwa and effectively close the end of the engagement area. There are some goat trails that we could use in Hummers to resupply, but most of the resupply would be by air," Provost said, pausing for a moment. "None of these courses of action will allow us to concentrate artillery support, so each brigade would have to rely only on its own 105 battalion. Corps artillery may be able to back up some of our battalions, but not by much. We will be relying on the attack aircraft and tac air," Provost concluded.

Peters stared silently at the map for another minute. Finally, he said, "Colonel, I like course of action two. Course of action one has us too far back and not taking advantage of the depth to get the infantry hitting them. We can wear him down in course of action two and stop him with the brigade to the rear. Our deep battle can engage him for some time before he reaches our front-line units. Let's get it flushed out and run it up to CENTCOM and brief the brigade commanders. I'm going to move the Saudi brigade to cover that third avenue to the coast. We just don't have the combat power to cover that avenue as well. With CENTCOM's permission, I want us moving into positions as soon as possible and getting away from this airfield before it gets hit again."

Chapter 7

A Legend Is Born

12 September 1990
495th Tactical Fighter Squadron "Valkyries"
Hurghada International Airport
Hurghada, Egypt

Major William "Gunslinger" Kidd sat in his chair as he watched
Captain Wolf from the 1N shop stand up to give them his portion of the
mission brief. The 1N shop was the air force's intelligence group,
similar to the Army S2 or G2 intelligence shops. The last few weeks'
missions had been tough on the squadron. They'd lost four of their
sixteen aircraft—one to enemy ground fire and three shot down by
fighters. Worse, none of the aircrews had been recovered yet. They
knew one of the planes had blown up with the crew still in it, while the
aircrews of the other three planes had managed to eject. They were
presumed prisoners for the time being.

"This next attack is going to be against the 7th Iraqi Division near
Tabuk. We hit this unit pretty hard a week ago. The latest intelligence
reports indicate they've just been refitted with some new equipment
and replacements. They also appear to be getting ready to link up with
the 37th Iraqi Division just as the 7th and 5th Republican Guard
Divisions are gearing up to make another hard push against Medina
ridge. Those poor blokes in the 82nd can only withstand so much.
They've been getting pounded with enemy artillery, mortars, and
sporadic attacks for more than a week. Just last night they got hit by an
enemy air raid," Captain Wolf explained.

"Now it's our time to hit back. What you guys need to be on the lookout for are any additional SA-13 Gophers, SA-19 Grisons, and those damn SA-6 Gainfuls. Try to use the terrain to your benefit as much as you can until you clear the mountains and ridges. Also, one other major thing I need to tell you about. We're still trying to gather intelligence on this, but there's apparently an Iraqi squadron called 3rd Squadron. We don't know a whole lot about them other than they fly MiG-29s and they're apparently in this neck of the woods. What we do know is these pilots are damn good. Two of their pilots have already reached Ace level, having each scored in excess of five aerial kills. Near as we can tell, this squadron has scored some twenty-nine aerial kills since the start of the war. Nineteen of those kills have come against us, so don't think they're just getting lucky against planes parked on the ramp. Whoever these pilots are, they're damn good and know what the hell they're doing."

Major Kidd interjected, "Captain Wolf, this is good information. Knowing this, what kind of fighter support do we have? Also, are we going to have some Wild Weasels flying ahead to clear us a path through the SAMs?"

"As a matter of fact, yes. We have a dedicated E-3 Sentry along with a flight of six F-4 Phantoms who'll run ahead of you as Weasels and three flights of two F-15Cs as fighter cover. Oh, just so you're aware, the fighters are coming from the 71st Fighter Squadron out of Langley. They just arrived in Egypt a week ago and are flying out of Berenice International Airport," Wolf explained. "OK, if no one else has further questions, then that concludes my portion of the brief."

As Captain Wolf left, Major Kidd walked up to the lectern. "OK, this is it. Our seventh mission in ten days. We've all learned a little bit about what works and what doesn't on these missions, so let's put that to good use. As you know, we're still waiting for our new squadron commander to arrive, so for now, I'm still it."

Their squadron commander had gotten shot down deep inside Saudi Arabia a week ago. For the time being, Kidd had taken over.

"Once we cross into Saudi, I want everyone to do their best to hug the terrain features like we have in the past and stay ready for whatever may come next. We're going to go in just like we have the last two missions. That trick we've been playing on them seems to be working, so let's stick to it. I want Karma Four-Two with me. Karma Four-Three and Four-Four, you guys are going in the chute second. Karma Four-Five, Four-Six, you'll be going in third, followed by Karma Four-Seven, Four-Eight, Four-Nine, and Five-Zero closing the show out. Remember, you closers will be plastering the area with cluster munitions. That means you need to drop your ordnance with at least two thousand feet of altitude. The rest of us will be carrying eight sticks of Mk 84 heavies. We have a lot of enemy vehicles in the area spread across a wide area. We're going to need the heavies if we're to mess things up for them."

Several of the pilots let out a few whistles at the news. They didn't usually carry the heavier two-thousand-pound dumb bombs. Those kinds of weapons were typically good for carpet-bombing-type missions by the BUFFs. Then again, dropping sixty-four of them across the Iraqi divisions' positions pretty much counted as a carpet-bombing mission.

Ninety minutes later, the Valkyries had just topped off their tanks compliments of a group of KC-10s as they loitered over the Red Sea. The Wild Weasels from the 81st Fighter Squadron had just gone in ahead of them. They were flying down the same flight path the Aardvarks would in a few minutes, clearing the path of enemy air-defense systems. If all went according to plan, the Iraqi SAMs would engage the Weasels, who were better suited to counter them and take them out. Then Kidd's fliers would zip in behind them down a cleared-out path to carry out their strike.

All of that was being covered from high above them by three pairs of F-15Cs from the 71st Fighter Squadron. If those enemy MiGs from the Iraqi 3rd Squadron showed up, the Eagles would give them a run for their money. Prior to getting airborne, Major Kidd looked at the entire mission package for this mission. They had a total of thirty-nine aircraft involved in supporting just one single mission. Quite a bit when you thought about the number of individual airmen needed to make a single mission fly and work.

The radio in his helmet crackled to life. "Karma Four-One, Eagle Two. We're showing clear skies, no enemy aircraft. Panther element is ten mikes into the chute. We're not showing any signs of SAMs. You are cleared hot to enter the chute."

Kidd smiled; it was time to go earn their keep. "Eagle Two, Karma Four-One, that's a good copy. Karma elements will begin entering the chute as outlined in the package. Out."

Switching over to his internal squadron net, Gunslinger related the attack order and information to the other eleven pilots. It was time for them to head in and hammer this enemy division.

Angling his aircraft towards his new heading, Gunslinger began dropping in altitude. His aircraft steadily moved from angels fifteen down to just a hundred meters above the deck as they crossed over onto land. His heads-up display or HUD's navigation unit guided him down the path he needed to travel. In moments he saw the valley entrance and knew exactly where he was. They'd flown through this path once before on a mission a few weeks back. It didn't have too many curves to it, which made it easy enough for their larger, fast-moving aircraft to navigate while still shielding them from ground radars. When they emerged from the valley, they'd be less than five minutes from their target.

As they zipped through the valley, he'd already swept their angled wings back, reducing their drag and further reducing their radar cross-signature. Looking down at his altimeter, he saw he was fluctuating between ninety-six meters and one hundred and five meters at a speed of 610 knots. They weren't cruising at supersonic speeds, but they weren't far off either. As he looked outside his canopy, the ground and terrain around them whipped by in a blur. They were traveling so low and so fast you just couldn't make out the finer details of what you were flying past. If you looked off in the distance or further ahead of you, you could see those details.

For the next fifteen minutes they rode in virtual silence. Gunslinger's bombardier and copilot, Captain Tommy "Kung Fu" Hansen, continued to run through his checks, making sure everything was ready.

Gunslinger liked Kung Fu. The man was a beast in the gym and an amazing martial arts instructor, which was how he'd earned his nickname.

He'd been teaching many of the pilots in the squadron various self-defense tricks they could use in case they had to eject.

As they approached twenty-five minutes to the target, their radios crackled to life. No one was speaking to them directly, but they could hear the excited chatter going on with the Panther element. From what Gunslinger could tell, they were in a real fight. They were calling out one SAM or gun truck after another, with the code word, Fox Three, being called in quick succession. They were apparently sending one HARM or high-speed antiradiation missile after another at the targets.

"Sounds like the Panthers are giving them the business," said Kung Fu.

"Yeah, it sure does. I hope it means they'll have cleared the area out for us. I'd like us to get through this mission without any further losses."

"Agreed, it's kind of hurting morale."

"Five minutes till we're out of the chute," Gunslinger announced over the comms.

"Roger that, Gunslinger. We're ready to bring the pain!" came the excited voice of his wingman. These kinds of missions were what pilots like them lived for. They'd spent their entire Air Force careers up to this point training to do this exact type of mission across Germany and Europe in case the Russkies decided they wanted to get froggy and ignite the Cold War. Now they were doing these kinds of missions for real.

"Holy crap! Look at that!" Kung Fu blurted out, startling Gunslinger.

Looking up, he saw exactly what his friend had shouted about. In the distance, the battle was raging just beyond the end of the chute, which they were rapidly approaching. They saw strings of red and green tracer fire crisscrossing the sky. Normally you wouldn't see this level of clarity with tracers during the day, but the sun had largely been obscured by dense cloud cover, so it was a bit darker than normal for this time of day.

The tracer fire was thick, too. It was intermixed with little puffs of black smoke, which they knew instinctively was flak. That meant the enemy not only had SAMs and gun trucks set up—they'd also moved in some anti-aircraft artillery equipment to the area. AA and SAM fire was one thing; introducing triple-A to the mix was a whole new ballgame.

"Whoa, we're going to need to change things up. Spin up our EW pod while I let the others know what we're about to fly into."

Gunslinger let his fliers know they were about to fly into a huge straight-up mess and likely an ambush by the Iraqis. They must have figured they'd be gunning for this same division because they had moved a *lot* of additional guns over to protect them.

"All Karma elements, FRAGO. I say again, FRAGO to original plan. I want everyone to pull out of the chute and go supersonic as we climb to angels twenty and reapproach the enemy from position beta."

Just as he'd applied more power to the engines, pushing them past Mach 1 as he climbed for altitude, one of the Panther aircraft exploded off to their right. He didn't have a lot of time to glance at it, but he saw it just long enough to see the two pilots eject and their chutes open. *Thank God, at least they made it out of the plane.*

As his aircraft climbed, pushing past angels ten, his RHAW or radar, homing, and warning system blared in their ears. It told them a single SAM site had locked on to them. Moments later, the tone from the RHAW changed as a SAM had fired. Then the sky around them filled with gunfire as some of the radar-controlled gun trucks tried to blot him from the sky.

"Missile launch! Five o'clock and closing," Kung Fu announced. He was working their EW pod, doing his best to jam the enemy missile's radar lock.

Meanwhile, Gunslinger was doing his best to maneuver his way deftly through the gunfire around them while at the same time trying to put some distance between himself and the missile that was chasing after them.

Giving the engines more juice, he clawed at the air for more speed. Then it dawned on him that he still had his entire stick of ordnance attached to him. Aside from the weight, it was killing his maneuverability. Checking his position, he saw he was just now crossing over top of the enemy division. Without giving it another thought, he hit the arming button on the bombs and released the entire stick.

Of course, racing across the sky at Mach 1.1 at an altitude of thirteen thousand feet meant his stick of eight two-thousand-pound bombs would be spread wildly across the area. He just hoped they caused some damage.

With the bombs no longer slowing him down, his jet took off even faster. He pushed it for all it was worth as the missile warning alarm continued to blare, letting him know the damn thing was still chasing him. As he angled the large aircraft into a slight roll and dove for the deck, he felt the tension in the airframe from the massive g-forces he was putting it and himself through.

As they flew lower, dropping below fifteen thousand feet again, they found themselves back in range of the AA gun trucks once again. Their radar-controlled vehicles directed the guns to open up on him, sending renewed bullets right after them.

On the ground, he saw one of the enemy gun trucks explode when a HARM missile slammed into it. He also saw a SAM vehicle blow up a minute later. He was glad to know the Wild Weasels hadn't moved from this enemy trap and were still doing their best to cover the bombers. He just hoped the rest of his guys did better than he had in going after their targets.

"That missile is still on our tail."

"Not for long. Watch this," Gunslinger said as he pulled up hard on the flight controls. The big Aardvark pulled out of its steep dive and then spun into a climbing corkscrew of a move as it sought to regain the altitude it had just lost. The SAM that had been on their tail moments earlier slammed into the ground, exploding harmlessly.

"Hot damn! Now that's some flying, Gunslinger!" Kung Fu congratulated him.

Before either of them could say anything, a string of cannon shells zipped right across their cockpit, scaring the hell out of them. Then the aircraft shook hard as more than a handful of the shells slammed into them.

Gunslinger turned the aircraft to the right and changed their altitude rapidly to throw the gun crew on the ground off as another group of shells just missed them once again. While he was doing that, Kung Fu was checking their gauges to make sure they hadn't sustained any serious damage.

"I think it's time to turn back for home. Our luck's just about run out."

"Yeah, I agree. I think I'm going to need to change my flight suit. That was close."

Turning to head back home, Gunslinger counted his pilots. While the mission had gone sideways and they hadn't been able to hit the Iraqi division like they had planned to, they hadn't lost any aircraft. They'd still delivered their ordnance (though the results looked a bit mixed from their vantage point). Sadly, the Panther unit flying the Wild Weasel mission ahead of them had suffered the brunt of the ambush. They'd lost two aircraft while two more had taken damage. In exchange, they'd succeeded in destroying nine AA gun trucks and five mobile SAM trucks. Taking out that many enemy air-defense vehicles meant the next mission would have that many fewer resources from which to defend the division.

Once they returned home, they'd regroup, assess what had been damaged, and then work up another mission to go hit the exact same division. This time he'd advocate for them flying across more of the desert and approaching the enemy from the rear. This way they wouldn't be flying right into the hornet's nest like they had this time around.

Chapter 8
Plans Are Adjusted

13 September 1990
Iraqi Army Forward HQ
Abu Dhabi, United Arab Emirates

General al-Dulaymi had called a meeting with his division commanders at the Presidential Palace in Abu Dhabi. The Al Ras Al Akhdar was one of the most luxurious palaces in the world, with a private beach, yacht basin, manicured lawns, several swimming pools, and tennis courts. The opulence was amazing and, in al-Dulaymi's mind, made the palaces in Baghdad look cheap and tawdry. He was rather enjoying the opportunity to stay in such fine accommodations. As each of the division commanders came in, they were directed to the central conference room and served an assortment of tea, coffee, and milk, along with a selection of fruits and pastries.

"Gentlemen, if you will be seated, we can begin today's meeting," announced a colonel and member of al-Dulaymi's staff. As each commander took a seat, Colonel al-Baghdad pulled up a map on the overhead projector, depicting the corps sector and the location of each of the divisions.

"General al-Tikrit, you are the northernmost division, so let's start with you outlining your positions," General al-Dulaymi said.

"Yes, sir... in the very north, the terrain is rugged, too rugged for any mechanized or armor force. It is my understanding that the American 82nd Airborne and 101st Airborne are in Jeddah dealing with a similar type of terrain. They've shown that an infantry force can hold down a superior force pretty well, especially if they have attack helicopters. Seeing how this has played out, I have only one battalion there operating out of Ras Al-Khaimah. Moving south from there along the border to the ocean is also very restrictive terrain. However, around Fujairah there are good port facilities and a major highway through the mountains into the heart of my sector. We seized the naval port at Fujairah, and it is ready to be turned over to the navy for their use, whenever they get here," he said. His sarcasm was noted by the others.

"I have positioned a reinforced brigade along that coastline and requested additional long-range artillery and air defense to counter a possible amphibious landing by the American Marines. The hydrography will support an amphibious landing with a wide beach of sand that could support track vehicles. I am preparing the beaches now with the corps engineers to create obstacles along the beaches, but we are talking many miles of beach with easy egress off them. Our defensive positions will be in buildings, and we are moving the local population out of the homes and buildings within two kilometers of the beach," General al-Tikrit concluded.

For a moment, General al-Dulaymi said nothing but studied the map and rubbing his chin. "General, you probably have the most dangerous avenue of approach into the corps. I want you to move your entire division to the Fujairah area. General Ujayll, your division will assume responsibility for his previous sector. I know that is a large area, but with the Strait closed to the Americans, you have little threat until they force entry. Any questions?" General al-Dulaymi asked, directing his question at both commanders.

"No, sir," was the unanimous response from both generals. They knew better than to question his order on this matter.

"General Asaad, please discuss your defensive plan," General al-Dulaymi requested. After his latest meeting with Saddam, he needed to make sure his commanders were as ready as possible for what might be coming with the Americans. He didn't need more grief from the boss. He needed to win some battles and pray to Allah the Americans would see reason and pursue peace.

"Sir, the terrain forward of my sector is very rough, with only one major road coming from Oman, Highway 7. The rough terrain stops about fifteen kilometers short of the border in the north to fifty kilometers from the border in the south. The city of Al Ain unfortunately sticks like a finger out to the border, exposing three sides. We seized the military installation in Al Ain, an air wing, with no difficulty. There were no aircraft there, however, and it appears they likely flew them to Oman. My intent is not to occupy the area but to build my defenses in the Al Ain area. I intend to keep my tank force mobile and ready. This way they'll be ready to respond to any movement by an attacker's force once I identify where the main attack will be coming from. Although Al Buraimi is on the Oman side of the border, if we see any major force coming on Highway 7, I will attack first to occupy Al Buraimi and deny the enemy the ability to close unmolested right up to my defensive positions," General Asaad explained in great detail and with a few maps.

"If you must do that, do not employ your artillery in Al Buraimi. We want to win the hearts of the people, not turn them against us. Understood?" General al-Dulaymi pointed out.

"Yes, sir, understood" came the expected response.

Turning his attention to General Dairi, commander of the 6th Nebuchadnezzar Mechanized Division, al-Dulaymi explained, "General, I am most concerned about your sector. We are placing a lot of faith in the Empty Quarter deterring an attack from that direction. That means you are the only unit protecting our flank from that direction. While I am more concerned with an attack out of Oman from Tan'am and Fahud, we cannot fully dismiss the idea of the Americans attempting to move through this sector. Keep in mind the dunes in this area parallel the avenue of advance and will help mask their movements if they opt to go that route."

General Dairi countered, "The dunes will also conceal our positions as well. We have ample depth to see into Oman and identify where they are going to attack from. This is not easy terrain to try to cross with a large military force. The distance between the dunes is anywhere from one and a half kilometers to three kilometers, creating rectangular boxes running east to west. It would be very difficult for any mechanized or armor force to move through this area unnoticed."

Continuing, General Dairi added, "What I believe they will do is look to capitalize on the one paved road that parallels the border north to south and then turns west, right to my positions. Our infantry forces will have time to reposition if necessary, and my armor forces will be positioned to respond as they approach. I suspect the Americans will come at me in the right flank, where the larger, more pronounced dunes do not exist and the more open ground provides good mobility for their tanks, in hopes of cutting our forces off, leaving us bottled up in the UAE."

Al-Dulaymi grunted at the blunt assessment. "See that you do not let him come that way, then. The last thing we want is to get a division or a corps cut off in the UAE. Now, I'd like to hear about the intelligence we are receiving about the American buildup in Oman, General," he said, acknowledging a brigadier general that had been sitting in the background.

His uniform indicated he was from the 8th As Saiqa Special Forces Division. The other division commanders had sort of forgotten about the Special Forces Division after they had bypassed the important oil refineries.

"Sir, the 8th As Saiqa Special Forces Division has been operating in Oman since June, acting as dockyard workers and other laborers. This has given us an opportunity to observe what the Americans have been doing as well as the British. It has also given us an opportunity to determine targets for demolitions and attacks when the time comes." He paused as he moved to the map of Oman that had been projected on the screen from the overhead projector.

"Currently, the Americans have ships unloading at the Said Bin Sultan Naval Base located in Al Mudayq, eighty-seven kilometers north of Muscat. They have some ships, the RoRo ships unloading in Liwa and ships unloading cargo and containers in As Sultan Qaboos Port. We have people at both of these locations recording the amount and type of equipment coming into the country. In addition, it appears that one US Marine Division is unloading at Dhuwwah on Masirah Island, using landing craft and their LST transport ships to load over the beach as well as hovercraft to bring supplies ashore. There are no major port facilities on Masirah Island, so moving supplies and people ashore with the hovercraft and the landing craft is necessary. There is a facility just off the airport that we believe they are going to use as their headquarters. We're trying to get some workers to infiltrate it so we can verify that and potentially sabotage it. I also want to note that at the airfield, we spotted a squadron of Marine Harrier jets. They are being stored in the hardened aircraft bunkers on the airfield.

"One of my commanders believes he may have found the Americans' primary headquarters location. They believe it's being established at the Oman International Exhibition Center and Oman Tourism College. These are located just outside the Muscat

International Airport, where some American aircraft have been landing and offloading military personnel. This places them close to the Omani government and the airport itself. It's also large enough for their enormous staff to work out of. We've managed to get a couple of people into the catering staff and janitor service. Again, once we have official confirmation that this is in fact the primary location, and you've given us permission, we'll look to carry out some sort of attack on the facility to see if we can kill some of the senior leadership."

Before anyone else could ask a question, the Special Forces commander quickly added, "I also want to bring your attention to this. This is a set of warehouses that have just been secured in the Ghala Industrial Estate. Some are being used to house people and others for stockpiling supplies. I bring this to your attention because it is now becoming abundantly clear that the Americans are planning to launch the bulk of their military operations against us out of Oman, not the Saudi port area of Jeddah."

One of the generals then asked, "What about these Harrier jets? I've heard they can land and take off like a helicopter, making them incredibly versatile. Do we know where else they are being held?"

Nodding at the question, Colonel Hassani explained, "Yes, we did find another location. Here, in the vicinity of Sohar, we spotted some Harrier jets that had landed. We could not determine if they were American or British, as they landed shortly after dark and were quickly covered. In Sohar there are three cantonment areas being prepared for military use—the Sohar Major Industrial Park, the Dunes Cricket Grounds in Majan and the Towel Workers Camp. Across the highway from the Towel Workers Camp is a school that has been turned into a headquarters for what we believe will be a division. There are two palaces northwest of the airport and adjacent to the airport that we believe will become the Marine headquarters and another division headquarters. As things progress and more intelligence is gathered, we will continue to provide it to you," Colonel Hassani concluded.

"Thank you, Colonel, for that intelligence update," General al-Dulaymi said. Colonel Hassani gave a slight bow and headed for the door. The generals around the table looked impressed with the detailed assessment their Special Forces had been able to provide. It was exactly what they had needed and wanted.

Turning to the division commanders, al-Dulaymi asked the group, "So, gentlemen, what is your assessment based on what our Special Forces have been able to acquire for us?"

"Sir, I think the 2nd al-Medinah Armoured Division will be taking on the US Marines. It appears to me that they are building up an amphibious force to make a forced landing. The question is, where? I think there are three important places that they'll need to conduct their combat operations. The first is the port of Fujairah as it is the major fuel offload site and they are going to need fuel for their armor forces. The second location is the port of Khor Fakkan as it is the only port that has a container offload capability anywhere along the coast besides the As Sultan Qaboos Port in Muscat, which is a long way off and not as capable as Khor Fakkan. Lastly, they will want the airport at Fujairah as it is the only multi-runway airport in this part of the country. Those are the three centers of gravity for the Americans," General al-Tikrit said confidently.

"I think your analysis may be correct, General. I will expect you to develop a plan to defend this area and get back to me within the next couple of days. I want to see one brigade moving into the coastal area very soon and engineer work commencing as soon as you have a plan developed," al-Dulaymi said. Then he turned his attention to General Ujayll.

"General Ujayll, I want you to work out a plan on how you are going to reinforce General al-Tikrit if the main attack comes against him and how you will reinforce the others as well. I would like that within a week with priority to the 2nd Division. Any questions?"

"Sir," General al-Tikrit asked, "I only have two brigades and I see the defense of this sector, which is twenty-seven kilometers long, as requiring a minimum of three brigades and preferably four."

"I think you may be right, General. When the 18th Brigade is refitted next week, I will send them to you as soon as it arrives," General al-Dulaymi explained, looking at his aide to make sure he made a note of that order. "Now if there is nothing else…," al-Dulaymi said as he stood and left the room.

Chapter 9
Lieutenant Takes Charge

14 September 1990
As Sultan Qaboos Port
Muscat, Oman

Second Lieutenant Ainsley Fitzgerald was about as new to the
Army as one could be. Six months ago she had been standing with her
beaming parents at graduation from the University of South Florida in
Tampa with her diploma in hand and her Army ROTC commissioning
only moments away. The following week it was off to the Basic Officer
course at Fort Lee, Virginia, for supply officers. She had gone through
the course with ease, especially the physical fitness portion. She'd
played goalie on the local ice hockey team and could take the blows as
well as give them. None of her classmates had wanted her for a
sparring partner in the hand-to-hand combatives. Some of the male
students had thought she would be easy. They'd all found out the hard
way. Standing only five foot three and weighing a hundred pounds,
she'd whooped their butts each time, but they'd all loved her for her
looks and her intelligence.

Her chain of command had soon realized that with her looks, her
brains and her personality, this young lady had a bright future ahead of
her in the service. She had only joined her unit the week before and was
now standing in an empty warehouse in As Sultan Qaboos Port,
Muscat, Oman. The warehouse sat between the first two piers in the
harbor. Both piers were capable of handling bulk and container cargo,
and a bulk carrier was just pulling into port. This ship had containers.

The container yard was adjacent to the warehouse, and it was presently empty.

"Lieutenant, don't just stand there. We have work to do getting this place organized and set to start receiving stuff. That ship will be secured in about an hour and it'll be brought directly here. How do you want to lay this place out?" the platoon sergeant asked in a less-than-respectful tone. Fitzgerald just stared at him for a minute, but he could see it wasn't a deer-in-the-headlights stare. *Oh, no, I screwed up with this one* went through his mind.

"Sergeant," she finally said, "we haven't really had an opportunity to work together yet, have we?" Before he could answer, she continued, "No, we haven't, so let's get one thing straight. I do the thinking and directing and you get the job done. Right now, I'm thinking. Do you know what I'm thinking about?" Again, before he could answer, she continued, "I'm thinking, what the hell is on that ship that we have to store? We aren't going to be emptying those containers. No one has given us a manifest yet, so until they do, how do we know what we're storing, what's shipping out in the container, where it's going and whether there are any special considerations for storage? Until we get that information, how do you propose we lay out this warehouse or the container yard?" she asked. He didn't respond. "Cat got your tongue, Sergeant Murray?"

"No, ma'am. I see your point," Murray hesitantly responded.

"Good. Now you get the platoon together and get the forklifts in working order while I go find someone that can get me the manifests, so we know what we're going to be putting in here. When I get back with that information, be ready to get this place organized. Oh, also see if you can get some spray paint," she directed and then turned on her heel to get a move on.

"Spray paint, ma'am? Yes, ma'am," was all he could say as she walked out the warehouse doors towards the dockyard.

An hour later she came back with a clipboard and papers. Following her was another sergeant. She made the introductions.

"Sergeant Major, this is my platoon sergeant, Sergeant Murray," she said. Murray didn't say anything, but the two noncommissioned officers exchanged handshakes.

"The sergeant major is in charge of the stevedores from the 7th Trans. They're working with the locals in unloading the ship. Most of the containers are bound for the 24th ID and consist of God only knows what. So, we're going to rack and stack them in the yard until transports arrive to haul them to the 24th's cantonment area. As each container is placed in the yard, I want you to note it on the manifest and then mark on the doors with spray paint which unit it's assigned to. That way it'll be easy for the unit to identify specific containers and easier for us to pull a specific unit's containers if they need it. Any questions, Sergeant Murray?"

"No, ma'am," he replied as a smile crept across his face. The thought of being stuck with a green butter bar of a lieutenant faded as he realized she might actually know what she was doing.

"Good, I'm going to go find out when those trucks are going to roll in here and start getting these containers out of my yard," she said, turning on her heel and walking off.

"Sergeant Murray, it looks like you have a thinking lieutenant there. That could be dangerous," the sergeant major said with a grin.
****

"Sir, I was told that all my problems could be solved by coming to see you," Lieutenant Fitzgerald said. She was addressing a two-star general in an open bay office area with about twenty other officers behind their desks, which were arrayed around the general's desk in the middle. She had originally started at some distant office in the dock area and hadn't liked the answers she'd gotten, so she'd had gone to the next higher level until two hours later she was standing before this general.

"And who told you that, Lieutenant?" General Sullivan asked, a wry grin forming on his face. He liked an officer that showed initiative.

"It was that colonel sitting over there, sir," Fitzgerald said, pointing to an overweight colonel who was trying not to look in her direction. He hadn't thought she would really go speak to the general after he hadn't given her the answer she'd wanted.

Looking at the colonel with a glare that said, "We'll talk later," General Sullivan motioned for her to sit down. "OK, what's the problem that only I can solve?" he asked.

"Sir, I'm in charge of the container yard at As Sultan Qaboos Port. Our first ship came in about three hours ago and began offloading. I've been asking when I can expect to have trucks arrive to start moving those containers as I have another ship due in tonight and another tomorrow. That yard isn't that big. No one seems to be able to answer my question about the trucks to move stuff, which means my yard is going to pile up to the point that I won't be able to offload any more ships. That means the ships will get stuck in port and future ones won't be able to dock and so on," she said, respectfully stating her case.

General Sullivan stared at her for a moment, a smile spreading across his face. This was the kind of officer you latched onto, groomed and mentored for higher ranks.

"Why isn't your company commander or battalion commander in here getting the answers for you?" Sullivan asked.

"Sir, it's my yard. It's my problem to fix," was her simple response.

Picking up the phone, Sullivan said, "Get me the contracting office." He waited. "Contracting, General Sullivan here. What's the status of the contracts for the trucks to haul containers?" He paused. "Well, if you don't know, get me someone who does know and pronto." He paused again. "Yes, I'll hold." He covered the receiver with his hand and looked at Ashley. "We should have an answer shortly.... Yes, I'm still waiting." He shook his head. "Chambers, hello. What's the status of the contracts for the trucks to haul the containers out of the port's container yard? Next week? Shit, the containers are arriving today.... Not a priority, my ass. Make it a priority. I want those trucks at the port tomorrow hauling that stuff out of there. They're to report to Lieutenant Ainsley Fitzgerald when they get there and no one else," General Sullivan said rather forcefully. Whoever Chambers was, he must have said the wrong thing. "Chambers, if those trucks aren't there in the morning, you'll be on a flight back to the States tomorrow night with your request for retirement in hand. And if they're not there by 0900, Lieutenant Fitzgerald is going to call me personally. Do I make myself clear? I don't care if they're gouging us on the price. Get the damn contract signed and today. Do you read me?"

Sullivan laid the receiver in the cradle and picked up a pen and a piece of paper.

"Lieutenant, you call me at 0900 tomorrow and let me know the status of the trucks," he said, handing her his phone number. "Now, is there anything else?"

Standing, Fitzgerald came to attention and saluted. "No, sir, you've been the savior of all my problems today. Thank you, sir." She turned and walked out. Everyone watched her leave the building, in a bit of awe at the bravado on her.

Chapter 10
Planning Guidance

15 September 1990
CENTCOM Forward HQ
Military Technological College
Muscat, Oman

The building that had been given to the US to act as their main headquarters was beautiful. After some hemming and hawing back and forth with the government of Oman and the group in charge of providing security, the military technological college had been officially designated as the new US Central Command Forward Headquarters and Joint Allied Headquarters for this war in the Middle East. This crisis in the desert would now be managed at the military college. The facility was perfect for such an effort. Aside from having multiple large buildings that could house everyone, it had a solid perimeter and limited access to and from the compound. It also had a lot of empty land surrounding it, thus allowing them to establish a host of tents to house personnel and room to both establish a localized quick-reaction force and host several air-defense units.

The compound also provided them quick access to the international airport and was close enough to meet with the King and other members of the royal family. It was about as ideal a location as they could have come up with.

General "Stormin'" Norman Schwarzkopf had finally arrived in-country on 1 September. After making the perfunctory stops and visits with the local dignitaries and members of the royal family, to include the exiled emirs and royals, it was time to get down to the business at hand—the business of waging war and winning the peace.

As he walked into the main auditorium, which was going to function as the primary briefing room, a junior officer, who happened to be a colonel, called out in a booming voice, "Atten-shun!"

As everyone jumped to their feet, Stormin' Norman called out, "At ease, gentlemen, and take your seats." He walked down to the seat at the head of the bottom of the auditorium and looked up at the stage where a briefer stood, ready to begin his presentation once he gave him the nod.

Turning around so he could see everyone, Schwarzkopf noticed how the rows of chairs and the desks sitting in front of those rows had been labeled by directorate, service branch, and/or allied branch. This allowed him and anyone else to quickly see who they were talking to and be able to direct their immediate questions to them.

Once everyone was settled, he began, "Now that we have our headquarters established and, more importantly, the army is officially en route to our positions, it's time to issue you smart guys some planning guidance. This war kind of caught everyone by surprise. It took off really fast, and it's been running at full speed ever since. We've also been thrown a huge curveball with the Soviets seemingly getting involved at every level. In many ways, this conflict appears to have been engineered by them almost as a way of forestalling their impending collapse. However, I'm confident in our defensive plans at this point. You all have done an outstanding job in preventing the Iraqis from seizing all of Saudi Arabia and pushing into Oman. No easy feat. But what we have to do next, well, that's the hard part. What I haven't seen from you guys yet is our offensive plan to throw the Iraqis back across their own border."

Many of the officers nodded in agreement. They knew it had been a mad dash to stop the Iraqis from taking over the Middle East. Now it was time to figure out how they were going to get them to give up and go home.

Schwarzkopf continued, "I want you to start putting an offensive plan together immediately. As I see it, there are three options. One, a penetration at some point with all our combat power focused on one point. Enough to break through into the enemy's rear. To do that, we have to generate the power to overcome the front-line force and hold the shoulders. Second option is an envelopment of their forces to get into their rear area. But to do that, we have to fix his front line to prevent them from turning on us. The third option as I see it is a frontal attack—put pressure on the entire front, find a weak spot and punch through." He paused looking to see who the notetakers were among his staff and give them a chance to also catch up.

Continuing, Schwarzkopf said, "Now, before we can do any of those options, we first need all of our forces in-country and acclimated. Second, we need our logistics in place to support the operation through the duration and beyond. Third, we need air superiority. Fourth, we need a good reconnaissance of the Iraqi positions, minefields, obstacles, things like that. Fifth, we need to fix his secondary forces in place so they can't counterattack our lead elements. Sixth, this needs to be a phased ground operation with the liberation of the UAE first, the liberation of Saudi second, then the liberation of Kuwait, and finally the attack on Baghdad. Lastly, I want to minimize collateral damage to the civilian population. I do not want to win the war and lose the peace because we bombed the hell out of them indiscriminately. Understood?"

"Sir, question," General Schless asked.

"What is it?"

"Sir, what is our final strategic objective? We need to know that, so we have some idea of our force and logistical requirements."

"Now, General, that is a very good question, and when I get that question answered by the bureaucrats in Washington, then I will be sure to let you know," Schwarzkopf said with frustration. "I'm sorry, Jim, I've been asking that question since the day we arrived here, and all I'm getting is hand-wringing and 'wait one for answers.' I've suggested several options to them, such as the high ridge overlooking Kuwait City and even Baghdad. Thus far, all my suggestions have fallen into the cone of silence. So, for right now, let's say it's Baghdad and plan accordingly. We can modify that later if we get a decision out of Washington."

Sitting in the room were six officers that were attending the School of Advanced Military Studies, or SAMS for short, at the US Army Command and General Staff College. These were some smart majors that had completed the one-year course and been held over for a second year for advanced studies in the operational level of war. The operational level of war focused on the movement and employment of divisions and corps and Army groups in the offense and defense. The instructors at the Army Command and General Staff College understood the operational level of war versus the tactical level better than anyone. The SAMS program was now teaching a selected number of officers in more detail than what they received attending the regular one-year course. When the call had gone to deploy CENTCOM, a decision had been made to get some of these smart majors to come along and join the planning cell to gain some real-world experience in a major war.

Looking at the small group of Jedi majors, as they were referred to, Schwarzkopf said, "I want you six to put together a plan for us to go on the offense with the current force we have. I want to see a concept for the ground plan based on the three options I just covered and your recommendation for the best option. And you only have the forces currently in-country or en route. If you can't do it with the current forces, I want your recommendation on what else we need. Any questions?" Schwarzkopf asked. The six majors looked at each other to see who would speak up. Finally, Schless, who they would be working for, answered, "No, sir, we got it."

"Good. I'll expect a brief in five days."

****

After Schwarzkopf left the room, General Schless and the six majors sat for a few minutes in silence, each lost in his own thoughts. Finally, one spoke up. "Sir, he is kidding, right, about putting an offensive plan together with the current force structure?" Major Rumgay asked.

"Major, General Schwarzkopf does not kid around," Schless replied calmly.

"I know, sir, I worked for him once before when he was a brigade commander," Rumgay said. "He's tougher than a woodpecker's lips."

A few of the majors chuckled at the simile.

Getting down to brass tacks, General Schless explained, "Alright, for planning purposes, let's look at the following to work with. We have the 82nd and 101st on the ground in the west. They're backed up with the 8th, 10th and 45th Saudi Brigades. We have the 24th with the 197th Brigade here in Oman. The 1st Cav and the 3rd Armored Cav regiment are offloading as we speak. We have the 1st Marine Division ashore and the 2nd Marine Division afloat. The British 1st Armoured Division is available, and we've been told we may get two Egyptian divisions, but you can't count on them yet. The Saudis have created a task force that's under the command of General Khalid bin Sultan and consists of two Saudi mechanized brigades, an Omani brigade, a UAE mech battalion, a Kuwaiti brigade with an additional mechanized brigade, a brigade of the Saudi National Guard and a battalion of Saudi Marines."

The majors were writing this down and making sure they understood the basics of what they had to work with.

One of the majors, Major Stube, joked, "If that ain't a mixed bag of worms, I don't know what is." Stube was an infantry officer and had been a scout platoon leader in Vietnam. In his younger days, he had been a college football player at St. John's University when it had won the Small School National Championship. He still wore his championship ring.

"Agreed, but we play the hand we're dealt. Next question," Schless countered.

"So, sir, if I understand this right, what we have is two light divisions, the 82nd and the 101st located several hundreds of miles away from us with little chance of linkup or the capability of supporting an attack by our heavy forces. We have seven heavy divisions and an armored cavalry regiment for conducting an offensive operation against six heavy divisions in the first defensive belt and three heavy divisions and three light divisions in the second belt, with eight more divisions sitting around Riyadh and a few more divisions in a third belt before Kuwait. And that's not counting their reserve corps in Iraq. Is that about right, sir?" Major Peters expounded to everyone.

"That's about right, Major," General Schless replied as he nodded his head in approval.

"Sir, an offensive operation can't be done and reach the strategic objective that General Schwarzkopf outlined with the current force structure we have," Major Stube finally proclaimed.

"Well, that's your initial opinion. But let's do this: look at how you can employ our naval and air assets to aid our offensive punch and see if that might succeed in changing the outcome and pushing us closer to our victory. Remember, if you can't meet the entire objective, outline what you can meet and what more you'd need to finish it. After that we'll see what additional forces we'll need to reach our strategic goals. With that, I'm off to meet some folks for dinner near the coast, so you all have fun. Give me a shout when you're ready to brief your plan to me," General Schless said to the chagrin of his Jedis and left the room.

Needless to say, the Jedi majors would be burning some midnight oil working up a plan.

****

As the night progressed into the next day, the six Jedi majors were looking for every possible planning consideration they could find. Items like the terrain and environment had to be examined and understood. The enemy disposition and force structure were examined in detail from intelligence reports and satellite photos. Enemy tactics were following Soviet doctrine, which these guys were well versed in, so that was the easiest piece of the puzzle. One of the more trying pieces was the capabilities of the Egyptian and Saudi forces. How did these guys operate? What capabilities did they bring? A thousand questions had to be asked and answered.

"What time is it?" asked Major Rumgay.

"It's 0230 hours," answered Jack Stube.

"Guys, let's call it a night and come back at say… 0900. I think we'll all be better off with some sleep instead of staring at notes and blank paper," Bob Peters suggested. No one objected, and the group turned out the lights and headed to bed.

A loud pounding on the door woke Rumgay and Stube, who were sharing a room. "Rise and shine, ladies," Bob Peters said as he opened the door with a pot of coffee and two cups.

"What time is it?" Stube grumbled.

"It's 0815 and you have forty-five minutes to get ready and be in the shop. Me and McClain are heading over there now, and Fred and Mike will be over when they finish eating breakfast. See you over there," Peters said as he closed the door, leaving them with the fresh pot of coffee.

"How can anyone be that chipper this early in the morning?" Stube asked as he yawned.

"I don't know, but if he's going to wake us each morning with a pot of coffee, let him stay chipper."

At 0900 everyone was assembled, and they started their meeting. "OK, I recommend we come up with two courses of action like the general put in his guidance. Let's look at the option that's just what we have right now in-country and then look at a second plan if we could get some stuff that we don't have and identify what those additional forces should be. Jim, Jack, and Mike, want to tackle the second option, and me, Roy, and Fred will tackle the first?" Peters asked. "I'll also go find out some information on the Arab forces that we have and get back to both teams."

"Sure. Sky's the limit on the second option, right?" Jim asked with a grin.

"Think outside the box," was Peters's response as the teams separated to opposite sides of the conference room and started developing the courses of action. Ideas were placed on paper and then tossed out. Slowly, two options with a couple of courses of action each began to form. Late in the afternoon, they'd settled on two courses of action. When General Schless came back to check on them, they'd be ready to brief him. In the meantime, Major Stube continued to look at one Iraqi fighter squadron in particular. It was being called 3rd Squadron. What everyone was struggling to figure out was what made this squadron so special? Something about them was uniquely different. The way they flew their aircraft, the way they engaged the Americans, the way they flew in formations, they just flew differently than the other Iraqi squadrons. They were proving to be incredibly deadly compared to the other Iraqi Air Force squadrons.

****

Three Days Later

"Good morning, sir," Major Stube said as General Schless came into the room. Major Stube was acting as the group leader for the six Jedi majors. Everyone was already standing behind their respective chairs, waiting to get started. General Schless moved to a chair in the front row of the briefing room, which was arranged like a small auditorium with thirty seats. Only six were presently occupied.

"OK, guys, let's get on with it. Show me what you managed to come up with," Schless said.

"Yes, sir. As you know, this is our first go at this. We've developed two courses of action for each option that we'd like to brief this morning. In addition, we will discuss the force structure needed to accomplish the course of action that you choose in order to reach the strategic objective. I will just say right up front, sir, that with the current force structure, we cannot reach the strategic objective of capturing Baghdad. Furthermore, in both cases, we believe we can successfully seize only the first objective, recapturing the United Arab Emirates and thoroughly hammering the Iraqi forces from the air," Major Stube stated and then waited a minute for the general to provide a rebuttal.

Stube had half expected to receive a major ass-chewing and then a dressing-down by the general. But when he didn't proceed to challenge their assessment, Stube pressed on.

"Sir, we'll discuss the assumptions we've made thus far. First, we will and must have air superiority in all courses of action for both options. Second, we must negate the Iraqi air-defense systems. Third, we assume that the 82nd and the 101st can continue to hold the area around Jeddah and Yanbu but cannot come to our assistance in the east. Their position will really be meant more for tying the enemy down. Fourth, logistical resupply from the outside will continue uninterrupted, to include logistic units. Fifth, the British 1st Armoured Division is of equal capability to the comparable US units. Sixth, the forces of Saudi Arabia and others are probably inferior to the Republican Guard of Iraq but equal to or superior to the Iraqi forces in general," Major Stube explained.

"All good assumptions, Major. We may have to add a couple more before this is over. Please continue," General Schless said.

For the next couple of hours, the Jedi majors went over everything they had come up with. Of the major challenges they had to figure out how to overcome, the logistics and air superiority over the battlefield were at the top of the list. The latter was still probably the most important factor and would likely tip the balance of the war in their favor. They went over in great detail the challenges faced in obtaining air supremacy over the Iraqis, namely the fact that the Iraqis had been outfitted with a lot of tier-one Soviet equipment both prior to the war, thus enabling the crews to be adequately trained on the equipment, and then apparently during the second week of the war, when more than a handful of Soviet freighters had already been in the area, waiting to offload their equipment refits in the newly captured ports.

This caused the group to digress into an hourlong conversation to discuss this so-called "lend-lease" program the Soviets had signed with the Iraqis at the end of 1989 and going into the first half of 1990, all the way up to the start of the war. What the Soviets had essentially done for the Iraqis was a one-to-one swap of nearly all of their existing military equipment for front-line tier-one Soviet equipment. This had both cut the maintenance costs of several Soviet Army corps and outfitted a battle-hardened military with the best tier-one equipment they could acquire just before the start of this war.

Worse, there had been a real priority placed on the modernization of the Iraqi air-defense systems and their air force. This meant when the war had started, their ground units had been able to advance with the best possible air-defense vehicles to protect them as they'd raced across the desert. What still baffled the Jedi majors was three specific Iraqi Air Force squadrons. The first was 3rd Squadron, which operated the vaunted MiG-29 Fulcrums; the second was 6th Squadron, which flew the MiG-25 Foxbats; and the third was 7th Squadron, which flew a mix of Su-25 and Su-24 attack aircraft. These particular squadrons had scored above-average sortie rates and kill or engagement rates. Several pilots in the 3rd and 6th Squadrons had already achieved fighter Ace status.

General Schless interrupted their conversation at this point to say, "This information you're asking about these Iraqi squadrons is very interesting. It's something that's been brought up at the highest levels as well. It's becoming quite the anomaly, and there are some suspicions, some outright accusations by some, that these squadrons are not being flown by Iraqis but in fact straight-up flown by Soviet pilots, who are operating these aircraft to aid them."

None of the majors said anything at first. Their faces all looked like they had just sucked on a lemon. This was a consideration they had thought about but hadn't given a lot of credence until the general had mentioned it.

"Sir, if these are actual Russian pilots flying these aircraft, that may account for why we've been unable to secure air supremacy. If the Iraqi Air Force is being reinforced with Soviet aircraft and pilots, essentially fighting the war for them as proxies or contractors, then this will seriously complicate our efforts at achieving air supremacy," Major Stube commented softly, almost unsure of what he was saying.

The general nodded slowly. "It does. This is a large political problem the folks back in Washington will have to sort out. For now, it's incumbent on us to devise the best possible strategy to defeat the enemy given the resources and capabilities we have at hand. With that knowledge once again moved to the forefront of our minds, let's get back to devising a strategy we can present to the boss, shall we?"

Chapter 11

1st Marine Division Stands Up

17 September 1990
1st Marine Division HQ
Masirah Island,
Oman

Masirah Island lay 475 miles from Fujairah by sea. The island of rock and sand and very little vegetation was just forty miles long at the longest point and about ten miles wide at the widest point. A paved road circled the island along the coast, but only an occasional dirt road cut into the interior. There was nothing in the interior except rocky mountains, so no need to pave a road there. It did have a major airport capable of accommodating a squadron of Marine fighters. It was in the process of being modified so it could handle a few more squadrons that'd start to show up in the coming weeks.

For the time being, during the buildup, access to the island had been limited to residents with proof of residency. Several ferries came over daily from the mainland, bringing additional workers, cars, trucks, and supplies as needed. These ferries had the capability to ramp right on the beach, just as a military landing craft could do. The island also boasted a similar hydrography to the beaches in the vicinity of Fujairah where it was rumored the Marines would come ashore. This made it an ideal place to practice their amphibious operations before having to do it for real. For the time being, the island was also becoming the temporary home of the 1st and 7th Marine Expeditionary Brigades, which would comprise the 1st Marine Division.

"Sir, the final elements of the 1st MEB will be here tomorrow," Colonel Hocklighter, the G-3 for the division, explained.

"Good, I want to make sure we give our Marines time to adapt to this environment before we start some large-scale training. Right now, the units can focus on small-unit tactics until everyone is acclimated. The Sultan has practically given us the entire island to train on, but we don't have permission to employ live fire as of yet. I think CENTCOM is working on that one. General Schwarzkopf's guidance is to have as little impact on the locals as possible. He doesn't want to win the battles but lose the peace. Be sure the commanders understand that," General Hopkins said. General Hopkins was the commander of the 1st Marine Division. He was hell-bent on making sure his Marines didn't stir the pot in the wrong direction. Marines had a reputation for being a rowdy bunch.

Colonel Jasper, the division supply officer, pointed out, "Sir, as you're aware, we have very limited facilities. The 7th MEB has been here the longest and morale has been slipping. Our Marines literally have nowhere to go and nothing to do, stuck living in some austere environments all while being in a dry country. With the 1st MEB closing in, the warehouses that we're housing people in are totally inadequate for our needs. The sanitation is almost nonexistent; they're overcrowded, and with the hundred-and-twenty-degree heat, the guys are burning up in those places. In addition, with the troops in the warehouses, we have no place to store supplies as they're being delivered."

Colonel Hocklighter nodded. The situation had been getting pretty bad and was looking to get even worse in the coming weeks and months.

"Sir, may I propose we start moving people out into the field? We have tentage now for the units, and the troops will be more comfortable out of the warehouses and in the field. They can sleep during the day and train at night when it's cooler. At least the breeze will help them cool down, which is not happening in the warehouses. The new arrivals can move into one warehouse for the first twenty-four hours before we notify their units and ship them out. The Maritime Prepositioning Squadron Two has brought in enough vehicles that we can start resupplying units in the field, and the supply and service units are about up and running and ready to get to work. If you'd like, we can coordinate with the amphib fleet and start making arrangements for some training and developing a combat operation as well," Hocklighter offered. He was hoping the general would let them start to get some sort of training going. If nothing else, it'd help to keep the men busy for the time being.

General Hopkins sighed as he listened to the report on his Marines. He was not happy about the morale issue. He knew that'd need to get sorted sooner rather than later. "Has CENTCOM given us any idea of what their plan for us is going to be?"

Hocklighter smiled as he replied, "Sir, we have been notified to attend a meeting the day after tomorrow, along with Admiral Joy, at CENTCOM headquarters in Muscat. Admiral Joy will be flying in to pick us up, so you and him will have a chance to go over some things prior to the meeting and then on the way back. I'll be going with you, and he's bringing his Ops guy as well. I suspect there'll be a logistics meeting shortly after this meeting. We'll probably be getting an idea of what we'll be doing after tomorrow."

"OK, get a plan together to move the 7th MEB on the north side of the island and the 1st MEB on the south side. They can start small-unit training until we get more of the vehicles ashore. What's our vehicle status at this time, Jasper?" Hopkins asked.

"We currently have thirty-one M60A1 tanks, two M60A1 tank-dozers, twenty M198 Howitzers, five LVTC7A1 and sixty-two LVTP7A1 assault amphibious vehicles, thirteen LAV-25s, forty-two TOW Humvees and thirty-three weapon carrier Humvees. The problem we're having is that this was all planned to be offloaded in a prepared port, which we don't have here, so a lot has to be loaded and brought over the beach," Colonel Jasper explained.

"Well, let's do the best we can. I suspect once we get it all ashore, we're going to have to develop some plans for combat loading it for the next phase."

"Sir, we have a bigger problem right now," Colonel Jasper said.

"Oh, do tell, Colonel."

"Sir, we have a Class I and Class III problem. We can get hot As, but we don't have the field kitchens ashore to cook the food yet, and I don't expect to see them for a couple of days. What fresh produce and meat we do have is going bad in this heat, as we don't have refrigeration for all this food," Jasper explained.

"And the Class III?" General Hopkins remarked.

"Sir, what fuel is coming to the island is coming by civilian barge, and they don't have the capability of supplying us with enough fuel for the vehicles we have ashore now. I would like to get the engineers going on building a POL farm over at the airfield so we can get tanker aircraft in here to fill them and service both our aviation assets and the ground vehicles. The other problem is the PrePo vehicles are in need of lubricants and services, and we don't have enough lubricant to service all of the vehicles. In addition, we haven't been able to locate the containers that have the mechanics' tools and equipment needed to service all the vehicles."

"Do we have any service support people, fuel handlers on the ground yet?" Hopkins inquired. He realized fast how quick this could screw things up for them.

"Fuel handlers should be arriving sometime today if the flow sticks to the manifest and plan," Colonel Hocklighter interjected.

"Good. As soon as they arrive, marry them up with the engineers and let's get that fuel farm built. I'll talk to MARCENT about getting us some refrigerated vans for food storage. Sending in the shooters with no support is not the way to do business. There are some lessons to be learned here."

Chapter 12
Transition

17 September 1990
3rd Squadron
Abu Dhabi International Airport
Abu Dhabi, United Arab Emirates

Major Popkov was exhausted. Their squadron had just relocated from the western desert of Iraq to the Abu Dhabi airport. Their intelligence said the Americans had moved a substantial number of new squadrons to Oman and bombers out of Diego Garcia. It was obvious they were building up forces to make a major play on the Iraqi forces in the UAE. The powers that be wanted their top fighter squadrons moved into the area to blunt the American's latest efforts.

Normally he'd be ticked off about being pulled away from a front he was responsible for so thoroughly dominating. Then he'd been told a new squadron of Russian volunteers had arrived in-country and would be taking their place. He liked that idea a lot more than some of these subpar Iraqi pilots. Some of the Iraqi pilots were actually pretty decent—they'd learned a lot from the Russians—but many of them needed more training time, and that wasn't going to happen with the war. Still, the near-constant missions and stress were starting to wear on him and his comrades.

Once his squadron had relocated to their new home, they had been given two full days off. He and his pilots had spent most of their time at the beach, swimming in the water and just forgetting about the war. They knew when they returned, they'd be thrown back into the grinder.

Right now, his pilots were being housed in the most amazing hotel in the city. They'd each been given a penthouse-style room to bunk in, full room service and just about everything they could want or need to unwind from the day's missions. The hotel fortunately wasn't located too far from the airport. With limited civilian traffic on the roads, nothing was really that far from the airport. When they either left the hotel or headed to the airport, they were driven in luxury sedans and given a military escort, not that they needed it. There hadn't been any civil protests or issues thus far.

One of the key differences at the airport Popkov noticed immediately was the deployment of the Soviets' S-300 surface-to-air missile system. Near as he could tell, they had deployed close to a battalion's worth of the systems in and around the city and the airport. He was glad he didn't have to fly against them. The S-300 was a beast of a system. The Americans were in for a rude surprise when they finally got their act together and started going on the offensive.

Walking into the squadron briefing room, Popkov noticed a lot more brass around than usual. For the last week, his squadron had largely been flying combat air patrols near the border and over any large troop movements. The Americans had for the most part kept their fighters on their side of the border, and the Iraqis had largely done the same. The southeastern front near Oman was, by all accounts, a quiet front compared to the active fighting taking place out west near the Red Sea. That front saw near-constant air battles raging between the two sides.

Taking his seat near the front of the room, Major General Sokolov, flanked by an Iraqi Air Force general, finally got the meeting going.

"Good morning, everyone. I wanted to meet with you personally to discuss with you the importance of the coming weeks and months. Later today, the Americans and their British lackeys are going to bypass the UN Security Council and push forward a referendum declaring the actions of the government of Iraq as illegal, claiming that the Iraqis have waged an illegal war against their peaceful neighbors. They are also pushing forward a second vote pending the first one passes to create a United Nations peacekeeping force, similar to what they did during the Korean patriotic war to form a military force to oust the Iraqis from their captured lands."

Popkov didn't like where this was going. It likely meant the Americans were not going to be willing to negotiate a peace to end this war. More likely they were going to form an alliance under the guise of the UN to oust them by force.

The general continued, "The Soviet Union, along with China, has vehemently opposed this move. We have even gotten the French to agree with us. However, the Americans are determined to assert their control over the oil nations of the Middle East and are pushing forward with their resolution. While Mother Russia cannot intervene directly in this conflict, the first secretary is going to allow more Russian volunteers to come to the aid of our Iraqi allies. Over the coming weeks, these new volunteer units will begin to arrive in Baghdad, where they will form up and then be sent forward to the front lines."

I hope they know what they're doing. This war could envelop the entire motherland if they are not careful, Popkov thought privately.

"What I need you all to do is work tirelessly to keep the American Air Force off the Iraqi forces' backs. It's important that they are able to build up the defenses needed to repel what we all know is coming—an American-led invasion. Continue to do what you do best, shoot down

Yankee fighters. That is all," General Sokolov concluded and then left their briefing room with the Iraqi general.

Once everyone had left, Popkov stood and took his own place at the head of the room. "Well, that was a complete waste of our time. It's not like they told us anything new. Of course we're going to kill Yankee fighters. We get paid a handsome bonus for each kill."

This elicited a few hoots and hollers of excitement. They were getting rich off this assignment, that was for sure.

"OK, here are the flight assignments and rosters for the next week. This is subject to change if we receive any new intelligence or there is a major American offensive. Continue to work together and look out for each other. Let's show these Yankees *this* squadron knows how to fight."

Chapter 13

Option 2

17 September 1990
CENTCOM Forward HQ
Military Technological College
Muscat, Oman

"I trust everyone had a decent lunch," General Schless said as he entered the conference room. The Jedi majors just smiled.

"OK, let's get started. This is option two and envelopment, correct?" Schless asked.

"Yes, sir," Major Stube said. "First slide." And the first slide came up.

"Sir, as you can see, we have had to add a few more assumptions. One, that the US Navy can dominate the Iraqi Navy in the Persian Gulf. The Iraqis have acquired some very fine coastal patrol boats with the latest in Soviet anti-ship missiles that'll need to be neutralized before any sort of amphibious assault takes place. It also appears that the Soviets sold the Iranians at least one Kilo-class submarine. That submarine was able to sink two supply ships. It also needs to be hunted down and sunk. Two, we have to have the Strait cleared of any minefields. Three, we need intelligence on the hydrography of the shores around the UAE on both the Gulf side and the Arabian Sea side. And four, we're assuming that the Gator Navy can support an amphibious assault." Major Stube indicated.

"So I take it you're looking at an amphibious assault along the coast somewhere," Schless said, nodding his head in approval.

"Yes, sir," Major Stube answered confidently.

"Please continue," Schless directed.

"Next slide." As the slide came up, it showed a large map of the battlespace. The slide also denoted the various friendly and enemy units. The subsequent slides would outline the course of action for each unit and task force.

"Sir, the course of action we're recommending is as follows. We recommend our naval amphibious ships move through the Strait and come to an embarkation station between Dubai and Abu Dhabi. This move has been designed to be a feint, a false attack. Our hope is to fix forces in that area, primarily the 1st Hammurabi Division and 2nd al-Medinah Division, with the threat of an amphibious assault so they won't be able to redeploy to stop our primary assault. The real amphibious assault will take place shortly after sunset, when JTF East will attack with the 1st Marine Division, conducting an amphibious assault in the vicinity of Fujairah, and continue to attack along E-84 towards Sharjah. This combined land and amphibious assault will be joined by the 2nd Marine Division, who will attack along Route 5 from Al Wajajah to Dubai International airport."

As Stube talked, more slides with maps showing the exact movements appeared. It painted a much bigger picture of how each attack would unfold and how each attack supported the next attack and so on.

"As the Marines and JTF East move, Task Force Sa'al—this is a combined force of what's left of the Kuwaiti, Bahrain, and UAE forces along with the Omanis—will fix the 3rd Tawakalna Division in Al Ain. Then one division will attack on right flank south of Al Ain and seize the objectives in the vicinity of Abu Dhabi with a division in the center and the last division on left flank. We'd then have the 3rd ACR screen forward of the left flank division to Al Mirfa." Major Stube paused for

112

just a moment as he looked at the map and the units he'd just been pointing to and their paths of attack before looking confidently at General Schless, concluding, "This constitutes the main attack to remove the Iraqis from the Gulf States prior to lunging into Saudi Arabia."

General Schless studied the maps and the proposals silently for a moment. Then he said, "We're putting a lot of faith in the Navy's minesweepers getting here soon. Honestly, the Brits have the better minesweeper fleet. Maybe the Navy can get them on board right away to help with this. Good brief, everyone. What else you got?"

Major Stube smiled. "Now for our next course of action." He brought up the next slide. A second course of action appeared with the map outlining the situation much like the first. "Sir, this is a single envelopment with Joint Task Force East attacking with three divisions abreast followed by the two Marine divisions, all driving on Abu Dhabi and continuing to Dubai. Task Force Sa'al will hold elements of the 3rd Tawakalna Division in Al Ain with the 3rd Armored Calvary Regiment screening the left flank for a possible counterattack from the 6th Nebuchadnezzar Division," Major Stube stated. "It's a bit more simplistic in its design, but it's also the brute force method of the two courses of action we've developed."

"I agree. This course of action appears to be a penetration move more than an envelopment. You left the amphibious assault option out," General Schless commented. The general looked like he was thinking pretty hard about the plan before he added, "Tell you what, put an amphibious assault in this course of action with one Marine division making the assault between Abu Dhabi and Dubai. The second Marine division will follow the division on the right flank. This will be the course of action we'll present to the general. It's straightforward, with a

113

bit less in the way of moving parts to it so even the crayon eaters can't screw it up."

His last comment elicited a few chuckles from the Army officers.

"Write it up and get the Air Force and Navy on board. This won't get us to Kuwait, but it'll at least free up the UAE and give us a lot better logistical network to leverage for the follow-on campaigns. I also want to hear from the logisticians and know that they can support the two courses of action and for how long. Let me know when you're ready to brief General Schwarzkopf and the staff. Any questions?" General Schless asked as he stood to leave.

Major Stube looked to the rest of his team to make sure they didn't have questions before he confidently replied, "No questions, sir."

****

CENTCOM Forward HQ
Military Technological College
Muscat, Oman

"Well, what did the Jedis come up with?" General Schwarzkopf asked General Schless as the man walked into his office an hour after he'd met with them.

General Schless smiled at the bluntness of Schwarzkopf. It made him relatively easy to work with. He took a seat as he explained, "With what they have to work with, they gave us two viable plans. I personally like the double envelopment or brute force plan the best. It could work, but it'll work only in liberating the UAE. It's going to take everything we have just to do that. Once we've managed to bring substantially more forces from the US, we'll have the combat power needed to finish the job. But this'll get us going and moved in the right direction."

"Good. Honestly, I don't know if we will go into Iraq, although that makes sense. My orders right now are to kick them out of Kuwait and Saudi Arabia," Schwarzkopf replied, easing into an overstuffed chair and indicating for Schless to do the same. These chairs were much more comfortable than the ones next to his desk. "Before you sit, pour us a drink. The bottle is on the sideboard over there," General Schwarzkopf indicated with a wave of his hand.

General Schless fixed two drinks, Cokes, handing one to Schwarzkopf. Oman was a bit more liberal about the consumption of alcohol than Saudi Arabia, and being inside a US compound, they really didn't care. However, one of the first orders that was put out to all US forces was that no alcohol would be consumed while in the CENTCOM AOR.

"You say the Jedi majors have a good plan," Schwarzkopf said in a matter-of-fact manner as he took a sip.

"I said they have a plan that's the best we can expect with the forces we have. It includes a penetration that drives north and an amphibious assault that drives south but depends on the Navy clearing the minefields and opening the Strait, and having a sufficient number of ships." Schless countered.

"Hmm, that'll piss off the Iranians," Schwarzkopf mumbled.

"After their sub just sank two of our supply ships, we should initiate Praying Mantis II and wipe out their entire navy," Schless declared angrily. He sighed before adding, "If we keep the mine clearing to the southern side of the Strait, they can't bitch too much, especially if we don't cross into their waters," Schless explained.

115

"You know those ragheads consider the entire Strait their domain, and there still isn't any definitive proof that it was an Iranian sub that sank those supply ships and not an Iraqi one," Stormin' Norman countered.

No one spoke for a moment. Then Schless pontificated, "I wonder if they consider it their domain enough to get into a shooting match with us. That would bring a lot more nations into this fight. Oh, speaking of more nations, I got word today that Canada and Australia are going to be sending naval ships and fighter aircraft to join us. The Canadians are sending two frigates and a resupply ship and an air task force of CF-18 aircraft and the First Canadian Field Hospital. I thought we would have them support 1st UK Armour."

"Good idea. Keep the Queen's own together."

"The Australians are sending two frigates and a resupply ship as well as an EOD dive team and a task group medical support element. I'd recommend putting the medics aboard the *Comfort*," General Schless explained.

"What about ground forces? Are they sending any?" Schwarzkopf inquired.

"A contingent of the Australian 16th Air Defense Regiment will be aboard the resupply ship as she has no air-defense weapons, but that's about it," Schless stated, sipping his drink.

Everyone wants Saddam out of Saudi Arabia and Kuwait, but no one wants to get their hands dirty. Fucking Allies, Schless thought privately.

Chapter 14

Piling On

20 September 1990
CENTCOM Forward HQ
Military Technological College
Muscat, Oman

"Atten-tion!" a noncommissioned officer said in a loud commanding voice as General Schwarzkopf walked into the room.

Stormin' Norman, as he was known to his troops, was a bear of a man, but dearly loved by those that had served under him over the years. The briefing room was packed with commanders and key staff for this major briefing. The CENTCOM forward headquarters had only been in Oman for the past thirty days. They were still in sorting things out mode as they got themselves brought up to speed. Figuring out what units were in-country, what units were en route to country, what had been delivered and what was going to be needed for future operations was an enormous challenge.

"Alright, let's get started. I want to know what the Iraqis are up to, what we have on the ground, what we have on the ground that's combat-effective, and what we have in the air," Stormin' Norman said as he pulled out a chair and took a seat.

"Morning, sir," said Brigadier General O'Donnell, the G-2 for CENTCOM. Without waiting for an acknowledgment of his greeting, O'Donnell launched into his presentation. "First slide. Sir, this is a laydown of the Iraqi forces in the eastern provinces and the UAE." The slide showed the various Iraqi divisions, where they were located, and

117

essentially what intelligence believed they were up to. The next couple of slides outlined what major ports were in the UAE and their status.

O'Donnell paused long enough for Stormin' Norman to study the map, then went on to explain, "We also have some indication that the 4th Al Fao Infantry Division is moving to secure the port at Khor Fakkan, which is one of the few ports in the area capable of container offloading."

"What about the port at Fujairah?" General Schwarzkopf interrupted.

O'Donnell shook his head dismissively. "Sir, that port is strictly a petroleum terminal. They have no capability for containerization."

Schwarzkopf furrowed his brow as he looked around the room. Notes were being taken, but he wanted to make sure the right notes were being taken. "Gentlemen, we need to keep this in mind when we go in. We're going to need both of those ports; they each have a needed function for sustaining our offensive."

"Duly noted, sir," was all O'Donnell said before moving on. "In the other parts of the UAE, we see the 6th Nebuchadnezzar Mechanized Division sitting tight on the edge of the Empty Quarter and the 3rd Tawakalna Mechanized Division reinforcing his positions around Al Ain. It appears that the 1st Hammurabi Armoured Division will be the Republican Guard reserve if needed."

"Is this an opinion or fact?" General Schwarzkopf asked.

"Opinion, sir," O'Donnell said without hesitation.

"I think you're right. Let's plan on it being fact."

"Sir, one other item of note. We've confirmed that three Scud launchers and missiles were offloaded in Saqr Port recently and have been deployed into the mountains. We have inserted three teams to find them and put them out of action with air strikes as soon as they are located." As O'Donnell spoke, he pointed at the map of the suspected locations.

"Good. I want them taken out as quickly as possible. Any indication the Iraqis have moved their chemical weapons?"

"No, sir. All indications are that they have not touched their chemical weapon stockpile," O'Donnell responded. "Sir, do you have any other questions on the eastern front?"

"Yes. I want to know more about these Iraqi Air Force pilots and squadrons. I find it incredibly hard to accept that they're this effective against our own guys. What's going on?"

This was a question being asked by a lot of people. It had led to more than one speculative response.

General O'Donnell appeared a little uncomfortable at the question but looked to tackle it head-on. "Sir, there are some rumors that some of the Iraqi squadrons are actually being flown and operated by what appear to be contractors. Not actual soldiers, but private Russian contractors."

Stormin' Norman held up a hand to stop him right there. He'd heard the same rumors, but he wanted to operate on facts, not disinformation. "I've heard the rumors too, but if these are contractors, where are they coming from? Who are they? Let's start to flesh that out a bit, because that's a really big deal."

"I agree, sir. We've tasked several of our intelligence groups with figuring this information out. We're also working with our embassy personnel in Moscow to see if they're hearing anything about contractors. What we know so far is the civilians appear to be former military pilots. I... I probably shouldn't say this, but one of my junior analysts said he believes these may in fact be Soviet pilots who have either temporarily or permanently left the air force to fly in these private squadrons. If that's the case, it would explain their effectiveness—"

"Sir, if I may," General Schless said interrupting. Schwarzkopf nodded for him to continue. "If there are Soviet pilots in those fighters, they should be treated for what they are—mercenaries. Mercenaries are not afforded the protection of the Geneva Convention and never have been. We call them contractors today, but they are mercenaries. If we capture them, we should ring as much intelligence out of them as possible and then put them before a firing squad. That will make them think twice about volunteering for duty."

"Hold your horses there, General. We are not going to stand anyone up before a firing squad. Downed pilots, regardless of their nationality, will be treated as prisoners of war. First, I don't want to draw the Russians into this conflict, and shooting their "volunteers" might just do that. Second, we don't want to open the door to equal treatment to our downed pilots. No, let's get to the bottom of who these pilots are and then look at our options. Is that understood?" Schwarzkopf asked looking around the room for affirmative answers.

Turning back to General O'Donnell, "OK, General. It sounds like this needs to be further vetted. So let's circle back to this when we have more information on it. In the meantime, let's talk western front."

"Sir, on the western front, the 2nd Republican Guard Corps has gone into a defensive posture on a line from Medina south. The combination of the 82nd, tac air and 101st attack helicopters pretty much stopped him. However, coming down from the north is the 2nd Iraqi Corps with three divisions, the 7th, 37th and 51st Infantry Divisions. The 2nd Infantry Division is sitting in Tabuk and the 14th Mechanized is limping back towards Tabuk after the air strike caught it in the mountains," O'Donnell said, pausing for a comment. None came.

"The 4th Iraqi Corps is sitting in the area of Buraydah and not moving. The 9th Corps is in the Al Hofuf area, with the 45th Infantry Division in Al Jubail and the 49th Infantry Division in the Dammam area. We suspect that these two corps may be creating a second line of defense in the event of our counterattack."

"Fact or opinion?" Schwarzkopf asked again.

"WAG at this point, sir," O'Donnell said with a smile.

"Might just be a good wild-ass guess if you ask me. Let's watch them, though."

"Moving over to the air campaign, we're achieving some air parity with the Iraqi Air Force. They're flying some of the latest Soviet fighters, which we didn't expect, and they've shown some very good combat tactics in some cases. We're still getting a higher kill ratio, but they have more aircraft in the region. Combine that with their enhanced air-defense capabilities that we're seeing, again the latest in Soviet equipment, and our aircraft have taken a toll," O'Donnell indicated.

Schwarzkopf turned to General Horner. "How about coming by and let's discuss this separately? We've got to get air superiority or at least total air parity before we can launch any sort of ground operation."

"Yes, sir, I'll get on your schedule," General Horner said.

"Anything else, General?" Schwarzkopf asked.

"Aside from the sinking of two Navy supply ships, the naval activity in the theater has been minimal. Primarily just the mining of the Strait by both the Iraqis and Iranians. We're still looking for that submarine that sank our ships, but thus far, nothing," O'Donnell concluded.

"Do the Iraqis or the Iranians actually have a sub?" Schwarzkopf asked.

"On the Iraqi side, not that we're aware of. The Iranians recently received a Soviet Kilo-class diesel boat, which was located at Bandar Abbas. They have a limited capability in the Persian Gulf but can operate in the Arabian Sea and Gulf of Oman," O'Donnell stated.

"Let's find that sub and keep track of it. Last thing we need is a carrier taking a fish or an LPH taking a hit," Schwarzkopf directed.

"Sir, that concludes my portion of this morning's brief. I will be followed by General Schless."

General Schless was a West Point graduate. He was your typical career staff officer. He'd never commanded anything above the brigade level but had held a few deputy positions and assistant division commander roles. He was fine working behind the scenes as opposed to being out front, taking shots for his decision. He was very comfortable making recommendations and doing the grunt work when it came to research. He just had no desire to be the one making final decisions.

"Morning, sir. Our current disposition of forces is as follows. The XVIII Airborne Corps minus the 3rd Armored Cav Regiment and the 24th Infantry Division are ashore in Jeddah. Also in Jeddah are the 82nd Airborne Division, 101st Airborne Division, and 1st Corps Support as well as a battalion minus from the 11 Air Defense Artillery Brigade and a unit from the 7th Medical Command. The 24th Infantry Division personnel and equipment began arriving last week in Liwa and are moving into an encampment around the town of Fahud, which is to the south but keeps them separated from other forces we're flowing in at this time."

Schless paused for a moment as he pointed at the map. "The 197th Infantry Brigade's equipment is arriving in As Sultan Qaboos Port this morning and their people started arriving two days ago at the Muscat Airport. They're currently housed outside the city, waiting for their equipment and getting acclimated before we move them out to join the 24th Division," he said. "The 1st Cavalry Division should be arriving the day after tomorrow and the ships carrying their equipment arriving three days later. We need to examine where to locate them. Truthfully, sir, we're running out of room here in Oman."

"Agreed, but I want it understood they do not, do *not*, go any closer to the border. I do not want them seen from the border, is that understood?" Schwarzkopf said, looking at General Yeosock, who nodded his head.

"What about the Marines?" Schwarzkopf asked.

"Sir, the 1st and 7th Marine Expeditionary Brigades are ashore on Masirah Island and are beginning training for amphibious operations. They're going to be under the command of the 1st Marine Division. The 4th Marine Expeditionary forces are afloat at this time. The 5th MEB is preparing to load and will be at sea in a week or so as soon as the President gives the release. Once in theater, they and the 4th will be redesignated as the 2nd Marine Division."

"Good. They'll be playing a major role in this operation along the coasts. But first we need the sea lanes opened through the Strait. What's our status on minesweepers?" Schwarzkopf asked, looking at his naval staff officer, Rear Admiral Cockren.

Cockren was a salty-looking individual with heavy folds and crow's-feet around his eyes from being on deck in the sun too much over the years. He had a scar on his left cheek and reminded everyone of Captain Ahab from *Moby-Dick* if he had a beard. His eyes, however, were ice blue and appeared to cut right through whoever he was talking with.

"Sir, we currently have four minesweepers in the region, with the USS *Avenger* being the newest. The others are older models, and to be truthful, we're having trouble keeping them in operation. The Navy hasn't given much thought over the years to countermine operations, and the ships show it. The best minesweeper force is the British. If we could get a couple of those guys—" He didn't finish before General Schwarzkopf cut him off.

"Well, damnit, request them. If we don't ask, we'll never get them," Schwarzkopf said. "What do we have to support operations right now as for Naval forces?"

"Sir, the Carrier Battle Group *Saratoga* is on station in the Red Sea and the *Kennedy* in the Gulf of Oman. They're going to be joined soon by the *Ranger*, *America*, *Roosevelt*, and *Midway*. All are at some point en route or preparing to come in the very near future," Admiral Cockren stated.

"Good, what about our amphibious forces?" Schwarzkopf asked.

"The Persian Gulf Group and Amphib Group Three are on station off Masirah Island. We have on station eight amphibious assault ships and twenty-eight landing ships to support the operation. The Persian Gulf Group will have the battleships *Missouri* and the four minesweepers with the battleship *Wisconsin* steaming to join the group," Admiral Corkren acknowledged.

"Between the *Kennedy* and the *Saratoga*, we have four squadrons of F-14 Tomcats, two squadrons of F-18 Hornets, two squadrons of A-7 Corsairs, two squadrons of A-6s Intruders, and two squadrons of E-2C Hawkeyes watching the skies. The 1st MEF will also have a wing of aircraft, which is currently located with the Marines on Masirah Island and the Sohar International Airport."

"General, if I may," General Horner interrupted.

"What is it?" Schwarzkopf asked.

"Sir, one problem we're having is finding airfields for our forces. Oman is lacking really badly in that department. The Fahud Airport and Ghaba Qarn are single-runway paved airports with almost no support facilities. Debba Airport is nothing more than dirt strips. The Adam Air Base is part of the highway system with no support facilities there. Muscat International is about the only modern airfield with support facilities that we can use. We have the 71st Squadron sitting over in Egypt, but we really have a need for some airfields here. Positioning all our Air Force assets at the Muscat International Airport is really putting all our eggs in one basket. Right now, I'm thinking we position our C-130 fleet at Fahud and Ghaba Qarn airfields. We can put some fighter aircraft at the airport in Salalah. Crews and maintenance people aren't going to be happy, but not much we can do about it at this point," General Horner went on to explain.

"Do what you have to do, is all I can tell you," General Schwarzkopf said, not too sympathetic to the discomforts of the Air Force personnel. *I'd wager they'll have air-conditioned sleeping tentage up and running before the maintenance tents are up.*

"Gentlemen, I'm becoming more confident as we continue to build our forces, but we're going to need more if we have to dislodge Saddam from the UAE and Saudi Arabia. General Schless, let's prepare a request for the 1st Brigade of the 2nd Armored Division, and III Corps Artillery. We're going to need someone to support those folks, so let's get 13th Corps Support Command as well. The 18th right now has the bulk of the attack helicopters, so request the 12th Combat Aviation Brigade and the 3rd Armored Division Aviation assets as well," Schwarzkopf directed. "I'd like to see if we could get VII Corps to join us as well."

"Sir, you realize that this request for additional forces, especially out of Germany, is going to ruffle some feathers," Schless pointed out.

"What else do they have going on right now? The fight is here, so they should be here. Hell, this is just the first volley. By the time this thing goes down, half of the US Army is going to be here," Schwarzkopf said.

Chapter 15
Oval Office

28 September 1990
White House
Washington, D.C.

The sun was shaded in clouds on this late September afternoon as the President sat in the Oval Office working on a bill that Congress had sent over for his signature. The bill, the Crime Control Act of 1990, contained another rider, the Gun-Free School Zones Act. Questions about the constitutionality of the Gun-Free School Zones Act were being raised, and the President's advisors were sure that it would be challenged.[2] He was of the opinion that it was an important piece of legislation and was strongly considering signing the bill.

"Mr. President, Mr. Cheney, and Mr. Baker are here," the intercom squawked.

"Send them in, please."

The door opened, allowing his two most important cabinet secretaries to enter. As they did, another less used door opened. A steward appeared carrying a tray with three coffee cups, a pitcher of coffee and sugar and cream. *How the hell does he know every time?*

---

[2] *The Gun-Free School Zones Act was declared unconstitutional by the Supreme Court in 1995 in* United States v. Lopez, *514 U.S. 549 (1995). This was the first time in over half a century that the Supreme Court limited congressional authority to legislate under the Commerce Clause. Wikipedia. Gun Free School Zone Act.

thought the President. The stewards always seemed to know just how many cups would be needed for each meeting he had and approximately how many creams and sugars his guest would use. It was incredible the attention to such little details the White House staff put into things.

"Thank you, Chief," he said, acknowledging the steward.

"Your welcome, Mr. President," the steward responded and left through the door he'd entered through.

"Sit down, guys," the President said, motioning for them to take the couch while he took his single chair.

After everyone had claimed their respective coffee cup and were seated, the President asked, "OK, what have we got? Tell me Saddam has come to his senses after this UN resolution authorizing military force against him and is going to pull out of Saudi Arabia and the Gulf states."

Mr. Cheney had a dour look on his face as he replied, "I'm afraid not, Mr. President. I would have thought that after it passed nearly a month ago and the reality of it finally set in, he would have seen reason. Maybe come to an understanding that he wasn't going to be allowed to keep these nations. But it only seems to have caused him to dig his heels in further."

"Damn."

"We do have some good news, however," Mr. Baker chimed in.

"Well, don't keep me in suspense. What is it?" the President asked, leaning forward in his chair.

"General Schwarzkopf called and said that British forces have started arriving. The British 1st Armoured Division, with their support elements, is starting to flow in-country, and the British Navy is en route with the *Ark Royal* serving as the flagship," Cheney explained optimistically.

"That is good news, and Margaret said they're going to fully support us in ousting Saddam," the President responded before sipping his coffee.

"That's not all, Mr. President. I spoke to Mubarak again and Egypt is sending two divisions. As we speak, they're moving to Port Said for embarkation and they're opening up more airports for us to use. CENTCOM is working out where to send these new units and how we can best utilize these new air bases. We're thinking the XVIII Airborne Corps might be best served with the reinforcements. They've been in a hell of fight there against two Iraqi corps, and holding their own I might add," Mr. Baker said.

"They've also sustained some horrific casualties, Jim. A lot of folks on Capitol Hill and the media are asking a lot of questions about why we aren't getting them more reinforcements or help," the President commented. Several journalists and a film crew were now embedded with the 82nd Airborne and the 101st, and the stories and images they were sending stateside were quite gruesome and sobering.

Cheney bristled a little at the mere mention of the media. "It's being addressed, Mr. President. The reinforcement of the 82nd with the 101st has allowed us to hold the area. The air units we have in place along with the helicopter support will ensure we don't lose any further ground. This is a war. We're going to take casualties when we fight the enemy. But your help in getting Mubarak to back us and send forces to assist us helps to defuse the argument the Soviets have been making that we're meddling in a regional dispute. Not all Arab nations agree with or welcome what Saddam has done. Many wonder if their nation is next."

"You're right, Dick. I know you guys are doing all you can and I'm glad Mubarak is proving to be a staunch ally. I thought he'd help, especially after Saddam humiliated him in the eyes of the rest of the Arab nations. Putting that aside, what do we know about these two divisions they're sending?" the President asked.

"They'll be coming under the command of a Corps headquarters," Baker said, referring to his notes. "A Major General Ahmed Bilal will be bringing the 3rd Mechanized Division and the 4th Armoured Division. General Bilal is en route to Muscat to meet with General Schwarzkopf and work out details of the integration of those divisions. We've worked with them in the past in the biannual Bright Star exercises, so we've got some good history working together," Baker went on to say.

"That is good news. We're still staging aircraft out of Egypt, aren't we?" the President asked.

"Yes, sir. We're now basing aircraft at Aswan International Airport, which has hardened aircraft bunkers and a squadron of Egyptian fighters; Hurghada International Airport, which has two runways and hardened bunkers; and Luxor International Airport, which also has two runways and hardened bunkers," Mr. Cheney explained.

"What about using airfields in Oman?" asked the President.

"Sir, Oman has only one or two satisfactory airfields for military use. The Muscat International Airport is one. Salalah is the other. The rest are pretty much one-runway airfields with little to no support facilities. There are a couple of airfields in Saudi that haven't been overrun, Jeddah and Yanbu are two, but they're well within Iraqi air strike range and are frequently attacked. We'd rather keep our aircraft out of Iraq's range and use air-to-air refueling to bring them into the combat zone," Mr. Cheney explained.

"How's the deployment of heavy equipment going?" the President inquired next.

"'It's going' is about all I can say. We haven't done anything like this since—well, since World War II or Vietnam. I mean, we've had some exercises like REFORGER that deployed forces to Europe, but nothing on this scale. Frankly, I'm surprised it's going as well as it is. Every day, it seems that the ship loading goes a bit better. Soon there'll be a ship every fifty miles from the East Coast to Oman carrying our equipment and supplies," Cheney added.

"And the airflow?" the President brought up next.

"Much better than the heavy equipment. The civilian air fleet has really stepped up and is moving troops from all over to the theater. The flight crews are volunteering and really taking care of the soldiers on those flights. This portion of the deployment started off good and has only gotten better. We've even let Arrow Air back into the Civil Reserve Air Fleet. But we're keeping them restricted to cargo loads only," Mr. Cheney pointed out.

"Oh, why's that?" asked the President with a curious look. He didn't really know much about the Civil Reserve Air Fleet other than that when the country faced an immediate wartime emergency, many of America's commercial passenger planes could be quickly brought into the fleet to assist the Department of Defense in moving tens of thousands or even millions of soldiers across the globe.

"They were the ones that lost the plane in Gander that killed over two hundred soldiers from the 101st Airborne Division after returning home from a six-month deployment to the Sinai," Cheney elaborated. It was a terrible tragedy and the worst loss of soldiers in peacetime in a single event.

The President sat back in against the couch for a moment, thinking about something. Finally, he directed his question to Secretary Baker. "Tell me about the Russians. What the hell is going on with them?"

"This is tricky, Mr. President. On the face of it, the Russians aren't intervening in the war. However, as you know, the CIA and the Defense Intelligence Agency noted the massive 'lend-lease' program the Soviets put in place with the Iraqis nearly a year before this war broke out. Since the war has started, the Soviets have continued to supply, support, and assist the Iraqis," Baker explained.

"A few weeks back at the UN, I pulled Foreign Minister Shevardnadze aside and showed him the images one of our Keyhole satellites had taken of their naval base in Syria. I showed him images of vehicles, munitions, and other supplies being moved by rail or truck from Syria into Iraq. Heck, the Soviets are the only ones being allowed into the Gulf right now, and even there, we're seeing their freighters offloading supplies at the ports. I told him we knew what they were doing, and we're telling them it needs to stop."

The President placed his cup of coffee down on the table, asking, "What did he say in response, once you showed him the images?"

"He told me Iraq was a Soviet ally, and they were honoring some previously arranged trade deals. He said America doesn't get to dictate to the rest of the world who they can be friends with and who they can do business with," Jim said.

"Did you tell him that providing the Iraqis with material support that's being used directly against us, that's essentially them participating in the war?" Cheney asked.

"I did. He said that they knew we had worked out a deal with the Saudis to collapse the price of oil in order to starve the Soviet Union of oil revenues, and he told me in no uncertain terms that America and the West had been engaged in unrestricted economic warfare against his nation for nearly a decade now, so no, they would not stop supporting their ally," Baker recounted.

No one said anything for a moment. Cheney looked like he wanted to say something, but he seemed content to wait to see what the President would say to that. Finally, the President said, "OK, I get it. Then let's look for ways to go after some of these logistical nodes that are being used to supply and support them."

Bush turned to look at Cheney. "Maybe we can have some of our submarines and aircraft mine the ports in the Gulf they're using. I mean, if the Gulf is closed to traffic, then let's make sure it's unusable for them as well. Let's also see if we can't come up with some missions to bomb these logistical routes that the Soviets are using from Syria to Iraq and from Iran into Iraq. If they aren't going to stop supporting them, then let's do what we can to negate the support they're providing."

"Yes, Mr. President, I'll send the word down to the Air Force and the Navy to develop some target packages that address this issue. Uh, there is one other thing we need to discuss."

"OK, out with it. I thought this was too cheery of a meeting," the President said with a sigh.

"Well, General Schwarzkopf has submitted a request for additional US forces, and it's not a small number either. We've already run it by the staff earlier and they recommend approval given what he's facing, but I can tell you there are reservations, especially from Colin, as some of what he's requested is coming out of Europe," Cheney explained.

"Hmm. So, Jim, is this going to cause a problem with our European allies?" asked the President as he took another sip of coffee.

"No, sir, surprisingly our allies are in support of what we're doing—all except the French, but they like to oppose us just for the sake of opposing us. I guess our European friends figure they would rather have us send troops before they're asked or roped into sending troops of their own," Jim replied.

"OK, so what is Schwarzkopf asking for?"

"He's asking for the 1st Brigade of the 2nd Armored Division, which is located in Garlstad, Germany, plus III Corps Artillery and the 13th Corps Support Command, which are at Fort Hood Texas, as well as 12th Combat Aviation Brigade and the 3rd Armored Division, the last two being located in Germany as well," Cheney replied as he briefly referenced his notepad.

"My God, does he want the kitchen sink too? This is a lot of soldiers. If we approve all this, will that give him the forces he needs?" the President asked, a bit surprised at the size of the request. *This must have been what Johnson thought when Westmoreland made his troop request in Vietnam.*

"Mr. President, if we're going to get Saddam to move, we have to show a superior force. He's got to be convinced that we're serious and are going to drive him out of Saudi Arabia and Kuwait. Putting in only a token force there will not convince him to move. Especially with how well their units have fought against ours around Medina and how effective their air force has been thus far," Cheney pointed out.

"Well, what's his plan to move them out right now with what he has?"

"Sir, I've asked for a ground offensive plan, but the response is always the same. 'We don't have the forces to go on the offense yet,'" Cheney said.

"Well, why don't we have the general get back here and brief us on his plans, then? I don't like the idea of just giving him a blank check on this," the President countered.

"We can do that. That might be best. I'll talk to Powell and get a briefing set up for you and have them brief the proposed air campaign, as that's really in action now in the area around Jeddah and Yanbu, and the proposed offensive ground plan. Then we'll have a better assessment of the forces he needs."

"That sounds good, let's do that as soon as we can. Get it on my calendar," the President said and stood, thinking the meeting was over.

"Sir, there's one more thing, and this is a bit unusual," Cheney said. The President resumed his seat. "We've been short ships for the amphibious force. We only have thirty-six ships available, which, best guess, can move two marine expeditionary brigades. If we could find more, that would be helpful."

"Well, where are you going to find some…? The mothball fleets? Hell, it'll take nine months to get those ships operational. Why the hell we keep them baffles me," the President said.

"Sir, several years ago we had a request from Evansville, Indiana, to acquire one of the old landing ship, tanks or LSTs, as that's the town where most of them were built for the war. They wanted a floating museum to the ships and the workers who built them, which at the time consisted of a large number of women, part of the whole Rosie the Riveter program. The ships were built there and then transited down the Ohio River until it linked up with the Mississippi. We granted their request, and they've maintained it and run it up and down the waterways, giving guided tours to schools, etc.," Cheney was explaining.

"You mean they actually have a working ship?" the President said with some surprise.

"Yes, sir. It's maintained by former naval personnel or workers on the original ships, or just veterans interested in maintaining history. They have a full crew as well, all civilians or military retirees," Cheney went on to explain.

"Damn, I'd like to visit that someday," the President expressed with a broad grin.

"Well, sir, you may get your wish very soon. They've contacted Admiral Kelso and want to have the ship rejoin the fleet, with the current civilian crew. They claim she's fully operational and is standing by for duty," Cheney explained with a grin. "Of course, we're not going to allow—"

He didn't get to finish before the President interjected, "Why the hell not? What better way to show the people the support for this operation than to allow volunteers to join the force? What does Kelso say?" The President stood and grinned like a kid with a new toy.

"Sir, the admiral said he would have to put a Navy crew on board and give it a full inspection," Cheney answered.

"Bullshit! We have civilian crews on the military sea transport ships, don't we? That crew is now, effective immediately, part of the military sea transport system. Tell Kelso to get an inspection team over there and give that ship a once-over. If it's good, then get it moving. In fact, tell Kelso to put an inspection team on board and move the ship immediately to New Orleans for deployment. What's the name of the ship?" the President wanted to know.

"Sir, LSTs were seldom named. They were numbered instead. She's the LST-325. Today they call her the USS *Memorial*," Cheney said, in a bit of shock at how fast that decision had been made.

"Well, she's named and recommissioned. The USS *Memorial* sails again," the President declared as he picked up the phone to connect him with the White House switchboard.

"Yes, get me the mayor of Evansville, Indiana, on the phone. I have a ship commissioning ceremony to attend."

Chapter 16
Early October

2 October 1990
CENTCOM Forward HQ
Military Technological College
Muscat, Oman

"Sir, General Powell is on the STU," Schwarzkopf's secretary said as he pointed to the secured telephone on the general's desk.

Schwarzkopf lifted an eyebrow at that. He hadn't expected a call from Powell. He picked up the receiver. "Colin, Norm here. How's the weather in D.C.? And don't tell me it's too cold," Schwarzkopf joked.

"It's fine, Norm. I'm calling about the situation over there. The President would like someone to come here and brief him on the planned air campaign. I've looked over what you sent, and it looks outstanding. I've been talking it up with him and the staff and he'd like to get a full-blown brief. Chuck Horner and Buster Glosson have done a great job putting this together. I want you to send the team back with the air campaign," Powell explained. After a short pause, he added, "And I also want you to send an offensive option back."

Immediately Schwarzkopf objected, "Look, I've told everybody all along we do not have the forces on the ground to conduct an offensive option, and if we do conduct it, there's only one possibility and that's a penetration right to the heartland of the UAE, where we will sit. If the Iraqis choose to reinforce, we're out of options, we have no reserve, we have no other forces over here and we could just as easily be destroyed."

Powell retorted, "I understand that, and you've made your position clear. What you're going to do is present an offensive option for the President and show the White House exactly what it is we're dealing with. Once they see that, it'll add validity and credibility to your request for those forces in Germany. Right now you're just sending massive troop requests along with no plan of action for how you're going to use them. That's not going to fly. Furthermore, the XVIII Airborne Corps is getting the shit kicked out of them and you keep pushing for more soldiers in Oman while ignoring the battle you already have going."

Schwarzkopf knew Powell was under a lot of pressure over what was transpiring here. Still, it stung to hear his comments.

Reluctantly, he agreed. "Alright, I'll fly over tomorrow and present the briefing myself. I can—"

Interrupting, Powell said, "That's not going to work. If you show up, it will be all over the nightly news. We can't keep anything secret around you. Send someone else to do the brief."

"You aren't trying to make this easy on me, are you?" Schwarzkopf said, pausing for a moment. "Suppose I send my chief of staff, Bob Johnson, to give the brief. Will that work? And when are we looking at doing this?"

"It's on the President's calendar for the sixth of this month," Powell said. "I look forward to seeing it. Have a good day, Norman." Then the call ended, leaving Schwarzkopf to stew on the news. This was not something he wanted to deal with on top of everything else that was going on.

****

Bob Johnson had just finished going over the briefing with General Schwarzkopf for this October 6 meeting at the White House. The brief was short and direct, used a lot of maps and presented the gravity of what they were facing.

Major General Bob Johnson was a US Marine officer who had joined the CENTCOM staff in early June and developed a great working relationship with Stormin' Norman just before everything had kicked off in the region. CENTCOM by all accounts had largely been a backwater combatant command when compared to the three major theaters of operation: Europe, facing down the Soviets and the Warsaw Pact, the Pacific, dealing with the Soviet Pacific fleet and the Koreas, and Central and South America, dealing with the narcos and the continued Soviet meddling.

Johnson was a unique Marine officer. He'd been born in Edinburgh, Scotland, migrating to the US in the mid-1950s as a teenager when his family had left the UK. Despite his thirty-plus years in America, he still maintained his Scottish accent. During his time in the Corps, he'd had all the usual assignments for a Marine officer as well as a few "plum" assignments. But CENTCOM was looking to be his final assignment.

Schwarzkopf nodded in approval at the end of the brief. "Excellent job, Bob. Do it just like that when you're at the White House," he complimented, handing two slides back to him with some notes scribbled on them. "These are the last two charts I want you to show the President. They're the only offensive option we can launch right now given the forces we have. But I do not recommend this course of action. It's my opinion that this is the wrong course to take. If and when we go on the offensive, we want it to be fierce and with a force large enough to crush the opposition. This will likely force the enemy to give up or surrender en masse."

General Johnson looked at the first slide and then the second before reading it out loud. "This plan is not recommended, and if you do want to eject the Iraqis out of Kuwait, it will take considerably more force on the ground that we presently have." When he finished reading it, he looked up at General Schwarzkopf.

"Sir, you really want me to show this?" He asked.

"Stick to this brief, though don't overemphasize it—otherwise I'll terminate your military career!" Schwarzkopf said, half joking, half serious. "There are going to be bureaucrats at the briefing that have no military experience but plenty of opinions that they will attempt to dazzle the President with. He needs to hear my position plainly. You're there to impart my opinion and not make any decisions or changes. Clear?"

"Very clear, sir."

Continuing, Schwarzkopf said, "When you brief this, you are going to be interrupted and questioned. Stick to the script. As you get into it, you're going to be dodging bullets from all sides of the room. Chances are, by the end, the room will be screaming that this is a terrible plan, and that is exactly what we want them to think. We want them to recognize that we're not going to be able to take back the countries with what we have. We need more ground forces.

"Now, another thing. Colin is not going to give you any support. He's for containment and waiting Saddam out. He isn't going to support additional troops that could give us an offensive capability. There are only three options. A, we attack up the middle, hey diddle diddle, in a penetration at a selected point, hope we can overwhelm the immediate forces, hold the shoulder, and get into the enemies rear. B, we do an end run in an envelopment or double envelopment and get into his rear. And C, we do a frontal assault across the entire front, which we just don't have the forces to do. What those Washington armchair quarterbacks don't understand is you have to have a minimum of a three-to-one ratio in your force to take out a well-entrenched defender, and preferably a five-to-one force. Now, get out of here and enjoy D.C. and grab a large, fat, juicy steak and a couple of beers for me while you're at it," he finished with a wide grin of jealousy.

****

"Sir, General Powell is on the line," the aide said. Schwarzkopf had just gotten in bed and was exhausted.

"What time is it?" the general asked, barely able to contain his yawn.

"It's 2330, sir," the aide responded, holding out the receiver for him to grab.

Sitting up, Schwarzkopf took the phone. "Colin, do you know what time it is here?"

"Yeah, are you in bed already?" Powell asked, a hint of humor in his voice.

"No, I was getting ready to go out to a dance tonight with the King. What do you want?" Another wide yawn escaped before he could stop it.

"Well, the briefing just finished, and I wanted to go over it with you and give you an update."

"That couldn't wait until morning? OK, never mind. How'd it go? How did Johnson do?"

"Oh, Johnson? He did great. Good call on sending him. The brief on the air campaign went very well. However, the brief on the ground campaign was horrible. General Johnson got a minute into it when the sharpshooters started in on him. All we were hearing was, 'Well, what about this?' and 'Well, if you don't do this, how can you do that?' To Johnson's credit, he stood in there and took a lot of hits. That last slide you sent was ineffective. Everyone was already convinced that this ground plan couldn't work," Powell explained.

"Look, I've told you that we don't have a viable plan with the size force you've given me. A penetration is the only possible option, and with the 82nd and 101st locked up over in Jeddah, the chance of success is nil. We could punch through the Iraqi lines, but they'd have us boxed in and surrounded in the UAE. We could end up losing the whole thing. It would be a bloody disaster. Right now it appears we're able to hold our own should they look to invade, but if you people want us to move Saddam back to his own territory, then I need a larger force. Without it, I'm just whistling Dixie. Now, if you don't mind, I'm going to get some sleep, Colin. We can talk in the morning if you'd like. Good night," Schwarzkopf said and enjoyed a restful night of sleep. Mission accomplished.

Chapter 17
Preparing for the Games

8 October 1990
101st Airborne HQ
Yanbu International Airport
Yanbu, Saudi Arabia

"OK, let's get started," Major General Benny Peters said as he walked into the briefing room. The division HQ had taken over most of the airport and turned a few of the rooms into briefing rooms. The division had set up a base camp on the northeast side of the airport in the open desert. The division staff had taken up residence in the haji tents permanently installed in front of the terminal building. What civilian air traffic came into the airport utilized the old terminal on the south side of the runway.

Looking over the assembled officers, General Peters was confident in the division's ability to execute the mission. However, he knew some of these officers would not be present at the next briefing, especially some of the infantry battalion commanders once their units deployed to the field.

"Gentlemen," he said, "the 2nd Iraqi Corps is on the move and heading this way—slowly, but they are coming. The Air Force is going to hit them with a B-52 strike to try and slow them up, but whatever survives that strike is going to be our responsibility to stop. This will not be an easy fight, but it's one I'm confident we will win. OK, Colonel Cordray, let's hear the intel," Peters said as he took his seat.

"Sir, the enemy situation is as follows." He pointed at a map of the area of operations. "The 2nd Iraqi Corps has five divisions—the 7th

Infantry Division, the 37th Infantry Division and the 51st Infantry Division are moving south. The 2nd Infantry Division is sitting in Tabuk and the 14th Mechanized is limping back to Tabuk after getting the shit kicked out of it in the mountains southwest of Tabuk by the Navy A-6s. The 7th ID is located at Masader with the main body and has pushed out reconnaissance elements as far south as Arar, located here. The 37th ID has moved south and is now located in the vicinity of Mogayra and Fadhia. The 51st ID is located south of Al Jadid and is moving south. Of note, each of these divisions has been allocated additional tanks, but they're all experiencing a shortage of fuel. The fuel problem has become so severe it appears they've parked the additional tanks and aren't even using them for the time being.

"In addition, the BTR-70s they received appear to be suffering from maintenance issues. We've seen several maintenance yards with a higher-than-usual number of vehicles. In the past, these three divisions moved by truck, and the BTRs are new to their organization. We suspect that they haven't had enough time to be fully trained and proficient in maintaining them properly and repairing them quickly," Cordray paused, expecting some discussion.

"Bob, could they be parking their tanks just to have them in reserve and waiting until they come upon a need or better tank terrain?" General Peters inquired.

"Sir, that is a possibility, but we believe it's more of a fuel issue. The 2nd Iraqi Corps has come a long way over some really tough terrain. They had few opportunities to take on fuel in their drive from Iraq to Tabuk. They were able to resupply at Tabuk, but they haven't had many places to get additional fuel from Tabuk to their present location, so their tankers are making long hauls to keep them supplied. To make matters worse, Tabuk is out of gas from what we're seeing, so they're having to go clear back to Iraq or Al Jubail on the west coast to get fuel. The closest major gas station for them is Yanbu and the refinery there. Even the 51st Division, which is in good open tank country, has circled the wagons on their tanks and left them at Al Jadid."

Grunting at the assessment, Peters countered, "So they're having a logistics nightmare, is what you're telling me, and it's across the entire corps."

"Yes, sir. It appears they've prioritized fuel to their air-defense systems, self-propelled and towed artillery, and their fleet of infantry BTRs. The tanks look to be a low priority for fuel," Colonel Cordray replied.

"OK," was all General Peters said.

"Air defense for the 2nd Iraqi Corps has been upgraded. Normally we see four ZSU-23-4 and four SA-9 with each regiment. Now we're seeing double that number with each regiment and some SA-6 missiles being integrated as well. Although in this terrain their effectiveness will be limited except in the area around the 51st Division, which is wide-open terrain, they're posing additional dangers for our helicopters and aircraft. They also have an abundance of SA-7s and we believe it was an SA-7 that took out the little bird from the Cav unit the other day," Cordray said.

Looking over at the Cav commander, Lieutenant Colonel Hawk Roe, Cordray said, "Sorry for your loss, Hawk." Hawk just nodded in appreciation.

Cordray turned back to General Peters. "Terrain in the area of operations favors the defense as it's rugged and steep, channeling an attacker into narrow passes and impassible terrain for armor and vehicles," Cordray noted.

146

As he spoke, an overlay of acetate was placed on the map, color-coded to indicate impassible terrain and roads. Wadis that could support vehicle movement were also highlighted.

"Sir, in the vicinity of Fadhia, there's a road that initially appears to be going west but in fact turns north and heads almost back to Tabuk and into some very nasty rugged terrain. They got their nose punched good a couple of weeks ago when the 14th Mechanized Division attempted to cut west through the mountains and we hit them with multiple air strikes," Cordray explained, expecting some discussion. When none came, he continued.

"From Fadhia to Masader is the main highway moving south. There are no exits off this road to the west. From Mogayra east of Fadhia, there's no road to Masader, but the terrain will support BTR wheeled vehicles. However, when they reach the vicinity of Masader, they have no avenue of approach and must come back to the road out of Masader. From Masader for ten miles south, there's a narrow gorge that the highway passes through before coming out on a wide wadi.

"The wadi is twenty-four miles long and six miles wide at the widest point. The town of Abu Haramel is at the end of the wadi and appears to have a population of fifteen hundred to two thousand inhabitants. Buildings are typical of Saudi Arabia—concrete block, one- and two-story. There are two roads that go west from the town but go into some very rough terrain. If they have local knowledge or recon elements, they may find a way to move through this area to the coast. From Abu Haramel to Jada'ah south for forty miles, they'd have open ground to disperse their force and then move into the more restrictive terrain for the next forty miles. That would take them into the flank of the 82nd," Colonel Cordray explained, stopping a few times to point out some of the terrain features and paths the Iraqi units could take on the big map. It helped to paint them a better image of the battlespace they were fighting in.

"Well, we can't let that happen, now can we, gentlemen?" General Peters said. "OK, Bob, what about the 51st Division? How does it look for them?"

"Sir, the 51st has open ground from Al Jadid south for fifty miles. He can disperse his force over a wide area with easy movement cross-country. At that point, the terrain is going to start restricting him somewhat to the road for eleven miles before it opens up again. He will have some maneuver room for the next nineteen miles before it starts closing up again. The ground is rocky but BTRs should be able to cross it. Tanks definitely can cross it. His mobility will be impeded to some degree, but he'll have greater mobility than his compadres in the west," Cordray said.

"So what you are saying is this guy, the 51st, may be the biggest threat because our infantry won't be as effective in this area as in the west," General Peters deduced.

"Yes, sir. He's going to have a mobility advantage over our infantry in this area. But we may have a great opportunity here. We could hit him with our attack helicopters before he reaches the restrictive terrain, then have our infantry hit him from the hillsides while the birds rearm and refuel. When he gets to the next open area, we lift the infantry out and move them back to the next restrictive terrain twenty miles south while the birds go to work on him again," Colonel Cordray indicated.

General Peters mulled that over for a minute, "OK, let's look at that as a possible course of action. Now, what about enemy air activity?"

"Sir, it appears that our air is gaining parity with the Iraqi Air Force and at times we may have air superiority but not complete as yet," Cordray replied. General Peters studied the map for a few minutes.

"Hawk, do your boys have eyes on this 51st bunch?"

Hawk Roe had had his boys watching the advance elements for two days now. "Yes, sir, we do. His lead elements are about twenty miles south of Al Jadid as of two hours ago. They're moving fairly slow."

Turning to the G-3, Colonel Eric Provost, Cordray said, "Eric, let's see if we can get a B-52 strike on this unit when it reaches this open terrain north of Al Eshash. If we can catch them in there with a strike, that ought to hold them up for a bit," Peters explained.

"Yes, sir, I'll get a request in right away," Colonel Provost said, and one of his battle captains was out of the room and heading to file a request.

***

The B-52s were in a flight of three aircraft at thirty thousand feet. They were accompanied by a flight of twelve F-18s that had met them over the Red Sea. They were part of the *Saratoga* battle group. Two EA-6 electronic jamming aircraft were in the package as well.

They were twenty minutes away from weapons release when they detected the first signs of trouble.

****

Republican Guard SA-10 Battalion
Prince Mohammed Bin Abdulaziz International Airport
Medina, Saudi Arabia

Major Vasily Ivanov moved to the sergeant's chair when the man raised his hand, indicating he needed to speak with a supervisor.

As he approached the man's chair, he motioned for his Iraqi counterpart to join him. *These people will never learn how to use this weapon properly if they do not pay attention and try to learn,* Ivanov thought to himself. He was growing frustrated with the Iraqi officers' lack of initiative. He'd been told the soldiers in the Republican Guard were supposed to be better, but he was having a hard time telling the difference between them and the regular army soldiers he'd been training for the last year.

"It looks like a major raid, Comrade Major," the sergeant declared.

"It sure does, comrade."

Ivanov turned to face his Iraqi counterpart, wanting to see if the man had learned anything up to this point. "What do you see, Comrade Major?"

The Iraqi major didn't like to be referred to as comrade. He wasn't a godless communist. "I see several groupings of aircraft. These smaller, more numerous objects appear to be fighters or escorts. These larger objects are likely bombers,"the Iraqi major said.

Good, he is paying attention Major Vasily Ivanov was thinking before he asked "This small group of fighters—they appear to have broken off from the main force. They look to be heading towards us. Tell me, comrade, why are they doing this and what should we do about it?"

"If I recall from our previous conversations, this group breaking off should either be Navy A-6 Intruders, likely carrying AGM-88 HARM missiles, or they could be either F-4G Wild Weasel Phantoms or F-16 fighters equipped with the HARM Targeting System," the Iraqi major replied after studying the screen for a moment.

"Good, so these fighters are now one hundred and eight kilometers away and closing. The main group, likely the ones with the bombers, look to be one hundred and eighteen kilometers away. I believe we should have Battery A engage the fighters closing in on our radar and then Battery B look to engage the bombers," the Iraqi major offered.

Ivanov smiled. His weeks of lessons appeared to be taking root. "Excellent, Major. What should we do with Battery C?"

"Battery C we hold back in reserve to protect the airport and our main radars until Batteries A and B have had time to reload."

Ivanov nodded in approval. "And here I had feared you were not listening to me during training. Good job, Major. I should be able to sign off on your certification after this engagement. Would you like me to spend some time at any of the batteries before I return to Baghdad?"

"Let's talk about that after we see the performance of the battery commanders from this first engagement."

Ivanov watched as the Republican Guard officer then went into action, showing more signs of life now than he had the previous four weeks of training. He was issuing orders and making sure his people knew what to do.

Maybe these Republican Guard soldiers really are the best soldiers the Iraqi's have

****

801st Bombardment Squadron
Saudi Arabia

151

Major Luke Duke, call sign Duke, was getting nervous. Beads of sweat were running down his face despite his best efforts to try to keep the cockpit cool.

Their RWR was telling them a very powerful search radar was tracking them. That meant they were likely going to be targeted by some sort of high-altitude missile system.

"What do you think? SA-2, or SA-5?" Duke asked his electronic warfare officer below the flight deck.

There was a momentary pause in response, causing Duke and his copilot, Captain Paul "Pancake" Haven, to get more nervous.

"Um, Duke, I'm not sure it's either. The range on that search radar is huge. I think they may have moved an SA-10 to the Medina airport," Captain Tim "Iggy" Igor, his electronic warfare officer or EWO, announced.

"If they moved an SA-10 into the area, Duke, that could cause us some serious problems," Pancake declared.

"Whoa, did one of you guys say those Iraqis may have an SA-10? How'd they get those?" one of the other crewmen said.

"It doesn't matter. If they fire a missile at us, we'll just deal with it. In the meantime, we have a mission to do," Duke declared as he sought to push his own fears down and reassure his crew.

Their bomber droned on for another few minutes before the tone of their RWR changed to a more urgent one. A missile had locked on to them.

"Yeah, that's an SA-10. No other missile has this kind of range," commented their EWO.

"Can you jam it? What do you need me to do to help you?" Duke asked urgently, trying to hide the fear rising within him.

They'd trained for penetration missions into the Soviet Union, and while training for something does help, it doesn't compare to having a giant missile fired at you from over a hundred kilometers away, racing after you at a speed of 5,400 miles per hour.

"Hang on. I'm trying. See if you can get ahold of the Raven flight. Their EW pods might come in real handy right now."

Duke switched channels to connect him to the Raven flight. They had a flight of two EF-111 flying cover with them. The Spark-Varks weren't kitted out to carry bombs like the other Aardvarks. Instead, they carried the AN/ALQ-99E airborne electronic warfare system tucked away in the bomb bay with the jamming pods mounted on the top of the rear vertical stabilizer and little nodules along the wings.

A handful of minutes later, the single missile targeting them appeared to have lost its lock. Duke and his aircrew breathed a sigh of relief. They watched with bated breath, hoping no other bomber took a hit. Then they saw it.

"Oh Jesus. Conga's plane took a hit." Pancake pointed to the stricken bomber. The missile looked like it had taken out two of their eight engines.

"Come on, dump your ordnance. Lighten the plane," Duke found himself whispering softly to himself.

"He's dumping his bombs," Pancake finally announced.

Stick after stick of five-hundred-pound dumb bombs fell from the bomber.

Pancake then pointed to something. "Oh, damn! There's another missile right there!"

The missile had flown almost straight up and slammed into the bottom center of the lumbering bomber. Moments later, the entire thing exploded in the largest airburst any of them had ever seen. As they were taking in the scene, five of their F-18 escorts were also destroyed, unable to evade or throw off the deadly missiles.

When the original missiles fired at the bombers lost their locks on the giant planes, their seeker head began scanning for the next best thing it could find. Unlike the B-52s, the Hornets didn't have a dedicated electronic warfare officer or advanced EW equipment built into their airframe. The bombers were built to penetrate Soviet airspace. They had a very strong EW capability of their own. Couple that with a Spark-Vark and they were hard to hit.

"We're coming over the target. Keep it stable, Duke," called out their bombardier.

A few minutes later, the fourteen remaining bombers of the squadron released their sticks of bombs. Once they'd released their load, the bombers made a wide arc out of Saudi Arabia, heading closer to the Jordanian border, which kept them out of range of the SA-10 near Medina. Until the Air Force or Navy was able to suppress that system, this would likely be one of the last deep penetration missions they'd run for a little while.

Chapter 18
Find the Scuds

8 October 1990
ODA 5226
InterContinental
Muscat, Oman

Sergeant First Class Mike Weekly wasn't just tired, he was bone-tired. His body ached all over. He and his team had been conducting a recon along the Oman-Saudi border, observing the activities of the Iraqi forces in the vicinity of Al Ain. In a way, his team had it easy. They would go out on patrol for a few days, then return to this totally awesome hotel the embassy had set them up with months ago when they'd first arrived in-country. It was a far cry from the medieval fighting taking place out west, near Jeddah.

Sitting in his hotel room at the InterContinental along the coast, Weekly was excited about the arrival of SOCCENT Headquarters. The advance party had arrived the day before and was finally settling in. With SOCCENT in theater, they'd finally have a buffer between them and General Yeosock. Sometimes Big Army and Special Forces didn't speak the same language. Additional SF elements were finally arriving in theater, which hopefully meant his ODA would start to receive some better, more SOF-specific missions. Playing recon games along the border was a big misuse of their skills.

"Hey, Weekly, are you in there?" Staff Sergeant Donovan asked while knocking on the door.

"Yeah, now go away," Weekly responded, not wanting to leave his bed.

"The LT wants us downstairs for a briefing in ten minutes. I was told to come and get you," his friend replied.

"OK, I'll be right down," Weekly said as he rolled out of bed and headed to the shower. He was feeling the past month in his bones. *I'm getting too old for this stuff,* he thought as the hot water ran down his back and shoulders.

Weekly was thirty-two and had risen quickly through the ranks. Joining the Army at seventeen to be an infantry soldier, he had excelled in basic and advanced individual training, earning a slot to Airborne School. Upon graduation, he'd been approached by a Special Forces recruiter. The recruiter hadn't begged him to join Special Forces; instead, he'd offered him a challenge like no other. Knowing these kinds of offers didn't come very often, not in the 1980s, he couldn't turn it down and accepted on the spot.

For him, the problem wasn't the physical endurance but the classroom and book work. Language school was a real challenge considering he had a hard enough time with English. One thing he'd quickly learned in Special Forces was that it left little time for a home life or a love life. You were constantly training or deploying. Which to a young single guy was cool, but as you got up there in years, you started to want those things you saw your siblings and families having. Hell, at thirty-two, he only needed five more years until he was eligible for retirement and having the safety net of that pension. It wasn't enough to live on unless you had low expectations; still, it was enough to make life with a second career very comfortable.

Drying off, he got into his uniform and headed out the door. Standing in the elevator, he was already salivating at the thought of grabbing a fresh cup of joe. The hotel had incredible coffee, ready for them at nearly all hours of the day, whenever they needed it.

In the past three weeks, the hotel had been taken over by Special Operations Command, Central. The Special Forces command had been given carte blanche by the government of Oman to billet their personnel out of and conduct their briefings from the hotel.

No other guests were able to stay at the hotel as it'd been completely rented out by SOCCENT. In the span of a week, the command had the entire place up and running as a fully operational military base, funded and paid for by the King of Saudi Arabia, who was seeing to every need of these brave warriors sent to liberate their Kingdom. All the soldiers had to do was order something from the menu or have it sent to their room and it was paid for. Even the bar did a good business despite Schwarzkopf ordering no alcohol for the troops in theater.

When the elevator dinged and opened, Weekly stopped in the lobby only long enough to grab a fresh cup of coffee and a Danish that'd been placed next to the coffee. Moving down the hall to one of the rooms designated for his unit, he put the danish in his mouth and held it with his teeth so he could open the door.

"Ah, there you are, Sergeant. Glad to see you could make it," Lieutenant Harris said as he pointed to an empty seat. It looked like the others had been specifically waiting on him, which made him feel kind of bad for not having rushed a bit more to get down here.

"Now that you're here, we'll get started." There was a major seated next to Lieutenant Harris. He hadn't seen this person before, which made him wonder what was going on.

"Sir," Harris announced, letting the major know they were all here and accounted for.

Standing in front of the operators, Major Reynolds cleared his throat as he began, "Gentlemen, your team hammered the hell out of the 1st Hammurabi Armoured Division last month. I mean, you guys thoroughly slayed names and stacked bodies. In light of that, we have a unique, special mission that's perfectly suited just for you. As a matter of fact, it'll give you guys a fresh chance to sneak around inside Saddam's backyard again."

As Major Reynolds spoke, he pointed to a map of the UAE. "Here's the port of Saqr on the Persian Gulf. Two weeks ago, a ship arrived and offloaded what we believe to be four Scud-D systems, given what we're seeing in the aerial reconnaissance photos." He showed them some images of the Scud launchers and some of the support vehicles parked near the freighters. "During the dead of night, and with some cloud cover obscuring our satellites, they disappeared. We believe they may have been moved to this area due east of the port in these mountains, and specifically in this wadi. That places them in range of every military installation in Muscat. I don't have to tell you how big of a threat it would be to start having Scud missiles raining down on CENTCOM HQ, our little pad here or the airport."

"Damn, hoss, you aren't joking. In Afghanistan, between March and June 1989, three Afghan firing batteries fired some four hundred missiles in support of some of their garrisons under attack. They used these Scuds extensively last year and into the start of this," one of the senior NCOs said.[3] He'd spent some time working in Afghanistan as an advisor to the mujahideen fighters.

---

[3] FAS, Intelligence Resource Program, Afghanistan. Wikipedia, https://irp.fas.org> threat> missile > Afghan

"Exactly. That's why your new mission is to insert into this area and find them. When you do, you will contact us, and we'll send an air strike your way to take 'em out. Any questions?"

"Sir, how do you see us being inserted? Helicopter's going to make a lot of noise in those mountains, and it's too far to walk with our gear," Lieutenant Harris asked. In his heart, he already knew the answer.

"You'll be conducting a HAHO parachute insertion. A C-130 will parallel the border at thirty thousand feet. As soon as you exit, activate your chutes and navigate to a point here. We've calculated your rate of descent and will drop you in favorable winds to move you along," Major Reynolds explained.

The team had practiced high-altitude, high-open drops at night, but this was a first for them in combat. Anxiety levels just went up a notch.

"And for the extraction, sir?" Weekly pressed.

"Helicopter noise for the extraction won't be a problem, so we'll come for you with aircraft from Task Force 160th," Major Reynolds responded. The team had frequently worked with the famed Night Stalkers. They were hands down the best night-flying pilots around.

"The aircraft will also have two other teams on board who will be jumping at points along the flight path. Once you leave the aircraft, you will not have contact with them as they're landing at other points to do the same as you—find the Scud launchers. If you find a launcher and can destroy it yourselves, do it. If not, call in an air strike before they can move it again. Scud missiles are important, but without the launchers, what good are they? We want the launchers destroyed."
****

30,000 Feet above the Desert

First Lieutenant Harris looked at his team with satisfaction. With a couple of missions now under his belt, he felt a lot more confident leading his team. He'd leaned on Sergeant First Class Weekly at the outset, but steadily he was taking more initiative. Heck, in a week, he pinned on captain, so he better start feeling more confident about leading them.

"Six minutes," the C-130 loadmaster yelled. The warning caused Harris to snap out of his private thoughts and return to the present.

One of the Air Force crewmen who flew exclusive Special Forces missions walked over to the row of seats Harris's team was situated on and shouted loudly, "Stand up."

The soldiers climbed out of the webbed seats, struggling a bit with their parachutes and all their necessary equipment strapped to their bodies as they did.

"Check equipment," came the next command. Each of the operators went to work, their muscle memory taking over as they went through the process of checking and rechecking the equipment of the man in front of them.

In addition to their parachutes, each operator had his weapon, rucksack, load-bearing equipment, oxygen bottle and mask, a double combat load of ammunition, and enough food and water for a week. It was a lot of equipment to travel with, but it meant they could go at least a week without needing a resupply.

At this altitude, it was necessary for them to carry a small oxygen bottle and mask. Inside the pressurized C-130, they breathed normally. However, when the doors opened they went on the oxygen bottles. Once they dropped to ten thousand feet, they'd be able to breathe normally again and removed the masks. The advantage of jumping and then deploying your parachute from this altitude was your ability to glide across long distances without being detected. One new piece of equipment they'd recently added to their inventory was the small Garmin handheld GPS receiver. This would help them navigate during their glide phase and make sure they landed at or near their intended landing point. These devices were so new to the military they were being purchased directly from the manufacturers for the Special Forces units.

Calculating the exit point, Harris figured they would be able to glide approximately seventeen miles to a touchdown point. If the Iraqis had radars tracking the aircraft, they certainly wouldn't track them. The men and their parachutes were too small of a return to show up on the kind of radars they were using. Even if they did, they would appear no larger than birds.

As they finished their final checks of themselves and each other, the sound of the ramp being lowered caused all eyes to turn to the rear of the aircraft. No matter how many of these HAHO jumps one did, the view was always the same. Tonight was no different. It was dark behind the plane, the full moon illuminating some of the ground below but leaving the canyons and valleys pitch black in some of the more remote areas. The full moon would make for a nice jump, and as the area was uninhabited, there was little chance they'd be spotted.

Walking towards the ramp as they finished their final checks, Harris and Weekly stood side by side at the edge of the ramp.

When the green light came on, they both leaned forward and dropped from sight. They were quickly followed by the rest of the team. Within seconds each jumper was stable and activated his square canopy chute and turned to the heading that would lead them to their intended touchdown point, seventeen miles away.

They floated for what felt like an eternity. The trip down did give them a good view of everything about them. For the most part, the ground below was black. However, they did spot a couple clusters of lights. Not a lot of lights, maybe just a handful. Some would flicker off only to flicker on again. This became a lot more noticeable as approached the ground. Still, they looked to be miles from their drop zone. The lights likely meant there was an army unit there, or maybe a Bedouin encampment. It'd be worth investigating later, Harris thought privately.

Approaching the ground, they were even more pleased to see it was bathed in moonlight. This made spotting any possible obstacles a hell of a lot easier. The last thing they needed at this point was a twisted ankle, or worse. As each member neared the ground, they dropped their rucksacks and applied the brakes to the parachute, causing them to all make stand-up landings and quickly collapse their chutes. No tucking and rolling on these landings, at least not if you did it right.

Although the ground was perfect for the landings, it was hard, compact ground, almost as hard as concrete. Once on the ground, Harris attempted to dig a hole to put the parachutes in. *Sad waste of a new parachute at the cost of a thousand dollars each*, he thought. He quickly realized that this was not going to work, as the ground was too hard for their small entrenching tools.

He waved his hands to get his second-in-command's attention. "Weekly," Harris said in a loud whisper, getting the senior noncommissioned officer to look at him.

"Sir," Weekly responded in a low voice. At night in the desert, sound traveled easily.

"See if you can find some soft area to bury the chutes. We'll be here all night if we keep trying to bury them in this soil."

While Weekly tried to figure out a better way for them to hide their chutes, Staff Sergeant Donovan established comms with SOCCENT and gave them a status report.

The team landed in a large wadi that flowed from the Oman-UAE border north to the Persian Gulf and the Port of Saqr. Their touchdown was only five miles from the port area. Between them and the port was a retention basin that captured water runoff from two large wadis. The other team jumping with them landed in another wadi to the south of their location. Between the two of them, they'd be able to scour the area near the mountains along the Oman-UAE border.

After an hour, the chutes were finally buried, and the team struck off to the north. Because of the large retention lake, which pretty much blocked the entrance to the wadi, they weren't too worried about anyone driving up the wadi towards them. On the other side, however, they would have to move carefully.

"Weekly, the first order of business is to find a hide position that we can operate out of and observe the approaches," Lieutenant Harris said. Weekly, being the most experienced of the two, knew this but felt that Lieutenant Harris was looking for confirmation of his decision rather than giving instructions.

"You got it, sir." Weekly pulled out his map. In the bright moonlight, it wasn't necessary to turn on a flashlight. While they took a moment to study the map, the remainder of the team set up a 360-degree perimeter around them, with each member kneeling and looking outward for any sign of an approaching threat.

Weekly noticed some key features that he began pointing out to the officer. "Sir, we have two good ridges on both sides of the retention pond, but I think we would have a better view from this one south of the wadi. We could set up a hide position on this forward slope in some of these crevices," he explained as his finger traced the areas he was talking about.

"Yeah, but we have to pass by this town to get there, and the damn dogs will start raising hell as we approach," Harris acknowledged.

"Yes, sir, but we'll have that same problem on this northern ridge as well—worse, we won't have nearly as good a view of the area as we would from the southern ridge," was Weekly's gentle reply.

"Hmm. Yeah, you may be right," Harris finally acknowledged as he continued to study the map and looked towards both ridgelines. He knew a decision was necessary and quick, as daylight was only six hours away. They didn't want to be caught climbing the ridges in daylight. Although the UAE was overrun by the Iraqis, there might be sympathizers that would love to turn his team in for any rewards that were being offered.

"OK, we'll head to the southern ridge and set up there. And for God's sake, let's be as quiet as possible going past this town. I don't want us to wake up every damn dog in the place," Harris said as he rose to his feet.

The soldiers manning the perimeter stood when they saw their leaders stand. They were ready to move; they just needed to be pointed in the right direction.

Once everyone was up and had adjusted their loads, Harris whispered, "OK, let's move out. Justin, you take point."

From where they landed, they had to move a klick and a half to get to the base of the ridge. The climb to the top was another klick. Once on the flat ground, they'd cover the distance to the hide site rather quickly, but the steep climb at the end was going to tax their physical endurance, especially getting to the top before sunrise.

Chapter 19

Raid on the Harbor

9 October 1990
As Sultan Qaboos Port
Muscat, Oman

Lieutenant Ainsley Fitzgerald was getting comfortable in her new role of container yard commander. She and her platoon sergeant had a good working relationship after being at the As Sultan Qaboos Port for a month. The container yard was organized and flowing smoothly, with tractor-trailer trucks picking up loads in a timely manner and getting them out of the yard. Ships were being unloaded quickly by the stevedores, and her people were marking and accounting for the containers. When a unit rolled in looking for containers, her people were able to take them right to the container and get them loaded and out the door. Life was good. The only flaw in the system was that she had requested a security element be assigned to keep looters out, but all she got was a few unarmed local hires in uniform to walk around the yard at night. Nothing had been stolen yet, but she was still uncomfortable with the arrangement.

To rectify the situation, she'd exercised some initiative and had her platoon sergeant develop a guard roster. Needless to say, that did not make the troops happy. Soldiers were pulling two-hour guard shifts in two two-person teams, to include herself and the platoon sergeant. The two teams would conduct roving patrols along the perimeter of the yard with the local security in the interior. Her teams were armed with their M-16s, and she required them to wear a helmet and a bulletproof vest that wasn't really bulletproof. It protected you from grenade fragments, not bullets. No one really cared for the vests. They were hot, and they didn't actually stop bullets. Then again, her soldiers were logisticians, not front-line soldiers.

Fitzgerald stood in the doorway of the warehouse where her office was located, holding her morning coffee. From that doorway, she could observe most of the yard. She noticed one of the civilian workers along the fence line. *What the hell is he doing over there instead of marking the containers? Hmm, that seems odd.* As she watched the worker move away from the fence, her thoughts were interrupted by another file being dropped on her desk, adding to the never-ending mountain of paperwork waiting for her. She was being drowned with all the stuff being sent to her yard, and then trying to make sure it got sorted properly and sent to the right units was a real challenge.

She looked at the clock. They had another ship due to arrive that afternoon, and after reviewing the manifest, she knew this load was going to need to be disbursed faster than normal. *Ammunition is arriving... a lot of ammunition.* Some of the munitions could be left outside in the yard for a short period until it could be delivered, like the artillery shells, but a lot of the other stuff would need to be housed directly inside the warehouse.

Seeing her NCOIC walk in, she called out, "Sergeant Murray, I'm going out to the warehouse to look at how we may want to stack the incoming ammo load. If you hear anything more about the ship, like any special requirements for the ammo, let me know as it might change the way we store it. I wish we had hardened bunkers for this stuff. Kind of makes me nervous storing this much ammo unprotected," she said as she donned her cap and departed.

"Yes, ma'am, I'll call the ASP and ask them to be standing by to come get it this afternoon or tonight," Sergeant Murray replied as she started to walk outside. "Oh, ma'am, don't forget your gas mask and weapon. CENTCOM policy, you know. You make us all carry them, you should too," Murray said with a *gotcha* smile, to which Fitzgerald responded with a stink-eye look as she picked up her weapon and mask.

The ASP, or Ammunition Supply Point, was responsible for getting the ammunition from her warehouse and yard to the Corps ammunition storage areas. Sergeant Murray had been working on all his contacts and schmoozing abilities to get their two units singing from the same page of music. They were now moving like a well-oiled machine.

Walking over to the warehouse, Fitzgerald was pleased with how the yard was laid out. Unit-identified equipment was all stacked together along with vehicles rather than everything just thrown together. Supply items were grouped by class of supply into ten separate areas, each identified with the roman numeral designation for the supply class, with Class I, III and V being the most important to the front-line troops when things got hot, and not from the environment. Class I was food, so pallets of Meals Ready-to-Eat or MREs were stacked in one location. Class III was petroleum products, in this case limited to canned oil and lubricants, as she didn't have the storage capacity for fuel. She didn't want the Class III next to the Class I for fear of contamination, so Class III was at the opposite side of the warehouse and at the opposite end. Class V was ammunition, so pallets of small-arms ammo and pyrotechnics were near the Class I, but the larger ordnance was located in the yard. The quicker it was out of there and transported to the ASP, the happier she'd be.

When she was done with her inspection, she walked back to her office on the other side of the yard. *What the hell?* she thought as she observed the same guy pacing across the yard. This time, she stopped

168

and stared at him as he walked. About halfway across the yard, he looked up and noticed he was being watched. He quickly picked up his pace and started looking at his clipboard as he moved out of sight around a container.

****

Unit 999, 2nd Battalion
Muscat, Oman

Captain Malik al-Masih felt a sudden surge of excitement now that it was dark. The darkness was providing them with the opportunity he needed to finalize the plans for what he hoped would be the beginning of many sabotage and hit-and-run attacks to come.

His battalion, the 2nd "Saudi Arabia" Battalion of Unit 999, had finally been given the go order to start their missions against the coalition forces now forming up in Oman.

Lying prone on the ridge, Malik looked down at the sprawling supply depot. The main yard looked to be about two hundred meters from the American soldiers' barracks, or the building they were using for barracks and administrative functions. The massive warehouse was another one hundred meters beyond that building.

Malik and his team of six had been on the ridge since the local national workers had left at the end of their shift. While the civilian contractors' work had ended, the soldiers assigned to the yard continued theirs, unloading the ammunition ship and sorting it in the yard and warehouse.

"Are you sure these measurements are correct?" Malik asked one of his teammates, the soldier that had a day job working in the container yard.

"I paced the distance off myself, sir, except for this one. I thought the female officer in charge of the place was watching me, so I had to quicken my pace. If it's not correct, it's only off by a few meters," the lieutenant explained. It was the distance from the fence to the artillery rounds storage area.

"Alright, then. Call this back to Sergeant Ahmed and give this to him. I want him to lay four mortar rounds per tube on the sleeping area. That should give us enough time and cover to get out of the yard and back through the fence before Ahmed shifts fire to the part of the yard with the artillery rounds. I want him to hit that area with another four rounds per tube. This should ignite the entire place. Now go, Lieutenant, and make sure he fully understands his orders and the sequence of how this needs to happen," Captain Malik explained.

The lieutenant scampered off to the field telephone they had strung from the ridge to the mortar team not far away. The mortar team was located on the other side of the ridge near a road that would give them a clean getaway to the safe house near the capital.

***

Placing the field phone down, Sergeant Ahmed motioned for his team of three soldiers to circle around him. Looking at their faces, he explained, "The lieutenant just called. They've given us the final coordinates for our fire mission." He handed the coordinates for the troop barracks to the soldier who would be responsible for sighting in the mortar tubes.

"The first fire mission is for a four-round spread. We're to pace the rounds we drop by approximately thirty seconds per round. Once these rounds are complete, Jawad will sight both tubes in for the next target. It's supposed to be a yard that contains recently unloaded artillery rounds. Once a total of two minutes have elapsed after the end of the first fire mission, we're to drop another four-round spread on the yard."

Sergeant Ahmed then looked at Jawad. "When we finish dropping those rounds, I need you to grab that bucket of water and slowly pour it over the tubes. We need them cooled down a bit before we throw them in the back of the van. The rest of you, make sure we grab everything and throw it in the van. We don't want to leave anything behind if we can avoid it. Now, get to it. We have a supply depot to blow up."
****

"Lieutenant, we have a problem," Sergeant Murray said as he walked into the barracks area. Most of the platoon was eating chow except for the two soldiers working the guard mount and a couple in the yard directing the loads coming off the ship.

"OK, what is it?" Lieutenant Fitzgerald asked as she looked up from her T-ration meal.

T-rations were served in large metal trays, twenty-five servings per tray. Cooks weren't typically needed other than someone who could boil water and pull the heated trays of food out of it every twenty minutes. When the trays had been removed from the boiling water, they'd be opened up with a can opener and served. There were three kinds of tray for each meal—a meat tray, a starch tray, and a vegetable tray. If you were really lucky, you might even get a dessert tray. It wasn't the most wholesome of meals, but it sure beat the heck out of MREs. A person's bowels could only take so many weeks of living on MREs before most folks developed some sort of problem.

Sergeant Murray explained, "The ship is unloading faster than we can keep up with now that the locals have gone home for the day. If we're going to get this done tonight, I'm going to need everyone in the yard and warehouse now or it'll take us till breakfast before we're done."

As he spoke, the soldiers of the platoon nearby heard his comments and collectively groaned. They were tired and just wanted to eat and hit the rack.

Standing, Fitzgerald turned to face the platoon. "OK, you heard the man. If we want to get to bed, we need to finish this job. As my dad used to say, many hands make light work. So grab your weapons and vests and get out to the yard. You all know your positions, so get to and start directing where it all goes. You guys on the forklifts, watch yourselves and keep your headlights on. Everyone be careful of the heavy equipment moving around out there. We don't need someone getting run over."

As she spoke, those still eating were shoveling the last mouthfuls of food into their faces. They knew it'd be hours before they could even think about coming back for more food.

"Sergeant Murray, I'm going to head over to the warehouse. Why don't you watch the yard? That way we'll have both areas covered and can unscrew things that might happen," Fitzgerald said as she headed out the door with Murray hot on her heels.

"Yes ma'am. Catch you later. Have you got your walkie-talkie with you?" He asked.

"Yeah, let's stay on channel ten," she replied.

The military hadn't issued them civilian handheld radios, but Fitzgerald had recognized a need for them and taken the initiative to just purchase them on her own and solve another problem— communicating. While she only had two of them, it allowed her and Sergeant Murray to stay in touch with each other while out in the yard.

****

Captain al-Masih withdrew his wire cutters and snipped the bottom of the chain-link fence. Standing quickly, he snipped the top of the same wire as the bottom and lay back down. The area was well lit, but with containers stacked four high, they were providing a nice shadow for his team to move about the area. With the top and bottom cut, he simply pulled hard on the wire and the fence opened wide enough that a Mack truck could go through. His team moved through the hole. Once everyone was through, two of his soldiers used some zip ties to rejoin the cut portions of the fence so it looked good as new. This way, if a roving patrol came by, they'd likely not notice that it had been tampered with. This would also allow them to exit the same area quickly once they were ready.

Al-Masih looked at his soldiers and motioned for them to get to work. They didn't have much time. They all knew their assignments and took off at a quick trot.

Al-Masih and three other soldiers moved to the warehouse. Al-Masih and one soldier would set the demo charges on the Class III and V items stored there. They only needed to place a few charges next to the petroleum products to get that pile going. Once it was, it'd burn nicely. The two other soldiers would set charges on the Class V munition products in the warehouse. Two other soldiers moved to the entrance of the port and yard. They were going to neutralize any guard force they found at the location. This would further aid them in their escape. He hoped they'd be able to subdue the guards, but ultimately, if they had to kill a few people on the night shift, then inshallah.

Al-Masih checked his watch. He saw they had one minute before the mortar rounds would impact the barracks. That would be the signal for everyone to break and run to their respective targets. The impacting mortar rounds would cause enough confusion for his men to complete their sabotage mission. If all went according to plan, they'd thoroughly jack this entire warehouse and yard, putting a further kink in the coalition forces operations.

Maybe I'll get a chance to kill some Americans too. They have no business sticking their nose in the Middle East, he thought as he stood in the shadows, waiting. A smile crept across his face. He heard the faint sound of a mortar round sailing over his head, barreling through the night sky seconds before it would crash into the barracks building.

That was the signal. He took off at a sprint towards his objective just as his eyes registered the flash of the explosion in the night sky and his ears picked up the blasts of not just one explosive but also a second one moments later. By the time he'd sprinted the fifty meters he needed to cover to reach the warehouse, another pair of explosions erupted behind him. Reaching down, he grabbed the door handle and yanked it open. Now he had to get his explosives planted and get out of the area.
****

Lieutenant Fitzgerald was completing her stroll through the warehouse when the first round hit the barracks. She immediately squatted down at the sound of the explosion, not sure of what had just happened. When the second round hit, there was no doubt in her mind what was going on. What she didn't know was what was causing the explosions or what exactly was blowing up.

She'd been directing four of her soldiers as they used a forklift to help them stack and sort some large crates of ammunition. The soldiers all looked at her for guidance on what to do next.

"Get down, grab your rifles and cover the doors," Fitzgerald screamed as she dove behind a pallet of MREs and a stream of small-arms tracer fire suddenly appeared. Whoever was shooting at them had sent a torrent of bullets and tracer fire down the center aisle of the warehouse attempting to pin them down. Two of her soldiers froze, unsure of what to do, or maybe they just hadn't heard her instructions. Suddenly one of them spun around and stumbled; it looked like he'd been shot. The other soldier finally dove to the side for cover.

Fitzgerald pulled her M-16 to her shoulder. It suddenly dawned on her that her little fiefdom was under attack. She had intruders inside the wire, they were inside the warehouse, and they'd just shot one of her soldiers. Looking above the stack of MREs she'd hidden behind, she saw four figures run through the large warehouse doors.

She brought her rifle to bear on them, placing her sight picture on one of them as they started to split up, presumably to carry out their mission. Flicking the safety off her rifle, she squeezed the trigger just like she'd been taught to do. The figure she'd fired at clutched at his chest and stumbled for a brief moment before collapsing to the ground. Her Tennessee mom, who'd taught her how to shoot, would have been proud. The other figures dropped behind pallets, looking for cover as she started firing at them next. Her two remaining soldiers were exercising the shooting technique of "spray and pray" firing wildly and randomly all over the place.

"Damnit, Fowley and Sprig, take a breath and try to aim before you fire. They're over there, behind the Class V pallets." *I need to get some help in here now*, she thought when she heard the sound of something hard hitting the floor near them.

"Grenade" was all she had time to say before it detonated, sending shrapnel across the room. Fowley and Sprig said nothing, but she could see that they weren't moving. The grenade looked to have landed between them.

As if on cue, a figure jumped up and began moving down the center aisle, shooting at Fowley and Sprigs's position. Fitzgerald didn't flinch or hesitate; she brought her rifle up and fired several shots into the attacker's chest. The Iraqi went down with a scream and thrashed about on the floor, blood rapidly pooling around him.

Two down, two to go.

Just then Sergeant Murray ran through the open doorway to see what the hell was going on.

"Lieutenant, are you OK?"

Before she could answer, red tracers whipped around him as a handful of bullets tore into his chest. Murray's body was flung backwards from the force of the bullets.

"No!" she heard herself shouting at what was happening around her. One of her soldiers was wounded, two more had been killed, and now her NCOIC was dead.

She couldn't see where Murray's executioner had fired from. All she knew was she had to move before she got flanked. Getting to her feet, she sprinted to the other side of the warehouse and ducked behind a stack of pallets in the Class III area, hoping she hadn't been spotted.

Looking back at her old position, she watched a burst of automatic weapons fire tear into it. They'd figured out where she was, and they had worked to flank her. She let out a loud moan and almost cried from the emotional shock of what was happening around her.

"Pull it together, Ainsley. You got this," she muttered softly as she reapplied her metaphorical war paint. She was going to kill these bastards.

Then she heard someone moving cautiously but quickly down the warehouse, right towards her. He stopped and knelt down on the opposite side of the pallets she hid behind. Looking between the pallets, she saw him squatting right in front of her, looking down. *Son of a bitch*, she thought, *is he placing a charge on my pallets?* She raised her weapon slowly until it was pointed right at him. Then he looked up and right into her eyes. It was the last thing he saw before she pulled the trigger and his head exploded.

Seconds after she fired her single shot, she heard more shooting at the entrance next to the Class V section, as some of the other platoon members had now converged on the warehouse. The last remaining attacker was dead.

"Don't shoot, I'm coming out," Fitzgerald yelled. *The last thing I need to do is get shot by my own soldiers.*

"Lieutenant, are you OK?" one of them called out as he ran up to her.

"Yeah, but how is Sergeant Murray?" she called out as she walked around the dead attackers. She assumed they were likely Iraqi soldiers, though they weren't wearing any uniforms. Who else could they be?

"He's dead, ma'am," was the response.

Sighing, she nodded at the news. "OK, this last guy looked to be setting some demo charges. I want you guys to start searching the warehouse for any of them. If you find them, let's grab them and move them to the far side of the yard, away from everything." She pointed down to the charge her attacker was planting. "These are clearly some sort of plastic explosives, so they aren't going to detonate if you touch them or move them. Just get them out of the warehouse if you find any, got it?"

"Yes, ma'am," came a chorus of calls from a few of the soldiers, who set about looking for more charges.

Moments later, Lieutenant Fitzgerald found herself alone. She walked around the pallets to the man she'd shot. She'd never seen a dead person before, and certainly not one that she had killed. As she stood there looking down, she began to feel queasy. She noticed the top of the Iraqi's head was missing. That was when she regurgitated her dinner. Her legs became weak, and she braced herself on the pallet, thankful that she was alone and no one was there to see this display of weakness. After a few minutes of deep breaths and a drink of warm water from her canteen, she felt that she could resume her duties. She began to prioritize what needed to be done, knowing she would be taking on more responsibility until she could get a replacement for Sergeant Murray.

Walking out of the warehouse, she saw the building they had been living and working out of on fire in a couple of places. The building was wrecked. Nearly all the windows had been blown out, and a couple of fires were slowly smoldering away. It was a real mess. Walking out of the building were some soldiers, clearly helping some wounded.

Seeing the wounded, she made her way towards them. Someone had gathered the wounded and placed them in one location. A couple of her combat medics were doing their best to treat the wounded. A few soldiers continued to move in and out of the building, either carrying or helping a wounded person out or bringing a dead body out. Seeing what had happened to her people almost made her want to retch again.

As she moved towards them, she ran into Staff Sergeant Robinson. He was the Third Squad leader and the highest-ranking soldier after Sergeant Murray. He was also a damn good NCO himself.

"Staff Sergeant, how you doing?" she asked, still feeling a little weak.

"Good, ma'am. How about you?" he replied, concern in his voice.

"I think I'll be alright. Right now I need you to take Sergeant Murray's place. Once we're sure the area is cleared of any other attackers, let's focus on making sure we find and collect our wounded."

As she was talking, the sound of police and fire engine sirens grew in intensity. Help was finally on the way. Hopefully her wounded could get treated at one of the local hospitals and get the treatment they needed.

"Sergeant, take over for the moment. I'm going to call headquarters and let them know we've been attacked and taken casualties," she finally said before walking away.

Chapter 20

The Western Sky Lights Up

10 October 1990

Yanbu, Saudi Arabia

Red Sea

Captain Abeer al-Maloof slowly broke the surface of the dark waters of the Red Sea, made so by the moonless night. It had been a long swim from where the small nondescript fishing boat had dropped him and his team into the water. They still had three hundred yards to go to reach the tanker ship docked at one of the petroleum docks in Yanbu.

The SS *American Trader* was a T-2 tanker left over from World War II and still supplying oil products to the American Fleet. This was to be her last trip before going to India to be scrapped. Her thirty-man crew of mostly foreign seamen would deliver the ship to India and then the company, C.F. Sharp Shipping, would fly them to their home port of Okinawa to sign them off. All were anxious to get back to another ship, as the extra pay for being in a declared combat zone was well worth the time they spent. Besides, Iraq had no navy, and the US air cover precluded an air strike against them.

Yanbu, with its excellent seaport and three oil refineries, was a strategic port. It was the best seaport in Saudi Arabia on the Red Sea, even better than Jeddah. The airport had just received the first of the American forces with the 101st Airborne Division arriving that morning. Planes were landing about one every hour, and already a full infantry brigade was on the ground. The follow-on support elements were beginning to arrive along with more attack helicopters from the 2nd of the 17th Cav Squadron and the 3rd Battalion (Attack), 101st Aviation

Brigade. The 1st Battalion (Attack), 101st Aviation Brigade, had already drawn blood in the Battle of Medina Ridge and was in the process of moving to Yanbu to join the rest of the division.

As Captain al-Maloof observed the ship, he noted that no security guards were visible on the deck. He also didn't see any patrol boats moving around the harbor. To the north, there were other tankers at the loading docks, but that was another mile swim. The currents had moved his team south of where they should have been.

This single ship, however, was within range, and that sealed his decision. He motioned to his teammates, and they slowly sank below the surface and activated their electric miniature sleds on a due east compass heading, staying twenty feet below the surface. As they progressed eastward, they noticed visibility increasing due to the lighting along the dock. The water was crystal-clear to begin with. Al-Maloof made the decision to drop down to thirty feet as he and his team approached the ship. He slowed his approach as the hull of the ship became visible, with one two-man team heading for the bow and him and his teammate heading for the stern.

Being an older tanker, the SS *American Trader* didn't have a double hull like modern tankers had. The double hull prevented an oil spill if the ship ran aground. As al-Maloof reached the stern of the ship, he followed the propeller shaft back into the hull. The thinnest metal on a ship is located in the stern around the propeller shaft. A limpet mine attached at this point would open a larger hole, and even if the ship could be saved, it wouldn't be going anywhere with a damaged propeller shaft. He knew that the ship would sink from their mines and that would foul up the harbor for subsequent freighters. What he wanted was a spectacular explosion that would rip the entire dock and port area apart.

The forward team went deep under the ship and came up to place two mines, one on each side of the ship just below the waterline. This would open the side where the fuel holding tanks were located. When the charges detonated, the fuel vapors would ignite and create a huge fireball, engulfing the ship and possibly destroying the docks.

****

Private Hayes was a member of Alpha Company, 1st Battalion, 327th Infantry Regiment. He had been on the first plane landing early that week and was dog-ass tired. The heat was sapping his strength as well. Sure, Fort Campbell, Kentucky, was hot and muggy in the summer, but this dry heat was something else. It was like walking around with your sister's hairdryer blowing in your face. Normally his fatigues would be soaking wet with perspiration in the heat. The desert fatigues were made of heavy canvas and designed to cause one to perspire. The dry air would cause evaporation to occur quickly and thus keep the body cool, or so the design engineers had explained. Private Hayes doubted that the engineers ever came to the Middle East, however.

About every thirty minutes, someone was handing him a liter bottle of water to drink, and yet he noticed when he urinated it still wasn't clear. It was on the darker side, indicating his body was becoming dehydrated. As he walked his one-man guard post along the dock in the Yanbu port, his mind wandered.

"What the hell are we doing guarding a dock, and why are we so dispersed?" he said to himself, since no one else was around. He went over what they had been told earlier. Sergeant Williams, their platoon sergeant, had told the guards to stay in sight of each other but not to buddy up as they walked their posts. Their sergeant had even gone so far as to use spray paint to designate the start and end of each of their posts, so they knew exactly where it was. The soldiers were all disappointed that they weren't being allowed to have a buddy on duty with them. Patrolling something like this on your own was incredibly boring. You spent hours upon hours alone, unable to talk with anyone to help pass the time as you just paced between the two spray-painted points.

I wonder what my flyboy Air Force brother is doing right now. Can't believe he really joined the Air Force to be a boom operator on those tankers. Talk about a soft job. He probably would have washed out of the infantry. His brother was a bit of a book nerd and soft.

As he continued to walk his post, he glanced up at the night sky. Although the lights of the dock and refinery diminished the intensity of the night sky, the Milky Way was clearly visible.

When I get off tonight, I need to sit down and write Billie Sue a letter. I know she must be worried about me. Oh, it would be so nice to be with her tonight in the forward cabin of her dad's sailboat. I never realized what you could do in that small cabin riding on anchor until she showed me, he reminisced as his mind began to wander again.

He smiled at the last time they'd gone to the movies together. It was a double feature, with *Bird on a Wire*, starring Mel Gibson and Goldie Hawn, and the much-anticipated release of *Back to the Future Part III*. They'd laughed pretty hard during the first show before having a little fun of their own, her sitting on his lap, her breasts pressed against his face. *I wonder where she learned those moves. I'd like to have her on my lap right now. Oh, the way she ground down on me... hmm. Damn, I'm getting a hard-on right now.*

Grunting to himself, he was glad he was alone right now. He'd never hear the end of it from his platoonmates. Getting a hard-on while on duty wasn't exactly standard operating procedure.

****

Twenty feet below the surface of the water, Sergeant Asif Abd al-Rashid started easing towards the surface. He and Sergeant Danish Abbas were responsible for setting the limpet mine on the dock side of the ship. This would help ensure the ship essentially sunk right alongside the dock, making the dock useless until they were able to refloat the wreckage and move it, effectively rendering one of the critically important pieces of the port inaccessible.

Coming out from under the keel of the ship, Sergeant Asif noticed the clarity of the water right away. The lighted docks illuminated the area and the water next to the ship so clearly he could even see the brightly painted, large and bold letters that said NO SMOKING. He was still twenty feet from the surface.

Slowly, Asif and Abbas moved up the side of the ship as they wanted to place their mines just below the surface. Once they were attached, they would set the timer and then get out of there as quickly as possible. This job required two mines, which was why each of the divers carried one. They weren't leaving anything to chance. Their orders were to make this harbor as impossible to use as they could.

Still, Asif was a bit conflicted about the placement of the mines. They'd been taught that the best place for anti-ship mines was along the keel of the ship, where they would break the primary strength and support structure of the ship, causing it to sink. But if a large explosion was the desired effect, then the mines should be placed above the waterline, where the fire and explosion would have sufficient oxygen to ignite the fumes of the JP-8 aviation fuel the tankers were taking on. Sergeant Asif was concerned about the sudden inflow of water suppressing the flames and inhibiting the fuel fumes from igniting.

When he'd brought this concern up the captain, he had been told in no uncertain terms to stop questioning the advice of his superiors and just execute the orders given to him. That kind of attitude bred a lot of distrust between the officers and the senior sergeants.

As Sergeant Asif and his fellow diver rose toward the surface, he smiled, knowing that the captain wasn't around to micromanage them. His divers would plant the mines the correct way, a couple of feet above the waterline, not below. *We just need a few minutes and the mines will be ready.*

****

Now that the sun was starting to set, the heat wasn't as bad. Still, drinking a liter of water every hour was beginning to place a strain on Hayes's bladder.

Damn, I haven't pissed this much since that night drinking at Cat West back in Clarksville. It'd almost be easier to just leave my dick hanging out so I can piss when I feel the urge, he thought to himself as he laughed at the image of that.

Walking up to the edge of the dock to relieve himself, he unbuttoned his trousers' front section and whipped his penis out. Just as he was about to start peeing, he saw something that caused him to pause.

What the hell? Is there some sort of big fish near the tanker? That's an awful lot of bubbles. It's almost like there might be some sort of diver under there...

"Oh shit!" Hayes yelled loudly in surprise just as a head cleared the surface of the water. In that moment, his training took over as he yanked his M-16 from his shoulder.

When he yelled, the diver in the water seemed startled and looked around for the source of the noise. In all his frantic searching, he never looked up. With his rifle now in his hands, Hayes flicked the safety off his M-16 as he pointed down at the diver. Then the man in the water peered up through the water and their eyes connected. There was an expression of surprise on his face, but then he pulled something metallic out of the water.

In the blink of an eye, Hayes's finger had moved from the foregrip of the trigger guard to the trigger as he started firing. He saw his first three-round burst of fire land near the diver, but it missed. He readjusted faster than he'd thought was possible, placing his sight picture right on the face of the diver, who at this point had raised some sort of pistol of his own right back at Hayes.

Pop, pop, pop.

The three-round burst of his M-16 thudded right into the diver, who instinctively fired his own pistol twice, sending a couple of bullets sailing right next to Hayes's head, causing him to flinch.

Hayes continued to fire three-round bursts at the diver, whose body now appeared to be lifeless, steadily sinking deeper into the water. He didn't care, though. The bastard had nearly killed him, and for all he knew there were more divers down there, so he kept pumping rounds into the water.

At this point, several soldiers from Hayes's platoon came running towards him, their rifles in their hands, ready to join him if needed.

Corporal Johannsan shouted to Hayes as he dropped his spent magazine to the ground and was in the process of slapping a fresh one in its place. "What the hell are you shooting at, dumbass!"

As the two soldiers came right up to him, panting from being out of breath. Hayes pointed to the water below. "Right there! There was a diver right down there. I pumped at least three rounds into his chest before he fired two rounds at me."

"Whoa, you're saying you actually saw a diver down there?" Specialist Berry said. A little further away at the entrance to the pier was a vehicle racing down towards them.

"Oh, great, here comes Sergeant Billings. You better be right, Hayes, or Billings is going to have your ass for emptying a magazine into the water like that," Corporal Johannsan added.

Crinkling his eyebrows in frustration, Hayes shot back, "I know what I saw."

Just then, the vehicle racing towards them came to a halt. Staff Sergeant Billings stepped out and marched right towards Hayes, with a look on his face that said this had better be good.

Staff Sergeant Billings was a large black man that took good care of his men, but he didn't tolerate misbehavior or slacking. He ran a tight team, keeping them out of trouble and always being the first to finish a task assigned to them.

Approaching the three, he demanded, "OK, someone explain to me why I heard gunfire a few minutes ago."

Johannsan and Berry slowly stepped back from Hayes, making it obvious who was the guilty party.

"Hayes, you have a story for me?" Billings said, not really asking.

"Sergeant Billings, I was getting ready to take a piss over the side of the dock, and as I looked down into the water, I saw these bubbles coming up. Next thing I know, some diver's head pops up, and I yelled. The guy looked around, but he hadn't looked up yet. I managed to unsling my rifle and aimed it at him. I was about to tell him to surrender when I saw him bringing something metallic out of the water. At that point I fired a three-round burst at him but missed. Then he fired twice at me before I hit him with another burst. That's when I decided to keep shooting around him, in case another diver was still down there. I think someone may be doing something with the boats tied up here," Hayes explained.

"Did anyone else see this guy?" Billings asked, looking at Johannsan and Berry.

"No, Sarge," Johannsan said, though he was now looking down into the water and along the side of the ship.

"I was down that way, so I didn't see anything," Berry said, pointing to where his guard position was.

Billings walked over to the edge of the dock and peered into the dark waters. As he looked down into the water, he couldn't see much. The sun was nearly gone, which meant they were relying more on the lights along the pier. Then he spotted something. A single bubble broke the surface.

With a puzzled look on his face, he kept staring at the location the bubble had just come from. Then he saw a small cluster of bubbles break the surface. Now he believed something was amiss. He just didn't know what.

Turning his head slightly while still keeping his eyes on the water, he called out, "Corporal Johannsan, get on the radio and call the headshed. Tell them we may have enemy divers near the pier and this ship. Tell them one of our guards believes he shot and killed one of them. We need a diver down here right now to investigate this out further. Private Berry, get your ass up on the ship and find a ship's officer right now."

"Yes, Sergeant!" came the quick reply from Berry as he took off at a run to the gangplank leading to the ship.

Several sailors were along the rail now, watching the activity on the dock below them. They'd heard the shooting, and when they saw Berry take off, it didn't take much for them to realize what was going on. Almost immediately, as one, they started running for the gangplank. They wanted off the ship now.

Billings looked over at Hayes. "OK, I believe you, Hayes. Ya done good," he said, a determined look on his face.

"Thank you, Sergeant," was all Hayes managed to say. The reality of just having shot and likely killed someone was starting to set in.

Johannsan came up. "Sergeant, the headshed wanted to know what's going on and I told them. They said for all of us to get off this dock but secure the road approaching it."

"OK, you round up Berry and Hayes here and get moving. I'll follow along in the vehicle and pick you up, but I want you away from here. Now move it, troop."

Hayes and Johannsan didn't have to be told twice.

As Berry and a ship's officer approached, Berry noticed his two compadres running down the dock. Billings just looked at him and pointed towards the others. Berry took off after them.

"I first mate on ship. What matter?" the officer asked. It was clear English was not his first language.

"Sir, I believe we killed a diver who was attempting to put a limpet mine on your ship. I would recommend you get your crew off until we can get some divers to check out the ship," Billings said.

"I finish load jet fuel. Then go."

Billings shook his head. "Sir, I have asked that divers be sent down to look at your ship. It would be safer if you waited just to make sure everything is OK."

189

"I have schedule. Diver come before I go, OK," the office said and in his native tongue relayed something to the crew that had disembarked. Reluctantly, the crew climbed back aboard and returned to their duties. Billing shrugged his shoulders and got back in his vehicle. Driving down the dock towards the mainland, he picked up the three exhausted soldiers.

They'd driven down the dock towards the shore for only a few minutes when a bright flash erupted behind them. Then a massive blast wave slammed into the rear of their vehicle, shoving it forward like a child's toy. Billings fought like hell to keep the vehicle from flipping over or rolling. The heat from the blast had been so intense, it singed the exposed hairs on their skin. Next came the ringing in the ears which would make communicating that much harder until their hearing returned back to somewhat normal again.

Steering the vehicle to a safe spot to stop, Billings put the vehicle in park. As he got out, he saw the run-flat tires on the vehicle had been shredded. The vehicle's paint had been burned right off. Hell, he looked down at his arms and could see singed hair on them. Turning, he looked back at the ship. There was nothing left save for a few large chunks of the hull, rapidly sinking next to the dock. Everything was ablaze. The oil pipelines that fed out to the ship were spewing flames as more fuel continued to pump out of them. Someone would get that shut off shortly.

Turning to look at his guys, he saw they were a little shook up, but aside from some minor cuts and burns and the fact that hardly any of them could hear anything, they all seemed to be alright.

Billings walked up to Private Hayes and put a hand on his shoulder. "You probably just saved all our lives, Hayes," he shouted." I'm putting you in for a medal, son. Damn proud of you."

Hayes just gave a goofy smile and pointed to his ears. Billings just smiled. They'd just dodged death by the slimmest of margins. They'd get their hearing back, but they wouldn't have gotten their lives back if Hayes hadn't spotted that enemy diver. Still, he felt bad that the captain of the ship hadn't heeded their warning. Not that it mattered. They likely wouldn't have gotten far enough away from the ship when it blew.

Chapter 21

CAV Out Front

12 October 1990
101st Airborne Division Headquarters
Yanbu Airport
Yanbu, Saudi Arabia

Hawk stood, studying the map hanging on the wall of the G-3's office. Lieutenant Colonel Hawk Roe had commanded the 2nd Battalion, 17th Cavalry Regiment, 101st Airborne Division (Air Assault), for the past year. His combination of OH-58A Kiowa and AH-1S Cobra aircraft were the eyes of the division. Scouting out in front of the division's forward positions, the Cav earned its motto of "Out Front."

Typical of all Cav officers, Hawk displayed all the bravado and bluster of an independent-thinking, take-charge leader. That was the kind of leader required to command a unit that was forward of the division, operating in unknown territory and facing a hazy intelligence picture of the enemy. It was the Cav's job to bring that hazy intelligence picture into clear focus.

"Hawk, how are you doing this morning?" Brigadier General Sheldon asked, joining him at the map.

"Good, sir, except for that loud explosion last night. Scared the hell out of me. I couldn't go back to sleep after that. Any idea what it was?" Hawk inquired.

"Yeah, it seems some UDT swimmers breached the security net in the harbor and laid a couple of limpet mines on a tanker full of aviation fuel. Blew the damn ship sky-high and destroyed the dock. Luckily, one of our privates managed to shoot the diver, but we think another diver probably got away. We're going to get a Coast Guard detachment in here to start running patrol duty around the terminals now."

"Wow! Still, that was the loudest explosion I'd ever heard in my life. Did we lose anyone?" Hawk asked, concerned for the welfare of the soldiers who were on guard duty there.

"No, thank goodness. The NCO in charge of the guard force got the people off the dock just before it blew. The crew on the ship, however, were all killed. Seems the ship's skipper didn't take the warning seriously." Sheldon shrugged. "Such is life."

Getting the hint that this discussion was over, Hawk asked, "Well, sir, what have you got for me? My boys are tired of sitting around here getting acclimated to the climate. They're ready to go hunting."

Sheldon pointed at the wall map. "Intel tells us that the 2nd Iraqi Corps has three divisions coming this way from here. The 7th Infantry Division is located around Masader, here. Then we have the 37th Infantry Division in the vicinity of Madain Saleh and Al Atheeb, and the 51st Infantry Division is around Al Jadid." As he spoke, he pointed at each location.

He paused for a second before adding, "With that corps and those divisions to the northwest of us and this mountain range that spreads across this entire area, it means they've come down from Tabuk to get through the mountains and try to get at us. This mountainous region is actually a godsend for us as it's giving the enemy very few options to get to the Red Sea and us. It also means their supplies are stretched big-time across this entire area of northwest and western Saudi."

"Damn, that's a lot of tough terrain to move through with tanks and armored vehicles," Hawk commented.

"It is. What's odd is somehow it seems they're fat with tanks, tons of T-72s. But as their lines stretched, they started getting real short on fuel trucks, so they're having a problem with large movements. From what we've seen with the satellite photos and a few U-2 flights, it looks like troops are traveling in trucks to keep up with the tanks. So that gives you the fifty-thousand-foot view of the situation. What I need you to do is start helping us get a lot deeper into the weeds. Start finding their lead elements for each of these divisions if you can. Then I need your choppers to help us find any logistic centers, supply depots, and artillery positions. We don't have the force to take on a corps, so I want to leverage our helicopters to do what we can to nail their supply lines. If we can starve those tanks and vehicles of fuel, they'll become paperweights. Combat-ineffective and we won't have to worry about them. But the trick, Hawk, is your boys are going to have to fly pretty far out there, most likely alone and without much in the way of support or help."

Studying the map, Hawk finally spoke up. "Sir, this is a big ask and these positions are a long way out. I think we can make it work, but I'm going to need to set up a forward area rearm and refueling point if we're going to run an operation like this. Am I going to be able to get some help with that?"

Sheldon nodded as a smile spread across his face. "I'm already on it. I spoke with Division Support Command and they're going to establish a FARRP in the vicinity of Al Ais. A security company from 2nd of the 327th will fly out in about two hours and set up the area to receive the CH-47s that will bring out the fuel and ammo. The DISCOM folks will be on that flight and will operate the FARRP. They understand that they're the ones refueling your aircraft and rearming them, so there should be no problems."

"Yeah, I remember my first exercise last year in Venice, Florida, when we were doing the night insertions into Avon Park and the DISCOM folks didn't think it was their responsibility to assist in fueling the aircraft," Hawk mused under his breath.

"Well, they understand now, so it won't be a problem. How soon do you think you can be off?" Sheldon asked.

"Well, as soon as the FARRP is established, we'll be out of here. I'll lead off with one troop and have the others on standby. I'll look to rotate them in so my pilots have some downtime. Unless we're running continuous life-and-death combat missions, I really don't like to push my pilots too far past their allowed flight hours per week. If you burn them out too quick, you won't have that reserve built up to call on later when the shit really hits the fan." Hawk paused for a moment as he traced his finger around the FARRP and then the positions where the enemy was likely to be. "I think I'm going to establish my CP at the FARRP for now. Once we have a better bead on the enemy, I may jump it forward if we need to move the FARRP forward," Hawk explained.

BG Sheldon nodded in approval. "Good. It sounds like you know how you want to run your operations. Just get me the intel I need, and good hunting. Oh, if you do find a lucrative target, do not hesitate to call tac air in on it. I'd rather you use tac air than let the Iraqis know you may be operating nearby. These guys have some serious ADA assets set up, and I'd hate for them to start figuring out your flight paths and you guys suddenly find yourselves flying into a hot mess."
****

Iraqi 2nd Corps
Al-'Ula, Saudi Arabia

Major General Izzat al-Douri had been dispatched from Baghdad to link up with the Iraqi 2nd Corps and find out what some of the problems were. Saddam had specifically sent him to be his personal eyes and ears and then report back to him once he felt he had enough information.

When he'd arrived a week ago, he'd set up his command post in Al-'Ula, between the 7th and 37th Divisions. He wanted to take a few days to gather some information, talk privately with certain commanders and some soldiers, and then begin to formulate an opinion of what was happening here. The more time he spent here, the more he was starting to understand the enormity of the problem they were facing out west. Saudi Arabia was just a vast country that, while having a decent infrastructure built up in places, still had swaths of the country with little to no infrastructure.

When Izzat had first arrived, he'd thought he would be moving and setting up a new position every few days as the headquarters moved forward. Instead, he was growing increasingly frustrated at the slow advance the corps was making. 2nd Division was sitting in Tabuk guarding their overextended supply lines. The 14th was also back there, a shell of what it had been after enduring multiple devastating air strikes while attempting to move to the coast. Now the problem was fuel and maintenance.

The extra tanks the divisions had been given were great for engagements when they happened. But they were eating fuel as if there was a gas station around every curve. What the division lacked was fuel trucks. The divisions just didn't have a sufficient number of fuelers to feed the tanks and the organic supply trucks need to keep these massive army formations moving. On top of that, maintenance issues were taking their toll on the vehicles. The fine sand got into everything and ate machine parts up. Repair parts were stocked, but not at the rate that they were being needed. This problem was going to be a subject of today's meeting with the division commanders. He'd finally gotten frustrated with the current leadership in charge and had opted to exercise some of his own special authority given to him by Saddam and get his hands dirty, so to speak.

Today, the three division commanders would finally arrive at his office to talk privately. This would be an informal meeting over tea. No staff officers would be present. No need to muddy the waters with staff officers trying to get face time with a general from Baghdad.

"Good afternoon, gentlemen, have a seat," al-Douri said as the three division commanders walked into the room. He had four overstuffed chairs arranged around a center coffee table. The table had a thermos of hot tea and some sweet cakes and fruit. The air conditioning held the room to a comfortable ninety degrees, a significant difference from the outside temperature of 128 degrees. Once the handshakes were exchanged and everyone had their tea and was seated, al-Douri started.

"Gentlemen, I have asked you to come here today so we may discuss our logistic problems in private. From what I've been able to gather, we have two problems. First, a shortage of fuel for the vehicles, and second, a shortage of repair parts." Three bobbing heads seemed to be in agreement with him. "Let's address the fuel problem first."

Major General al-Sabbag, commander of the 7th Division, interrupted, "Sir, when we started this operation, we had sufficient fuel to reach Tabuk, but we also had gas stations along the way that we could tap fuel from. Once we headed south, there were almost no fuel stations, and those that used to be there had been destroyed by the retreating Saudis before we got to them." The others nodded in agreement.

"That is a good point, but what is the solution to the problem we now face?" al-Douri countered.

"Sir, if I may," Major General Harb Tikrit, commander of the 37th Division, tried to answer, "we have a sufficient number of tankers for the trucks that are organic to our divisions. When we received the new tanks, that was wonderful, but they did not bring any fuel tankers with them. That is the cause of our existing problem. I would recommend that we prioritize the fuel in the tank trucks to our organic transports for the soldiers. The tanks can come along until they run out of fuel and then they can sit and wait until we seize a fuel depot at Yanbu or Jeddah. The fact is we are an infantry division, and we fight with infantry. If we feel we need the tanks, then we leave some behind and transfer fuel from those we are leaving into the few that will accompany us."

"What do you think of General Harb Tikrit's idea?" al-Douri asked, looking at the others.

Major General Zogby, who commanded the 51st Infantry Division, seemed to speak for himself and the other division when he said, "I think it is a very reasonable idea, sir. Plus, when you look at the terrain we are having to travel through, this isn't exactly ideal tank country. The fact is the tanks are slowing us down. If we had gone back to our roots and focus on light, mobile and fast infantry tactics, we would already be in Yanbu instead of stuck here with scores of tanks waiting on fuel."

General Zogby then went on to add, "As we move towards the Red Sea and the positions where the Americans are entrenched, we aren't facing large tank or even mechanized units. We're facing light infantry airborne units. They may have some armor near Jeddah from the 10th Saudi Mechanized Brigade, but nothing serious. We probably do not need all the tanks we have. Between our close-air support, our attack helicopters, and the few tanks we should take, we can leave the others behind and save fuel for those going forward."

The room fell silent for a moment as each commander was lost in his own thoughts. This was exactly the kind of information al-Douri had been looking for and what Saddam had sent him out here to find.

Finally, al-Douri asked, "Alright, what are the negatives to this course of action?"

"The negative is we continue the attack with only a quarter of our armor force," Al-Sabbag said. "But what good is it if we attack with everything only to run out of fuel before we join in battle—or worse, join in battle and then run out of fuel?"

"A very good point, General," al-Douri conceded. "So it is decided. We fuel only one-quarter of our tanks to continue the advance and leave the others until we find a sufficient amount to send the tanker trucks back." Everyone nodded in agreement.

General al-Sabbag was about to speak when al-Douri cut him off. "I think I know what you are going to say. We need to get the Corps commander to approve. Let me handle that. Right now, let's focus on the second challenge we are facing to taking Yanbu."

The three generals smiled and nodded.

"Now let's address our repair parts problem."

"Sir, if I may," MG Zogby said, "I have already started cannibalizing vehicles for repair parts. If a vehicle goes down and we do not have a part to fix it, the vehicle is then stripped of its parts to keep other vehicles operational. When parts arrive, we put them on the cannibalized vehicle and get it back up and running. It is better to have one vehicle down than four vehicles, each waiting on one part that we can take off the cannibalized vehicle."

"What is your vehicle availability, General?" Al-Douri asked, pleasantly surprised to see they had come up with this idea on their own and were already implementing it.

"If I had not initiated this program, I would be at forty percent availability. By doing this I am at seventy percent," Zogby explained with a satisfied look on his face.

"General Zogby, that was ingenious. With forward thinkers like yourselves, I am confident we'll take Jeddah before too long," al-Douri complimented.

"Thank you, Zogby, for sharing that. I hadn't gone that route yet, but hearing of your results, this sounds like it'd solve a lot of maintenance challenges my guys have been dealing with," commented General Harb Tikrit.

"I agree. When I return to my division, I'm going to initiate this idea right away," General al-Sabbag added.

Smiling, General al-Douri explained, "Gentlemen, it appears we have solved the two critical problems that have plagued your corps for nearly two months now. Two months of lost time we can never get back. What I'm going to do now is communicate this solution to Baghdad and let them know we have found a workaround to our problem, but that we still need those repair parts and fuel/tankers ASAP if we're to get this corps fully moving again."

****

0200 Hours

13 October 1990

Al Ais was a small town surrounded by high peaks and rough terrain. The only reason there was a town here at all was that the main highway from Masader to Yanbu passed through it, creating a waypoint of sorts through the mountains.

The town had a population of maybe fifteen thousand people. The town's buildings were typical concrete block, the same you saw in much of Saudi Arabia. On the north side was a wide wadi that came out of the mountains. It was near the town but isolated enough. This was the site chosen for the FARRP base. It was wide and flat enough for them to store their equipment and big enough that it could house roughly a dozen helicopters at a time if needed.

At 0200 hours, unbeknownst to the locals, half a dozen CH-47 heavy utility helicopters flew over the sleepy town and headed towards the wadi. Being out of the monsoon season, this was a pretty safe place to use—at least it would be until the spring rolled back around. No one had bothered to tell the local officials that the 101st was coming to town.

Twenty minutes after the CH-47s arrived, the last of them pulled pitch and departed, heading back to Yanbu to pick up the next load of equipment needing to be brought forward.

Captain Grobe, the officer in charge of this little outpost, surveyed his soldiers, who were scattered in a circle. With the last helicopter departing, groups of soldiers began getting up and moving out to create a perimeter around the open area. They had to have the area secured in thirty minutes for the next flight of aircraft to come in.

"Sergeant Crandall," Captain Grobe called out.

"Sir," came a reply in the night.

"Let's get this PZ marked for the next flight. I want the fuel blivets positioned on the east side of the area. Use IR chem sticks to mark those locations."

"Roger, sir, I'm on it. Pathfinders have the comms up now and are ready for the aircraft to call in," Sergeant Crandall, Pathfinder platoon sergeant, said.

As Captain Grobe squatted and studied his map, orienting himself with his surroundings, First Sergeant Simmons approached him.

"Cap'n, the boys are getting it done and have pretty much secured the perimeter. Should have it shut down tight in thirty minutes."

"Good, last thing we need to have is an aircraft in here refueling and a suicide car comes rolling in. Let's get an OP out a klick or so off the side of this road and be watching for any vehicles coming from the northeast. Need a checkpoint as well to stop any vehicles coming into this place. Chances are when the sun comes up, we're going to have some visitors wanting to check this place out," Captain Grobe added.

"Already done, sir. I had 1st Platoon establish an OP as soon as we landed. That young lieutenant knows what he's doing. He better— he's prior service and a scout platoon member back in the five-oh-deuce last year."

"Outstanding, Top. Thank you for staying on that. Oh, when our Saudi liaison folks get here, let's make sure we keep a couple of them near the OP. They'll be able to help explain things to the locals better than we can."

A few hours later, as the call to morning prayer commenced, it was drowned out by the sound of three CH-47 helicopters with the sling loads of fuel blivets. Elements of the DISCOM had already set out the pumps and hoses, so all that was needed for their little combat outpost to be operational was the fuel.

A ground guide was standing by to bring in each aircraft and show them where to set the blivets down. The CH-47s were bringing in four of these five-hundred-gallon blivets of JP-4. This was just a drop in the bucket of what was going to be needed to keep the helicopters fueled for what was certain to be a *lot* of aviation missions over the coming weeks.

While Captain Grobe and First Sergeant Simmons enjoyed a cup of coffee, a young private approached them.

"Excuse me, sir," he said, rendering the proper hand salute.

"Whoa, Private. Don't ever salute an officer in the field. Especially the captain. Got it?"

A little taken aback, the private blushed and nodded.

"What is it, Jarvis?" Captain Grobe asked, looking up at the baby-faced soldier who'd made the grievous error of saluting an officer while deployed in the field near the enemy.

"Sir, there's a car at the checkpoint, and they're yapping in Arabic and waving their arms. I don't think they're happy to see us," young Jarvis replied.

Standing up with his cup of coffee still in hand, Grobe said, "OK, I'll be right down. Come on, First Sergeant, you have nothing better to do right now. Let's go meet the locals."

Sighing, Simmons grumbled under his breath about being roped into a meet-and-greet with the locals. Everyone knew the first sergeant had a temper and didn't suffer fools lightly. The two of them followed Jarvis down the trail to the entrance of their little combat outpost.

Approaching the group of Saudi civilians, Captain Grobe extended his hand and in his best Arabic offered, "*As-salamu alaikum.*"

Smiling with a surprised look on his face, the elderly man that had come out to greet them countered, "*Wa alaikum as-salam.*"

"Hal tatakalam bial'iinjlizia?" Captain Grobe asked, exhausting his Arabic vocabulary as he sought to see if the man spoke any English.

The Saudi officials looked at each other. Grobe wasn't sure if he'd said the right thing or if something was wrong. The Saudis began what appeared to be an argument between them. Finally, one stepped forward while another ran back to the car and drove off. The one coming forward placed his hand over his chest. "Abdullah al-Ais." He repeated the words again, patting his chest this time.

"Sir, I think he's telling you his name," First Sergeant Simmons said.

"Captain Grobe," the captain said, imitating the chest patting. Abdullah smiled. *Now we're getting somewhere.* Abdullah motioned for everyone to sit down on the ground, which the remaining Saudis did. Grobe and Simmons followed suit, still clinging to their coffee cups.

"Captain, they're staring at our coffee cups. Should we offer some to them?" First Sergeant Simmons asked in a low whisper.

"Oh shit, now we have to entertain them too," Grobe said between clenched teeth. Looking at Abdullah, he pointed at his coffee and smiled. "You want coffee?"

Abdullah looked at the cup and then smiled and nodded in the affirmative.

"Jarvis, see if you can come up with three cups of coffee for these gentlemen," Simmons ordered.

"First Sergeant, where am I going to find three canteen cups for them, or the coffee?" Jarvis lamented.

"Jarvis, just do it. Anyone gives you shit, send them to me. Now go, boy."

Jarvis arrived back ten minutes later with three canteen cups and a thermos of coffee. No cream and no sugar. The Saudis seemed pleased that they were getting coffee, but as polite as they were, they would not have objected.

As everyone sat, some conversation was attempted but nothing was understood by either side. *I need to get an interpreter assigned to us. This is just not working*, Captain Grobe was thinking when the car returned and another Saudi gentleman was practically dragged out of the car. Words in Arabic were excitedly exchanged.

"I apologize that I was not here when you arrived, Captain Grobe. I, Hassan al-Ais, am the schoolmaster in our city. My father"—he pointed to the elderly gentleman who had introduced himself earlier— "is the mayor of our city."

"Your English is very good, Hassan. Tell your father that I am glad to meet him," Captain Grobe said with a slight bow to the old man, who returned a head nod. The old man commenced speaking to his son in Arabic. When he finished the long dissertation, Hassan turned to Captain Grobe.

"Captain, my father welcomes you. He has many questions. How long will you be here? What are your needs that we can assist you with? How many of you will come here?" Hassan asked.

"I don't know how long we will be here. I was told just to get here and set up a refueling point for our helicopters. How many Americans will be here, I don't know, but I can tell you that many Americans will be passing through your town in the coming days. As to what you can do to assist us, what we need is fresh drinking water. If you will allow us, we might be able to send a few soldiers into your town to purchase some food items," Captain Grobe said, looking at the old man the whole time.

Hassan immediately translated and the old man responded.

"My father says your soldiers are most welcome to purchase food in town, but he asks that they observe our laws and customs," Hassan explained.

"My soldiers have received a briefing about your laws and customs and will honor them. If they do not, then they will be punished by me," Captain Grobe replied, again looking at the old man with a very determined look.

The old man got the message without a translation. As they conversed about the town and the Americans, two Cobra helicopters and two OH-58s circled overhead before landing to begin refueling. In less than five minutes, they were off and heading northeast.

****

"Condor Two-One, Viper One, over."

"Viper One, Condor Two-One, go ahead."

"Viper One has what appears to be a recon element at coordinates…"

The Viper pilot read off the location to their operations group at the airfield. He'd found what he was hoping was the lead element of a larger force some ten miles south of Masader in the small village of Arar. Viper One was an OH-58 Kiowa helicopter hiding behind a small ridge one mile west of the village, which was astride the major highway from Masader.

"Roger, Viper One, let's move back to the west and then north and see what's up around Masader. How's your fuel?"

"Condor Two-One, sounds good. I'm good for another thirty minutes on fuel. Turning back."

"Roger, I have you in sight."

The two aircraft joined up and moved west for seven miles before masking behind mountainous terrain and proceeding north. Flying contour allowed them the greatest speed while maintaining a low profile.

When they turned east again, they would resume nap-of-the-earth flight, which would not only mask them but provide the slowest speed to approach an enemy position. The flight north to a point west of Masader was short, as it was only eight miles before they turned east and began NOE flight mode towards Masader. Once they turned east, they immediately spotted what they were looking for.

"Condor Two-One, Viper One, do you see what I see?"

"Do I ever. The Old Man is going to be buying tonight."

"Condor, he buys only if we call it in first. I am QSY to higher and will call it."

"Roger, Viper, Condor standing by."

Viper One switched frequencies to the squadron operations frequency. "Sabre Three, Sabre Three. Viper One, over." After a moment that seemed like forever to Viper One, they got their response.

"Viper One, Sabre Three, go ahead."

"Sabre Three, Viper One, sitrep."

"Viper One, roger, go ahead, ready to copy."

"Time: 0830 today. Location: west of Masader one klick." Viper One then sent the UTM coordinates electronically to Sabre Three. "Activity: Iraqi fuel truck farm. Approximately twenty tanker trucks. We are observing. Remaining time on station, one-five mikes. How copy?" Viper One asked.

"Viper One, we have good copy. You are the first. Understand you will break station in one-five mikes. Sabre Three, out."

****

"Son of a bitch. Viper One found something and reported it," Chief Warrant Officer Sinkey said to his copilot, Warrant Officer Ken Schuessler. Sinkey was a chief warrant officer, fourth grade as he'd cut his teeth flying in Vietnam in 1970. He enjoyed flying and had several thousand hours in helicopters and was qualified in almost every helicopter that was in the Army inventory and a few that weren't. Warrant Officer Schuessler, on the other hand, was new to flying, having just graduated from flight school in the spring, and was in his first assignment. He was front seat on the AH-1S Cobra.

"Well, they did have the shortest distance to travel to get to where the bad guys might be," Schuessler said over the intercom.

Switching to transmit, Sinkey said, "Viper One-Two, Condor Three-Five, over." Viper One-Two was a quarter of a mile in front of him and hugging the terrain as they flew north. The longer distance wasn't going to give them much time to conduct a reconnaissance.

"Condor Three-Five, Viper One-Two, go ahead."

"Viper, did you hear? Viper One found some refueling tankers."

"Yeah, I heard it and plotted it. They're just east of us, around Masader. I'm coming up on Fadhia and am going November Oscar Echo to their position."

"Roger, we have you covered," Sinkey replied and immediately switched to intercom. "OK, Ken, he's going NOE, so we need to be sure to have him covered."

"Roger," Ken replied and focused the M-73 gun sight just behind the little bird.

Viper One-Two commenced his NOE flight pattern, hugging the ground, though it looked more like he was hovering with motion than flying. He was literally peeking around hillsides and over hilltops

208

before sprinting to the next position that offered some concealment. As he eased up the side of a small hill, the vast wadi became exposed to him. The paved main highway from Madain Saleh to Masader lay before him. A few agricultural areas could be seen in the familiar round patterns common to the area. What really interested him was the large parking area with tanks in neat rows.

"Condor Three-Five, we have hit the mother lode. Shit, I'm looking at maybe fifty tanks all parked in a neat formation. We've got to get an air strike in on this one."

"Viper One-Two, pull back and send a sitrep. You'll probably need to get some altitude, so let's pull back a few miles."

"Roger, let me just get a good count and location. Wait one."
****

Sergeant Bassra was an infantry soldier in the 21st Armoured Brigade. He was assigned an SA-7 shoulder-fired anti-aircraft missile to use to protect the tanks. He didn't care for this assignment one bit. It was hot as hell out, and he was just sweltering in this heat. But infantry soldiers in an armored brigade were used for all sorts of ash-and-trash jobs as the tankers were the golden boys. And to make things worse, he now had to carry this weapon in addition to his own AK-47.

At least we aren't moving for some time. We're flat out of fuel, he thought with a grin at how these golden boys were nothing without fuel.

Sighing, he realized sitting here on the outskirts of Fadhla wasn't too bad. He had a roof over his head, clean water, and fresh food, not the army combat rations. The people, however, were not all that friendly. They weren't hostile either, so he supposed that counted for something. As his mind started to wander to thoughts of home, he thought he heard something.

What in the name of Allah is that? Sounds like a helicopter, but none that I have heard before, he was thinking when he rose and walked to the edge of the palm grove.

Looking southwest, he saw the small helicopter skirting along the ridge and then beginning to climb.

Whoa, that's an American helicopter.

Fumbling with the SA-7, he quickly got it off his shoulder and was attempting to recall the firing procedure for the weapon. As he mounted it on his shoulder, he initiated the launch sequence. When he heard the tonal sound indicating the seeker head had a solid lock on the helicopter, he pulled the trigger.

Whoosh...

The rocket leapt out of the tube, haphazardly at first before the main engine kicked in and it took off after its target with lightning speed.

He watched in stunned, satisfied silence as the missile left a small white trail as it streaked towards the helicopter. It changed course slightly to focus on the helicopter as it tried to make a maneuver at the last minute.

Boom!

The missile either got close enough that its warhead went off or it slammed into the helicopter. In either case, it blew it apart. The burning wreckage fell to the earth in a display of fire and black smoke.

Bassra couldn't believe it. He'd just singlehandedly shot down an American helicopter. He unceremoniously broke out in a happy dance before making a beeline back to where the rest of his unit and his commander were.

I need to tell my commander the news. I might get promoted for this. Might be able to get a transfer back to an infantry unit. Allah be praised, I finally did something right, something big.

****

"Viper One-Two, Condor Three-Five, over." Condor repeated the call two more times, with no answer. He hadn't seen Viper go down as he'd turned to head home. As he looked back in the direction where Viper had been, he saw something—a column of black smoke rising in the direction of where his friend had been. Viper One-Two was gone.

Chapter 22
Scud Attack

14 October 1990

ODA 5226

United Arab Emirates

They'd been on the ground now going on five days. In that timeframe, they still hadn't found the Scud launchers they'd been sent to destroy. They'd found several missile trailers, so they knew the launcher had to be nearby. They were also starting to run low on food. If they didn't find the launchers in the next two days, they were going to call in an air strike on the missile trailers. That would at least deny the launchers more missiles to fire.

Crawling up next to Weekly, Lieutenant Harris whispered, "Is there some other place we should scout or look at to find that launcher?"

Weekly had been asking himself that question a lot for the last forty-eight hours. They'd found a good hide location, and they'd spotted half a dozen missile trailers, which meant the launcher had to be close. But where?

Turning slightly to look at Harris, Weekly replied, "I think we're going to have to. We've got maybe an hour of light left. Unless you're opposed, I'd like to take AD with me and scout this other ridge over here. I'd wager that launcher is probably hidden here."

Harris looked at the ridge on the map, doing a quick calculation. "That's like six kilometers away. You'd be a long way from help if you ran into trouble. You sure you just want to take AD with you?"

AD or Accidental Discharge, aka Staff Sergeant Joe Bruiser, was their resident sniper. He'd earned his nickname during sniper training when he had an accidental discharge of his pistol at the range. It had embarrassed the guy to no end, but the nickname had stuck. Now he wore it like a badge of honor.

"Yeah, if it's just the two of us, we can move faster. Also, if we happen to find that launcher and we see it getting to fire before we can get an air strike called in, then maybe he can disable it before they're able to launch it," Weekly explained to Lieutenant Harris.

"OK, do it. Just make sure you bring an extra battery for the SINCGARS radio. I'll let HQ know where you'll be headed so they'll be ready in case you find something and need to call in a strike."

A few hours later, Weekly and AD left the hide location and started their six-kilometer hike to the next ridge, where they believed the launcher vehicle was waiting.

****

A Battery, 2nd Rocket Battalion
United Arab Emirates

Major Yousef smiled as he listened to the order. He'd finally been given permission to launch his first salvo of Scuds at the Americans. His battery of four launchers had been twiddling their thumbs in the desert now for nearly two weeks, waiting for these orders. When his battery had left the port, he'd split them down into three sections—his launcher section, missile section, and headquarters and service sections. All three had set up shop in a different wadi. This was done to disperse his force.

Six days ago, one of his soldiers thought they had heard the sound of a helicopter. It had turned out to be nothing, but it had caused him to break his launchers up. He'd had a launcher paired with their three missile trucks and support elements. Now he had the launchers all together, where he could concentrate his limited air-defense assets to protect the launchers themselves. Without those vehicles, the missiles were useless.

"Did we finally get our launch orders?" Captain Ibrahim asked.

Turning to face his executive officer, Major Yousef replied, "We did. I need you to work with the fire control officer and make sure they get these coordinates entered in. Also, once we fire this first volley, I want the launch vehicles moved to the next position. Make sure we have another missile for each launcher standing by at the location. We're to expend all twenty-four missiles before dawn."

Captain Ibrahim nodded slowly at the command. It was a tall order. It could take upwards of half an hour to an hour to reload a launcher. If they were supposed to launch all four missiles for each launcher, it'd take roughly four hours just to get them reloaded. That didn't take into consideration moving them to a new location after each launch.

Seeing the look of concern on his executive officer's face, Major Yousef knew what he was thinking. "You don't have to say it. I know, and I agree with you that it is going to be impossible to launch all four missiles if we have to relocate after each launch. I do not think it is safe for us to stay put for all four launches, but I do believe we can move forward by launching two missiles from each firing position. Go ahead and place a call to our missile trucks and have six trucks drive to our location."

"I think that is a wise choice. I fear once we launch these missiles, it won't be long before the Americans will send helicopters or fighters to come search for us. Muscat is not that far from our positions for a fighter plane or a helicopter."

Yousef agreed with that thought as well. This first day's worth of launches would likely be the only launches they'd have before the enemy started to scour this area looking for them.

"I will get everything ready now. We should be able to commence our first launch within the next twenty minutes," Captain Ibrahim declared and then headed out the tent to see to it.

****

Weekly extended his hand down to AD, who grabbed it, allowing Weekly to pull him up. They were nearly to the top of the ridge where he thought the launcher vehicles were located.

Suddenly the SINCGARS handset crackled to life. "Blue One, Blue Six."

Taking a knee, Weekly grabbed the handset and depressed the push to talk button. He waited for the familiar beeping sound, letting him know the frequency-hopping radio had synched.

"Blue Six, Blue One, send it."

"Blue One, we're seeing movement. Six launcher vehicles just started moving. I believe they may be headed towards you. How copy?"

If they are sending vehicles this way, then those launchers really are nearby. But if they're sending the reload vehicles this way, that means they must be readying to launch. Crap, we need to find those vehicles ASAP, he thought.

"Blue Six, that's a good copy. We're almost to the top of the ridge. See if you can raise headquarters and get some birds in the air. If we find the launchers, we may not have much time to take them out before they fire."

"That's a good copy. Keep us apprised. Out."

****

Standing outside his command tent, Major Yousef looked at his watch. It was 2049 hours. They were nearly ready to launch. His ears told him the missile trucks had arrived.

"Sir, we're ready to fire. Just waiting on your final orders," Ibrahim informed him.

"Excellent. Good job on getting them ready so quick. Which targets are we firing at first?" Yousef wanted one final check before the missiles fired. Once they were on their way, they couldn't change their targets. The 985-kilogram or 2,100-pound high-explosive warhead would pulverize whatever it hit.

The Scud-Ds they were firing were a much-improved version of what they'd had during the Iran-Iraq war. Back then they had been making do with the Scud-Bs, which had a range of three hundred kilometers and a CEP or circular error of probability of four hundred and fifty meters. The new D variants their Soviet allies had given them had a CEP of fifty meters and a range of seven hundred kilometers, making this variant of the missile a hell of a lot more deadly.

Ibrahim replied confidently, "Two missiles are targeted at the coalition headquarters building located on the military technical college campus, the other four missiles at the Muscat International Airport. Once the missiles impact, the Unit 999 members will give us a BDA assessment so we can adjust the coordinates when we move to the next firing location."

"Once again, Captain, you continue to impress. When I am promoted to battalion commander, I will be able to rest easy knowing you will take my place here," Yousef said.

Moments later, the first Scud missile fired. It lit up the night sky for a brief moment as the missile continued to gain altitude. Seconds after the first launch, the five subsequent missiles took to the sky, racing after the first.

****

Weekly had just made it over the top of the ridge when the darkness of the evening was broken by the sudden flash of the missile's ignition and then its steady stream of flame as it now accelerated into the sky. Moments later, it was joined by five additional missiles.

Damnit, we're too late, Weekly thought, angry at himself for not having tried to come over here earlier.

"Let's not worry about this one, AD. We need to try to disable those launchers before they fire any others," Weekly said to his friend and teammate.

"I just need a clear line of sight and I'll disable those missiles," the sniper replied.

It took them a few minutes to get in position, but once they had a solid view down into the wadi below, they spotted what they were looking for. Despite the moon being largely hidden in the high cloud cover, they could still make out some of the vehicles. They had some low-light running lights on and a few ground guides.

"You see that, Weekly? I count six launcher erectors, six missile trucks reloading them right now, and then over there"—he pointed to the far side of the wadi—"that has to be the fire control and headquarters element. Those two BTRs have a lot of antennas on them."

"Yeah, I see 'em. Look to the right of them. You've got at least one SA-9 Gaskin and a ZSU-23. Those air-defense vehicles would make it tough for a helicopter or low-flying aircraft to attack them."

"What do you want to do? Call it in or try to disable the missiles?" AD asked.

"I'm going to call them in. As much as I want you to just shoot the missiles in hopes of disabling them or even blowing them up, if you open fire, it'll give away our position and the rest of the team. There has to be at least two hundred Iraqis down there, which means they likely have at least a company of infantry supporting them. If there's a company, there's a battalion nearby. We're not going to lose an ODA team to take out a few Scuds. We'll call in the flyboys and let them make a run," Weekly said in frustration. This was not how he wanted things to go down.

Weekly pulled out his map and got a rough idea of where the launchers were. In minutes, he was on the horn with their headquarters element. Lieutenant Harris had already relayed what was going on and there was a flight of four F-16s inbound to their location. They'd arrive on the scene in less than twenty minutes.

****

"Major Yousef!" a sergeant shouted as he burst into the command tent.

"What is it, Sergeant?"

"Sir, we just got a message from the Dubai air-defense group. They said they spotted at least four American planes headed our direction," the sergeant blurted out.

Damnit, I was hoping we'd get a couple of missiles off before this happened. "Alert our own air-defense vehicles, now go!" Yousef ordered. "Captain Ibrahim!"

"Yes, sir," Ibrahim said as he came into the tent.

"We have inbound American aircraft. Get our missiles fired as fast as you can. It's time to break camp and get the hell out of here," Yousef ordered as he moved to pack up a few things. The soldiers around him were already breaking down the inside of the tent and the tent itself. They needed to get out of the area.

****

"It looks like they're getting ready to fire. When are those fast movers supposed to get here?" AD asked.

Weekly looked at his watch. "Soon," was all he said.

AD shook his head. "I'm going to try and put a bullet into each of those missiles. Maybe I can damage something."

Weekly reached a hand out, placing it on AD's arm. "Don't. I know you want to. I do too, but we'll give away our position. Right now they have no clue we're here, which means we can keep raining air strikes down on them. That's more important than trying to put a bullet in each missile."

AD struggled with that decision, but eventually he nodded.

Moments later, two more Scuds lifted off into the air. Then a third missile took off. Before the remaining three could get airborne, all hell broke loose around the wadi.

The ZSU opened fire with their quad 23mm autocannon, sending red tracers into the night sky. The SA-9 fired off one missile, then a second, before it exploded into a giant fireball.

Two black objects whipped past their heads at lightning speed. Seconds later a series of explosions erupted on the ground.

The ZSU swiveled its turret and continued to fire after the two fighter planes. Then the ZSU exploded when a missile slammed into it. Two more black objects flew over the area, releasing more bombs across the wadi.

The three missiles that hadn't been fired were destroyed, blown up on the ground before they had a chance to get airborne.

As the fighters flew back to base, more aircraft came over the radio, asking for more possible locations to bomb or look for more launchers. Weekly spent the next ten minutes directing them to a handful of places where he thought they might be. Seeing the fighters attack a couple of other positions made him feel good about not having AD try to snipe at the missiles. They were causing far more damage calling in air strikes and directing fighters than they could have done on their own.

Chapter 23

National Guard Makes Their Case

16 October 1990
Situation Room,
White House
Washington, D.C.

"Good morning, gentlemen, keep your seats," the President said as he walked into the morning briefing.

All the key players involved in the war were present, along with a few others that had been asked to attend. Chief among them was Lieutenant General Conway, Chief of the National Guard Bureau. He had been vocal about the National Guard combat and round-out units in particular not being called up yet. Usually when their parent unit deployed, they went with them to fill in any gaps and augment the division, like the 48th Infantry Brigade with the 24th Infantry Division and so on.

In August, someone had made the decision not to deploy the 48th Infantry Brigade with the 24th ID like they were supposed to have. Instead they'd deployed the 197th Infantry Brigade at Fort Benning, Georgia, with the division instead. Several active-duty divisions were manned at two brigades, with the third brigade being a National Guard brigade. The National Guard brigade trained with the active-duty division on division exercises, to include TEWTs, so it was odd for them not to go with their parent units.[4]

Turning to the briefing officer, Lieutenant Colonel Atwell, the President gave the "go ahead" nod.

"Good morning, sir. Today's brief will cover actions in the past forty-eight hours, naval forces in the region, Air Force assets being employed, and issues to be resolved with the National Guard call-up. First slide, please."

As it appeared on the large screen in the front of the room, Atwell continued, "Sir, in the past forty-eight hours, the situation has been somewhat stable. CENTCOM continues to receive forces and is positioning them throughout the region where needed. The 82nd Airborne, located in Jeddah, has continued to hold the line. They're still heavily outnumbered, but air and helicopter support have continued to prove vital in blunting each Iraqi assault. At this point, we believe the Iraqis are looking to just dig in and hold where they are."

A red dot appeared on the map slide of Saudi Arabia, indicating the location of Medina Ridge. "The 101st Airborne Division, Air Assault, has moved from Jeddah and has established itself in Yanbu. It's moving forces to the east to block the roads into Yanbu and Jeddah." Again the pointer moved to indicate the location of Yanbu and the positions the 101st was looking to capture and hold.

"Excuse me, Colonel, but is the entire 101st Division deployed now?" the President asked.

---

[4] TEWTs, or Tactical Exercises Without Troops, were generally command post map exercises for effectively training brigade and division staffs.

"Yes, sir, their last combat unit is in the air as we speak and should be landing in Yanbu in three hours. That will complete their deployment," Colonel Atwell replied.

"Please continue," the President directed.

"CENTCOM continues to position forces in Oman, with the 24th Infantry Division being headquartered in Fahud and the 1st Cavalry Division being headquartered in Falaj. These two units, along with the 197th Infantry Brigade, which is serving under the 24th Infantry Division, have had some of their vehicles delivered and should be completely deployed by the end of the month. The 1st Brigade of the 2nd Armored Division is under the command of the 1st Cavalry Division."

Before Colonel Atwell could continue, Lieutenant General Conway jumped in. "Sir, if I may."

The President turned in his chair. It took a second for him to recognize who had spoken. When he did, he gestured for the general to continue.

"Sir, both the 24th and the 1st Cav have round-out brigades from the National Guard that should have been called up and deployed with those divisions. Instead, the Army leadership attached two active-duty brigades and sent those with the two divisions. This is a breach of faith with the National Guard and needs to be corrected. National Guard units and divisions fought with distinction in World War I, World War II, and Korea. In World War II, the 29th was in the first wave at Normandy. The 35th landed in southern France and fought all the way to Austria. The 40th and 45th fought in Korea. They shouldn't be shut out like they were in Vietnam." The more he spoke, the more his emotions rose.

Looking at General Powell, the President said, "Care to explain this one?"

"Sir, we did deploy two active-duty brigades in place of the National Guard Brigades. Your Executive Order 12727 ordered a selective reserve call-up of two hundred thousand personnel for a ninety-day period, not a full call-up to last for the duration of the crisis. In light of this, we felt there would not have been sufficient time to mobilize those units and have them undergo certification at the National Training Center and deploy before their ninety-day clock would be up. As of right now, we have nineteen National Guard units in-country with four hundred and eighty-two soldiers from thirteen states. We believe that if we go to partial mobilization that would lock people in for a twenty-four-month period, then we can call up these other combat units. Right now, Mr. President, General Schwarzkopf is calling for support units, not combat units."

"What are some of the units currently deployed from the National Guard?" the President asked.

"The 1241 Adjutant General Company—it's a postal unit—the 1207 Water Purification Company, the 1158th Movement Control Detachment and the 382nd Public Affairs Detachment have all been called up. The 719th Transportation Company is deploying right now and will be attached to the 101st to assist in ground transportation for that unit."

Interrupting, Conway countered, "Those units were low priority for call-up and yet they were the first to go."

With a touch of anger in his voice, Powell said, "Those, General, were the Guards with personnel and equipment ready for deployment. As a matter of fact, we're seeing a pattern of the National Guard Bureau trying to fix all its broken unit equipment by moving units up on the deployment list, so when they link up with their active-duty counterparts, they have to be issued new equipment just so they can operate and function with the rest of the division."

"Alright, gentlemen," interjected Mr. Cheney, "we'll take this up after this meeting in my office. Continue, Colonel."

"Marine units in theater are the 1st Marine Division and the 2nd Marine Division. The 1st Marine is located on Masirah Island and is conducting training there. The 2nd is afloat at this time." Atwell paused so the red dot could point out where Masirah Island was located.

Colonel Atwell pointed to western Saudi Arabia again. "Ground activity in the past forty-eight hours has been minimal. The 101st Air Cavalry Squadron is conducting a reconnaissance to the east, locating units of the 2nd Iraqi Corps. The 2nd Republican Guard Corps is maintaining its positions around Medina. In the east, the 1st Republican Guard Corps has established positions across the UAE. It appears that they're moving one division to the area around Kalba, Fujairah and Khor Fakkan. This gives them nearly a corps level of forces along the Gulf of Oman and the entrance to the Strait of Hormuz." Atwell paused long enough for this information to register with the President.

Bush then asked, "What about naval activity? It was either them or the Iranians that managed to get lucky and sink a couple of supply ships. Have we hunted them down yet?"

Admiral Kelso answered this question. "Not yet, Mr. President. I've tasked a few submarines to work on that. They're just now starting to arrive on station and will begin to prosecute the hunt."

Colonel Atwell waited for a moment before continuing. "Sir, recent naval activity in the area allowed the USS *Florida* to follow a freighter through the minefield in the Strait of Hormuz. Although the Iranians claim responsibility for the Strait, this minefield was a joint venture by the Iraqi and Iranian navies. Once the *Florida* completed its passage, it was then ordered to sink the Russian bulk carrier *Kuzma Minin* as she was suspected and confirmed to be carrying Scud missiles that were offloaded in Saqr.

"The *Florida* deployed SEAL Team Two, which did the job nicely with all team members recovered. The *Florida* is currently awaiting further orders. On the negative side, it appears that an Iraqi underwater demolition team got into the port of Yanbu and blew up a tanker ship that was taking on aviation fuel. The crew, the ship and the dock were all lost. No soldiers were lost; however, there were only three docks at this port, so this attack effectively took out a third of its capabilities. CENTCOM is requesting some Coast Guard Port Security units with patrol boats to be dispatched," Atwell concluded.

"That's probably a good idea," the President opined, and the notetakers made a note of it. "Those units were activated back in August, the twenty-second, if I recall. Have they not been sent over yet?" He looked at Admiral Kelso.

"Sir, I can't say. The Coast Guard is under the Department of Transportation, so I've had no visibility on those units. With your say-so, we can pull them under DoD for this operation," Mr. Cheney interjected.

"Make it happen and get them over there pronto. We can't have ships being destroyed while in the harbors and dockside," the President directed. "Admiral, you were going to cover ships in the area today?"

"Yes, sir. Currently we have the *Saratoga* Battle Group in the Red Sea supporting XVIII Airborne Corps. It consists of the USS *Saratoga*; the *Biddle* and the *Philippine Sea*, both guided missile cruisers; the *Spruance*, a destroyer; the *Sampson*, a guided missile destroyer; and the *Elmer Montgomery* and the *Thomas C Hart*, both frigates.

"In the Arabian Sea we have the USS *Kennedy*, though she'll be replaced by Battle Group Alpha at the beginning of next month. The USS *Midway* will be the new flagship and have a complement of ships equal to the *Saratoga* Battle Group."

"I thought the *Eisenhower* was in the Red Sea. Did *Saratoga* replace her?"

"Yes, sir, *Eisenhower* was at the end of a six-month deployment in the Med. We rushed her to the Red Sea until we could get *Sara* there," Admiral Kelso said.

"What about the battleships? Are we going to be using them in this fight?" the President asked.

"Yes, sir. One is on the East Coast and one is on the West Coast. We're forming up battle groups around them and they'll be heading out shortly. They'll be linking up with the amphibious fleet soon and exercising with them."

"OK, what does the Air Force have in-country now?" the President asked, looking at Colonel Atwell.

"Sir, the Air Force has the 14th Air Division, which has A-10, F-15, F-16 F-111 and F-117 aircraft. They're located for the most part in Egypt and Oman. The 15th Air Division has RF-4C, F-4G antiradar aircraft, EC-130 Compass Card and E-8A Joint Stars aircraft. The 15th is also split between Oman and Egypt. The 1610 Air Division has C-130 medivac aircraft and is operating out of Oman. The 7440 Composite Wing is in Incirlik, Turkey. We're still negotiating with Turkey to allow us to use them when we start hitting inside Iraq."

"Is there a problem with Turkey?" the President inquired, an eyebrow raised at this sudden development.

"Sir, there's always a problem with Turkey," Mr. Baker said. "They feel that they should have been consulted about our actions before we got into it with Saddam. They feel that he's the strongest leader to keep the Kurds in check and really don't want to see him hurt or removed from power."

"Well, tell them to talk some sense into Saddam. If he leaves Saudi, the UAE, and Kuwait, this entire thing ends," the President said with heat to his words. Looking back at Colonel Atwell, he asked, "Do we have any B-52s involved?"

"Yes, sir, and they're under the 7th Air Division based out of Diego Garcia."

After a momentary pause, the President looked at Powell. "Have we received an assessment from Schwarzkopf on what he thinks he's going to need if we have to push Saddam out of Saudi Arabia and Kuwait?"

"Sir, we have, and it's going to be a much larger package. If he has to move against the Iraqis, he feels he'll need the VII Corps from Germany and the 1st ID from Kansas. In addition, he wants three more brigades, which are going to have to come from the National Guard, along with two field artillery brigades, also located in the National Guard. The active Army doesn't have eight-inch artillery any longer. It was all transferred to the National Guard, and all the multiple rocket launchers outside of divisions are located in the National Guard now as well."

"Don't we have this stuff in the Army Reserve?" the President asked with some frustration in his voice.

"Sir, the bulk of our combat units are in the National Guard. The bulk of service support units are in the Army Reserve, and we've called up several of those units to assist as backfill in Europe and stateside," Mr. Cheney answered.

"But Schwarzkopf hasn't asked for the additional combat forces yet, has he?" the President asked.

"No, sir, he has not, but we anticipate he will soon," Cheney countered.

"OK, Dick, Colin, let's continue this conversation in my office this afternoon. But before I leave to get ready for this next meeting with the Department of Energy, I want to know more about this Scud attack from the other day. Since it wasn't included in this brief, which I find odd, how bad did we get hit?"

A few of the generals squirmed in their seats a bit at the question. Colonel Atwell, for his part, just looked at General Powell. Finally Cheney asked, "Do you want to tell him, Colin, or should I?"

General Powell let out a sigh as his shoulders sank a little bit. "I'll do it." Powell turned to look at the President, who now had a curious look on his face. "Sir, last night around 2100 hours local time, the Iraqis initiated their first Scud attack of the war. This was a weapon they used extensively during the Iran-Iraq war to the tune of a little more than five hundred missiles. At the time they were using the Scud-B missiles, which honestly were terrible missiles. The Soviets, however, have provided them with the Scud-Ds, which have much greater accuracy. This greatly increases the likelihood of hitting their intended target. The D model also has an improved range of up to seven hundred kilometers."

The President held a hand up for a moment to stop Powell. "I get it. They launched some missiles at us. Get to the point. How many did they launch, what did they hit, how bad is our damage, and did we manage to locate and destroy any of the launchers?"

The slight pause in responding to his question let the President know something bad had happened.

"Mr. President, during the night, a Special Forces A-Team managed to find the location of one Scud unit, but not before they were able to fire off a volley. The soldiers then called in an air strike, which successfully managed to destroy all six launchers. They continued to scour the area for more launchers and did find a few more, not too far from this first group, and destroyed them as well."

"Ah, this sounds good, General. So I take it they got some licks in too?"

Powell grimaced. "They did, and it was bad. Four missiles hit the military technical college General Schwarzkopf had established as his CENTCOM headquarters. One of the missiles scored a direct hit on one of the buildings being used as a barracks. It struck around 2123 hours, so a lot of folks were already in the building. They're still sifting through some of the rubble, but current death count is three hundred and ninety-one killed and another two hundred and forty-eight injured. There are still another one hundred and twelve missing, likely still buried in the smoldering ruins."

"Jesus, Colin. The media is going to have a field day with this once they learn how many people died in this attack. Tell me this was the worst of it," the President said, a bit taken aback by the staggering number of killed.

"I'm afraid not, sir. We had another one hundred and twenty-two killed from the other three hits the campus took and another three hundred and eighty-four injured. The airport took six hits. We didn't have as many casualties at the airport, but we did lose a number of aircraft. Twelve fighters were destroyed outright with another twenty-nine aircraft sustaining some sort of damage. The port also took three hits. We didn't lose any ships, but one of the missiles did hit a nearby warehouse housing ammunition. The entire dump went up, which caused two more nearby warehouses to explode. All told, we had some six hundred and seventy-two killed, and another eight hundred and ninety-two injured," Powell explained.

The President just shook his head. Finally, he asked, "How many people have we lost in this war? I mean, we're a little more than two months into this thing—how are we doing?"

"Um, I'd have to get back to you on the exact specifics," Powell replied.

Lieutenant General Conway blurted out, "If you include the KIAs from the Scud attack, it brings our total KIAs up to two thousand, one hundred and fifty-seven. Add in our wounded and it's another five thousand, six hundred and thirty-two more."

The President nodded at the National Guard commander, almost surprised that he readily knew the number and Powell had not. Shaking his head, the President stood. "Gentlemen, I think we've covered what we needed to for this meeting. I need to leave now for a meeting with some folks from the Department of Energy. We now have an oil crisis to handle on top of this."

****

Later That Same Day

"Come in and have a seat," the President indicated as Cheney, Powell, and Vuono entered the Oval Office, followed by Sununu. "Where's Conway?"

"Sir, for this meeting, I thought it best that we not have him present. The man gets a bit emotional, and while I can't blame him, we don't need that at this point," Powell said.

As if on cue, the side door opened, and the steward entered with a tray of coffee and cups, the correct number. *How does he know every time?* the President wondered.

After the steward poured the coffee and departed, the President asked, "OK, what's the story with the National Guard units? Why didn't we follow the planned procedures?"

Cheney fielded the question. "Sir, this whole war started really quickly and kind of left us with little initial choice. What the active Army does well, the National Guard does not, and what the Guard does well, the active Army does not. The two have an integral function and role in supporting each other. The active Army does fire and maneuver very well; the National Guard units do not. When the war initially broke out, that's what we needed right off the bat.

"With the National Guard, each year at their two-week summer training, they're evaluated by active Army officers and NCOs. When we review the after-action reports, it's obvious that the National Guard units aren't up to par in most cases. A lot of pressure is put on the active Army evaluators to make the reports glowing as it's all political in the Guard with officer promotions. Case in point, last summer an infantry battalion from the 35th Infantry Division was rated as bad as it gets, with the evaluator pointing the finger at the incompetence of the battalion commander. On the last day of the two-week drill, the battalion commander was relieved, promoted to full colonel and put in charge of their public affairs office. His brother was the governor. The summer before last, General Marsh was senior evaluator for a National Guard division. His summation was, and I quote, 'I can think of no national emergency to include nuclear war that would warrant the activation of this division.' The only real time they have to train is on the two-week summer exercise. One weekend a month is just not sufficient as some weekends are taken up with off-the-wall stuff—company Christmas party as an example."

"OK, I'm getting the picture. What was Conway saying about taking low-priority units and deploying them before higher-priority units?"

"Sir," Vuono said, "we have a TPFD, Time Phased Force Deployment schedule, and it has prioritized units for deployment based on the plan developed and the TPFD designed for that plan. Naturally, those units with the higher ratings for personnel, training, and equipment have the higher priority. Each night, CENTCOM sends us what type of unit they need. The next day at FORSCOM, they pull up the TPFD and see what the top priority unit is to fill that need. If it's a National Guard unit or a reserve unit, FORSCOM contacts Guard Bureau or OCAR[5] and tells them that we're going to activate that unit. With the Guard Bureau, they'll come back and offer another unit that generally has a lower priority because of lack of equipment or personnel. They're attempting to get their units all fixed by having us activate the unit and then get them the equipment they need to be in C-1 status. Sometimes they use the excuse that they want to get every state involved and therefore don't want to take too many units from one state."

John Sununu interrupted to add, "To be honest, General, from a PR standpoint, that's not a bad idea. Having the National Guard units from the various states increases public support for the war if we get into a shooting match any greater than what we have right now."

---

[5] Office of the Chief of Army Reserve.

"OK, I understand the priority issue now. What about the round-out brigades? Why did we not deploy them with the parent divisions?" the President pressed.

"Sir, the three brigades were the 48th, the 155th, and the 256th. First, they're not fully trained and should have a rotation at the National Training Center before we send them over. To send them over in their current state of training would result in a higher-than-average number of casualties if they went into combat. We recommend that each of those brigades go through a rotation at NTC and pass the tests before they're deployed. To do that, they'll have to be mobilized, which will be a one-month process, then deploy to the NTC, which is a ten-day exercise. Then two weeks for the exercise and another ten days to return to home station. All told we're looking at a month and a half. On a ninety-day call-up, they couldn't even get in-country before we would be bringing them home."

"And you're confident that they lack the degree of training needed for this operation?" the President asked.

"Yes, sir. The last evaluation of the 48th recommended that the brigade commander be relieved as the evaluators considered him unstable.[6] When the 256th was last evaluated, it was noted they had poor morale issues,"[7] General Vuono said. "Sir, a big argument on the

---

[6] When the unit was activated and sent to the NTC, the brigade commander was relieved by his executive officer for stress-related issues.

[7] When the unit was activated and sent to Fort Hood, over fifty members went AWOL and then complained to the press about poor living conditions and food. Investigation found they were eating and living in the same conditions that active-duty soldiers live in year round. They received no sympathy from the active-duty soldiers.

National Guard side of the coin is that they feel that if we do activate and send their units over and they do well, then Congress will reduce the size of the active Army as the National Guard can do the same job at a much cheaper cost."

"So eventually we're going to have to activate them, is what you're telling me," the President replied.

"Probably, sir," Cheney interjected. "Another part of the problem is education. The officers and noncoms haven't had the military schooling that the active soldiers have. They have the opportunity just like the active soldiers to attend, but they don't because of civilian jobs or family. Thus, in many cases, when activated, they have the rank but not the knowledge to do the jobs. They can do the job adequately on weekend drills and the two-week summer training exercise, but for sustained combat, they lack the education. Now in some MOSs, they're on par with the active-duty soldiers. For instance, their helicopter pilots are as good as and, in some cases, better than the active pilots as many of the National Guard pilots are full-time pilots with police departments, fire departments, medical evacuation units or even airlines. We do take them on an individual basis. Their aviation mechanics are excellent, especially one Guard aviation maintenance unit from Maryland."

"OK, I get the picture. But when this is over, we need to rework the issue so this doesn't come up again. Either they're round-out brigades and deploy with the unit or they aren't and can wait to be called up," the President said. "Anything else we need to discuss?"

"Sir, what do we tell Conway?" Cheney asked.

"Tell him to sit tight. They'll get the call." The President rose and turned to the Resolute desk, signaling that the meeting was over.

****

Once everyone had left, the President asked Sununu, "John, what's going on with the price of oil? That meeting with the DoE people didn't exactly make me feel good."

"Obviously having the Strait closed and most of the Middle East oil closed off has put a crimp on the supply. Fortunately, the oil fields in West Africa and Venezuela are starting to pick up the slack. Heck, now that we've allowed our own oil production to increase, we should see the supply start to meet the demand."

"I think I'm going to open the strategic oil reserves. The price of a barrel of oil has gone from twenty-two dollars a barrel prior to the war to seventy-five dollars. We need to bring it back down," the President announced.

John didn't say anything right away. Finally, he asked, "Do you think that's wise? This war is likely going to drag on for some time. Why not wait and see how things play out?"

Bush shook his head. "Reagan started this effort to depress oil at the end of his term. I've continued it. The policy is working. The Soviet empire is about to crack and fall apart—look at Germany and Poland. No, we need to keep the pressure on them. The last thing we need is seventy-five dollars a barrel becoming the new norm, or worse, the price moving higher. It's bad enough that they're becoming the primary supplier in Europe. We can't let this oil war bail them out, not with them on the ropes like this. We need to think long-term, John. This war is a distraction they've instigated. Let's not let them win."

Chapter 24
Bastogne Brigade

20 October 1990

1st Brigade TOC

Vicinity Tara'ah, Saudi Arabia

Colonel Tom Hall, the commander of the 1st Brigade, 327th Infantry Regiment, was in his command post, which had, along with the rest of the brigade, moved into their assigned sector some thirty miles south of Masader.

He and his infantry battalion commanders along with the artillery commander had looked at their mission, their assigned sector, their assets, and the enemy's capabilities in developing their defensive plan. One of the limitations placed upon them was the use of attack helicopters. General Peters had warned all three brigade commanders that the attack helicopter battalions were his for the deep battle mission. They needed to build their defensive plans around the likelihood of not receiving any attack helicopter support.

Colonel Hall was a solidly built individual. He had served as a scout platoon leader in Vietnam and followed the usual path for an infantry officer. His career had taken a turn when he'd been selected to be the aide to the Chief of Staff of the Army at the time. That position had put him in contact with the Army's senior and rising leadership. To say Colonel Hall had learned the politics of the Army would be an understatement. He'd learned it well and played it well. He was intensely loyal to those around him, almost to a fault, and he would accept no criticism of his staff, even when they weren't functioning well. All three battalion commanders had questioned the brigade staff's decisions, and all three had been bitten in the ass.

Hall had called the battalion commanders in to discuss their battle plans as well as the overall brigade defensive plan. Major Clauson, the brigade operations officer or S-3, was responsible for development of the overall plan, which had been slightly modified after Lieutenant Colonel Dan Cory, the 3rd Battalion commander, and Colonel Thomas, the 2nd Battalion commander, had massaged it with Hall.

"Sir," Major Clauson started, "the brigade defends the sector with three battalions abreast. 1st Battalion defends from Al Marameh to Abu Haramel; 3rd Battalion defends in sector from Abu Haramel to Sulailah Juhainah; 2nd Battalion defends in sector from Sulailah Juhainah to a point at…" Clauson read off the military grid coordinates. "The main effort is to 3rd Battalion. The commander's intent is to strike the attacking forces early with long-range fire and close-air support and prevent a penetration of the brigade sector."

Lieutenant Colonel Cory had combat experience in Vietnam as a helicopter pilot. After Vietnam, where he'd received his commission to first lieutenant infantry, he'd slowly transitioned out of flying assignments and into infantry assignments. He had commanded infantry companies in Fort Lewis, Washington, and an airborne infantry company in Alaska. He taught airborne tactics at the infantry school and corps and division operations at the Command and General Staff College. Hall deferred to Cory on many occasions when it came to tactical plans.

Cory had covered his tactical plan with Hall and the other two battalion commanders and the artillery commander. In short order, they'd see if his and the other plans were actually worth a damn. After all, the enemy always gets a vote.

****

Twenty-four hours earlier, Cory had visited each company and discussed the company defensive plan. Company A was located in the town of Al Muraba'a with the main highway from Masader to Yanbu passing through the town. Unfortunately, an attacking force could bypass the town to the south but not the north due to the terrain. To the south, it was 1,173 meters of open ground to the next major terrain feature, well within the range of the TOW missile system and within the range for the most part of the Dragon weapons system, a shoulder-fired antitank system with an excellent sight, capable of thermal imaging targets at night. The biggest drawback, however, was the fact that the gunner would be exposed when firing the system and he had to hold the sight on the target for the entire flight of the missile. Scattered throughout this open area were some orchards and palm groves. Cory didn't want his infantry in those groves as they would have no escape route if surrounded. Artillery was planned for both areas, and both were assigned target reference points or TRPs.

As Cory and Captain Mulford, the A Company commander, walked through the town, Alpha Gators, as Company A was known, were preparing the town to become a defensive strong point.

"Had any problems with the locals, Mulf?" Cory asked, using Captain Mulford's nickname.

"No, sir. Most left forty-eight hours ago. I guess they needed little encouragement when told what was coming and the fact that the King was going to rebuild their town when it was over," Mulf said.

"When did the engineers arrive?" Cory asked, noting an engineer vehicle cutting a ditch across the road.

"They arrived last night and have been going at it nonstop. I told them the priority was to level the buildings on the perimeter. They set charges and blew them all early this morning."

"I was wondering what the noise was this morning. You should have advised the TOC you were going to blow them. Scared the crap out of the chaplain," Cory chuckled.

As they walked, Captain Mulford began to point out some of the actions they had taken to strengthen their defense. "Sir, each of the two-story buildings has plywood with nails and concertina wire prepared to cover the stairs to the second floor once the infantry moves in and occupies the building. Claymore mines have been hung under the eaves of those buildings that had overhanging eaves. Doorways are booby-trapped to kill anyone that attempts to enter after the boys have gone in. Holes have been prepared through the exterior walls to shoot through," Mulford pointed out.

"That's important. Those windows will attract enemy fire," Cory noted. Cory had taught Defense in Built-Up Areas while an instructor at the infantry school. He also taught those classes to each of his junior officers.

Captain Mulford continued, "Additional ammo was stockpiled in each building designated a prime position. Field wire has been run between buildings so radio traffic would be minimal and field phones would be used in case the enemy was to use electronic jammers," he said.

"Good point. We haven't had any reported in use, but we don't want to be caught flat-footed. I see that you have the main highway blocked with concrete barriers and a ditch being dug just in front of them with the spoil behind them," Cory observed.

"Yes, sir, that way they can't push the spoil into the ditch as well as the barriers and refill it. It's going to be difficult to get to the spoil to fill the ditch back in. I also have several Dragon positions overwatching that barrier," Captain Mulford proudly stated.

He and Cory had a strained relationship up to this point, and any brownie points he could score would be helpful at this point. Captain Mulford had gotten the company when Colonel Cory had had to relieve the previous company commander for inefficiency. To raise the spirits of the company, Captain Mulford did a few things that the boys liked but that put Cory's ass in a sling with the division chief of staff. Not the kind of visibility a career officer wants.

"Good. The main highway is blocked, and this should get the advancing enemy to attempt to bypass the town to the south," Cory said. "Good job, Mulf. Now, don't blow it in the execution." Cory turned and climbed into his waiting vehicle.

Driving across the open area south of the town, Cory checked his map for the location of the antitank company CP.

"Lester, let's head for Delta Company CP," Cory directed.

Specialist Bob Lester had been Cory's driver since being alerted to deploy to the desert. Lester was in his early twenties and was a quiet man from Michigan. His mom wrote to him often, but he never heard from his dad since his parents had divorced.

To Cory, Lester was more than a driver. He was a companion and confidant, always there for Cory, taking care of anything the colonel needed. He was also someone Cory could vent to and knew it would not be the next days gossip. When they stopped at night, they slept where they stopped, and while Cory got a last call into the units, generally at 0400 after walking a patrol with a junior officer, Lester would have his air mattress inflated and his sleeping bag laid out. After two hours of sleep, Cory would wake up to a hot cup of coffee, compliments of Lester. When Cory was sleeping, Lester would monitor the radios and decide if a call was important enough to wake Cory. Lester didn't have to look at a map to know where Cory wanted to go. He had it memorized.

"Yes, sir. They're up on that ridge over there." Lester turned the vehicle to head towards the CP location for the Delta Dawgs. As they pulled up alongside Captain Nick Stein's vehicle, Stein jumped out of his vehicle with a shit-eating grin on his face. Stein had been commander of Delta Company for about a year.

"Morning, sir," Stein said but didn't bother to salute. Cory had put the word out—no saluting on the battlefield as it made it too easy for a sniper to identify a leader and pick them off.

"Nick, give me a rundown of your positions," Cory said as he laid his map out on the hood of the vehicle. Stein pulled out his map and laid it beside Cory's.

"Sir, as you can see, I've laid out the range fan for each weapon system and have identified the dead space for each weapon."

Stein's map indicated the location of each weapon, a fan for each weapon and striped areas where the terrain created dead space within which the weapon could not engage a target.

"Looks good," Cory complimented, studying Stein's map. As he did, Stein pulled a clear piece of acetate out of his map case. It was color-coded with green and red fans.

"Here, sir, I've identified the overlapping fires of each weapon, and as you can see, every weapon position has a secondary weapon covering their sector of fire," Stein explained as he adjusted the overlay. Cory could see that each weapon system fan was covered by at least one other weapon. Removing the first overlay, Stein laid down and positioned a second overlay.

"These are each weapon system's alternate positions and the fans, dead space and supporting weapons systems coverage. As you can see, we have good coverage over the entire open area with multiple systems covering each other's area of responsibility. At both the primary and alternate position, we've stockpiled additional ammo, and each of the companies that we're co-located with has provided a squad with a vehicle to provide security and assist in the ammo reloads," Stein pointed out as he indicated each position. "You will note, sir, there are no TOWs with the Gators, as it would be a waste to put a system in the town," he concluded.

"Yeah, I agree," Cory said as he continued to study Stein's maps. "Have you forwarded this to the TOC?"

"Yes, sir, and Badger integrated it with his fire support plan," Stein said.

"Good, I want to make sure that we aren't dropping artillery when you're firing and having the artillery cut your wires. When you engage, give us a minute to cut off the artillery or shift it so that doesn't happen," Cory directed.

"Yes, sir. Badger and I talked about it, and when they hit the FASCAM field, he's going to put in HE airbursts one time and then shift fire. When he shifts, we engage. Already worked it out with him," Stein explained.

The Family of Scatterable Mines, or FASCAM for short, was a series of both antitank and antipersonnel mines that were delivered by artillery or aircraft. The Remote Anti-Armor Mines, known as RAAMS, and the Area Denial Artillery Munitions, or ADAM, were both delivered by the 155mm howitzer. There was one system delivered by aircraft, the GATOR mine system, and two systems delivered by various vehicles, the Volcano and GEMSS mine systems. The MOPMS or Modular Pack Mine System was a manually emplaced mine dispenser that was remotely detonated and had seventeen antitank mines and four antipersonnel mines. The mines had a life span of four hours to fifteen days depending on the system.

"So that's the reason for the shit-eating grin. Already worked it out without me. Damn, you guys make my job easy. Sounds good. I'll catch you later," Cory said as he climbed back into his Humvee. He spent the rest of the day visiting each company commander and going over each plan, ensuring that each defensive position could accomplish their portion of the battalion plan. When he was satisfied, he told Lester to head for the TOC for a cup of coffee. It would be a long night and not much sleep for a little while.

Chapter 25

Showtime

Morning Hours

22 October 1990

Battleforce Engagement Area

Al Muraba'a, Saudi Arabia

Once the brigade battle plan was developed, the battalions positioned and assets allocated, the combat role for the brigade was one of monitoring the battle, conducting deep battle and being prepared to reallocate assets and move units as required.

"Colonel, Battleforce has identified a battalion approaching his positions with an unidentified follow-on force. Because of the dust from the lead element, he can't determine what's coming behind the first, but he suspects it's probably two more battalions."

"All right, let's get some tac air. With the attack helicopters all over to the east, we're going to be hard-pressed. Do we still have that little bird playing FO for us?" Colonel Hall asked.

"Yes, sir," responded his S-3, Major Clauson. "Battleforce has already called for close-air support to hit the follow-on forces."

"Good. Pass this information on to the FO and see if he can identify and locate the follow-on force. If he can, have him hit them with the MLRS battery when they're in range. And keep hitting them. Put tac air on them as soon as it shows up. God, I wish we had some attack helicopters," Hall fumed.

****

"Battleforce Six, Scout Six, over."

"Scout Six, Battleforce Three, go ahead," Major Billy Wells answered. He was the battalion operations officer.

"Roger, sitrep. I'm showing a BTR battalion passing through Sulailah Juhainah. Rate of movement is ten kilometers. Break. I count five-seven vehicles. Break. Second element is five kilometers behind, but with the dust, I cannot determine the size. Over."

"Roger, good copy on all. What are your intentions? Over."

"Oh, we're just going to hunker down and continue to watch. Over." Lieutenant Al Stahl had been scout platoon leader for only a couple of months as the battalion had shifted officers in the early summer due to some departing the battalion for schools and some new officers coming into the battalion. Although he was new to the job, Al was absolutely the right person for it.

At sixteen, he had become a guide for duck hunters on the Mississippi Flyway. In hunting season, his freezer was always stocked with game supplied by him or his very capable hunting partner, his wife. There wasn't much about stalking that Al didn't know, and he brought those skills with him to the job. He was also prior service enlisted and a fine leader.

"Roger, be safe. Over," Major Wells said, handing the hand mic to the battalion radio telephone operator or RTO, Specialist Mahnken. Specialist King manned the radio that connected the battalion to brigade.

"King, notify Brigade that we have eyes on what appears to be an enemy BTR battalion with follow-on elements of unknown size. Pass along the location as well," Colonel Cory directed as he sat in the jump TOC overlooking Al Muraba'a. The jump TOC or TAC CP consisted of few people, mainly the commander, the operations officer, the two RTOs and two drivers along with the fire support coordinator. The main TOC was located across the valley on the south side and was manned by Major David, the battalion executive officer, along with the rest of the TOC staff, consisting of assistant operations officers, intel officers, communications officers and NCOs.

Turning to the fire support officer, Colonel Cory directed, "Badger, let's lay in the FASCAM now."

"Roger, sir," Badger responded. Badger was Captain Harrison, but Colonel Cory had nicknames for each of his battle captains. His own was the Old Man, a nickname Cory wore with pride as he was the oldest person serving in the battalion at the age of forty-four. His gray hair only added to the nickname. Of course, no one ever referred to him by that name in his presence except by accident, and Cory would usually just chuckle.

"Captain Avery, let's get some tac air out in front to wear them boys down," Cory said, addressing the TACP team chief that was with him.

"Roger, sir, I believe we have a flight of A-10s just waiting for a target. Do you want them on this first bunch or the follow-on?"

"Hit the follow-on. We may be low on ammo and firepower once we take out this first bunch. I'd rather hit the second group if they can see them through the dust." Cory explained.

Captain Avery got on the radio and started submitting their tac air request ASAP. There wasn't a mission more desired by a ground attack pilot than a column or two of enemy vehicles waiting to get shot up.

Colonel Cory took the hand mic from Mahnken. "All Battleforce elements, Scout Six has enemy battalion with BTR vicinity Sulailah Juhainah. Break. Anticipate your engagement area in one hour. Break. Do not engage until enemy is hit by the FASCAM. Acknowledge."

247

"Roger, Gator Six," the A Company commander, Captain Mulford, said.

"Bulldog Six, roger," Captain Grubich, the Bravo commander, acknowledged.

"Charger Six, roger," the Charlie Company commander, Captain Agather, replied.

"Dawg Six, roger," Captain Stein acknowledged. Dawg Company, with its twenty TOW weapons, was the principal antitank weapon for the air assault infantry battalion. The line companies had the Dragon weapons system, but the TOW, with its three-thousand-meter range, was the relied upon weapon against tanks.

The TOW vehicles were arrayed in the hills overlooking Al Muraba'a, with one-third on the south side, one-third to the west of the town and one-third north of the town. Delta Company also had three strong officers. The company commander was one of the best in the brigade. In addition, he had a captain as a platoon leader who had transferred out of the battalion to attend the Special Forces course but dropped out and returned to the battalion, taking any job Colonel Cory would give him just because he wanted to go into combat with the battalion. An antitank platoon was all that was left and needed to be filled. The young captain took it. In addition, the company executive officer was a positive influence and could easily take command if necessary.

Cory watched as the BTRs moved down the valley towards Al Muraba'a. Company A was in the town, and Cory hoped they didn't give away their positions until the enemy hit the minefield. Bravo Company was located on the south side of the valley twelve hundred meters from the edge of town. Charlie Company was to the west of town, closing the western end of the minefield. Wherever the enemy vehicles moved, they would be within range of both the TOWs and Dragon weapons systems.

The sound of the flight of four A-10 aircraft passing over his head at low-level altitude grabbed Cory's attention. They were just above the hilltops and driving right for the enemy formation but bypassing the first elements. When they began unleashing their ordnance, Cory could hear the explosions but couldn't observe the damage they were inflicting.

"Captain Avery, ask them for a BDA if they can give us one when they're expended," Cory asked the Air Force captain. Avery was an F-16 pilot but had to pull a tour in the world of tactical air control party. He would much rather be flying in the conflict but accepted his role and did it well.

"Sir, I don't have comms with those birds. Brigade called up that air strike. They must have some eyes on the follow-on force," Captain Avery indicated. "I'll call the TACP at Brigade and see what they can tell me."

Cory and his S-3, Major Wells, were positioned to observe the engagement area and the entire defense plan from their hilltop position. As they watched, the first of the enemy's vehicles appeared.

"Battleforce Six, Gator Six, over."

"Gator Six, Battleforce Six, go ahead."

"Battleforce Six, enemy reconnaissance element is a klick east of our position and observing. It appears he's trying to decide which way to go. Over."

Shifting his binoculars, Cory could now see the reconnaissance element. Three individuals were in front of a BTR-60 and looking at a map. It appeared that there was a disagreement on which way to advance.

Come on, come on, this is a no-brainer. Bypass the town. Don't be stupid, Cory was thinking as he watched the reconnaissance team discuss the way to go.

"Battleforce Six, Scout Six, over."

"Scout Six, Battleforce Three, go ahead," Major Wells said. Major Wells had been the battalion S-3 or operations officer for only a month when the battalion had been alerted to deploy. In that short time, he and Cory had established a good working relationship but with some frustration for Major Wells. At times, he and Cory had a difference of opinion on tactics, which is not uncommon between infantry officers depending on background. Wells knew if he made a compelling enough argument, Cory would come around to his plan, but it took a convincing argument.

"Battleforce Three, battalion-size element passing through Sulailah Juhainah with fifty-three vehicles, four ZSU-23-4, four SA-9s. No tanks, no artillery. How copy? Over."

"Scout Six, good copy. Do you have eyes on follow-on force? Over."

"Battleforce Three, that's a negative. We do hear a lot of explosions and noise, but they're covered in dust at this point. I estimate they're three klicks back. Over."

"Scout Six, roger. Keep us informed. Battleforce Three, out." Wells turned to Cory. "Sir, did you get that?" he asked as Cory was still watching the recon element.

Turning to face Wells, Cory said, "Yeah, and that's not going to give us much time to take out this first bunch and reposition. I hope Brigade can slow them down a bit or we're going to have our hands full. Call the XO and have him ask Brigade if we can get some priority on tac air when the second element gets to us."

"Will do, sir," Wells said and reached for the battalion radio. Cory returned to watching the recon element. After a few more minutes, he noticed something.

"They're mounting up. Looks like they've made a decision," Cory said, still glued to his binos. "Hot damn, they're going to bypass the town."

"Battleforce Six, Gator Six, over."

"Gator Six, I see the recon element is bypassing your position, over."

"Roger, they're moving south and skirting the town. I intend to hold all fires and let them pass. Over."

"Gator Six, that's exactly what we want. Break, break. Charlie Rock Six, Charlie Rock Six, Battleforce Six, over."

"Battleforce Six, Charlie Rock Six, over." Charlie Rock was commanded by Captain Agather, nickname Flex. Flex was as skinny as they come, and the nickname was a play on him flexing his muscles. He was a physically fit officer but just didn't have the muscle definition that would indicate such.

"Charlie Rock Six, you have a reconnaissance element of ten vehicles approaching your positions. As we discussed, let them pass through and then take them out with your ambush. How copy?"

"Battleforce Six, good copy. All is ready."

Cory knew that Flex would have everything ready and carry out the mission as they had discussed. He returned to watching the reconnaissance element move south of the town and head due south towards Flex's position. Looking north, Cory could see the dust cloud approaching as the first enemy battalion moved forward.

"Badger, lay in the FASCAM," Cory directed the fire support officer.

"Roger, sir."

"All Battleforce elements, Battleforce Three, FASCAM is going in," Major Wells informed everyone. Each acknowledged that they understood. The valley floor was now covered in mines and trip wires. The combination of ADAM and RAAMS created an instant obstacle. Each company also had MOPMS but had not activated them except in Company A's sector.

Cory continued to watch the forward progress of the enemy battalion and the forward progress of the reconnaissance element. It was just reaching the forward positions of Charlie Rock, and Cory was holding his breath that it would pass through without detecting Charlie Rock.

"Battleforce Six, Charlie Rock Six," Flex said in almost a whisper.

"Charlie Rock Six, go ahead."

"Recon element is through my position. Ambush is ready in two klicks."

"Roger, let me know when it hits. Over."

"Roger, Charlie Rock Six out."

Turning to Major Wells, Cory said, "Flex says the recon element passed through his positions and it appears they didn't see him. His ambush is two klicks down the road. He'll let us know then they spring it."

"Well, sir, it appears that things are about to get lively. The lead elements of the battalion are about to run into the minefield," Wells pointed out, and Cory redirected his attention. In the open valley, they watched as the Iraqi battalion was in an anticipated formation of two companies abreast, with a third company following. Air-defense weapons were seen on the flanks for the ZSU-23-4 and the SA-9s array across the middle of the formation. As the first vehicle entered the minefield, all hell broke loose.

The first vehicle, a BTR-60, hit an antitank mine, designed to destroy a much larger and heavier vehicle. The BTR-60 set off the mine, which tore the BTR-60 into three large pieces and scattered the remains of those inside some distance away. Some landed and set off antipersonnel mines, which just added to the confusion. Almost immediately, Badger squeezed the mike switch, and the command for the artillery battery to open fire was given.

Moments later, airbursts could be seen over the enemy battalion, stripping off antennas and anyone outside the vehicles. As prearranged, the TOWs, all twenty, immediately opened fire at ranges varying from fifteen hundred to three thousand meters. The longer ranges required ten seconds to reach the target, but when one is buttoned up inside a vehicle with limited exterior views, finding a hide position quickly isn't always possible. Of the first twenty TOWs fired, sixteen found and destroyed targets. One was the Iraqi battalion commander's vehicle as TOW gunners always looked for the leaders' vehicles. In addition, three of the ZSU-23-4 were destroyed by two Dragon missiles and one by one of the four Vulcan 23mm anti-aircraft guns located with Cory's battalion. The second round of TOW missiles focused on the remaining BTR-60s, which were now seriously bogged down in the FASCAM minefield or being engaged by Dragons from soldiers located in the GATOR sector.

After fifteen minutes, Cory called Hall. "Bastogne Six, Battleforce Six, over."

"Battleforce Six, Bastogne Six, go ahead."

"Roger, engaged one Iraqi battalion. Destroyed fifty-two BTR-60, four ZSU-23-4 and four SA-9. How copy?"

"Good copy. Be advised you have a second force approaching your position."

"Roger, understood. Battleforce Six out."

Cory turned to Major Wells. "Billy, notify everyone that there's a full following brigade coming at us. Rearm, move casualties and be prepared for incoming. Have them report status of III, V, water and casualties. I got a feeling this next one won't be so easy," he said with a resigned voice. The lack of sleep was catching up to him.

****

"Colonel Hall, sir, the follow-on force heading for Battleforce has turned. The scout is reporting they held short of Sulailah Juhainah and then turned toward Sililah Anezah and are heading southeast towards 3rd Brigade," Major Clauson said. Hall quickly grabbed up the map and looked to where 3rd Brigade was defending.

The 3rd Brigade, 187th Infantry Regiment, was on the 1st Brigade's right flank. The bulk of his force was on a defensive line from the east side of the ridge, south of Al Muraba'a, to just east of Jada'ah. The terrain would channel an advancing division onto a very narrow front approaching Jada'ah.

"Excuse me, sir," Major Clauson said, "but Division just notified us that priority of air support now is with 3rd Brigade as well as long-range fires. That leaves us with our DS 105 battalion and that's about it."

"Well, we're just going to have to make do. It appears that most of the Iraqis are moving southeast and not coming into our sector. What's the status of Battleforce?"

"Sir, I spoke with Battleforce Six. They're good—a few light casualties but nothing that needs immediate evac."

"And No Slack and Bastogne?" Hall asked.

"Sir, they never really got into it as they were bypassed. This Iraqi division appears hell-bent on getting into it with 3rd Brigade."

"Yeah, but there's another division somewhere north that should be following this division. Get Division on the horn and see what they have intel-wise and what they're thinking about our next move. The Iraqis aren't coming this way, and there's no point in us just sitting here," Hall instructed Major Clauson.

Chapter 26
Battle in the Desert

Midday

22 October 1990

187th Infantry Regiment (Rakkasans)

General Rashid Hamdani, commander of the 12th Regiment, 7th Iraqi Division, did not like sacrificing his men. He knew when he committed the 1st Battalion that he was doing just that as they moved down the highway and wadi from Al Dhalyiah towards Shajwa. His regiment was the right flank of the division. The 13th Regiment was the left flank and had reported some enemy engagements. The black smoke columns indicated more than just some engagements. The 12th and 13th Regiments were to draw the enemy out and hold the shoulders of the penetration with 14th Regiment, pushing through the enemy's defense so the 37th Division could exploit the attack and break through to Jeddah and Yanbu. The enemy on the flanks was just light infantry, he was told, but they were proving to be a stubborn and resilient enemy. He had lost all contact with the first battalion.

Picking up the hand microphone, he called his 2nd Battalion commander. "Two-Six, this is One-Two-Six, over."

"One-Two-Six, this is Two-Six, over."

"Two-Six, you are to assume the right flank and probe along those hillsides. There should be more of this American unit hiding. I think we have lost One-Six. We must clean the Americans out of those hills," Hamdani said.

"One-Two-Six, understood. We have had negative contact since we passed Sililah Anezah. My lead element is moving towards Tara'ah," Two-Six reported.

"Roger, let me know when you reach there. One-Two-Six out," Hamdani responded. He did not like sending battalions off on scouting missions. That was not how they were trained to fight. *We fight as a regiment and not a piecemeal commitment*, he was thinking when the radio began crackling.

"One-Two-Six, Two-Six, over." Two-Six's voice was elevated.

"Two-Six, One-Two-Six, over."

"One-Two-Six, my lead element has been hit hard. We cannot get past this position and have dismounted but are meeting stiff opposition. Request assistance." In the background, Hamdani could hear the sound of machine-gun fire and explosions, very loud explosions. *I am not going to have my regiment destroyed in a piecemeal fashion*, Hamdani said to himself.

"Two-Six, what is the location of your lead element?" Two-Six gave him the coordinates, which he plotted on his map. They were held up at the first choke point on the road leading to Tara'ah. Hamdani noted that a bit south of the entrance to the wadi going to Tara'ah was another wadi that could bring a force south of the choke point and into the rear of the ambush site.

"Three-Six, One-Two-Six, over." He was calling the Third Battalion commander.

"One-Two-Six, Three-Six, over."

"Three-Six, move one wadi south of the wadi to Tara'ah and take it. You will come back to the road that Two-Six is on and behind the ambush site. Understood?" Hamdani passed the coordinates of the ambush site to the Third Battalion commander.

257

"One-Two-Six, understood." Third Battalion continued south before turning west to come behind the ambush site that had been decimating the second battalion. Now the 12th Regiment was fully committed.

****

"Son of a bitch, that hurts!" Private Billy Jones yelled when a bullet grazed his upper arm as he started to raise his Dragon antitank launcher.

"Hold still and let me see it," Specialist Williams said, grabbing his first aid bandage.

"Screw that, keep shooting. I'll be OK. Now I'm going to kill something. I'm pissed," Jones said, readjusting his Dragon and looking through the thermal sight. As he scanned quickly for a target, he saw a BTR-80 six-wheel vehicle with a whip antenna and a flag flying from the antenna. The vehicle appeared to be stopped, with other vehicles on the other side doing the same thing. *You're mine*, Jones was thinking as he adjusted his sight and fired. The exploding round leaped from the launcher and commenced what appeared to be an erratic flight towards its target. To those watching the flight of the round, it appeared that it was going everywhere and nowhere as it was designed to fly with small thrusters keeping the round inside a box that appeared in the sight. From Jones's perspective, the round was functioning perfectly as it zeroed in on the BTR-80.

****

BG Baghdadi, commander of the 13th Regiment, was intensely listening to his radios and reports from his subordinate commanders. He was serving on the left flank of the 7th Division and his mission was to find and fix the American positions and hold the shoulders to allow follow-on forces to penetrate the American defense. However, nothing was happening according to plan or going right in his opinion. The American TOW and Dragon weapons were decimating his vehicles. Around him, the sounds of explosions from incoming artillery could be heard as well as an occasional bullet bouncing off the side of the armored vehicle. He was thankful the Americans did not appear to have any heavy machine guns such as the .50-caliber that had been in the American arsenal since 1918. He was a bit miffed that he couldn't get some close-air support or attack helicopters as the division commander was saving them to support the penetration by the 4th Regiment. *Well, he better damn well commit the 4th now* was the last thought he had as the Dragon missile slammed into the side of the vehicle, causing it to explode. The 3rd Regiment was now leaderless, and confusion quickly set in.

***

"Damn, Billy, you nailed his ass. Good shooting," Specialist Williams congratulated his foxhole mate.

Billy didn't have time to celebrate but discarded the spent launcher, grabbed another launcher and attached the thermal sight, ready for the next vehicle that came within range. Picking up his M-16 rifle, he engaged individual targets who had already dismounted and were attempting to move up the hills to overrun his and Williams's position and the rest of the 1st Platoon, Company B, 1st Battalion, 187th Infantry Regiment. The platoon's position was laid out so each fighting position had interlocking fire with the positions on each side. The platoon leader and platoon sergeant had designated the location of each position and had marked each position on the ground with orange spray paint before the soldiers had moved into the area. They'd then

259

had two days to prepare their positions before the platoon leader and platoon sergeant had come and inspected the positions and questioned the occupants on sectors of fire, dead space and engagement areas. When they were satisfied, they moved on to the next position. The two days of preparing the positions were now paying off as the enemy was dying attempting to move up the hill to reach them.

****

"Bastogne Six, Eagle Six," MG Peters called.

"Eagle Six, Bastogne Six, go ahead," Colonel Hall, the 1st Brigade commander, responded.

"Bastogne Six, sitrep," MG Peters requested.

"Eagle Six, No Slack is in heavy contact at this time. Battleforce appears to be quiet now with eighty percent availability and fifty percent ammo status. He has requested an ammo resupply. Bulldog Six reports no activity in his sector as he was totally bypassed. How copy?"

"Bastogne Six, good copy. Move Bulldog to PZ posture. He's to be attached to Rakkasan Six to reinforce. Birds will be there in thirty mikes to commence extraction. How copy?" Peters asked.

Hall didn't like giving up one of his battalions but understood. The Rakkasans were becoming the main effort as they now had two regiments coming at him, one holding the shoulders of the penetration and the other preparing to punch through and roll on to Yanbu.

"Eagle Six, I have good copy. Will send PZ locations in one mike. Over," Hall replied while Major Clauson was reaching for the brigade command radio to alert 1st Battalion of their upcoming move.

Having notified 1st Battalion, Clauson turned to Hall. "Sir, I hope Division understands that if the follow-on division comes this way, there's nothing to stop him."

"Yes, and I guess the CG is willing to accept the risk. That's why he makes the big money."

Twenty minutes later, Bulldog Six was back on the radio.

"Bastogne Six, Bulldog Six."

"Go ahead, Bulldog," Hall responded.

"Bastogne Six, Bulldog is moving to PZ postures. We plan on taking all the infantry out first, then the TOW systems, Vulcans and any vehicles we can on the big birds. They're being prepared for sling loads," Bastogne Six stated.

"Roger, have you been in contact with Rakkasan Six?" Hall asked.

"Negative, Bastogne Six."

"We'll contact him for you and alert him to your arrival. Good luck, and keep the boys healthy."

"Roger, Bastogne Six. Bulldog Six out."

An hour later, Rakkasan Six received a call. Rakkasan Six was Colonel Bob Clark, who had previously commanded Battleforce before being sent to the US Army War College and promoted to full colonel. He was very familiar with standard operating procedures in the division.

"Rakkasan Six, Bulldog Six, over." Bulldog Six had never worked with the Rakkasans before, but the division operated with an SOP, which made things much simpler.

"Bulldog Six, Rakkasan Six, go ahead."

"Rakkasan Six, my first elements are on the ground and moving into position. TOWs and vehicles will be on the first lift of heavies. Understand you want me to establish a defense in depth behind Leader Rakkasan. Is that correct?" Bulldog Six asked, seeking confirmation on the FRAGO he'd received before departing his previous location.

"Bulldog Six, that is affirmative. They'll hit Leader Rakkasan in about one hour. He'll delay them for as long as possible but will gradually allow some to get through his position for you to hit. We cannot allow them to get through you, understood? How copy?" Rakkasan Six asked.

"Roger, Rakkasan Six. We'll be ready," Bulldog Six replied.

"Rakkasan Six out."

And with that, Bulldog Six commenced to discuss his plan with the battalion S-3. They had received the mission days ago as a "be prepared" mission, so everyone in the battalion had an idea of where they were going and what they were going to have to do. The wadi was six thousand meters wide and about seventeen thousand meters long from the rear of Leader Rakkasan's positions. Vehicles moving down the wadi would be out of TOW range if they stayed right in the middle, but single-file hey-diddle-diddle up the middle was not how the regiments attacked. They would be spread out, easily within range of TOW weapons. At the southern end, the wadi came to a choke point that was only two thousand meters wide. This was where the bulk of the Dragon weapons would be located. Bulldog Six also planned to emplace an air-dropped minefield there as well using Air Force CBU-89 GATOR munitions.

Bulldog Six's plan was to initially position seven ambush sites for his vehicle-mounted TOWs along the sides of the wadi forward of the choke point. Positions would engage and fall back past other TOW position to take up a new position around the choke point, a technique called bounding overwatch. The superior speed of the TOW vehicles and the range of the TOW missile would make it possible to quickly move out of the range of the main gun on the T-72 tanks or the machine gun from the BTR-80. In addition, seven more ambush sites were planned along the eastern side of the wadi, hiding in the edge of the wadi along the steep ridgeline from the choke point to the final defensive positions.

"What troubles me about these positions around the choke point is he's going to see this and should be smart enough to know we're going to be there. He'll use his artillery or tac air and attack helicopters to hit us hard. We've got to be sure to get overhead cover on the troops," Bulldog Six discussed with Bulldog Three.

"Sir, we don't have much time once we get the troops on the ground and really nothing to use for overhead cover," the S-3 pointed out.

"Well, let's be sure the company commanders understand the foxholes have got to be deep and commence work as soon as they're on the ground," Bulldog Six said, mumbling to himself, "Wish we had the damn attack helicopters working with us."

Chapter 27
Scud Hunting

22 October 1990
ODA 5226
United Arab Emirates

"Did you hear that?" Lieutenant Harris asked Sergeant First Class Weekly, cocking his head slightly.

"Yeah," Weekly said in a whisper. "Sounded like it was down in the port area. Hell of an explosion. Don't think it was an air strike."

Harris and his Special Forces team had been looking for three Scud launchers for the past thirteen days. After that initial Scud attack, finding any remaining launchers had moved to the top of the priority list. So much so that an unplanned resupply of food and water was made.

The first night they were inserted, they climbed to the top of a dominant ridgeline, from where they could observe the approach to the wadi from Saqr Port area. Only an occasional civilian vehicle was seen. It became obvious to Weekly and Harris that they were going to have to conduct a search of the wadis that branched off the main wadi.

"Guys, we may have missed some launchers being moved into positions, so…we're going to have to start searching," he informed the team. No one complained; they all took the information like the professionals they were.

"I'll take Justin with me, and Mr. Garrett will take Cardwell with him. Weekly and Donovan will stay here and maintain contact with us and higher. Any questions?" There were none as everyone had expected this after the first day when they saw no traffic.

After everyone had their respective gear and the sun had just set for the evening, Harris directed, "OK, let's move out."

As the two teams moved down the hillside, the descent was much easier than the climb and both teams made good time reaching the bottom of the wadi. It had been decided that Harris and Justin would search the wadi they had parachuted into first. Mr. Garrett and Cardwell were heading northwest up that wadi. Both wadis could be observed from Weekly's position except the last couple of hundred meters in each. Weekly's high position allowed for good communications with both teams.

"Hey, Donovan, you got good comms with higher still?" Weekly asked once the teams had departed.

"Yeah. This elevation and clear sky are giving us good comms for a change. I think a relay was established across the border to monitor all of us," Donovan replied. Four Special Forces teams had been inserted along the border to find these launchers. To maintain contact besides satellite communications, monitoring sites had been established on the Oman side of the border. Each site was monitoring the communications with two teams. Co-located at each monitoring site were two MH-60 helicopters from the Special Operations Aviation Regiment, TF-160. If a team got into trouble and needed to be extracted quickly, these aircraft were there to do just that.

"You think. Didn't you listen to the brief? You were told there would be, and the extraction aircraft would be co-located with the monitoring station, or did you sleep through that part of the brief?" Weekly jokingly asked.

"No, I had to take a dump and left for about ten minutes. They must have covered that when I was in the john. Did I miss anything else that was important?" Donovan asked.

"I'll let you know when the shit hits the fan and you start asking questions. Until then, why don't you get some sleep and I'll take the first watch? Four hours and I'll wake you at midnight. Sound good?" Weekly suggested.

"Yeah, I can handle that. Wake me at midnight and be sure there's a cup of coffee in your hand for me," Donovan said, yawning as he wrapped his poncho liner and shelter half around his body. His comment was not disrespectful to Weekly's superior rank but said with the familiarity reserved for comrades in this very professional organization.

Looking over the terrain on this clear sky night, Weekly was simply amazed at the number of stars in the heavens. From where he sat on the prominent ridge, away from any artificial light, he had a million twinkling lights above his head. He reached over to his kit, withdrew his PVS-7 night vision goggles and powered them up, looking skyward. The million points of light became two million as he could now see stars that were too faint for the naked eye. *My God, we really are insignificant in this universe. Which one of you has life on it, because we can't be the only ones out here?* he thought. His concentration on the stars was only broken by the faint sound of the radio.

"Base, Team One, over." Without removing his NVGs, Weekly picked up the hand mike. He noted no panic or shooting in the background of the call.

"Team One, Base, go ahead."

"Base, Teams One and Two have reached point alpha. Separating at this time, over."

"Roger, Team One. Have good copy. Base out." Weekly laid the hand mike down and recorded in his notebook that the teams had reached the bottom of the ridge and were separating to investigate their respective wadis. Transmissions were kept short so that a fix could not be made on the location of the transmitters. *God be with you guys*, he thought as he returned to observing the stars.

****

Mr. Garrett and Cardwell moved off to the north, skirting the west and north side of the pond. It was a man-made pond created by a dam across the mouth of the wadi and runoff from the surrounding mountains. Garrett stopped for a moment and took a knee. Reaching down, he cupped one hand, dipped it into the water and took a sip.

"How's it taste?" Cardwell asked.

"Like water," was Garrett's response. "I think it's good. We might fill up when we return and then boil it when we get back just to make sure." The last thing anyone wanted was to have diarrhea caused by drinking bad water, or something worse like hepatitis, even though they all had their shots up to date. As they moved around the north side of the pond, they came across a pumping station and deduced that it must be supplying fresh water to the villages further down in the wadi or maybe even Saqr itself.

The terrain was very restrictive on the north side of the pond, which forced the team to stay off the ridge. This escarpment rose a thousand feet above the floor of the wadi and was impossible for them to climb. As they approached the wadi, a cluster of agricultural fields and buildings were to their immediate right. They had decided after doing a map reconnaissance earlier and now confirming what the map had shown them that it would be better to cross the wadi and move up on the opposite side. The terrain sloped upward gradually on that side, and the area they wanted to see was on that side as well. This would give them an easier walk and allow them to avoid most of the locals. It also offered hide positions where they could hunker down for the day, as they were sure they couldn't do an adequate reconnaissance and return to Weekly's position in one night. However, Garrett decided to change the plan slightly.

"With this compound being so big, it offers a lot more concealment than if we cross right here. What do you think if we move north along the base of the escarpment for about five hundred meters and then cut over? We would only be exposed for about a klick in crossing instead of a klick and a half," Garrett said.

"*Es ist mir egal*, but let's just get a move on," Cardwell said, practicing his German. He did not like being exposed in the open. They started moving past the compound with it on their left and the escarpment on their right. They didn't want to move too high on the slope, as this might cause loose rocks to roll downhill and alert those in the compound. However, as they were on the far side of the compound and starting to breathe a bit easier, a dog started barking. The compound was enclosed in a chain-link fence, so the dog couldn't get out, but it was barking enough to wake the dead, and it did.

Someone came out with a flashlight and was shining it through the fence in the direction that the dog was facing, right at Garrett and Cardwell. Both had taken a prone position and pressed themselves into the dirt as best they could before the flashlight panned across them. After a minute of panning, the flashlight went out and something was said angrily in Arabic. The dog yelped. It did not return to its barking.

"Let's move," Garrett said in a whisper and slowly raised to a low crouch and began moving again to the north. The further they got from the compound, the taller they stood and the more they picked up the pace. There was minimal talking but constant head turning as they continued to scan for the elusive launchers. Wearing their PVS-7 night vision goggles certainly helped in seeing any potential problems early.

After moving five hundred meters, Garrett motioned for them to take a break and both immediately went to their knee. A drink of water was in order, as they had soaked their uniforms with sweat. Even late at night, the desert temperature was hovering in the nineties. Garrett pulled out his map and scanned it, noting their current location, the direction to move to cross the wadi and the distance across at this point.

Turning to Cardwell, he held out his map and pointed. "Here's where we are, and it's a klick across the wadi. We have to cross the road and it's pretty open around it. Once we get to the far side, there's some brush along the wadi that'll give us some concealment. We'll have a bit of a downhill walk to the road, then a level walk to the far side."

"Looks good to me. I'm ready when you are," Cardwell said, adjusting his backpack, which contained the radio.

"OK, let's go." And with that, Garrett stood and moved out on a heading of three hundred degrees. His pace had not changed, as this was a walk and not a race. The road was only one hundred and fifty meters away and an easy walk. As they approached, they realized that the road was slightly elevated. More concerning were the headlights approaching from the south and the direction of Saqr Port.

"Get across and hide," was all Garrett had to say. They half ran and half walked across the road and dropped down ten feet. The side of the road had a steep drop to the wadi, where it appeared that water in the rainy season had washed the side out. When they landed, they stayed lying up against the embankment. The vehicle continued to approach, with no noticeable change in the engine noise as it sped past their position. They both noted that this was no light civilian truck but a heavy truck, maybe a five-ton or bigger.

"I wonder where he's going," Cardwell said, peeking out to the side to see if he could follow the truck. As he watched, it entered the town and then he lost sight of it.

"Maybe when we get across and start going up the hill, we can spot it. Let's get going," Garrett said, adjusting his rucksack and continuing his march.

It took them an hour to cross the rocky wadi, as hurrying across it would mean risking a twisted—or worse, broken—ankle. Once they reached the far side, they changed course to due west. The spot they couldn't see from Weekly's position lay one klick due west and up a gradual slope, although the final location was set in a draw about five hundred feet below the crest they were climbing. It would be another two hours of hiking and climbing to position them in a location to observe at about 0400 hours. They moved out in silence.

Finding a hide position, Garrett and Cardwell dropped their rucksacks and camouflaged their position. It was in a small draw, and with the use of their camouflage rucksack covers, they appeared to be just more rocks, or at least they hoped they did, as it was still dark. Without the rucksacks, they could move faster and headed off the last two hundred meters to look over the escarpment and down into the valley. As they approached, they picked up a faint sound.

"Do you hear an engine running?" Garrett asked.

"No, I hear a generator running. Ten K, from the sound of it. Big," Cardwell said. They continued forward, and the sound grew louder. "That is definitely a generator," Cardwell said in a low voice.

When they were ten feet from the edge of the escarpment, they went into low-crawl mode and slithered up to the edge to look over.

There, five hundred feet below them, sat a large tent with a large generator next to it. An electrical cable ran from the generator out one hundred feet to another tent that appeared to be well lit inside.

"What the hell is this setup?" Garrett whispered as he looked down on the scene below.

Cardwell tapped his shoulder and pointed. Garrett followed his arm and gazed to where it was pointed. He saw nothing but rocks until someone moved. The Scud launcher was backing into a large, camouflaged cover over what appeared to be a shallow hole that allowed the vehicle to back in and out. Once inside, under the camouflage, the launcher was below ground level.

"No wonder they couldn't find it in an aerial recon. Sneaky little bastards they are," Cardwell said.

"Well, let's get some photos and the location and ease back. We'll call it in when we get to the hide position," Garrett said, pushing himself back from the edge.

****

Lieutenant Harris and Sergeant Lovett moved up the wadi they had parachuted into the night before. There was a small compound on the south side as one entered the wadi, so they elected to move on the northern side to avoid any locals or dogs. They hugged the base of the escarpment that created the north wall of the wadi until they approached another compound.

"Damn, another compound. Let's cross over to the other side and avoid this," Harris said and took off at a low crouch, jogging across the wadi to the south wall. It was only two hundred meters across and flat, so the crossing was made with little difficulty. They moved further into the wadi, another five hundred meters of which the last two hundred was actually behind a small rise that provided some concealment from the compound on the north side. Coming out from behind the rise, Harris raised his hand for Lovett to stop and dropped to his stomach. Lovett crawled up beside him.

"Whatcha got, Lieutenant?" Lovett asked.

Pointing to his front, Harris asked, "What does that look like to you?"

"Sir, that looks like either a well drill under camouflage or a Scud launcher, and I don't think a well drill would have tents and generators around it," Lovett said. As they lay there, both scanned the area with their night vision goggles. "Hey, Lieutenant, look to your ten o'clock and about three hundred meters. What does that look like?" Lovett pointed out.

"Shit, that's another Scud," Harris replied. "OK, let's plot these positions and get out of here. We need to call this in before they move them." Five minutes later, they were on their feet and heading back to link up with Weekly.

****

Reaching the top of the ridge just as the sky was turning pink in the east, Harris, soaked with perspiration, walked into Weekly's position. Earlier he had called Weekly and provided the information on the two Scuds they had found.

"Did you get through to higher and report the locations?" Harris asked as he dropped his rucksack and stretched his back. *Humping that damn rucksack is going to make an old man out of me one day*, he thought.

Handing a cup of coffee to Harris, Weekly said, "Yeah, we got the position of all three reported to higher. I suspect we're going to see some action around here sometime this morning."

"Three? I only sent you two," Harris replied with a questioning look.

"Mr. Garrett located one last night as well," Weekly replied with a smile.

"Is he coming back in this morning?" Harris asked, sipping his coffee.

"No, they hunkered down for the day and will come in tonight after the sun drops. I told higher we would need an extraction, and they were standing by to send us a bird."

Harris absorbed this information for a moment. "I don't like it. If those launchers get hit today, the ragheads are going to know someone spotted them and will be looking for us."

"Hey, Lieutenant, Garrett knows what he's doing. I'm sure he's in a good position for the day and set out early," Weekly assured him.

"Did higher say about what time the air strikes would go in?" Harris questioned.

"No, why?" Weekly asked, curious as to what the lieutenant was thinking.

"Get them on the horn. Ask if they can schedule the air strikes for just before sunset. In the confusion, Garrett will have a better chance of slipping away. Let's pick a PZ location that we all can move to for the extraction," Harris directed and pulled out a map to begin plotting their extraction.

******

As the sun approached the western horizon and the long shadows of the mountains brought an early evening to the wadis, three loud explosions could be heard as Maverick missiles slammed into the launchers, each with a missile erected. The sounds of the explosions reverberated off the walls of the canyons, making it sound as if several bombs had been dropped. The A-6E Intruder aircraft had flown well under the electronic eye of radar, taking advantage of the canyons, and thus entered and exited the area without a shot being fired at them. Thirty minutes later, the two teams were on the move to the preplanned extraction point.

Harris was not totally happy about the extraction point, but he wanted to make it easy for everyone to get to it. It was located halfway between the two teams and in the wadi along the main road coming into the area out of Saqr. Harris explained to Weekly that if they had an extraction around four in the morning, it would still be dark and the Iraqis might just be tuckered out, having spent the night looking for them in the area of the strikes. And so, having watched the strikes, the teams set out. Both had downhill routes to the extraction point. Garrett and Cardwell would have the more difficult and tiring hump as they would be walking cross-slope and down. Harris and team had a long downhill run and then flat ground, negotiation around a compound. Garrett didn't have that problem on his route this time. At 0200, both teams had reached their respective edges of the wadi. Some vehicle traffic had been seen on the road moving to and from the Saqr Port area. They were four hundred and fifty meters apart.

"Team Two, Team One, over," Harris called.

"Team One, Team Two, go ahead," Garrett responded as he pulled an IR chem stick out of a cargo pant pocket and cracked it.

"Team Two, did you just start an IR chem stick?" Harris asked.

"Roger, I believe I have you in sight as well. Over," responded Garrett.

"OK, the road is right in front of us. We're going to cross and come to your location and get away from these compounds," Harris indicated.

"Roger, we'll cover you," Garrett said.

Turning to his team, Harris gave a hand signal that everyone could see since they all had on night vision goggles. They then immediately spread out, and with the next signal, they all rose and crossed the road at the same time. On the other side, they assumed a wedge formation and proceeded to link up with Garrett. Promptly at 0358, the sound of a UH-60 Black Hawk helicopter could be heard, and at 0400, a cloud of dust covered them, created by the Black Hawk landing next to them. The flight home was uneventful, just the way soldiers liked it. Mission complete.

Chapter 28

Partial Mobilization Decision

22 October 1990
Oval Office, White House
Washington, D.C.

General Schwarzkopf was listening to the latest intelligence brief, and he did not like what he was hearing.

"Sir, as we speak, the Iraqi 1st Republican Guard Corps is moving one division from the north coast to Fujairah on the south coast. With the Strait closed, we believe they feel that an amphibious assault by the Marines is a major threat in this area. The hydrography of the beaches will support an amphibious landing, and Khor Fakkan Port, Al Quarayyah Port and Fujairah Port are the only ports that can support a major operation. Fujairah International Airport is also suitable for cargo jets. The beaches are four hundred feet in depth from waterline to seawall, which is approximately four feet high," the briefing officer said.

"Damn, I was hoping we could put the 2nd Marine Division in there unopposed, but that just went out the window. We're going to need two divisions to open that door. I foresee one Marine division conducting an amphibious assault across the beach and another division moving north out of Bu Baqarah, Oman, now to hit the Iraqi division in the flank. Can't send a Marine division across the beach alone against prepared positions and a dug-in Iraqi division," Schwarzkopf said, looking at the CENTCOM G-3, General Schless, who nodded in acknowledgment that what had just been said would have to be included in his war plan. "And I don't think we have the ships to support a full Marine division in a forced entry, do we?"

"Sir, I will have to defer to MARCENT to get an accurate estimate of what we could put into a forced entry," General Schless indicated.

"Is there any indication that Saddam is going to pull out? I really don't want to bring a lot of folks over and then have to turn around and send them home," Schwarzkopf asked the briefing officer and CENTCOM G-2, BG O'Donnell.

O'Donnell fielded the question. "Sir, there are no indications that he's going to withdraw. In fact, all indications are that he's reinforcing. I'm sure the G-3 will cover it in detail, but last night we took out three Scud sites in this area"—he pointed at the map—"outside the Port of Saqr, where the *Florida* took out that bulk carrier full of Scud missiles. No, sir, he's not pulling out but reinforcing."

"Sir, over in the west, 101st is in a major fight with the 2nd Iraqi Corps. It started this morning and is still raging. ARCENT just sent the first reports up to us. The 101st is holding but just barely," General Schless said.

Turning to Schless, General Schwarzkopf said, "See me after this meeting and let's review the war plan. I think we're going to need more forces."

****

Prior to going to General Schwarzkopf's office, General Schless stopped off in his office.

"Have you guys flushed out the plan?" he asked, coming through the door. "The Old Man wants to review it—now."

"Sir, we wrapped it up about ten minutes ago based on the latest intel. We also have a proposal for additional forces to support the plan. There's just no way to do this without more," Major Stube said.

"Good. Gather it up and come with me. You can brief the Old Man on it. Give you a little face time with him. I hope you have your shit together, Major," Schless said as he grabbed a pad of paper and led the way out the door.

Arriving at General Schwarzkopf's door, General Schless said, "Sir, we're ready to give you an update." He motioned for Major Stube to lay out the maps on the conference table.

As Major Stube laid out the maps, General Schwarzkopf asked him, "Jack, how you are doing this fine day?"

"Good, sir, thank you."

"Jack, I know our current disposition of forces on both sides, so we don't need to plow through that again. What I want is your best estimate of what additional forces I'm going to need to drive them out of Saudi and back to Iraq," Schwarzkopf stated.

"Sir, we've looked at his current disposition of forces. Starting in the UAE, we feel it will take two Marine divisions to clear the area of Kalba-Fujairah-Khor Fakkan, with one division coming over the beach and another striking the southern flank and overland from Bu Baqarah. We'll also need one division to strike Al Ain to hold those forces in place, and one division to strike south of Al Ain and encircle to prevent any escape or reinforcement. The bulk of the division at Al Ain is south of the city. In addition, we need one division to strike towards Asab. While the divisions are engaging, we use deep battle assets to hit the division in Abu Dhabi or at least hold him in place. That right there is five divisions, not counting the 101st and 82nd over to the west. Once successful, those five divisions will now have the IX Corps, which is still in Saudi Arabia, to contend with, and it has six divisions of which two are committed in Al Jubail and Dammam, respectively. Sir, we see this as a phased operation in the east, with phase one being the liberation of the UAE and the second being the liberation of Saudi. At a minimum, sir, we need ten divisions for the eastern campaign alone."

"And the western campaign?" General Schwarzkopf asked.

"The XVIII Airborne Corps is holding its own in that rugged terrain. We feel we should continue to just remain in a defensive posture there until phase one is complete. We can then reexamine the situation in the west and decide what additional forces we need there."

"You do realize that if we ask for more divisions, at some point, they're going to have to call up the National Guard divisions," Schwarzkopf said.

"Sir, that should not be our concern. We're the war fighters—the Pentagon and the DOD are the suppliers. They leave it up to us to prosecute this fight and it's up to them to supply us. How they do that shouldn't be our concern," General Schless said.

"Alright, draft up a message requesting additional forces. In addition, I would like to have III Coprs from Fort Hood and VII Corps from Germany as the control headquarters. We want mechanized and armored divisions. If they have to activate a National Guard division, so be it. Get it drafted and I'll sign it."
****

"You have got to be shitting me," Mr. Cheney said when he read the request that General Powell had just handed him. "He wants two corps headquarters and seven more divisions. Do we have seven more divisions to send him?" he asked.

"Sir, we have the 1st Infantry Division, the 2nd Armored Division and the 4th Infantry Division, here in the States. The 25th in Hawaii is committed to the Pacific, as is the 2nd at Fort Lewis. The 3rd Armored Cavalry Regiment is on its way over and the 197th Infantry Brigade is already there. The 10th Mountain at Fort Drum, New York, is about all that's left, and it's a light infantry unit," Powell outlined. "We have units in Europe we can draw from that'll strip them from NATO, which is going to cause problems with the other members."

"Well, they can just suck it up or join us. Their choice," Cheney said under his breath, making a note. "Colin, are you telling me we're going to have to activate National Guard units? Are we that desperate at this point?" he asked as he slumped into his chair behind his desk.

"Mr. Secretary, that's what I'm telling you—unless we can get the British and the Egyptians to send us more forces," Powell said.

Cheney sat for a minute and said nothing. Powell could see the wheels turning in the Secretary's head. Finally, Cheney reached for the intercom. "Mike," he called his military aide, "get General Conway and ask him to come over here for a meeting. Also see if the President can put us on his calendar for today for a sit-down, and see if Mr. Baker can join us." Hanging up the phone, he said, "Colin, have a list of recommendations for which National Guard units we want to activate. This is going to require a partial mobilization order from the President."

****

"Mr. President, I have here a request from CENTCOM for additional forces—seven more divisions to start with, which means a lot of supporters as well for those divisions from corps assets. We have some assets here in the States that we can send, but that's only the four divisions that are not committed at this time. The options are we could strip a division or two out of Europe or we could ask the British and the Egyptians for more assistance," Cheney said.

"Dick, I don't like the idea of stripping divisions out of Europe at this time. The Soviet Union is falling apart and there's no telling what some people will do in desperate times. Are there no other options?" the President asked.

"Sir, we could activate a National Guard division to make up for one or two of the shortfalls," Cheney said reluctantly.

"I take it you don't like that option," the President said, sitting back in his chair in the Oval Office while the others were on the opposing couches.

"Mr. President, it's an option, but one with a lot of strings attached. On the positive side, it would bring the nation into this war, and if the past holds, the nation will get behind this action as these are hometown boys getting into the fight. On the negative side is a train-up period to ensure we're sending trained units into the fight and not untrained men for cannon fodder," Cheney said.

"How long of a train-up are we looking at?" the President asked.

"Sir," Powell said, "to activate a division, move it to home station, in-processing procedures to include physicals, dental checks, and immunizations, we're looking at least two months. Then train-up and evaluations are another four months. At best, sir, it'll be six months before they could deploy to the theater. To do that, we're going to need congressional support and a partial mobilization order."

"Sir," Cheney interjected, "under Title 10, United States Code 12302, partial mobilization will allow for a call-up of one million reservists and National Guardsmen for a period of twenty-four months. Presidential call-up under US Code 12304 only allows two hundred thousand to be called up and for only two hundred and seventy days. That's not enough time, I'm afraid, to train up and deploy a National Guard division."

"So, gentlemen, what I'm hearing is a recommendation to bring congressional leaders in and go for partial mobilization. Where those National Guard divisions come from, however, is still up to us, correct?" the President asked, thinking out loud. Everyone nodded in agreement.

"We call up a National Guard division. Depending on how well they do at the National Training Center, we can send them to the theater, or we can send them to backfill an active division out of Europe. Am I correct?" the President asked.

"Yes, sir, it's your call on where we send them," Cheney answered.

The President was quiet for a moment, lost in thought. "General Conway, you understand our position on calling up National Guard divisions? I don't want to hear any pissing and moaning in the press because you or some of your staff are dissatisfied with what units are being called up or committed to where. Is that understood?"

"Yes, Mr. President," Conway said with a satisfied look. He'd gotten what he wanted—a large call-up of the National Guard.

"I hope you understand that they're going to get an evaluation at the National Training Center and there will be no patty-cakes. I want a realistic, tough evaluation. No one is going to be able to say we sent untrained, unqualified citizen soldiers to their death," the President added.

He turned to Mr. Sununu. "Call the House and Senate leadership and ask them to come over. We'll need to run this by them. And, Jim, see if the Brits and the Egyptians can send additional ground forces. Let me know if I need to weigh in on that. If there's nothing else, gentlemen..."

They all rose, knowing the meeting was over.

Chapter 29

Battle on the Flanks

22 October 1990

502nd Infantry Regiment

South of Al Muthalath, Saudi Arabia

General Peters monitored the engagement taking place on the western flank of 1st and 3rd Brigades. From the sound of things, the fight was going well, with the Iraqi divisions being torn up pretty good. He was concerned, however, about what was about to unfold on the right flank with 2nd Brigade.

The 2nd Brigade had inserted three battalions along the highway nine miles north of Al Eshash. The three battalions of the 502nd Infantry Regiment, which comprised the 2nd Brigade, were further broken down into company-size and platoon-size positions, all focusing on the defense of the TOW and Dragon weapons systems. Each position had a designated pickup zone to which the unit would move after engaging the enemy and make good their extraction and movement to their next fighting position. Every TOW and Dragon position was carefully chosen, with overlapping fires integrated with artillery target reference points. Mines were positioned at the end of each engagement area. Each kill zone was also covered by small-arms fire, to include the M-60 machine guns and squad automatic weapons or SAW. Small arms would not engage until Iraqi infantry dismounted and attempted to move towards the Dragon and TOW positions. These tactics had been tested extensively at the Joint Readiness Training Center and National Training Center. This was a fight the division was ready for. The final defensive line was located around Al Uqiylah.

"No Mercy Six, Sabre Six, over."

"Sabre Six, No Mercy Six, go ahead."

"No Mercy Six, we've stripped his forward recon element pretty good, so he has no eyes out front. He's moving with two regiments abreast and the third regiment following. I think his left-flank regiment is going to try to slip through the rough terrain in that big wadi on the west side. His lead elements are in the vicinity of Hafirat Al-Aida. Over."

"Sabre Six, good copy. No Mercy elements are moving into position and have it now. See you when you're back up."

"Roger, No Mercy Six, good hunting."

No Mercy Six, Lieutenant Colonel Dick Cody, had twenty-one AH-64 attack helicopters under his command. Cody had graduated from West Point in 1972 and had been commissioned as a transportation officer but concentrated on Army Aviation. By the time he'd graduated from flight school, the US Army had been pretty much out of Vietnam, so he hadn't gotten the chance to fly there. His entire career up to this point was in Army Aviation, and he was qualified in almost every rotary-wing aircraft the Army had.

"Eagle Attack Six, No Mercy Six, over."

"No Mercy Six, Eagle Attack Six, go ahead." Eagle Attack Six was Lieutenant Colonel Mark Curran, who commanded the other attack battalion in the 101st, the 3rd Battalion, 101st Aviation Regiment. He had eighteen AH-1F attack helicopters under his command, along with twenty-one scout helicopters, the OH-58 Kiowa. The AH-1F was armed with sixteen TOW missiles with a range of three thousand meters.

"Eagle Attack Six, did you monitor Sabre Six about the western approach?" No Mercy Six asked.

"Roger, I have it covered. I'm committing half my force at a time as he has little maneuver room. We'll keep constant pressure on him. What might get through will be able to join whatever gets through you and the grunts in the vicinity of where your road comes out of the mountains north of Al Eshash, but I don't think anything's going to make it that far. Over."

"Attack Six, I think you're right. We're going to commence engaging in five mikes. Over."

"No Mercy Six, Eagle Attack Six. Sounds good, will do same. Out."

The AH-64 Apache helicopters were each armed with sixteen AGM-114 Hellfire missiles. The AGM-114 was a subsonic laser-guided missile with a range of six point eight miles or eleven kilometers. It was capable of killing the heaviest of tanks. Besides the AGM-114 missiles, the AH-64 also carried a 30mm chain gun with twelve hundred rounds in the nose. Both attack battalions moved into firing positions behind the covered and concealed infantry positions. As the Iraqi lead elements moved with caution towards the mountainous terrain to their front, they did not expect what hit them.

"Specter Six, No Mercy Six. Slide your elements to the west and engage the flanks of the follow-on battalion. How copy?" No Mercy Six asked.

"Good copy, Specter Six."

"Break. Bearcat Six, No Mercy Six."

"No Mercy Six, Bearcat Six, over."

"Bearcat Six, engage lead elements on my command."

"No Mercy Six, Bearcat elements are standing by."

"Paladin Six, No Mercy Six."

"No Mercy Six, Paladin Six, over."

"Paladin Six, engage the left flank of the lead elements on my command."

"Roger, No Mercy Six, moving into position at this time."

No Mercy Six waited until each of his subordinate companies had moved into position. He knew the scout aircraft would have their laser designators painting the enemy vehicles already. Once he was sure they were in position, No Mercy Six gave the command.

"All No Mercy elements, this is No Mercy Six. Engage."

Still three miles from the protection that the mountainous terrain might offer, the first of the Iraqi tanks exploded. At first no one could understand why the tank would have exploded, but the other tanks and vehicles immediately closed their hatches and buttoned up their vehicles. Not only was the visibility for the following vehicles' obscured by the dust from the first vehicles, but now visibility for each vehicle was further reduced from being buttoned up. It seemed to the Iraqi commanders that as a vehicle would come out of the dust of the vehicle in front of it, they would be destroyed. Some vehicles on the flanks were being destroyed as well. In a matter of thirty minutes, the lead brigade on the right flank had lost just under three hundred vehicles to the No Mercy Battalion.

The Iraqi brigade on the left flank was faring no better as he was also still short of the protection offered by the terrain and was losing vehicles, with his air-defense vehicles being the first to be destroyed.

"Dragonslayer Six, Eagle Attack Six," Colonel Curran called.

"Attack Six, Dragonslayer Six, over."

"Dragonslayer Six, when you've expended seventy-five percent, let me know so I can have Archangel Six relieve you. Over."

"Roger, Eagle Attack Six, we are fifty percent expended at this time."

"Roger, Dragonslayer. Break, Archangels Six, Eagle Attack Six."
While the Dragonslayers were engaging elements of the 51st Division
on the Iraqi division's left flank, Archangels, Company C, 3-101
Aviation Regiment, had been sitting in a loiter position with engines at
flight idle, saving fuel.

"Eagle Attack Six, Archangels Six, over."

"Archangels Six, send the little birds forward to relieve
Dragonslayer elements. Be prepared for battle handoff in one-five
mikes."

"Roger, Eagle Attack, little bird elements are launching." From
the loiter position, six little birds came to full engine rpm and began to
lift off. They remained low, skirting the hillsides so as not to silhouette
themselves in the morning sun. As they came within view of the enemy
formation, each little bird communicated with the AH-1F they were
supporting, advising the attack aircraft on the enemy disposition.
Gradually, all the Dragonslayer little birds were replaced and
Dragonslayer attack helicopters were replaced on station by Archangel
birds. The Dragonslayers returned to the FARRP that had been
established to the southwest outside of Al Thamad.
****

Both No Mercy Six and Eagle Attack Six were prosecuting the
deep battle plan for the 2nd Brigade commander, Colonel Dean
Anderson. Colonel Anderson was an infantry officer, but in his younger
days he had also been an Army aviator before the aviation branch had
been formed. The 2nd Brigade had three infantry battalions of the
502nd Infantry Regiment, an artillery battalion, an engineer company
and an air-defense company. Reinforcing his brigade was a corps
engineer company and a battery of 155mm artillery that Corps had

provided. Arriving in sector, the engineers were put to use right away, placing obstacles across the road, where they could be covered by fires from the TOWs and Dragons. FASCAM minefields were planned as well, and they would be on call for the 155mm artillery to fire. Regardless of which avenue the Iraqi forces chose to come down, they were not going to have an easy time of it.

The 1st Battalion of the 502nd was positioned so Alpha Company would be the first to hit the Iraqi lead battalion on the left flank. The plan developed by LTC Jim Donald was to engage the lead battalion once it was in the kill zone, then hit them with artillery while his troops disengaged and moved to pickup zones. They'd be airlifted to their next position, which already had additional ammunition, and water pre-positioned behind Bravo and Charlie Companies.

Lieutenant Gentry was the scout platoon leader for the First Battalion, 502 Infantry. He was from Alabama and had probably learned to walk by following his father as he snuck through the woods, hunting out of season. Theirs was a poor family, and hunting was how his dad put meat on the table. Sharecroppers, as they were referred to, still existed in the Deep South, both black and white. Only difference today was that most of the land was owned by a billionaire living in Seattle that had never gotten his hands dirty in his life. He'd made a fortune in developing a computer software program and now was buying up any piece of land he could find. Of course he let the poorest work the land and he took the profits, paying them a pitiful wage.

"First Strike Six, Hunter Twenty-One, over," Lieutenant Gentry radioed.

"Hunter Twenty-One, First Strike Six India, over," answered the colonel's radio operator.

"First Strike Six India, it appears that lead elements were hit hard by the birds. The follow-on battalion is passing through to take the lead. Birds appear to be departing. Over," Lieutenant Gentry reported.

"Roger, Hunter Twenty-One, good copy. First Strike Six India out." Colonel Donald had been listening to the transmission. The scout platoon was screening along his left flank, ensuring that the Iraqi force didn't attempt to slip around to that side and play havoc with the pickup zone on that side of this defense. The worst thing that could happen was for the enemy to discover the pickup zone and hit it with artillery as the aircraft were withdrawing the soldiers.

A little over one thousand meters down the road, once it entered the rugged terrain, was an open area on the right side of the road. This was designated the first of several kill zones. The battalion had positioned the three rifle companies on the right flank in the rugged terrain and positioned its twenty TOW vehicles on the left flank. The plan was for the infantry companies to engage first with the Dragon weapon system, and when the enemy turned towards them, the TOW weapon systems would engage. The rifle companies were positioned a klick apart, so the first company would engage, then withdraw to their respective pickup zone and depart while the next company commenced engaging and so forth. The engagement range for the infantry and Dragon systems was six hundred meters downhill and for the TOW weapons a little over one thousand meters. This would be a short, violent engagement. Artillery would be called to cover the disengagement of the infantry, and the TOWs had a road that they could use to run parallel to the main highway. This route would take them to their next engagement area, which was just to the front of the 2nd Battalion, 502nd Infantry, which had a similar battle plan.

As the Iraqi column came together to move on the highway, its pace slowed. This was not the most ideal terrain for a mounted force to move through. They were gun-shy and had every right to be so.

"First Strike Six, Anvil Six, over," the Alpha Company commander called.

"Go ahead, Anvil Six," said Colonel Donald, who had taken the hand mike from his RTO. Donald was in his jump TOC, co-located with the TOW weapons. His main TOC was already located at his last defensive position, and the TAC CP was at the next defensive position.

"First Strike Six, lead elements are approaching EA Alpha," Anvil Six transmitted.

Each of the rifle companies had established company engagement areas within the battalion's overall engagement area. When Alpha Company reported the enemy in EA Alpha, all elements would know they would be engaging shortly. Anvil Six just had to sit and wait, looking over the ridge his company was occupying. In a low crouch, he went from position to position and offered words of encouragement and patience to his soldiers. Waiting is the hardest part of an engagement. Your mind begins to think too much. You wonder what it's going to be like. Is it going to be like a Hollywood movie or a nightmare? What is it going to feel like to kill someone or to be killed? The soldiers had been trained well to think that they were destroying metal machines moving down the road and not to think of the human cargo those machines were carrying. But, eventually, humans would empty from those destroyed and burning machines and then what? Each soldier was lost in their own thoughts as they watched the enemy armored vehicles move past them.

"First Strike Six, EA Alpha is occupied. Request permission to engage," the Alpha Company commander transmitted.

"Alpha Six, fire!"

Instantly twenty DRAGON missiles rained out of the rugged terrain on the right flank of the Iraqi column and nineteen vehicles exploded. The Iraqi force immediately turned towards the first and began engaging with the vehicle-mounted 14.5mm KPVT machine gun and the 7.62mm PKT machine guns. The 14.5mm KPVT was a heavy machine gun that chewed up those positions that it could find. As the vehicles turned to face their attacker, twenty TOW missiles leaped from their launchers and made the short flight to slam into the BTR-60s and other vehicles in the convoy. As those vehicles exploded, the Iraqi soldiers became confused about which way to fight. Some vehicles attempted to push forward to drive out of the kill zone, only to run into mines that had been placed across the road. As quickly as the attack had started with thirty-five vehicles burning, it stopped. The Iraqi soldiers breathed a sigh of relief as they looked at the carnage that surrounded them. Their relief was short-lived as artillery rounds, making the sound of freight trains, could be heard growing louder each second. The airbursts were devastating to anyone that wasn't in a vehicle or enjoying overhead cover, and there was none of that.

As the artillery suppressed the Iraqi forces in the kill zones, soldiers of Company A, 1st Battalion, 502nd Infantry, moved to preplanned pickup zones and began loading the UH-60 Black Hawk helicopters that would deposit them in their next fighting positions further south. This engagement was over for them for now as Bravo and Charlie Companies also had engagement zones to execute before the Iraqi forces would meet the 2nd Battalion, who had a similar battle plan. It was going to be a long day for the attacking Iraqi forces.

Chapter 30
Spiritual Needs

22 October 1990
Battleforce TOC
Al Muraba'a, Saudi Arabia

October in Saudi brings in cooler temperatures, so during the day it is very comfortable at ninety degrees. Nights are cooler in the sixties, but it feels colder. The sky remained clear, and green vegetation was evident where it had been lacking in the summer months. The men of the 3rd Battalion, 327th Infantry Regiment had remained in their positions around Al Muraba'a since the heavy fighting against the 7th Iraqi Division. Thankfully, the battalion had only lost a few soldiers, with another handful wounded and sent back to the rear. The biggest problem the battalion had after the fight was the burial of the dead Iraqi soldiers. Almost immediately after the last shot was fired, the battalion commander, Lieutenant Colonel Dan Cory, received a visit from the battalion chaplain.

"Sir, the chaplain is outside and needs to talk to you," the battalion executive officer, Major Bill David, said.

"Send him in," Cory said, turning his attention away from a map he had been studying in the battalion operations tent.

"Sir, he has a local with him," David said, looking around the TOC to indicate that it might be best not to have a non-US person seeing the maps and activities in the TOC.

"OK, let's see what they want. Do you know?" Cory asked, heading for the doorway.

"I best let him explain things to you," David said, not looking happy. Moving outside into the afternoon light, Cory had to take a moment to adjust his eyes even as he put his sunglasses on. Cory had a detached retina and bright light hurt most days. As he adjusted his eyes, he saw the battalion chaplain and an Arab, whom Cory quickly recognized as the imam from Al Muraba'a.

"Chaplain, what's up?" Cory asked as he walked up. Both the chaplain and the imam approached Cory. Placing his hand over his heart, the imam said, "*As-salamu alaikum.*"

Cory immediately answered, "*Wa alaikum as-salam,*" and shook the cleric's hand.

"Sir, the imam came and got me right after the fighting was over—"

"How did he know where to find you?" Cory asked, concerned as the chaplain could be a loose cannon at times with his "good deeds." Chaplain Sumbler had been an infantry officer in his early years but had left the military and become an ordained minister, although Cory couldn't figure out what denomination. The military recognized two hundred and forty different denominations, and Chaplain Sumbler was ordained in one. He'd attempted to explain it to Cory, but all he understood was that it wasn't one of the big six.

"Sir, I introduced myself to him when we moved into the area and told him where I'd be if he needed anything," the chaplain said. Cory and Major David exchanged looks and the message to Major David was clear if unspoken: *Get the chaplain under control.*

"OK, so what's the problem? I'm sure there's a problem," Cory said. Sumbler never came to him with solutions, only problems.

"Sir, in accordance with Muslim tradition, he wants to know when we're going to bury the dead Iraqi soldiers. First, we have to wash each body and then—"

"What the hell are you talking about? We ain't washing every dead Iraqi body out there. Are you nuts, Chaplain?" Cory looked at the chaplain and then at the imam. The interpreter that had accompanied the chaplain started to speak in Arabic when Major David cut him off.

"Sir, it's Muslim tradition that the dead should be washed and then immediately buried, preferably before the end of the day, with their hands folded in prayer on their right side and their head towards Mecca. I assured the cleric we would honor their traditions," Chaplain Sumbler said.

"You did what?" Cory asked, about to explode. "Chaplain, there are three, maybe four hundred dead Iraqi soldiers out there. We aren't washing one of them. If he wants them washed, he best get the locals to start scrubbing because I'm not having our soldiers do that. Look out there." Cory pointed to a tank ditch that had been dug before the fight due east of Al Muraba'a.

"Yes, sir," Sumbler said as he and the imam looked to see where Cory was pointing.

"Do you see those Iraqi prisoners that are being moved out of Al Muraba?" Cory asked.

"Yes, sir," Sumbler replied.

"Those prisoners are about to start gathering up the dead and tossing them in the tank ditch, which, when we have them all in there, will be covered up by a bulldozer as soon as I can get one here from Division. Now if you and the imam here want to wash everybody, then I suggest that you and he get the locals to start washing them as the prisoners drop them in the ditch. But not one drop of our bottled water is to be used. Do I make myself clear?" Cory said, attempting to maintain his composure. The imam still didn't understand what was being said, but he knew this wasn't going the way he had seen it unfolding.

"Sir, they have to be placed on their right side with their heads towards Mecca. It's the traditional way for a Muslim to be buried," Sumbler argued.

"Well, you're in luck, Chaplain, because that tank ditch runs east to west and Mecca is south of us. If you and the imam want each body on its right side with its head towards Mecca, then I suggest you and he get down there. In fact—no, that isn't right. You, Chaplain, are in charge of the Iraqi burial detail. You will report to Captain Mulford and take charge of the Iraqi prisoner detail. I will have Captain Mulford provide a security detail to you. You and the imam here will supervise the prisoners in placing each body in the ditch in accordance with the imam's instructions, but not one US soldier will touch one of those bodies. Do I make myself clear?" Cory said, slowly moving closer to the chaplain.

"Sir, I understand, but I really don't think I should be in charge of this. As the chaplain, I meet the spiritual needs of the soldiers, not take charge of details," Sumbler objected.

"Well, let me ask you something, Chaplain. If we were in the States, would you not meet the spiritual needs of our soldiers' families if a soldier died in a car accident?" Cory asked.

"Yes, sir."

"And aren't you in charge of our memorial service for our soldiers that were killed in this fight?"

"Yes, sir."

"And aren't burial services meeting the spiritual needs of the soldiers?"

"Yes, sir."

"And don't you meet the spiritual needs of all soldiers regardless of their denomination?" Cory needled.

"Yes, sir."

"And aren't you a commissioned officer in the United States Army, governed by the Uniform Code of Military Justice, which says you are to follow all lawful orders issued by your superiors?" Cory asked. Major David was attempting to hold back his laughter.

"Yes, sir."

"So you just answered your own question. You are meeting the spiritual needs of those Muslim soldiers by being in charge of the burial detail. God does not discriminate between our soldiers and the enemy. You need to have a little faith, Chaplain. I would suggest you get down there and take charge before they start tossing bodies in that ditch or else you're going to have to haul them out and start over. General Schwarzkopf said we would not win the war and lose the peace. I intend to support that position. I'm sure the imam and the locals will agree that we're keeping the peace by honoring the dead Iraqi Muslims. Thank you for bringing this to my attention, Chaplain. Is there anything else you need to discuss with me?"

At this point, Cory had a smile on his face. The imam was smiling as well, though he had no clue about what had been said. Chaplain Sumbler did not smile but saluted and left with the interpreter and the imam in tow.

As they watched the trio move off, Major David said with a grin, "Sir, Chaplain Sumbler does not look happy."

"Bill, in the future, Chaplain Sumbler will learn that if he has a problem he's bringing to me, he best have a solution as well. He'll learn," Cory said as he moved back into the TOC.

Chapter 31

Her Majesty's Support Arrives

24 October 1990
CENTCOM Forward HQ
Military Technological College
Muscat, Oman

"Sir, he's here," General Schwarzkopf's aide said, standing in the doorway.

"Good, show him in," Stormin' Norman said as he stood and moved around his desk. He was excited about meeting the man coming through the door. Sir Peter de la Billière, newly appointed commander, British forces, stopped five feet from General Schwarzkopf, came to attention and in stoic British fashion rendered a smart salute, palm out.

"General Schwarzkopf, British forces reporting for duty," he said. Schwarzkopf returned the salute and added a broad smile as well.

"And very glad to have you, sir," Schwarzkopf said, dropping his salute and extending his hand. Sir Peter de la Billière was a solid, very fit officer. He'd started his military career as a private in the Durham Light Infantry in 1952. In 1956 he'd been accepted into the Special Air Service or SAS and had over the course of his career seen combat action in Adan, Sudan and Malaysia. Now he commanded all British forces in support of Operation Desert Shield—and Storm, if it came to that. At this point General Schwarzkopf was almost convinced that the Storm was coming.

After they exchanged handshakes, General Schwarzkopf motioned for them to take a seat in two overstuffed chairs. As they conducted some initial small talk, the aide came in with a pot of coffee and served. Once the aide left the room and closed the door, Schwarzkopf revealed his feelings.

"Sir, I am truly glad to have the assistance of you and your government at this time. Truthfully, I do not expect Saddam to pull out peacefully. He has right now about twenty-seven divisions arrayed across Saudi Arabia and the UAE. His air force has been able to hold their own against ours, so we have air parity at this time. His air-defense systems are far superior to ours, an area that we've been remiss in the past and are paying for now. He has no naval forces outside of the Persian Gulf but has, along with Iran, managed to control the Strait with mines. We've found a way through as long as he doesn't change the minefield. Your forces are certainly most welcome," General Schwarzkopf stated.

"General, we are proud to serve as part of your coalition. My staff is waiting to give you a brief of what our capabilities are and what we're bringing to the fight. They have coordinated a presentation with your staff and are in the conference room to give that presentation at this time," Sir de la Billière said.

"Well General, let's not keep them waiting," Schwarzkopf said, standing and motion for Sir de la Billière to lead the way. Little was said as they moved down the hall to the conference room, which was full of officers from both nations. Already present were General Horner, USAF, General Yeosock, USA, General Boomer, USMC, and Rear Admiral Henrey Mauz, Jr., Commander US Persian Gulf Naval Forces, along with their primary operations officers.[8] On the other side

---

[8] Prior to Operation Desert Shield, no fleet number was assigned to those US naval forces operating in the Arabian Sea/Persian Gulf. Naval forces were under COMNAVCENT operating out of the US

of the table sat officers from Great Britain, to include Sir Michael James Graydon, Commander, Strike Command, and his deputy, Sir Kenneth William Hayr; Major General Rupert Smith, Commander, 1st Armoured Division; and Rear Admiral Roger Charles Lane-Nott, Royal Navy. As they entered, an American officer announced "Attention" and everyone stood.

"Sir de la Billière, this is your show, so sit here, please, at the head of the table," General Schwarzkopf said, motioning to the chair.

"Thank you, General," de la Billière replied, taking the chair. The briefing officer, a British brigadier general, was already standing behind the podium.

"Gentlemen, this briefing will focus on the British forces that will be participating in this operation. First slide, please," he asked. The slide appeared on the large screen in the front of the briefing room.

"Gentlemen, this slide shows the royal air assets that will be participating in this operation. Some are in-country at this time and some are inbound as I speak. There will be seventeen squadrons of Panavia Tornado fighters with each squadron having fifteen aircraft. The Panavia Tornado is a multipurpose role fighter and can employ the JP233 Runway Buster," he said before General Schwarzkopf interrupted him.

"Excuse me, General, but what is the JP233?" he asked.

"Sir, the JP233 is a runway-buster two-stage bomb consisting of two canisters. The HB876 is an antipersonnel canister with two hundred and fifteen mines, and the SG 357 concrete buster has thirty

---

Naval Support Facility in Bahrain. After the conflict, those naval forces became the 5th Fleet.

bomblets. These ignite first, rendering sizable craters in the runway, and then the HB876 ignites, causing problems for anyone who attempts to repair the runway. Nasty little things, sir."

"Thank you for explaining that, General," Schwarzkopf said. "Please continue."

"Yes, sir. There are three squadrons of SEPCAT Jaguars with twelve aircraft in each squadron. They are equipped with the Pave Spike laser designators to support Tornado strikes. Generally, we employ two SEPCAT aircraft with four Tornadoes in each strike package." The brigadier paused to see if a question was coming. When none did, he picked up the brief. "In addition, sir, we're bringing four squadrons of Hawker Siddeley Nimrods for maritime reconnaissance and one squadron of our Handley Page Victor heavy bombers," he stated.

"Excuse me," General Horner said, "but what's the payload of conventional weapons on the Handley Victor?"

"Sir, they're capable of carrying thirty-six one-thousand-pound bombs," the brigadier said.

"Thank you," Horner replied, making a note on his notepad.

"Are there any other questions about our air package?" the brigadier asked. After a moment and no questions, "I will now cover naval assets at sea at this time. Next slide, please." Unlike the air asset slide, this slide had a "to be continued" note at the bottom. Turning to Schwarzkopf, the brigadier was pleased to see the look on the general's face.

HER MAJESTY'S COMMONWEALTH FORCES

NAVAL

Aircraft Carrier	Frigates	Destroyers
HMS Ark Royal	HMS Jupiter	HMS Cardiff
	HMS Battleaxe	HMS Exeter
	HMS Brazen	HMS Manchester
	HMS Sheffield	HMS Gloucester
	HMS London	HMS York

Command Ships	Mine Countermine	Submarines
HMS Herald	HMS Ledbury	HMS Opossum
HMS Hecla	HMS Cattistock	HMS Otus
	HMS Dulverton	
	HMS Bicester	
	HMS Atherstone	
	HMS Hurworth	

ROYAL FLEET AUXILIARY

RFA Argus	RFA Regent	RFA Olna
RFA Orangeleaf	RFA Sir Bedivere	HMS Exeter
RFA Sir Percivale	RFA Sir Tristram	

"Sir," the brigadier explained, "you will note that we are bringing a sizable force. Her Majesty's ship *Ark Royal* has a full complement of Harrier jets along with Westland Lynx helicopters. The Westland Lynx helicopters are capable of supporting both land and naval operations. I know you're especially keen on our mine countermeasure vessels, of which we are bringing six. HMS *Dulverton* and HMS *Bicester* are the oldest vessels, and HMS *Atherstone* and HMS *Hurworth* are the newest, both having been commissioned in the 1980s." Again, he paused for questions and comments.

Turning to Sir de la Billière, General Schwarzkopf said, "Sir, when the time comes, we're going to be relying heavily on your minesweepers. This is one area that our Navy has overlooked for far too long. We are in serious need of upgrades."

"You will get no argument from me on that point, General," Admiral Mauz said with a smile.

"Continue, sir," Schwarzkopf directed.

"Sir, lastly, I would like to highlight the two Oberon-class submarines. They will be in support of SAS operations in the area. These are older diesel boats. They've been modified to support the SAS in their over-the-beach operations. This concludes my discussion of naval assets, sir. What are your questions?"

"I see you've brought support ships on your slide, sir. I thank you for bringing support ships to cover your fleet," Schwarzkopf said. "Supplying our own fleet was going to be a problem, and this will make it much easier on us."

"Sir, RFA *Argus* is a primary care or hospital ship, as I believe you refer to them. RFA *Diligence* is a ship repair vessel serving the fleet. RFA *Fort Grand* is a fleet replenishment ship. RFA *Regent* is an ammunition resupply ship. RFA *Olna* is a fleet tanker—"

Interrupting the brigadier, Schwarzkopf said, "OK, I got the picture. You've covered the bases quite well. I rest assured that you can support your fleet. What's next?"

"Sir, with your permission, I would like to cover the ground forces," the brigadier said.

"Please do," Schwarzkopf said.

"Next slide, if you please." Quickly the slide came on the screen, replacing the slide with the British support ships.

1ST (BRITISH) ARMOURED DIVISION

7TH ARMOURED BRIGADE HQ & SIGNAL SQUADRON (207)

Royal Scots Dragoon Guards (Carabiniers and Greys)	A Squadron, 1st The Queen's Dragoon Guards	40 Field Regiment, Royal Artillery
Queen's Royal Irish Hussars	1st Battalion, The Staffordshire Prince of Wales Regiment	21 Engineer Regiment, Royal Engineers

4TH ARMOURED BRIGADE

4th Armoured Brigade HQ and Signal Squadron (204)	1st Battalion, The Royal Scouts (The Royal Regiment)	40 Field Regiment, Royal Artillery
14th/20th King's Hussars; Royal Regiment of Fusiliers	3rd Battalion, Royal Regiment of Fuiliers	23 Engineer Regiment, Royal Engineers

DIVISIONAL TROOPS

16th/5th The Queen's Royal Lancers	26 Heavy Regiment, Royal Artillery	32 Armoured Engineer Regiment, Royal Engineers
4 Regiment Army Air Corps	26 Heavy Regiment, Royal Artillery	39 Engineers Regiment, Royal Engineers
26 Field Regiment, Royal Artillery	12 Air Defence Regiment, Royal Artillery	

"Sir, we're bringing the 1st Armoured Division with these units. The 7th Armoured Brigade has two armored battalions, the Royal Scots

Dragoon Guards and the Queens Royal Irish Hussars, each with fifty-seven Challenger tanks. Also, there is an infantry battalion, the Royal Staffordshire Regiment, and a reconnaissance squadron, A Squadron, 1st The Queen's Dragoon Guards." The brigadier stopped to take a drink of water, though the pause was really more in anticipation of the possibility of a question. When no questions were asked, he continued, "The 4th Armoured Brigade has one armored battalion of Centurion tanks and two infantry battalions. Divisional troops have one regiment of reconnaissance forces, the 16th/5th The Queen's Royal Lancers, and three artillery battalions. The 4th Regiment Army Air Corps has a combination of Gazelle and Lynx helicopters for antitank, reconnaissance and courier duties. What are your questions, sir, about the 1st Armoured Division?"

"Covered it very well, Brigadier. I have no questions," Schwarzkopf said.

"If you have no questions, sir, next slide," the brigadier called, pausing to allow the audience to study the slide.

HER MAJESTY'S
SUPPORTING UNITS

1 Armoured Division Signal Regiment	23 Parachute Field Ambulance
30 Signal Regiment	24 Airmobile Field Ambulance
2 Squadron 14 Signal Regiment (Electronic Warfare)	32 Field Hospital
1st Battalion Scots Guards	33 General Hospital
1st Battalion Coldstream Guards	60 Field Psychiatric Team
1st Battalion Royal Highland Fusiliers	205 General Hospital
One other infantry battalion	3 Ordnance Battalion Royal Army Ordnance Corps
Elements of 1st Battalion Queen's Own Highlanders	6 Ordnance Battalion RAOC
1 Armoured Division Transport Regiment Royal Corps of Transport	6 Armoured Workshop Royal Electrical and Mechanical Engineers
4 Armoured Division Transport Regiment Royal Corps of Transport	7 Armoured Workshop Royal Electrical and Mechanical Engineers
7 Tank Transporter Regiment Royal Corps of Transport	11 Armoured Workshop Royal Electrical and Mechanical Engineers
10 Regiment Royal Corps of Transport	71 Aircraft Workshop Royal Electrical and Mechanical Engineers
27 Regiment Royal Corps of Transport	174 Provost Company Royal Military Police
28 Ambulance Squadron Gurkha Transport Regiment	203 Provost Company Royal Military Police
52 Port Squadron Royal Corps of Transport	27 Group Royal Pioneer Corps
1 Armoured Field Ambulance	187 Company Royal Pioneer Corps
5 Armoured Field Ambulance	598 Company Royal Pioneer Corps
22 Field Hospital	

"Sir, these units will provide supply and services, transportation, medical support and engineer work in the rear areas. They will be the first units arriving to prepare the bases for the 1st Armoured Division when it arrives. The first unit, 52nd Port Squadron Royal Corps of Transport, should be arriving tomorrow by air along with the 174th

Provost Company Royal Military Police, and the ships are one week away. Sir, this concludes the briefing if you have any questions."

Schwarzkopf, always the gentleman with foreign officers, congratulated the brigadier on a fine presentation. He had known most of the information already but felt this would be an opportunity for those American officers seated in the gallery to learn about their British counterparts.

Standing, Schwarzkopf said, "Gentlemen, let's all move to the officers' mess for lunch." No one complained about the quality of the food that was awaiting them, and all moved quickly out of the room.

Chapter 32

Strike Brigade

24 October 1990
2nd Brigade Engagement Area
Al Majrdeh, Saudi Arabia

This fight had been going on for two days now. Everyone was tired. The Iraqis weren't pushing hard, almost fearful of leaving an engagement area once the fight there was over since they knew that another engagement area was waiting just ahead. Colonel Anderson sat in his vehicle and monitored the radios on the brigade command net. He had a second radio that he could use to monitor the communications of any single battalion as well, so he had a good mental picture of what each battalion was experiencing without having to nag the battalion commander for a sitrep. As he listened, it appeared that Alpha Company of the 1st Battalion was in the pickup zone and ready to be extracted. It would take one extraction of ten Black Hawk helicopters to get the entire company of infantry soldiers out of the pickup zone and in the new position. This was only half of the total Black Hawk fleet working for him. While aircraft were extracting Alpha Company, ten more aircraft were standing by to extract Bravo Company, who was about to engage the Iraqi forces. The 4th of the 101st Aviation Brigade would have to do. An hour later, the last of 1st Battalion was being extracted, having hit the Iraqi column two more times.

"First Strike Six, Strike Force Six, over," Colonel Anderson heard over the radio. The 2nd Battalion commander was calling the 1st Battalion commander.

"Strike Force Six, First Strike Six, go ahead."

"First Strike, passage of lines is complete. I have it now. Over."

"Roger, Strike Force Six, good hunting. First Strike out."

Colonel Anderson smiled to himself. The 1st Battalion had successfully handed the battle off to the 2nd Battalion, who had his own engagement areas established. These were delaying positions designed to engage and wear the enemy down. The main defense for the sector would be between Al Eshash and Al Majrdeh, a distance of nine kilometers, where the attack helicopters from the two attack battalions would concentrate their fire. The infantry battalion's final defensive positions were ten kilometers to the south in the vicinity of Ghamrah, where the mountainous terrain began again. The kill zone was ten by ten kilometers, flat, with few places for a vehicle to hide.

"Strike Six, Strike Force Six over," the 2nd Battalion commander, Lieutenant Colonel Chessley, radioed.

"Strike Force Six, go ahead," Colonel Anderson responded.

"Strike Six, we're commencing our engagement on his lead air-defense systems. It appears he's pushing them out to the front and flanks. Scratch two Zulu Sierra Uniform Two-Three-Four. Over"

"Strike Force Six, that's whittling them down to size. Strike Six out."

****

MG Daler Zogby, commander of the 51st Infantry Division, was facing his worst nightmare. Ever since the division had left Al Jadid it had been hounded by the American attack helicopters. American A-10 close-air support aircraft had also strafed and bombed his lead regiments. The air defense was able to keep most of the close-air support aircraft at bay, but some of the damn helicopters were operating outside the range of his air-defense weapons.

He turned to his operations officer and screamed, "Get me Colonel Aziz, now!" A few minutes later, Colonel Aziz, the air-defense commander, arrived with a Russian advisor, Major Adam Smirnov.

"Tell me, Colonel, why can't you keep the American attack helicopters off my vehicles?" Zogby asked in a less-than-pleasant tone.

"Sir, the American attack helicopter has a superior range over our air-defense systems. He can fire his missiles from eight kilometers away, and the range of our air-defense missile is four kilometers," Colonel Aziz said, pleading his case.

"Are you telling me that the SA-6 missiles do not have a range to reach the American attack helicopters?" General Zogby questioned.

"Sir, the SA-6 missiles are all located about the corps headquarters and supply depot as well as the tank park. They have the range, but these helicopters are flying below an acquisition height. The SA-6 cannot track them," Colonel Aziz stated.

"Well, we have to come up with something because they are destroying our regiments," General Zogby complained.

"General, may I make a suggestion?" Major Smirnov asked.

"Please do, Major," Zogby encouraged him.

"Sir, currently the ZSU-23-4 in each regiment are traveling two hundred meters apart and about four hundred meters behind the lead elements of the regiment. They are ineffective as the Americans are outside the range of their weapons system. Same for the SA-9 missile systems. What if we pushed them forward with the reconnaissance elements instead of holding them back to cover the main body? At worst they would be just as ineffective, and at best we may be able to provide better coverage as we move into the mountains, where the range advantage for the American attack helicopters will be greatly reduced," Major Smirnov recommended.

General Zogby thought about this proposal for a minute and finally said, "Do it. And, Colonel, you will be leading your weapons with the recon elements. We have got to get the American helicopters stopped." Major Smirnov thought Colonel Aziz looked a little pale when they left General Zogby.

****

Colonel Anderson positioned his tactical command post to the west of Ghamrah on a high mountaintop, which gave him clear visibility of the entire engagement area. To the north he could observe the forward progress of the 51st Iraqi Division not by seeing vehicle movement through the passes but by the rising columns of black smoke from burning vehicles. *The Division commander must be more afraid of Saddam than us to continue to attack through this ground with our attack helicopters pounding him*, Anderson thought.

"Strike Six, No Mercy Six, over."

Picking up the hand mike from his radio operator, Anderson replied, "No Mercy Six, Strike Six, over."

"Strike Six, No Mercy elements are on standby just waiting for your call."

"No Mercy Six, roger." Anderson had assigned the western side of the engagement area to No Mercy elements and the eastern side to Eagle Attack. Eagle Attack had already reported in that their elements were just waiting for the order to attack. Scout aircraft from both units were shadowing the progress of the two regiments or what was left of three regiments moving south. It appeared to the scout pilots that the regiments of the 51st had been so badly mauled that they had become intermingled into a steady stream of traffic moving south with no real combat formation. They were a bit surprised to see the air-defense weapons in the lead as well.

"Strike Six, No Mercy Six, over."

"Go ahead, No Mercy Six," Anderson said.

"Strike Six, little birds are reporting that on coming forces are leading with Alpha Delta Alpha systems. Over."

Anderson and his operations officer, Major Hurbert, exchanged looks. "What do you think, sir?" the major asked.

"I think the attack aircraft have eaten their lunch so bad that they've moved the ADA forward to attempt to keep the attack aircraft off their backs. I'll bet he has almost no ADA to his rear," Anderson said as he grabbed the hand mike.

"Eagle Attack Six, Strike Six, over."

"Strike Six, Eagle Attack Six."

"Eagle Attack, do you have eyes on the enemy formations?"

"Affirmative, Strike Six."

"Roger, where are you seeing his ADA? Over."

"Strike Six, it appears that his ADA is leading and on the flanks over."

"Roger, understood. Stand by. Break, break. No Mercy Six, Strike Six."

No Mercy Six, Lieutenant Colonel Dick Cody, was sitting on the ground with his flight of twenty-one AH-64 Apache helicopters in a wadi ten kilometers from the engagement area.

"Strike Six, No Mercy Six, over."

"No Mercy Six, Eagle Attack Six, I want you to engage the rear of the formation. Do not engage the ADA weapons but leave those for the Strike elements to engage. Engage the follow-on forces and let the Strike elements take out the ADA vehicles. How copy?"

"Strike Six, No Mercy Six, I have a good copy."

"Strike Six, Eagle Attack Six, roger, I like this." Eagle Attack had the AH-1F Cobra helicopters with the TOW weapons system and thus the shorter range versus the Hellfire system on the AH-64 Apache aircraft.

Anderson continued to watch the forward elements of the oncoming force proceed into the engagement area. He could see the lead elements from his observation position but not the follow-on forces because of the dust from the lead elements. Patience was needed at this point. The planning was done, the troops had been briefed and knew what had to be done. Now it was a matter of waiting while the enemy came forward. Waiting and watching was one of the hardest things in a battle.

****

Captain Hilliard commanded Company A, 3rd of the 502 Infantry Regiment. He was a graduate of Austin Peay University and commissioned through the ROTC program. He was a prior service soldier, having spent two years enlisted working up to corporal before he was accepted into the Green to Gold program. His whole time in the Army, aside from schools, was with the 101st Airborne Division. He considered it his home. His soldiers loved him as he had walked in their shoes as an enlisted soldier and now did it again as an officer.

His company had been occupying a position on the forward edge of Ghamrah. His company frontage was about one thousand meters across. He knew the enemy would be coming right at him, so he had made sure his soldiers were in the best defensive positions they could construct. Buildings were reinforced with sandbags. Claymore mines were positioned where there was a building overhang or a likely approach to a building or position. Stairwells were booby-trapped and wire strung down the stairs. Sectors of fire and range markers were designated and emplaced. From his position, he could see dust clouds approaching, but no vehicles as yet. He prayed that the TOW weapons systems of the battalion would take out the tanks before they reached his position. He understood his priority of fires for the Dragons was air-defense systems first, BTR-80 vehicles second. His biggest fear at the moment was the enemy artillery, which he had no chance of engaging and trusted that someone above his pay grade was wired in to take care of that threat.

"Gator Six, Rabbit One, over," the 1st Platoon leader was calling.

"Rabbit One, Gator Six, go," Captain Hilliard responded.

"Gator Six, my OP1 reports vehicles to his front. Reports two Zulu Sierra Uniforms Two-Three approaching TRP Three. Over."

"Rabbit One, roger. Contact Thunder One and engage," Captain Hilliard directed. Turning to his fire support officer, he said, "Bob, we have vehicles approaching TRP Three. Rabbit is calling the mortar platoon. Can we get some arty on that point too?"

"I'm on it, sir," his FSO said and began making a request of fire. As the TRPs had all been passed to the artillery battery already, it didn't take long to bring the guns to bear. In the distance to their rear, they could clearly hear five 105mm howitzers fire, followed by what sounded like a freight train passing overhead. The forward observer with Rabbit was adjusting the fire and on the second volley called for fire for effect. The effect was devastation as both ZSU-23-4 air-defense guns were hit.

****

Colonel Anderson watched as the two anti-aircraft vehicles were destroyed. At this point he was concerned about the enemy's artillery, which consisted of some excellent guns from South Africa and the Soviet Union. The most worrisome piece was the Al Fao artillery that had originally been designed in South Africa. It had a range of thirty-five miles and fired a 210mm projectile, slightly larger than the US eight-inch self-propelled artillery found at the corps levels. Thankfully, its rate of fire was low at two rounds per minute. He wanted to find the artillery and destroy it quickly. One of the missions for the Cav squadron was to find the artillery and direct tac air on their positions.

His other concern was the size of the advancing force. His brigade of light infantry was facing a division of motorized infantry. In theory, the attacking force must have a three-to-one advantage over the defender. Anderson's brigade was facing three-to-one odds and a motorized enemy at that. However, the weight of the two attack helicopter battalions and the cavalry squadron tipped the balance back to a more level field. He also had the advantage of conducting a delay through very difficult terrain for the motorized force. If he could just keep the attacking artillery off his positions, he felt they could hold.

"Sabre Six, Strike Six, over."

"Strike Six, Sabre Six, over."

"Sabre Six, I need you to concentrate on going deep and find his artillery. Once you do, hit it with whatever you have—artillery, air strikes, your gunships. We have to knock it out. How copy? Over."

"Strike Six, Sabre Six, good copy. Going deep now." With that, Sabre Six began contacting his three troops of seven attack helicopters and three little birds. Each troop had the AH-1F Cobra gunship and OH-58 light observation aircraft.

"All Sabre elements, Sabre Six, over."

"Annihilators Six, over."

"Head Hunters Six, over."

"Condor Six, over."

"This is Sabre Six. We are looking for his artillery locations. Once you find them, report and adjust artillery or request air strikes. Annihilators, I want you to screen the east side of the engagement area. Head Hunters, screen the west side. Condors remain in rearm-refuel and be prepared to relieve either Annihilators or Head Hunters. Any questions? Over."

"Annihilators, good copy on the go."

"Head Hunters understand and wilco."

"Condors are standing by."

"Sabre Six, good hunting, out."

Colonel Anderson had monitored the communications between Sabre Six and his troops and felt some relief knowing that there was an active search underway to find the enemy artillery. Now the question was whether the Cav would find that artillery before it began pounding the infantry positions.

****

MG Zogby could not take it any longer following behind his regiments and ordered his staff car to take him to the lead regiment. As they drove south, the carnage inflicted on his regiments was obvious as the driver was driving around and bypassing burning vehicles. When they reached the mountain passes, the driver had to slow to a crawl to avoid the damaged vehicles blocking the road. Finally, he reached the rear of the trailing regiment and called for it to halt while he spoke to the regimental commander.

317

Getting out of his staff car, a BTR-80 command vehicle, he exchanged salutes with Colonel Maloof, a young officer and a very good one. However, he was not a Muslim but a Christian and not considered an Iraqi as his family was from Syria, though he had been born just across the border in Iraq. If it hadn't been for these facts, he probably would have been in the Republican Guard divisions or been a general in the Iraqi Army.

"Colonel, what is the status of your regiment?" Zogby demanded.

"Sir, I am eighty percent strength in vehicles and men. My concern is for the lack of air defense around us. The American attack helicopters have done most of the damage. I am also running low on fuel," Colonel Maloof said.

"Have you not been resupplied with fuel?" Zogby asked.

"Oh, we topped off before the attack started, but our fuel resupply trucks are fifty kilometers behind us and reporting the road is clogged with wrecked vehicles. We can continue, but I like to anticipate problems, and fuel will be a problem if they don't get the road cleared," Colonel Maloof explained.

"That is not your problem, Colonel. That is behind you. You should be concerned with what is before you."

"What is in front of me, General, is more wreckage from the 1st Regiment and the lack of fuel in the future," Maloof knew he was pressing his luck antagonizing Zogby.

"Colonel, move the wreckage out of your way and keep moving. I want all three regiments together when we get to the open wadi. Now move it!"

Zogby stormed off and climbed back into his vehicle. *That damn Maloof is so damn smart, and he is right. If we don't get this mess cleaned up and push the fuel forward, we will die on the vine.* As his driver worked his way around wrecked vehicles, they finally caught up to the trail-end elements of the 1st Regiment, the lead regiment on the right flank. He decided to just follow and let the regimental commander do his thing without interfering.

Eventually, all forward movement stopped and Zogby decided to move forward and see what was happening. He found himself entering a wide-open wadi. To the left he could see a cluster of vehicles that appeared to be command vehicles, and he directed his driver over to them. As he approached, he recognized that both the 1st and 2nd regimental commanders were together, overlooking a map. *What now?* he thought as he stepped out of this vehicle and approached the group of officers. No one noticed his approach, so he stood back and observed.

"I'm telling you we must keep the ADA weapons on the flanks," Major Smirnov was attempting to explain. "The American attack helicopters will continue to use the cover of the ridgelines to engage with their TOW and Hellfire missiles. If we move the ADA systems to the center or behind the regiments, they cannot adequately cover the front or flanks," Smirnov said with some frustration.

"I understand what you are saying, Major, but in this open ground, the American close-air support aircraft is the biggest threat now and they will attack the center of our formations. We need concentrated firepower and not dispersed coverage," the 1st Regiment commander, Brigadier General Jawad, argued.

Brigadier General Hashem, the 2nd Regiment commander, nodded in agreement and added, "Colonel Aziz, let's move the ADA systems back into the formations."

Aziz didn't know what to do at this point. He just knew it was his neck on the line. "Gentlemen, I think—"

"I think we should do what Colonel Aziz and Major Smirnov have recommended, gentlemen," Major General Zogby interrupted. The others turned and immediately came to attention and saluted.

General Jawad spoke first. "General, we were just discussing the protection offered by the Air Defense force."

"I know what you were discussing, General, and about to direct. Are you also taking responsibility for the results if your decision and orders are carried out by Colonel Aziz?" Jawad did not answer. "I didn't think so. We will continue with the employment of our air-defense weapons in the manner prescribed by Colonel Aziz and Major Smirnov. What is the status of your regiments?" he asked first, looking at General Jawad, although he had a fair idea based on the wreckage he had just driven past.

"Sir, I believe I am at seventy percent strength," Jawad answered.

"Really!" Zogby said. "I counted your vehicles as I drove here and by my count I would be surprised if you were at fifty percent strength. You best contact your battalion commanders and get an accurate count." He turned to General Hashem. "And your strength?"

"Sir, I am at sixty percent at this time," Hashem said with some embarrassment.

"Well, at least Colonel Maloof has a good understanding of his strength and is ready to assume the lead. You will continue the attack and I will follow. At some point, you will turn out and hold the shoulders and Colonel Maloof with the 3rd Regiment will continue the attack and penetrate the enemy's defense. Now can we resume this attack and stop standing here with our thumbs up our asses?"

Like a covey of flushed quail, the commanders grabbed their maps and returned to their vehicles, moving to position themselves in their respective regiments. They had fairly open, flat terrain to their front for about twenty-one kilometers before they would be forced into the rugged passes again. The lead two regiments stepped off together and 3rd Regiment fell in behind the 1st Regiment on the right flank.

******

"Sabre Six, Head Hunter Six, over."

"Head Hunter Six, Sabre Six."

"Sabre Six, sitrep. One battery of Al Fao artillery located at…" Head Hunter Six provided the grid coordinates. They were outside the range for the division or corps artillery. Sabre Six knew that if one battery was discovered, two other batteries would not be far removed.

"Roger, Head Hunter, continue to observe. If you have one, the others are close by. Continue with mission but keep eyes on the one. We are requesting tac air."

"Roger, Sabre Six."

Anderson heard the conversation and picked up the hand mike. "Sabre Six, Strike Six, over."

"Strike Six, Sabre Six, over."

"Sabre Six, I monitored and we are requesting tac air. We will pass them to you and Head Hunter when they're on station. Over."

"Roger, Strike Six, understood."

Major Berry, USAF, in charge of the 2nd Brigade Tactical Air Control Party, was already sending the request up the chain to get some fast-mover aircraft on this target. He didn't care if it was A-10s or F-15s. At this point he would be happy if it was a Vietnam-era Skyraider, just something to bomb this target.

Anderson continued to monitor the radios and observe the dust cloud approaching from the north. Scout teams from the infantry battalions were positioned along the hills surrounding the wadi and gave constant updates on the forward progress of the opposing force as it moved south down the wadi. From his position to the first phase line was ten thousand meters. He would wait until the advance guard was three thousand meters before he would fire his artillery and commit the attack helicopters. The first to receive artillery fire would be those lead elements and it would be airburst artillery, stripping away antennas and killing anyone outside the vehicles. Then the ground TOWs would open fire and destroy the ADA systems and any vehicles moving forward. At one thousand meters, the Dragon systems would open fire as well, as would machine guns with the rifle companies. The division had just received the Mark 19 automatic grenade launcher, which was mounted on a tripod. It was very effective against troops in the open and added considerable weight to the supporting M-60 machine guns, especially with a range of over two thousand meters and a sustained rate of fire of three hundred and fifty grenades per minute.

Simultaneously, he would release the attack helicopter battalions against the follow-on regiment, which he believed was the strongest regiment. He hoped that tac air would be available to engage the first two regiments. The destruction of vehicles was the paramount concern. He was confident that his infantry soldiers could hold their own if they didn't have to contend with tanks or heavy vehicles, and that was the priority for the attack helicopters.

"Strike Six, Sabre Six."

"Go ahead, Sabre Six."

"Strike Six, we have his artillery positions. Coordinating with Tac Air now."

"Roger, keep me posted."

Looking at Colonel Anderson, Major Berry said, "Sir, I have three flights of F-15 and two flights of A-10s. The FAC is talking to Sabre and had identified the artillery positions."

"Good, taking out his artillery is first priority. Then go after the main body in the wadi," Anderson said, a bit more relieved and confident.

****

Captain Hilliard was on a rooftop observing the dust cloud approaching. He could now observe what was creating it. Two ZSU-23-4 vehicles and six BTR-60 scout vehicles were approaching his position. He had four of the battalion's TOW vehicles in his company area, but they worked for the battalion commander and were not under his control. He had coordinated with them for sectors of fire and agreed on priority of fires. His Dragons, on the other hand, were his, and he had directed them as well on priority of fires and sectors. Now it was a matter of waiting for the artillery to hit, which would signal the start of the engagement. The first artillery, however, was not outgoing but incoming.

The Al Fao artillery rounds passed over Hilliard's positions. As they exploded on impact, the ground shook and dust rose in columns, but each round overshot his positions, for which he was thankful. It appeared that they might be shooting counterbattery fire, attempting to take out the brigade's artillery before the brigade could fire.

The next sounds he heard were explosions and the rounds passing over his head, but this time they were outgoing and the sky to his front was suddenly filled with black puffs as the rounds exploded at one hundred feet above the advancing troops. Seconds later, ground TOW weapons opened from twenty different locations, impacting on direct-fire air-defense vehicles first and SA-9 missile vehicles second. The ZSU-23-4 could be used in a ground defensive role and the soldiers wanted to kill them quick. A couple of vehicles survived the initial onslaught of TOWs and came to a halt—for what reason was anyone's guess, but stopping was the wrong thing to do. Ten seconds later, those vehicles were destroyed as well. Hilliard was glad that none of his positions had to fire yet. He didn't want to give away his unit's location or expend ammo unnecessarily.

As things quieted down, Hilliard knew that the main body would be coming on soon. The dust clouds representing the bulk of the enemy force were still approaching. From the hillsides, he saw fleeting flashes of light as attack helicopters engaged the approaching force. In the dust he couldn't tell what they were shooting at or hitting, but columns of black smoke mixed with the dust clouds. The freight train sound of the artillery had commenced again, sending steel rain to fall amongst the enemy.

However, it was drowned out by a sound of what sounded like fabric being ripped. It came in short bursts, three to five seconds in length, almost like a *brrrr* sound that unnerved everyone that heard it. Then he saw the source of this terrifying noise. A pair of Air Force A-10 aircraft passed over his location, firing their GAU-8 Avenger 30mm Gatling guns. The effect was almost instantaneous as approaching vehicles were riddled with hundreds of depleted-uranium rounds that tore right through their armor. What surprised Hilliard more was the fact that no anti-aircraft fire was engaging the aircraft. From where he sat, the air-defense systems had been destroyed, but surely there must be more in the formation. Then again, maybe they'd gotten lucky.

****

MG Zogby directed his driver to place their vehicle in a low depression and stop. Naturally, when he came to a halt, the vehicles of his staff and advisors stopped. This included Colonel Aziz's vehicle.

In a low crouch, Aziz ran to Zogby's vehicle.

"Aziz, where the hell are your air-defense systems? The Americans are pounding the lead regiments," Zogby screamed.

"Sir, the ADA systems have been destroyed. They were taken out on the first salvo by those damned Americans. Only the 3rd Regiment has any air-defense weapons systems left," Aziz pointed out as an A-10 Warthog passed over his position and everyone dove for cover. This particular A-10 hadn't fired.

"Major Smirnov, what do you recommend at this point?" Zogby asked his Russian advisor.

Smirnov had been following Aziz and suspected that this was going to happen. They just didn't have enough air-defense weapons for the size of the American helicopter force in this area.

"Sir, at this point, with the losses that we have sustained in ADA trucks, I would recommend we withdraw into the mountains and encircle ourselves with the ADA systems the 3rd Regiment has. That or we get higher headquarters to send us a lot of air support to keep these American aircraft off our backs. If we continue the attack without proper air defense, those helicopters and now those A-10s will shred us to pieces."

As Zogby discussed the situation with his staff, they hadn't caught sight of the TV-guided Maverick missile coming right at them. Finally, they all heard the rocket motor sound and looked up. The looks on their faces were recorded just as the bomb exploded.

Chapter 33

REFORGER in Reverse

2 November 1990
US VII Corps HQ
Kelly Barracks
Stuttgart, Germany

It was getting cold at Kelly Barracks in Stuttgart, Germany. Winter was approaching on this November day. Sitting in the basement of one of the buildings was a small staff that had been planning movements and operations for the VII US Corps, commanded by Lieutenant General Frederick Franks Jr. since the last week in October. General Franks was a gentleman in every sense of the word. He was not a big man, standing just five foot seven, with gray hair and a gray mustache to match. He was a quiet man, an intelligent man, not full of a lot of bravado like some general officers, but he was a warrior. He had lost part of one leg in Vietnam but still managed to get around pretty well, and most people didn't notice he was missing a leg.

"Gentlemen, the decisions have been made on who is deploying to Southwest Asia," General Franks said. "The units that General Saint and I have chosen are the 1st Armored Division and the 3rd Armored Division. 2nd Brigade Forward will deploy as well and be attached to the 1st Infantry Division when it arrives in-country. The 2nd Armored Cavalry Regiment will deploy, and two infantry battalions from the 8th Infantry division. We're going to need a large support package, so the 2nd Corps Support Command will deploy early. They're going to be supplemented by one hundred and sixty-six National Guard and reserve units when they arrive in-country to make up for the host nation support we enjoy here, which will not be going to the Middle East. Any questions?" Franks asked, to the shock of his officers.

"Sir, when are we looking at for deployments to commence?" asked the G-4 logistics officer. He hadn't been included in the initial planning cell.

"Deployments will commence on 12 November and a deployment cell will be run by BG Daniel. The order of deployment will be 2nd Armored Cav Regiment followed by Corps headquarters, 2nd COSCOM, 1st Armored Division, 3rd Armored Division and lastly 2nd Armored Brigade. The 3rd Infantry Division will run port support activities at Antwerp, Bremerhaven and Rotterdam," General Franks said. "General Daniel will now cover some other details with you. General Daniel," he said as he turned the meeting over to his deputy commander.

"OK, we have a busy time ahead of us. Some of you will enjoy part of the holidays with your families, but I can assure you not all the holidays. We have ninety days to get everything in-country and operational. We have to move quickly. The CENTCOM commander would like to initiate combat operations during the winter months, which in their AOR is the best time of year to wage a war. It becomes unbearable during the summer months. Best as I have determined, we'll be moving some forty-nine thousand vehicles," he said, and immediately notes were being scratched out on pads.

"And we have seventy-three thousand soldiers to fly over, which is going to take four hundred and thirty-five aircraft." Transportation officers were writing notes as quickly as possible. "This is all going to have to be coordinated with the host nations of Germany and the Netherlands, so get to it," he said. "By 1300 tomorrow, I want an outline of what we're going to be requesting to move this much stuff and this many people. I suspect we're going to need convoy clearances, rail priority, and barges if necessary. The units are receiving their warning orders at this time and will receive the deployment notices tonight around 1800 hours. Any questions?" There were none, as the staff needed to start crunching numbers and fast. "This is going to require a lot of coordination. I'll see you all tomorrow," General Daniel said, dismissing everyone.

****

The next day at 1300, the staff was assembled. New additions to the staff included officers from the German Department of Transportation, officials from the Netherlands and the German police. All were going to be playing a major role in the movement of so many people and equipment. Members of each of the units were present as well as members from the 3rd Infantry Division. They weren't happy about being left out of the deployment. Brigadier General Daniel got things started promptly at 1300.

"Gentlemen, if you find a seat, we'll get this going," he said, looking over the audience. "First off, I want to thank members from the host nations for joining us and helping us pull off this deployment as painlessly as possible for your people as well as ours. Without your assistance, this would not be possible. We have all participated in REFORGER exercises. Think of this as a really big REFORGER exercise in reverse. I will be followed by the G-4."

"Sir, we're looking at a sizable movement operation," the G-4 said, "and I've asked representatives from the Department of Transportation of Germany and the Netherlands as well as the German police. We're going to need their assistance to pull this off. Right now, sir, we're looking at four hundred and sixty-five train cars, one hundred and nineteen convoys, and three hundred and twelve barges moving equipment. We will require four hundred and thirty-five aircraft and one hundred and nine ships to move everything in the ninety-day period." The host nation representatives' eyes looked like saucers.

"Excuse me, Herr General," said the representative of the German government.

"Yes, Herr Bergan," General Daniel said.

"Herr General, we will have to mobilize our reserve federal police just to handle convoy control and empty all barges from supporting civilian commercial operations. We will also not be able to move any freight on the German railway. I'm afraid this cannot be done," Herr Bergan said with a look of amazement on his face.

"Herr Bergan, the Chancellor has assured General Saint that Germany will give us full support in moving our forces. He would rather support us in Germany than have to commit German soldiers to the war in the Middle East. I suggest you work with us or leave, and I will request a replacement for you. I know this is going to be a strain on the German and Dutch workforce, but it must be done," General Daniel concluded. Herr Bergan did not know what to say, so he stayed quiet, looking around for support from others. He received none.

"Anyone else wish to raise a flag?" Daniel asked.

"Herr General, how soon can you provide me with the routes and timetable for your convoys?" asked Generalmajor Tesmar of the Bundesgrenzschutz. "Once you provide me with that, I will coordinate with the respective Landespolizei to be sure that your convoys will pass through their territory with little difficulty. I will also have the Bahnpolizei increase security along the rail lines and rail terminals. We have nine patrol craft that will be operational at all times in the port of

Bremerhaven as well. I would like to assign a liaison officer here so if a problem arises we can quickly deal with it, if that is acceptable."

"Generalmajor Tesmar, that is most welcomed," Brigadier Daniel said.

"Herr General Daniel," a tall man said, raising his hand to be recognized.

"Yes, sir, and you are…?" Daniel asked.

"Sir, I am Herr Hufnagal and I am the Bremerhaven Port manager. We have just cleared the yard where cars are prepared for loading on RoRo ships, so I can accept your rolling stock at this time. If you will have your people give me a schedule of when they anticipate rail loading and delivery to the port, we will make accommodation for them. I will need some soldiers to drive the vehicles on the ship. My people can drive cars, but a tank may be a bit much for them," he said with a chuckle.

"Sir, I thank you, and we will get that information to you as soon as we've worked out the load plans. Thank you," Daniel said. The rest of the meeting continued in a similar fashion, with host nation support coming to the forefront to assist in the deployment. The VII Corps would make its deployment times.

Chapter 34
Rotation of Units

5 November 1990

Pentagon

Washington, D.C.

"Holy shit!" Bob Daley said as he studied the latest download from Big Bird, the KH-11 satellite passing over the Persian Gulf and the UAE. Looking around the room, he spotted his boss, Cliff Jeffery.

"Hey, Cliff, you may want to take a look at this," he said, tilting his computer screen up for Cliff to look at over his shoulder.

Coming up behind Bob, Cliff looked over his shoulder. After ten seconds, he said, "Get up and let me see this. What the hell...? Is he pulling out of the UAE? Where the hell are those divisions going? And who the hell is this coming down from the north? What the...?" On the screen, a large force was moving from Al Hofuf south, with the units of the 1st Republican Guard Corps starting to move back into Saudi Arabia. The 6th Nebuchadnezzar Division had already left its positions around Al Waqan and was moving across the desert with some vehicles already on the paved highway to Haradh, southwest of Al Hofuf. Elements of what appeared to be the IX Corps were moving south from the Al Hofuf region along the coast road towards the UAE.

"I think he's replacing his front-line troops, the Republican Guard, with Iraqi Army units and putting the Guards in a counterattack position," Bob said, pointing at different units on the screen.

"Bob, you may be right. Get this written up and let's get it fired upstairs. This is going to get people hopping, I'm sure," Cliff said as he stood up. "I'll carry it up when you have it written up. You're going to brief it, so be prepared."

****

General al-Dulaymi had the four division commanders seated in the conference rooms sipping tea. All looked refreshed from the first time they occupied this room in the Royal Palace. Each had a clean pressed uniform, and all were in good spirits. *Time for them to earn their pay again*, he thought.

"Gentlemen, we have been ordered to return to Saudi Arabia. The IX Corps will be conducting a relief in place with us commencing at 0600 tomorrow. General Dairi, your division will be the first to pull out. The 10th Armoured Division will coordinate with you tonight for the exchange. Tomorrow night, General Asaad and the 3rd Tawakalna Division will exchange with the 1st Infantry Division. They are more suited for the city fighting that is anticipated if the Americans attack. General al-Tikrit, your division will coordinate with the 17th Armoured Division, and General Ujayll, you will coordinate with the 52nd Armoured Division. Al-Tikrit and Ujayll, I suspect your changeover will take a bit longer than the others, but try to make it as swift as possible. I will have more tomorrow on where you are going to be positioned. It is felt that if the Americans attack, and I believe they will, we are better equipped and trained to serve as counterattack force than the IX Corps units. The IX Corps can wear the Americans down and we can come in and finish them off. Logistic support for us has already begun moving back, and IX Corps is moving on the coast road. We will avoid them by taking the interior road north. Again, keep the track vehicles off the paved roads. Are there any questions?" al-Dulaymi asked. He knew there would be none.

****

LTG Juwad Assad Rasol Shitnah, commander of the IX Corps, had called a meeting of his four remaining commanders. The commander of the 45th and 49th Infantry Divisions were in Al Jubail and Dammam, respectively. They had not been called to this meeting as they were going nowhere but would continue to secure those two vital seaports. Shitnah had just returned from a meeting with LTG al-Dulaymi where they had discussed the relief in place of the 1st Republican Guard Corps by the IX Corps. It was time now to brief his subordinate division commanders.

"Gentlemen, we have been ordered to relieve the 1st Republican Guard Corps and assume their positions in the UAE," he said, noting the sudden smiles on the faces of his division commanders. He knew what they were thinking. *They expected to move into the luxury offered by Abu Dhabi and Dubai. Well, they have another rude awakening coming.* "I have seen their so-called positions in the UAE and they have none. They moved in and took over homes and hotels and the pleasures offered, lacking any defensive positions or preparation of the battlefield. The Americans—hell, the Saudis—could roll through the country and the anointed ones wouldn't even know it. They have no security outposts, no obstacles. They have done nothing to oppose an attack. We will not be so lax. The Americans are not going to attack major cities as they have concern for civilian casualties and the destruction of civilian property. They want to win the hearts and minds of the people and that cannot happen if you blow up their cities," he explained as the smiles disappeared.

Getting out of his chair, he walked over to a map on the wall. "General al-Barwari, I am placing your 1st Infantry Division in Al Ain.

Between the city and the escarpment to the south, you should be able to stop any force coming at you as they can only come on Highway 7 out of Oman and they will be committed in piecemeal fashion as the passes are narrow and they will only be able to commit a brigade at a time. Any questions?" Shitnah asked as he pointed at the map.

"Al Ain sticks out into territory claimed by Oman. The enemy can move out of the mountain passes and disperse before attacking in plain sight of me. Must I wait until he physically crosses the borders before I may engage?" al-Barwari asked.

"General, if you can see them, you can kill them. Is that plain enough for you?" Shitnah responded. The nod and the smile on al-Barwari's face said he understood.

"General al-Hiti, I want your 10th Armoured Division to take up positions between Al Dhaid and Al Madam," which he pointed out on the map. "They will come at you along Highway E84 through the mountains in the north and in the vicinity of Al Madam from the highway coming out of Hatta," Shitnah directed. General al-Hiti acknowledged his assignment.

"General al-Furayi, the 17th Division will take up positions south of Al Ain to the Saudi border." Shitnah traced a line along the border from Al Ain south to the border. "You have the widest sector. However, the terrain forward of your positions is rugged, restrictive terrain that offers few roads that the Americans could use. General Dairi will position the 52nd Armoured Division behind you and will reinforce you if it becomes necessary. I expect that when the Americans attack, they will make their main effort your sector, General al-Hiti. I believe they will attempt an envelopment from the north, cutting down across the country. They will attempt to hold everyone in place and get their forces through the mountains and on line to sweep

334

down to the southwest and towards Riyadh. The Americans have a thing for attacking to free cities. They think if they capture Riyadh that the war will be over and they will be in a position to sue for peace and our departure. With our forces arrayed in a good defense, they will not be successful and the 1st Republican Guard Corps will make the counterattack," Shitnah concluded.

"Sir, I have a very wide sector. Is there any chance the 45th or 49th Division will join us and we can place them on my flank and take some of my frontage?" General al-Furayi asked.

"In good time, General, in good time," Shitnah said, returning to his seat. The rest of the meeting was a discussion of logistics and movement of the units into the UAE.

Chapter 35

All-Star Revue

9 November 1990

CENTCOM Forward HQ

Military Technological College

Muscat, Oman

"Sir, General Powell on line one for you," the aide said, standing in the doorway.

"Thanks, close the door, please," General Schwarzkopf said, reaching for the phone. "Colin, I hope you have good news for me. I could use some right now. Have you seen the shift the Iraqis are doing in the UAE? You know they're moving the 1st Republican Guard Corps back to serve as a counterattack force, if we attack," Schwarzkopf said.

"That's what I'm calling about. We received the intel brief, and we came to the conclusion that you don't have the forces available to go on the offense. The President has decided that a larger force is needed. He met with the House and Senate leadership and, after some horse trading, got them on board. Your staff should be receiving message traffic shortly showing the increase in forces, but I can tell you it's VII Corps from Germany, and we're activating four National Guard divisions as well. For command and control, we're also sending Ivan Smith and the III Corps headquarters and logistics arm to you. III Corps is bringing the 6th Combat Aviation Brigade as well. General Franks has been alerted and will be flying down in a few days to meet with you and Yeosock," Powell said.

"So the decision was made for partial mobilization. That's good. That will let Saddam know we're very serious and the public will more than likely get behind this as well. What kind of divisions are these?" Schwarzkopf asked.

"We're activating the 29th, 28th and 35th Infantry Divisions and the 50th Armored Division. The 50th will be the first and we'll run them through an NTC rotation before we send them over," Powell said.

"NTC rotation! When can I expect them in-country?" Schwarzkopf asked, a bit concerned at the potential timeline.

"Well, the 50th will take about three months to get there, and then the others will follow on," Powell explained.

"So we're looking at a year before I have the entire force in place is what you're telling me. So for another year, we sit on our asses here and watch the Iraqis fortify the border. Send the National Guard divisions over now and we can do the train-up here. We can't wait a full year. The longer Saddam sits in Saudi, the more likely he wins. Even if he withdraws now relatively intact, he wins. The only units we've hurt to a draw are his 2nd Republican Guard Corps and the 2nd Iraqi Corps. The rest of his army is relatively in great shape. We can't wait to let him reinforce those two corps. We need the VII Corps and the 50th Division now and we need to get this thing going, *now*. We can't be sitting here playing this waiting game. Let me come back and give the President a brief and some facts without being filtered by Scowcroft and Cheney," Schwarzkopf argued. Powell was silent. *Colin is for containment and the status quo. I'll bet he fought these units being activated and VII Corps being sent*, Schwarzkopf thought.

Finally, Powell spoke up. "I'll see if I can get you on the President's calendar for that briefing," he said and hung up.

****

Lieutenant General Frederick Franks, commander VII Corps, arrived in Muscat and was quickly escorted to General Schwarzkopf's office. Lieutenant General Yeosock, the ARCENT commander and General Franks's boss for this operation, met him planeside. "Fred, I cannot tell you how happy we are to have you and your command joining us in this. We've been screaming at Washington since day one that we needed a bigger force, and all we've been getting is 'wait one.' Someone has been stonewalling our efforts to go on the offensive. We even had to prepare an offensive plan with the limited forces we have. Ridiculous. We still haven't been given a strategic objective for this operation or a timeline. Having you folks and with the shift in Iraqi forces, we're back to the drawing board on an offensive plan," Yeosock said.

"When did the Iraqis make the relief in place?" Franks asked.

"It started last week and is still going on. I wish we could have hit them when they were in the middle of it, but we just don't have the forces. We've run some air strikes, but the Iraqi Air Force is still formidable and we've been holding back to some extent until we're really ready to launch the offense," Yeosock said as their driver negotiated the Muscat traffic.

"When are we looking at starting the offense? It's going to take some time to get my force down here," Franks said.

"We were looking at the offensive operation starting in January, or at least the air campaign. Washington is sending the 50th Armored Division over and three other National Guard Infantry divisions and wanted us to wait. Norm told them no and to send the 50th right away and we would get them trained up. We can't wait a year to train up the National Guard divisions like we did prior to World War II. They're also sending over III Corps from Fort Hood to take command for part of the force. They will start arriving this week, too. Ivan Smith should be arriving tonight. You know him, don't you?" Yeosock asked.

"Yeah, Ivan and I served together in a couple of assignments in our early days and on the joint staff. Good man. We'll work well together," Franks said.

"Well, we'll let you get settled in for tonight, and in the morning both you and Ivan have a meeting with Norm. After that we'll give you a detailed brief on the Iraqis, and the logistics for your people. The boys in the plans are some of those Jedi majors you created with the SAMS program and they're coming up with a new offensive plan. They're prepared to give you a couple of courses of action that we're looking at and would like yours and Ivan's input. Oh, have you met Sir Peter de la Billière? He's the commander of British forces, to include the 1st Armoured Division," Yeosock asked as they arrived at the VIP quarters.

"I've met him, and we've been at several NATO conferences together. Very capable officer, I believe," Franks said.

"Well, he'll be at the brief as well, and so will Lieutenant General Boomer from MARCENT."

"With this all-star revue, it could be very interesting," Franks said as he exited the car and went into the VIP quarters, assisted by his aide.

Chapter 36

The Call-Up

12 November 1990

Across America

Larry Pyle had been married all of six months. Janie had dated him for almost two years before he'd popped the question, and she hadn't hesitated to say yes to his proposal. She had everything she could dream of in the marriage. Larry was a good provider with a steady job as a corporate attorney for a coal company. He'd been working there for the past two years after graduating from law school. He found corporate law to be his niche in the world of law and loved every minute of it. To help pay the bills, he had joined the National Guard and attended officer candidate school, receiving a commission to second lieutenant, infantry. He enjoyed his one weekend a month drilling at the armory or going to the rifle range at Fort Indiantown Gap northeast of Harrisburg, Pennsylvania, or Fort A.P. Hill south of Washington, D.C. In the summer, his two-week drill was a nice break from corporate law as he got to go camping with the guys, run through the woods and play soldier. What was not to like?

"Larry, you have a phone call," Janie called from the kitchen phone hanging on the wall as she was preparing dinner.

"OK, I'll pick up in the study," Larry called back. His study was really one of the three empty bedrooms upstairs in their Kingstowne townhouse. Kingstowne townhouses were pretty much the same, with every fourth house being identical. It was a planned community started in 1980 and was always expanding. Typical residents were military stationed in the D.C. area, government employees and young professionals.

"Hello, Larry here."

"Sir, this is Staff Sergeant Baker. Hate to call you this late, but this is a recall notice. Company assembly is 0900. Company commander would like you there at 0800," Staff Sergeant Baker said.

"What? This is some kind of joke, Sergeant? Who put you up to this one? I ain't biting on this hook. Did Triplett put you up to this?" Larry asked, almost laughing. Last year they'd played a prank like this on one of their fellow officers a couple of days before he was getting married. They'd all had a good laugh when he'd shown up at the armory the following morning in uniform with his fiancée, ready to beg and plead that he at least be allowed to marry her before he left.

"Sir, this is no joke. You have been notified. Duty uniform. Have a good evening, sir."

"Wait, are you serious, Sergeant?" Larry asked.

"As serious as a heart attack, sir. We've been activated. The President just announced it on the television. You can check it for yourself," Sergeant Baker explained.

Lost for words, Larry just mumbled something and hung up the phone. "Janie, turn on the television!" he said as he came down the stairs, taking them two at a time.

"Why, what's going on, dear?" Janie asked, drying her hands on a kitchen towel as Larry headed towards the television and switched on CNN, the only twenty-four-hour news station. He'd already missed the local nightly news. The CNN mouthpiece appeared very serious and rightly so. The National Guard and Army Reserve hadn't been called up since the Korean War.

"Ladies and gentlemen, the President of the United States with the consent of Congress has just announced that the nation will activate the National Guard units under Title 10 of US Code 12302. This allows the President to activate up to one million National Guard and reservists for a period of up to two years. As I am broadcasting this, some units are receiving their alert orders to report for duty as early as tomorrow. Which units are being activated has not been released to the press as yet. We will bring that to you as we obtain that information.

"In the Middle East, US forces continue to flow into Oman and portions of Saudi Arabia, but it appears that Saddam's forces are digging in and showing no signs of leaving. The President has continued to insist that Iraqi forces must leave both Saudi Arabia and Kuwait immediately, as well as the tiny oil-rich nation of the United Arab Emirates. US forces..."

Larry turned off the television and stared at Janie with a look of shock and uncertainty. She had the same look written on her face.

"Was that call... about this?" she asked, pointing to the TV, her eyes starting to well up with tears.

Larry didn't say anything right away. He just nodded, then he explained, "I have to report tomorrow morning to the armory. I suspect they're going to bring us in and give us an overview of the call-up. I don't think they'll look to activate us. I've heard the soldiers they need over there are largely support troops. You know, cooks, supply clerks, truck drivers and mechanics. I think that's what they're doing... I suppose I'll know for sure tomorrow." He paused for a moment, a couple of tears streaming down his wife's face. "I best call Jim and tell him I won't be in tomorrow morning. I hope he can take that meeting I have with the client."

Larry walked over and briefly hugged his wife. "It'll be OK. I'll know more tomorrow, and we'll figure this out. I need to go call Jim and explain what's happening. When I get done, help me get my uniform ready for tomorrow and let's work on making that little munchkin we've been talking about."

She wiped away a tear and headed off towards their bedroom. Turning, she looked at him. "Don't be too long, soldier."

****

Mike had been drawing unemployment checks for the past three months since the mill had shut down. Like almost everyone in Eleanor, West Virginia, Mike was out of work. Those that hadn't worked at the mill were beginning to hurt, as no one was really spending any money on eating out or retail shopping except to purchase liquor and groceries across the river in Winfield, which was also feeling the closure. Cigarettes and gas were still in demand, and unfortunately, so was the local drug dealer. The unemployment rate had been hovering around seven percent before the mill had closed. About the only people with steady paychecks were teachers at the two elementary schools, city employees and the guys operating the Winfield Locks on the Kanawha River.

Mike was a bit more fortunate than most, however. He wasn't married, so he didn't have a family to support. When he'd graduated from high school, he'd joined the Army right away to get away from West Virginia, and he had. But somehow, he'd wound up right back here two months after he was discharged. He intended to use his GI Bill for some additional training or college. He just wasn't sure what he wanted to do yet. He had ten years to use it, so he wasn't in a big rush. Guard drill did put some coin in everyone's pocket as almost everyone was a member of the local National Guard company. They were part of the 29th Infantry Division. His unit, Troop B, 1st Battalion, 15th Cavalry Regiment, was glad to bring him aboard as they hadn't had to retrain him, since he had already been a specialist four when he'd been discharged. He had been able to retain his rank and likely would make sergeant once a slot opened up.

The Prancing Deer was the local beer hall, the only watering hole in Eleanor, and on this night just about everyone was there soaking up suds and shooting pool. What else does one do when they don't have to go to work in the morning? The jukebox was playing, and between that and the conversations, one almost couldn't hear oneself talking. Then the jukebox went quiet.

"Hey, turn it back on. That was my song," a big fellow of about twenty said as he stood and turned towards the box. Then he saw who had unplugged it. "Oh, sorry, Sheriff."

"Alright, listen up, everyone. *Shut the hell up!*" That got everyone's attention. Besides being the county sheriff, he was also the Guard company commander. When things quieted down, he continued. "I want all you boys to drink up and head home," he announced. Subdued mumbling and complaints could be heard. "Tomorrow at 0800 hours you will all report to the armory with all your uniforms and TA-50 gear. Don't plan on getting home for supper tomorrow night because we have a lot of work to do, and no one goes home until it's done. Is that clear?" he rhetorically asked, knowing full well that they had no idea what he was talking about.

"Hey, sir, we don't have drill tomorrow. In fact, in two weeks it's Thanksgiving, so we don't have drill until next month," one young man pointed out.

"Daniels, I know we don't have drill tomorrow, and I know you already had drill for November. I also know that in two weeks it's Thanksgiving, but this ain't no drill. Effective about an hour ago, we've been activated under partial mobilization for the next two years," the sheriff said to stunned silence as everyone attempted to absorb what he'd just said. Then the shouts and cheers rose as everyone realized that they were going to start getting regular paychecks courtesy of the United States Army.

****

Lieutenant Colonel Steve Gooderjohn was sitting in his office sipping that first cup of morning coffee. The Headquarters and Headquarters Company were located in Silver Springs, Maryland. The other units in the battalion, all mechanized infantry companies, were located in towns across Maryland, to include Greenbelt, Frederick and Olney. He had been in command of the 1st Battalion, 115th Infantry, 29th Infantry Division for the past year. He was a full-time National Guard officer, having received his commission through ROTC and immediately gone into the National Guard rather than go on active duty. He enjoyed the fact that he didn't have to move like active-duty officers had to every three years, and the two weeks in the summer at Fort Indiantown Gap, Pennsylvania, were a fun time. It would have been more fun if the active-duty evaluators hadn't regularly buzzed around like flies on shit, but that was a small inconvenience. The evaluators' comments were seldom taken seriously unless it was a security issue. Gooderjohn had the same opinion as most Guard officers: "We haven't been activated since Korea, and there's nothing out there that's going to get us activated now."

"Excuse me, Steve," his personnel clerk, Bob Wilson, said, sticking his head in the door. Formal military rank was not applied during the week.

"Yeah, Bob?" Gooderjohn replied. Bob had been a full-time Guard employee for fifteen years and the battalion personnel clerk for that whole time as well. He worked daily at the armory, handling the building maintenance, logistic receptions and general paperwork. On drill weekends, he was the personnel clerk, working for the battalion personnel officer or S-1. Physical fitness was foreign to him as he was forty pounds overweight, and this was a constant thorn in the Army advisor's side.

"The State Ops officer is on the phone for you. That Steve Blum guy," the clerk said.

"OK," Gooderjohn replied. He set his coffee down and picked up the phone. "What line is he on?"

"Line one," Bob said over his shoulder as he walked away.

"Colonel Gooderjohn here, sir."

"Gooderjohn, I'm giving you a heads-up," Blum said a bit anxiously. Colonel Blum was a full-time National Guard officer as well. He had been a schoolteacher and in his second year of teaching had seen a presentation on the National Guard Special Forces program. Since he was a physically fit weight lifter, this had immediately grabbed his interest, and he'd signed up. He'd sailed through the officer basic course, Ranger school, and the Special Forces qualification program. He'd enjoyed it all so much he'd applied for and obtained a full-time position in the Maryland National Guard.

"At five o'clock today, the President is going on the television to announce enacting partial mobilization of the National Guard and Reserves," Blum said.

"Oh, bullshit. Who put you up to this one? I'll bet it was Harry over at Second Battalion, wasn't it?" Gooderjohn said, almost laughing.

"Listen, you dumbass peckerhead, this is no damn joke and your battalion, along with the rest of the 29th, is the first unit to be called up. You'll have a formal alert order delivered to your office by 1800 tonight. Recall will be tomorrow by 1200 hours. By 1700 hours tomorrow I need a full set of reports as outlined in the State Mobilization and Pre-deployment Requirements. You have read those, haven't you?" Blum asked with a bit of anger in his voice.

"No, we've never gone through this before. Why would I read that crap? You are serious, aren't you?" Gooderjohn questioned, still not convinced that this wasn't a prank.

"You're damn right I'm serious. Now I suggest you pull out the State Mobilization and Pre-deployment Requirements and read them before that alert order arrives. And you may want to start exercising your alert rosters and telephone trees. Your battalion will be rolling out on Monday to Indiantown Gap. Now get to it, I have a few more calls I still need to make. Goodbye."

Gooderjohn sat there with the phone to his ear, hoping to hear Blum start laughing, that this was another prank or joke, but all he heard was a dial tone.

Oh shit, this is real...

"Bob! Get in here," Gooderjohn called out.

Taking his sweet time, Bob strolled into Gooderjohn's office. "What's up?" he asked as casually as possible.

"Pull the alert roster and start calling the staff to get in here. I'll call the commanders and get them moving on recalling everyone," Gooderjohn directed as he began dialing the phone.

"Wow, what's going on? I'm not sure the staff alert roster is even up to date. Hell, everyone is at their civilian jobs today," Bob pointed out.

"We're being activated for the next two years. The President is invoking partial mobilization and we'll have the order this afternoon. Now start making the calls," Gooderjohn directed.

Bob walked out of his office and headed to his desk. Opening the file drawer, he pulled out a piece of paper he'd thought he would never need. The title of the paper was NON-DEPLOYABLE PERSONNEL. The first paragraph was headed MEDICAL. He smiled as his name was the first name on the list: overweight. Bob wasn't going anywhere. The second paragraph was headed CIVILIAN EMPLOYMENT and further subdivided into categories to include State Police, City Police, and Firefighters. All told, of the five hundred and fifty soldiers assigned to the battalion, one hundred and thirty were on the nondeployable rosters.

Chapter 37

Time to Reconsider

12 November 1990

3rd Brigade Engagement Area

Bulldog Six finally had his entire battalion minus some two-and-a-half-ton trucks, which were driving back towards Yanbu and would come up behind his positions. Monitoring the 3rd Brigade command net, he could tell that Raider Rakkasan was giving the enemy hell. The fight had been ebb and flow for the past two weeks, with the Iraqi forces pressing the attack, then hunkering down and then attempting to renew the attack. Both sides were getting tired. Rakkasan Six told Bulldog Six to be ready as Raider Rakkasan was going to allow a small force to pass through his positions and then seal the opening. Bulldog alerted his Delta Company commander.

"Delta Dog Six, Bulldog Six."

"Bulldog Six, Delta Dog Six, over."

"Delta Dog, Raider Rakkasan is going to allow a small force to penetrate and move into your engagement area. Are you ready?"

"Bulldog Six, Delta Dog, we will welcome them with open arms into the halls of Valhalla," Delta Dog Six announced.

"Roger, just watch out for this artillery or you'll be waiting in Valhalla for him. Over."

Moments later, Bulldog Six could see Delta Dog's TOW missiles being fired from four launchers at maximum range to the enemy. The time of flight was ten seconds, and four missiles impacted four BTR-80 vehicles. After a short delay of fifteen seconds, four more missiles were in flight, streaking towards the advancing rifle company for twenty vehicles. As those rounds impacted, four more missiles were launched from the opposite side of the wadi and destroyed four more vehicles. This fight was a minute old, and the Iraqi company had lost twelve of his twenty vehicles. As no artillery was being adjusted on Delta Dog's positions, it appeared that the Iraqi company commander might have been killed in one of the first engagements. As Bulldog Six was contemplating this, he suddenly realized why there was no enemy artillery as four MI-24 Hind attack helicopters popped over the ridge on the left side of the wadi and began searching for targets. One of Delta's vehicles didn't see the Hind-D when he fired his TOW missile. The Hind-D spotted the weapon and immediately engaged with rockets and machine-gun fire. Delta Dog's vehicle didn't stand a chance and exploded immediately.

"All Bulldog elements, cease fire and stay down. Hinds in the area," Bulldog Six announced on the radio. All the elements ceased shooting and hunkered down under their camouflage nets and fighting positions. Only the air-defense soldiers with their Stinger missiles and Vulcan 20mm cannon were going to engage. Everyone waited as the Hind-D helicopters approached their positions. The Hind helicopters maintained a racetrack flight pattern when hunting, with one aircraft following the other. Unlike US tactics, where the Apache hid behind a hill mass and hovered up to engage, the Hind flew with airspeed and strafed its target with 12.7mm machine-gun fire and rockets. Key in this engagement was being able to take out the first and second aircraft together, as they always flew in teams of two.

"Goose Gunner Six, Bulldog Six." Goose Gunner was a nickname that Bulldog Six had tagged his air-defense platoon leader with.

"Bulldog Six, Goose Gunner."

"Goose Gunner, you are cleared to engage."

"Roger, Bulldog Six, will be engaging the chase aircraft first."
Bulldog stayed low in his jump TOC position, watching the MI-24
Hind-D approaching. Suddenly, from behind and to the side, a missile
leaving a white contrail departed the hillside. As it raced skyward, it
adjusted its course ever so slowly, impacting on the point where the tail
boom connected to the main body of the aircraft. Almost immediately,
the aircraft began turning and continued to spiral in a flat spin,
impacting the ground and exploding. The first aircraft must have seen
the point of origin for the missile as he immediately turned in the
direction of the point of origin. A fatal mistake as both another missile
and a 20mm Vulcan cannon opened fire on the flying tank. The Vulcan
shredded the cockpit area, and the missile slammed into the tail section.
This aircraft did not have an opportunity to go into the flat spin but
simply exploded in flight. The remaining two MI-24 Hind helicopters
decided that the threat was too great and departed the area immediately,
which made the soldiers happy, but not Bulldog Six. He knew they
would report a serious air-defense threat in this area and the result
would be Frogfoot close-air support jets coming to his area.
******

PFC Bannion had joined the Army right out of high school. He
wanted to go to college and understood the need to do so but just
wasn't ready for it. He thought four years in the Army would be good
for him. It would allow him to mature some and finally decide what he
wanted to do as well as provide the GI Bill for college. Like most
privates, he'd never expected to be in the Middle East in a battle. He
had been assigned to a rifle company and was a "grunt" like every other
infantry soldier. They were called "grunts" because when they would
pick up their hundred-pound rucksacks, you could hear them grunt.

With their rucksack and combat gear, each man carried about one hundred and twenty pounds. He was always amazed at the "old soldiers" being able to hump that load and never complain about it.

"Hey, Bannion, get your ass over here and bring your entrenching tool. We've got to get this fighting position dug and dug quick. The noise you're hearing isn't the Fourth of July back on the block," yelled Sergeant Frazier, his team leader.

"I'm coming," Bannion responded.

"Hell, you aren't even breathing hard," Private Anderson said. Anderson and Bannion would be sharing a fighting position with Sergeant Frazier. Anderson carried an M-60 machine gun and Bannion served as the assistant gunner. Anderson had been in the Army longer but had been busted down from specialist to private because of a DUI. They were putting their position on a slope forward of a TOW vehicle, offering some protection to the TOW. Other TOW vehicles further north had already engaged the enemy and had withdrawn back through their position. They were now the tip of the spear.

Once the fighting position was near completion, Sergeant Frazier yelled, "Get down now!"

Diving for the fighting position, Bannion asked, "What's up, Sarge?" Then he heard the sound and knew what was up. The first of four MI-24D Hind helicopters were flying down the wadi, looking for targets. Anderson started to raise his M-60 machine gun.

"Don't bother with that. All you'll do is give away our position even if you did hit him. Thing is like a flying tank. Just stay low and let the air defenders take them out," Sergeant Frazier instructed just as a missile streaked from the far side of the wadi and slammed into the Hind-D. Almost immediately, a Vulcan air-defense cannon opened fire along with another missile on the second Hind-D. It went down in flames as well. The remaining two attack helicopters turned and exited the area.

"Damn, I'm glad they didn't spot us," Bannion said, slowly raising his head above the edge of the fighting position. "Oh, shit."

"What's wrong?" asked Anderson, picking himself up and looking to where Bannion was pointing.

Across the floor of the wadi were at least two companies of BTR-80s and some tanks moving south. Immediately, Anderson positioned his M-60 to engage the dismounted enemy soldiers as soon as they came in the predetermined kill zone. As they waited and observed, artillery from the battalion began hitting the formation with airbursts, which stripped away antennas and killed anyone outside of the vehicles. Then HE Quick rounds began impacting, throwing large chunks of shrapnel across the battlefield, which did not penetrate the vehicles unless it was a direct hit but did destroy the tires on the BTR-80, resulting in a mobility kill. Finally, the TOW positions opened with deadly accuracy using their thermal sights.

The Iraqi smokescreen was ineffective against the thermal sights. Iraqi soldiers started to realize that sitting inside the vehicles, especially ones that were disabled, was a sure way to die, so they dismounted into a hail of machine-gun fire. As they moved towards the machine-gun positions, small-arms fire intensified as they came within range. Bannion and Frazier were exercising fire discipline with well-aimed shots as opposed to the spray-and-pray shooting that the Iraqi soldiers utilized. After an hour, only occasional AK-47 shots could be heard. The sounds of battle could still be heard to the north, and Bulldog Six knew this wouldn't be the last of the action they would see as Raider Rakkasan was about to allow another Iraqi unit to slip through. This piecemeal commitment of the Iraqi regiment was a sure way of being defeated by a smaller force.

****

"Rakkasan Six, Raider six, over." His voice was elevated.

"Raider Six, Rakkasan Six, go ahead."

"Six, we have tanks pushing through my positions. Appears to be a battalion of T-72s. We can't hold them, over."

"Roger, Raider Six. We'll get some tac air to handle it. Let them through. How copy?"

"Roger, good copy. Raider Six out."'

Turning to his tactical air control party, Colonel Clark needed tac air now. *If we only had some attack helicopters*, he was thinking. "What have we got that we can put on this tank formation and quick?" Clark asked.

"Sir, the FAC has the tank force in sight and is bringing up a flight of Navy F-14s and Grumman A-6s. The F-14s are flying a cap and the A-6s will do the work. They should be ready to commence their runs in about five minutes," Major Bledsoe said. Major Bledsoe, like most TACP officers, was a pilot but had been on an assignment to the TACP when the war had started. He'd tried his best to get into a cockpit but had been denied at this point.

Turning to the operations officer, Colonel Clark said, "Get out a net call that we have friendly fast movers in the area and commencing a bomb run in five minutes. Hold all air-defense fire. Get confirmation that's understood." *The last thing I need right now is for one of our own to shoot down one of our own*, he was thinking.

"Also inform Bulldog that the priority of fire for his TOWs is ADA weapon systems. Let's protect those fast movers," he directed his operations officer. As Colonel Clark sat and monitored the radios, he was lost in thought. *Action, reaction, counteraction—so what's my reaction to that going to be? He sends in a battalion of tanks. I send in fast movers. He counteracts how? Air-defense weapons, interceptor jets. Well, the Navy has the F-14s protecting the A-6s, and I have the TOWs going after the ADA weapons systems, so what's left? Damn, as a brigade commander, I'm not in the fight but managing and allocating assets. Division has the long-range assets for the deep battle and they're all committed with the 2nd Brigade to the east. We really don't have any long-range artillery in any quantity such as MLRS—just the 155s and not a lot of those. All the battalions are committed and doing well, but this tank thing...the A-6s have got to stop them or they'll punch through.*

Sitting and waiting is one of the hardest things for a commander at the brigade level. He must visualize the battle, as his area is so large he cannot really physically see the entire battle. This was frustrating for him.

****

"Sarge, we got tanks!" Bannion yelled as he watched the billowing cloud of dust moving into and down the wadi. Almost immediately, the battalion TOWs were engaging. Their only saving grace was the range they had versus the range of the tanks demonstrating accuracy. A moving T-72 didn't have the accuracy of the TOW or the American Abrams tank.

Gazing over the rim of their foxhole, Sergeant Frazier noted that the TOWs weren't engaging the tanks but seeking out the ZSU-23-4 and the SA-9 vehicles. Looking over his shoulder at the TOW system closest to him, he screamed, "Take out the fucking tanks!" They either didn't hear him or ignored him as the next missile slammed into an SA-9 vehicle. *What the fuck?* Frazier was thinking when the ground in the wadi erupted with hundreds of flashes and the roar of the A-6 passing by could suddenly be heard. Each jet carried a combination of Maverick antiarmor missiles and fourteen Mk-20 Rockeye bombs. Each bomb carried two hundred and forty-seven individual bomblets, each capable of destroying a tank with a direct hit.

Frazier, Bannion and Anderson had never seen such a firepower demonstration and all three stood up in a daze, forgetting that they were still in a combat situation. Before them on the wadi floor were forty tanks and vehicles, burning or missing vital parts. Iraqi soldiers lay about the ground or hung out of burning vehicles. A few were wandering in a daze themselves, it appeared, not carrying any weapons and walking in circles. Some were crying. For now, it appeared the attack had stopped.

****

"General al-Douri, sir," the staff officer addressed the 2nd Army Corps commander sitting in the living room of a home that he had seized for the Corps headquarters in Al Jadedah.

"Yes, what is it, Colonel?" al-Douri asked, looking up from a report he was reading about a supply issue. The fuel he was requesting was not getting to him, and this was the logistics officer's weak excuse for why they weren't getting the fuel they needed.

"Sir, I have an update for you," the colonel said, but his facial expression did not bode well, al-Douri thought. "Sir, we have lost contact with General Zogby and the 7th Division is requesting to go on the defense. They have not been able to penetrate the American positions and are down to forty percent in vehicles. The 37th is reporting a shortage of fuel and cannot proceed forward," the colonel said, waiting for the backblast of anger from al-Douri.

"What are you talking about, Colonel?" al-Douri asked in confusion. "If the 7th has sixty percent of his vehicles, he should continue the attack. No—tell him no and to continue the attack. And send someone with the MI-8 helicopter to see what Zogby's communication problems are," al-Douri said, returning to his report.

"Sir, you misunderstood me," the Colonel said. "The 7th Division has only forty percent of its vehicles left. He has lost over half of his division, sir. And General Zogby was killed, as were the 1st and 2nd Regimental commanders. We have communications with the 3rd Regiment commander, and he says the 1st and 2nd Regiments were destroyed. He is attempting to gather up those who are left into his regiment. He said the American attack helicopters and tactical air are killing anything that moves. He is in the mountains but does not want to withdraw for fear of being attacked by the helicopters once he is in the open."

Al-Douri sat in silence, attempting to process all that he had just been told. Of his five divisions, two more had now been destroyed by the Americans and one could not move because of a lack of fuel. The 2nd Infantry Division was still in Tabuk, and the 14th was south of there being refitted and would not be ready for another month at least. He knew it would be futile to continue the attack at this point.

"Colonel, have the 3rd Regiment continue to pull in what remaining forces he can and then withdraw to Al Jadid. Have the 7th withdraw as well, back to Umm Shuquq. Have the 37th hold its present position. Move the headquarters to Fadhia. We must regroup and reassess the American air threat. And get me the damn air-defense colonel and the air liaison officer, *now!*"

Chapter 38

Mobilization Station

20 November 1990

Fort A.P. Hill

Virginia

Lieutenant Colonel Gooderjohn had never felt as tired as he was right now. Assembling the Headquarters Company, 1st Battalion, 115th Infantry, at the hometown armory wasn't a problem until it came time to take a head count. He hadn't seen a nondeployment list before and that came to bite him in the ass. Seems Bob Wilson hadn't provided him with accurate information on the status of nondeployable soldiers. Over twenty-five percent of the battalion was nondeployable for one reason or another, and they hadn't even gotten to their mobilization station for further screening. The powers that be were not happy when the nondeployable status was revealed, but this was common in the National Guard.

The next bit of confusion came when, instead of rolling out and heading to Fort Indiantown Gap, where they normally conducted two weeks summer training and had all the contacts, the mobilization station was changed. It seemed that the 28th Infantry Division, Pennsylvania National Guard, were mobilizing at that location. They were now heading to Fort A.P. Hill in Virginia. Gooderjohn's staff was not the least bit familiar with the fort or the people that normally worked at the fort year-round. Fort A.P. Hill, like Fort Indiantown Gap, was left over from World War II and had no permanent active-duty units located there. The entire full-time military population on the fort was about ninety people, the rest being civil service employees working in activities to maintain the fort. The biggest event each year was the National Boy Scout Jamboree, held here in the summer, and this ensured funding for the fort. Otherwise, it would be in serious disrepair.

At the main gate, Gooderjohn received a call on the unit radio net.

"Gunrunner Six, Gunrunner Three," his operations officer, Major Thornton, called.

"Gunrunner Three, go ahead."

"Gunrunner Six, HHC should proceed to Building 2700. That's the beginning of our battalion area. I'll meet you there. The command sergeant major is with the first sergeants and assigning billet to each company in that area at this time. Over."

"Roger, Gunrunner Three, I have a good copy. Over."

"Gunrunner Six, you have a meeting at 1800 hours tonight at the brigade headquarters. I can give you details when you arrive. Over."

"Roger, en route to your location now. Out," Gooderjohn lied. He was sitting on the side of the road with twenty vehicles backed up behind him while his driver searched a map looking for Building 2700. Finally, he found it.

"Holy shit, sir," the driver said.

"What's wrong?" Gooderjohn asked.

"Sir, this 2700 block of buildings is in the middle of nowhere. It's not close to the PX or theater or anything."

"Let's just get there before we wonder about the entertainment. Drive." Gooderjohn was in no mood for this right now.

****

At 1800 hours, Gooderjohn and the other two battalion commanders of the 115th Infantry Regiment, 29th Division were seated in the brigade conference room. The conference room was really the bottom floor of a World War II wooden barracks building that had seen little in the way of maintenance since the end of the Korean War. There was no air conditioning, but the windows did have screens. The coal furnace had been replaced by a gas heat system. The latrine was the four-shower, four-sink, four-toilet decor left over from World War II. Paint was the pea-soup green color and from the looks of things was probably ten coats thick before you got to the wood. The upper floor was the same and was occupied by desks for the staff. They were billeted in a similar building next door, but with twenty bunks on each floor in the open bay.

"Alright, let's get started," the brigade commander, Colonel Warren, said, looking at the brigade operations officer, Major Lucas. Colonel Warren wore a Combat Infantryman's badge, Airborne wings and a Ranger tab. He had seen action in Vietnam as a young officer. Coming home, he had been offered an early out for having extended his tour in Vietnam and had come home to a very lucrative job in an investment company in Baltimore. He had risen quickly through the investment house, met all the right people in state government and been encouraged to join the Guard. Promotions in the Guard came fast, and within fifteen years he was a full colonel and commanding the brigade. He had his eyes on the adjutant general's position for the state someday.

"Thank you, sir. I know you're all a bit confused about being here, but we got bumped out of Indiantown Gap because, along with us, the 28th has been activated too and so has the 50th Armored Division, who are at Camp Grayling. We just need to make the best of it. So... first off, everyone is restricted to the post," he said. Moans and groans were heard from everyone in attendance. "I know everyone wants to go home over the weekends and see the wife or girlfriend—well, there are no weekends. We have a schedule that's around-the-clock processing and training. As of right now, the post is closed to visitors as well, so your wives and sweethearts can't get on the base either. Have your people call them in the next forty-eight hours and explain that because in forty-nine hours, off-post calls will be shut down. We'll be going into a blackout phase," he said.

"What the hell? This isn't a secret mission or anything. Why all the security crap?" a battalion commander asked.

"Sir, I have no answer for you, but this is what we are being told. And it's not just here but at other installations as well," Major Lucas, the brigade operations officer, explained, to no one's satisfaction. "Next, tomorrow we begin in-processing procedures and I've provided a schedule for the day's events to each of your battalion operations officers. Some units will start the day with administrative processing such as reviewing wills, insurance papers, enlistment contracts." He paused. "You do understand that everyone is activated for two years regardless of their enlistment contract." That brought more moans and groans. "Those not going through admin processing tomorrow will be taking physical fitness tests conducted by a cadre from the Old Guard." Again, moans and groans.

"Sir, some of our people are pretty much out of shape. A physical fitness test is liable to kill them," another officer said.

"We'll find out tomorrow who can cut it and who can't. We're going to be going into combat and we need to weed out those that aren't fit," Colonel Warren said. "Continue, Major."

"Yes, sir. Tomorrow evening after chow, immunizations will commence for those units that took the physical fitness test. The next day, everyone flips, with those who haven't taken the physical fitness test yet taking it while the others go to admin processing." The rest of the briefing was a full calendar of activities for the week, with every minute planned out in detail. How soon people would get to bed at night depended on how fast they could get through the day's planned events. Dental exams were going to be the problem as most of the soldiers hadn't seen a dentist in the last decade, let alone every six months.[9] Finally, the question on everyone's mind was asked.

"Sir, any word on when, where, and if we're going to deploy?" asked one battalion commander.

"No, no word at this time, but CENTCOM needs divisions and mechanized divisions, so we're prime meat. Start a vigorous inspection program on your vehicles and the Bradleys. We don't want to roll off the ships with a bunch of broken vehicles. Getting maintenance support from the units already in-country is not going to be a problem. Any other questions?"

"Sir, I heard that we might have to go to the National Training Center for a rotation. Any truth to that rumor?" Gooderjohn asked.

"Some Guard units have been sent already, and it's been a disaster. The 256th Infantry Brigade was activated and sent to Fort Hood. They were going to get an NTC rotation, but fifty or so of the soldiers went AWOL and then complained to the press about their living conditions. They're getting no sympathy from anyone. I think the

---

[9] Dental exams were given prior to deployment in ODS. Over 13,000 were rated as fit for deployment but "probably requiring emergency dental care within one year." Captain Les Melnyk, *Mobilizing for the Storm: The Army National Guard in Operations Desert Shield and Desert Storm* (Washington, DC: National Guard Bureau, Office of Public Affairs, Historical Services Division, 2001), 16.

Army is now taking the approach of 'get them mobilized and shipped over. We can train up when we get there,'" Colonel Warren said. "For right now, let's concentrate on getting ourselves squared away."

The physical fitness tests proved what was suspected. Most were out of shape for combat. On the third day, each unit started the day off with one hour of physical fitness training. By the fifth day, people were complaining of sore muscles, sore backs, and sore legs. The morning run was initially a one-mile run, and before it was over, stragglers were three-quarters of a mile behind the lead soldier and walking. Nondeployable figures then started to increase. Colonel Warren was becoming concerned, as almost a quarter of the brigade wasn't fit for duty.

"Good afternoon, sir. Can I come in?" asked Major Osborne from the division G-1 shop or personnel office.

"Please do, Major. How's life on the Division staff?" Warren asked. Major Osborne had been the executive officer for one of the battalions before he had been dragged up to the Division staff, much to his displeasure, but he wasn't a full-time guard officer, so he didn't have a lot of pull.

"It's OK, sir, and the G-1 is an OK guy to work for. Right now he's really under the gun with the admin portion of this deployment and getting everyone's records up to speed," the major explained.

"Take a seat," Colonel Warren said, pointing at a folding metal chair. This office was best described as austere, not like his office back at the investment firm. "So what brings you to my doorstep?" he asked.

"Sir, I know you're down on deployable personnel, but I've brought you some relief. It seems the active Army has shaken the tree and found some homesteaders hiding in the trees as well as new recruits from the training centers. Over the next couple of days you're going to be receiving replacements in all ranks that will bring the brigade up to ninety percent strength. The privates are all coming from basic and advanced individual training centers, so they'll be in good physical condition. The junior NCOs are coming out of the Shake and Bake NCO[10] school, so they'll have the training and be in physical shape as well. The senior NCOs have been considered excess by their units and are coming in to fill our ranks. They're physically fit and have the training," Major Osborne explained.

"Why are these senior NCOs considered excess?" Colonel Warren asked.

"Sir, some have been in garrison positions such as range control or installation safety officer or installation communications—positions that could be taken over by civilians. Some are coming out of stateside medical facilities as it was felt that beefing up the front-line medics would be of more use. Surprisingly, most are volunteering to come to us. These are not the sick, lame, and lazy but good people."

"At this point, Major, I would take the sick, lame, and lazy, but I'll be sure we receive these people with open arms. When can I expect them to start arriving?" Warren inquired.

"Sir, the first group from advanced infantry training at Fort Benning are on Greyhound buses at this time and heading here now. They should be arriving sometime tonight. I'll get with your people to get them in-processed tonight when they arrive and release them to you in the morning. There are five buses coming, and that's just the first

---

[10] Shake and Bake NCO Course was a program used during Vietnam where a young soldier, Private through Specialist 4, could apply to a ninety-day course to become an E-5 Sergeant if he successfully passed.

load. I expect we'll have you up to strength by the end of next week," Osborne said.

"You have just made my day, Major," Warren said, extending his hand.

****

"All right, let's get the vehicles loaded on the flat cars," yelled Chief Warrant Officer Berger. Mr. Berger was the vehicle maintenance officer for the battalion. In the civilian world, he'd managed a heavy equipment maintenance facility in Townson, Maryland, repairing Caterpillar bulldozers and earth-moving equipment. Fortunately, or not, most of the soldiers under his charge in the maintenance platoon were auto mechanics, heavy equipment mechanics or full-time National Guardsmen that worked in the repair shops. To say his people were well trained in their jobs would be an understatement. On the other hand, they weren't too swift in NBC procedures or qualifying on their rifles. They were mechanics, not riflemen.

"Staff Sergeant, be sure every jeep has cardboard taped over the windshields, and I want the hoods on all the jeeps to be chained and locked. If we don't, the windshields will all be broken from kids throwing rocks at them on the overpasses and thieves will steal every damn battery and cut the cables. It's a short haul to Norfolk for loading, and the drivers will take off in the buses as soon as the vehicles are loaded so they can unlock and offload when the train arrives," Mr. Berger directed. The active Army was using the new Humvee vehicles, but the 29th still had the venerable M151 Jeep that had been around in one model or another since World War II.

Mr. Berger and most soldiers liked the vehicle as it was a simple design and easy to maintain in the field. On the negative side, repair parts were hard to come by since it was no longer in the active Army system, having been replaced the year before by the Humvee.

"Mr. Berger, do you think the jeeps will survive this war? I mean, we don't have a lot of parts for replacements," Staff Sergeant Abbot asked, wiping his hands on a rag that he always carried.

"Oh, I suspect they'll last for a bit and then we'll be replacing them with the Humvees. Now those are a real pain in the ass to work on, and I suspect we'll have our hands full if they start issuing those to us. Oh, be sure we have enough chain-link fencing so each vehicle can have a screen," Mr. Berger said.

"Sir, the screens for the Bradleys are in each Bradley and the ones for the jeeps are in the CONEX containers. Do you think the jeeps will be close enough to the shooting to have to worry about a screen to stop RPGs?" asked Staff Sergeant Abbot.

"No, the screens for the jeeps will be to lay down when they get stuck in sand and be able to drive over them. Sort of like a road rug for the jeeps. Gives them traction," Mister Berger explained.

"Well, sir, I guess we're about to learn a lot of new things in the next year," Abbot said as his attention was caught and he wandered off.

I just hope we don't learn too little too late, Mr. Berger was thinking.

Chapter 39
Never Too Old

20 November 1990
Cleaver Construction Company
Evansville, Indiana

Evansville, Indiana, was a quiet town on the banks of the Ohio River. Like any Midwestern town, it had its Veterans Day parade and fireworks on the Fourth of July. On Armed Forces Day, a serviceman couldn't order a beer or dinner that someone else didn't pay for. On Veterans Day, the heroes of World War II, and a few still around from the Great War, wore red poppies in their buttonholes. Even the Vietnam veterans were treated with quiet respect.

Mr. Cleaver was seated in his office overlooking Marina Pointe Park. He loved the view from his office window, as he could keep an eye on his pet project. By day, Mr. Bob Cleaver owned a construction equipment company selling Caterpillar tractors and other heavy equipment to the construction industry. He had built the company from the ground up after coming home from the Korean War at the age of twenty-one. He had served in the Navy aboard a Landing Ship, Tank, commonly known as an LST. He remembered those years fondly, and when the opportunity had come along to relive that time, he'd jumped at it. Bob and a group from the Chamber had purchased and restored an LST—the LST-325, who had seen action in the Normandy invasion. Over the years, the ship would cruise the inland waterways, stopping at communities along the way and giving lectures to anyone who came aboard. The admission fee helped maintain the ship. The crew were all volunteers.

His intercom buzzed. "What's up, Katie?"

"Sir, you have a call on line one," his secretary replied. "It's the mayor."

"OK, I got it," Cleaver said and punched the appropriate button on this desk phone. "Mr. Mayor, what do I owe the pleasure?" Bob asked. He was golfing buddies with the mayor, but he liked jerking his chain with the political title.

"Bob, you'll never guess who I got a phone call from. The President of the United States!" Mayor Zack said with some excitement.

"Wow! Does he want you to run for the office in two years?" Bob asked with a grin.

"No, he wants to activate our ship!" Zack said with excitement dripping from his lips.

"You're shitting me, right?" Bob said as he suddenly sat up straight in his chair. "He really bought into the bullshit story about the ship being available?"

"I guess so, because he's sending a Navy captain down tomorrow to see you. Be nice to him," Zack almost pleaded. "Call me when you see him."
****

The knock on the door got Bob's attention as he looked up from the newspaper article he'd been reading about the deployments to the Middle East that had been going on for the past three months.

"Mr. Cleaver," his rather attractive secretary in the tight skirt said. "There is a Naval officer, a captain, I think, here to see you."

Folding his paper, Bob was thinking, *So they really want to take her. Got to be something in this for us. We bought that ship, we restored it and did it all with our own money. Not about to just give it away, regardless of what Zack says. Hell, the city didn't even help us.* As the secretary turned and Bob followed the shape of her rear, he was thinking, *Oh, to be young again.*

"Send him in," Bob said as he stood and came around his desk. The Navy captain in his blue uniform with three rows of ribbons walked in with his white hat tucked under his left arm and his right hand extended.

"Mr. Cleaver, Captain Ambrose, sir. Thank you for seeing me."

"Captain, it's a pleasure," Cleaver said, noticing the firm handshake that the captain offered. "Have a seat, please. I understand you want our ship," he said, pointing to an overstuffed pair of chairs with a coffee table. "Would you like some coffee?"

"No, thank you." Captain Ambrose said, taking a seat. "Sir, I'll come right to the point of my visit. I do want your ship, LST-325."

"I heard," Bob said, attempting to cover any emotion.

"I should have said the US Navy wants your ship. It is operational, is it not?"

"Damn right it's operational, but why would the Navy want our ship? I don't understand." Bob was sitting on the edge of his chair, hands folded and elbows on his knees. He wanted to be sure he was hearing correctly.

"Mr. Cleaver, the US Navy is short landing craft in the Middle East. After Vietnam, the Boxer-class LSTs were put out of service. The Navy acquired a new class of LST, the *Ticonderoga* class, and those were phased out in 1979 for the LCAS ships. The bottom line is we don't have enough landing craft for our needs now. We're in the same boat with minesweepers. Your ship is one of four LSTs still afloat, and one of those is a derelict on the banks of the Columbia River. One is a ferry boat out of New London, Connecticut, and no longer capable of open ocean cruising. One is in Michigan and is also a ferry, but the bow doors are welded shut. Yours is the only one still, how do I say… combat-ready. We need it and we want it," Captain Ambrose said.

Cleaver sat in stunned silence. Finally, the questions began to flow. "How long do you want to keep her?"

"For the duration of operations in the Middle East… a year, probably."

"Sweet Jesus, a year. Who's going to crew her?"

"We'll put a Navy crew on board. We'll need a train-up as none of the crew is old enough to have served on board that class of ship."

"Who's paying for this operation and the maintenance on her?"

"The United States Navy will pay for the maintenance in our possession and any repairs that are needed after she's returned to you upon joint inspection."

Cleaver sat back in his chair and was silent for a minute. "Tell you what, Captain, you come back and I'll have an answer for you."

"Mr. Cleaver, you really don't have a choice…"

"Captain, a private citizens' group purchased that ship from the Greek government, so technically it wasn't the property of the US government when we got it. That same group raised the money to maintain that ship. You come back tomorrow and you'll find out if you're getting her peacefully or in a hostile takeover." Bob stood and motioned for the captain to head for the door.

"I'll be back in the morning, Mr. Cleaver," Captain Ambrose said, not too happy.

****

"OK, everyone, calm down and let's get to business," Bob said as he stood on the deck of the ship. One hundred men stood in front of him. Some were his age, some older, and some barely able to shave. They all had one thing in common: they were the crew of LST-325.

"I was approached today by the United States Navy. They want our ship right away." That brought on murmurs of "Oh, hell no," "Not going to happen," and "Not without me they aren't."

"Gents, you need to understand, they have the power to seize the vessel. But we may have some negotiation wiggle room. They don't have sailors that have ever sailed on this type of ship and they need it fast. Truth is they don't have enough landing craft to do the job." Bob paused. "Question—how many of you could sign on as crew for one year and be ready to leave in a week?" Slowly, hands started going up. Bob started counting.

"Bob, would we get paid if we sign on?" someone asked.

"I'll see that your civilian salaries are matched and will insist on combat pay on top of that," Bob answered. Several more hands went up.

"Bob, would our families have that government life insurance that soldiers and sailors get?"

"We'll insist that you're covered." A few more hands went up. Bob now had a skeleton crew, just enough men to man the ship.

"Bob, what about our jobs? Will we get them back when we return?" another asked.

"We'll make sure that you're covered just like the National Guard guys are covered and guaranteed their jobs back when they come home." More hands went up.

"Who will be the skipper?" another voice asked.

"I already spoke with Captain Harold and he told me that he'll take it to sea and he wants everyone's rank and positions to stay the same." More hands went up.

"Bob, can we call you in the morning after we talk to our wives?"

"Not a problem. Talk it over with your families and call me in the morning. If you're sure you're going, pack a seabag and wait for my call."

****

"Mr. Cleaver, Captain Ambrose is here," the secretary said, filling out her tight knit sweater. *Oh, to be young again*, Bob was thinking again.

"Please show him in," Bob said, approaching the door and extending his hand. "Captain, good morning. Please sit down." Once they were seated, he asked, "Captain, which is it going to be? A hostile seizure or a peaceful transition?"

"I'm not sure what you have in mind, Mr. Cleaver. I would prefer for this to be a peaceful transition," Captain Ambrose said.

"Well, if you play ball with me, it will be more than peaceful. Here's what I'm offering you…"

****

It was a sunny but cool Saturday morning. The air said winter wasn't far off. Soon ice would be forming on the banks of the river. LST-325 had experienced a flurry of activity for the past two weeks, with crew moving aboard, supplies being loaded, fuel being transferred. As she sat with her twin diesel engines softly running, the parking lot filled with townfolk. The local police were directing traffic to parking areas. The high school band was setting up. A stage with seats for

372

several dignitaries and a podium were set up with a loudspeaker system. Two Navy officers were already on the stage, along with Mayor Zack and Captain Harold, the skipper of LST-325. Finally, the time came for the dignitaries to start talking, and they did once the ship's chaplain gave the invocation, asking the Lord to give them calm seas and safe passage. One of the Baptist church choirs sang the national anthem as the high school band played. Once the dignitaries were done, Captain Ambrose stood and gave a short speech. As he concluded, he turned to Captain Harold and handed him a manila envelope.

"Captain Harold, sir, here are your sailing orders and your vessel's commissioning documents." As he did so, a boatswain's pipe sounded and the commissioning pennant was hoisted on the bow of the ship.

"Thank you, sir, and with your permission we will get underway," Harold said, saluting Captain Ambrose.

"Godspeed, sir," Ambrose said and returned the salute.

Harold stepped off the stage and walked to the gangplank of LST-325. Once he was aboard, the gangplank was withdrawn and a loud blast on the ship's whistle was heard. The water under the stern began to churn as the two big props began pushing the ship into the Ohio River current. A piece of canvas had been draped over the bow on both sides. As the ship began to move, the canvas was hauled aboard and exposed the name painted about the large white numbers, USS *Memorial*. Hundreds of small craft escorted the vessel as she pulled away from Evansville and the families left behind.

Chapter 40

Looking to the Offense

21 November 1990
XVIII Airborne Corps HQ
Jeddah, Saudi Arabia

General Luck was reading over the reports of the actions against the 2nd Iraqi Army Corps from General Peters. The 101st Airborne Division had stopped them with the help of Navy attack aircraft and the enemy's crappy logistics system. Everyone had known the first asset was going to be a powerful tool. No one had known how good, or in this case how bad, the Iraqi logistical system was. Having two of the world's largest gas stations, could the Iraqis be so incompetent that they could not fuel their vehicles? With respect to the 2nd Iraqi Army Corps, that was the case, but what about the other forces? Could the 2nd Republican Guard Corps be experiencing the same issue? They hadn't moved since the Battle of Medina Ridge.

Throughout the night and the next day, reports from the 2/17th Cav indicated that the 2nd Iraqi Army Corps was not only hurt but withdrawing back to where they started this attack from. Intelligence reports indicated that the 2nd Infantry Division and the 14th Division were still in the Tabuk area and not moving. Time to give General Yeosock some good news for a change.

"Sir, General Yeosock is on the line," General Luck's aide informed him, and he quickly reached for the phone.

"John, Gary here. How is your day?" General Luck said. Although Yeosock was Luck's boss, rank between lieutenant generals was like virtue among whores. In private, they were all equal.

"Right now, I could use some good news. I understand that the 2nd Iraqi Army Corps has stopped his attack," Yeosock said.

"Well, let's say he's resumed his attack…but he's attacking to the north," Luck said. It took Yeosock a minute to comprehend what he'd just heard.

"Wait, are you saying he's withdrawing?" Yeosock asked with a touch of excitement in his voice.

"He is, according to the Cav at the 101st. Seems he's pulling back. Don't know how far back he's going, but we're going to keep watching him for a while," Luck explained.

"That's great news. Give my congratulations to Peters, and I'll be sure Norm hears about this. What were Peters's casualties?" Yeosock asked.

"Not bad. Lost a couple of choppers and some of the infantry were roughed up, but overall he's in good shape. He attributes their success to three things. The first is their attack helicopters, which we all figured would be a boon to the fight. The second and third, however, were deal breakers, he feels," Luck said.

"OK, are you going to tell me or keep me in suspense?" Yeosock complained.

"Well, the second was the terrain. The corps couldn't operate in the mountainous terrain. Regiments were committed in piecemeal fashion. Whenever he could mount a two-regiment front, they would hit him with air strikes. The priority for the ground soldiers was to take out the air-defense weapons that for some reason in one division's case had been positioned in the lead and on the flanks," Luck explained.

"And the third factor? What was that?" Yeosock's interest was really piqued.

"Logistics, and specifically fuel. He's out of fuel. He parked a mess of tanks that were above his normal complement, and we think it's because he doesn't have the fuel to run them," Luck stated.

"You've got to be kidding me. He has two of the world's largest gas stations and he can't move it? Is that what you're saying?"

"Look, I don't know what it's like over in the east, but over here, the 10th Saudi Brigade did a good job of scorched earth when they pulled out of Tabuk. There are few roads in the interior coming south, and what gas stations and fuel farms there were, the Saudis destroyed. All his fuel has to come by truck from over on the east to Tabuk and then south to where he is. He can't get enough fuel for a major push now. I'm wondering if your intel people are seeing the same thing with the 2nd Republican Guard Corps or any other units," Luck questioned.

"No one has said anything, but I'll raise the flag on that one. That might just be the deal breaker. On another subject—and I want you to keep this close for now—I want you to start thinking about going on the offense. Norm's been notified that we're going to get the forces we want. Fred Franks is here now and bringing the VII Corps from Germany, and Ivan is coming in tomorrow, bringing in III Corps headquarters along with one National Guard heavy division. Three infantry divisions from the Guard are also coming. Thinking of giving you one of those infantry divisions for sure and maybe two. Think how you would use them all and get back to me in a week or two. OK?" Yeosock asked rather than ordered, but the message was clear.

Chapter 41
Everyone Is Asking

21 November 1990
Situation Room, White House
Washington, D.C.

The President was up at his usual time. The crisis in the Middle East was taking most of his time now, but there were still other matters that had to be dealt with. Congress wanted constant handholding and briefs on what was going on, and congressional leadership asked for constant updates. Half the members of Congress were grandstanding for the hometown vote, supporting mobilization, and the other half were paying lip service to supporting the effort while dragging their feet on bills to support the effort.

As he walked to the Situation Room, his mind was in a different arena. *This damn Budget Enforcement Act is going to be the death of me yet. Why in the hell did I ever say no new taxes? This is a damn good bill, and it's going to reduce the deficit over a ten-year period since we now have a major conflict on our hands that's costing us a pretty penny.*

As he approached the door to the Situation Room, the Marine sentry opened the door. "Thank you, young man," the President said.

"You're welcome, Mr. President," the young Marine responded. He would write home tonight to his parents to say that he'd talked to the President of the United States today.

"Keep your seats," he said when he'd cleared the door. "Let's get started. What've you got for me today, Colonel Atwell?" the President asked as he sat down and a military aide set a cup of coffee in front of him.

"Sir, we're going to cover some recent developments in the AOR, current status of the major forces and deployment actions. First slide, please," Colonel Atwell called. Two slides came up. The one on the right was a map of the western side of Saudi Arabia. The left slide was a satellite photo of the same area. Atwell continued, "Sir, in the last forty-eight hours, the 2nd Iraqi Army Corps with the 7th, 37th and 51st Infantry Divisions launched an attack south against the 101st Airborne Division in this location." A red laser point appeared on the map. "With assistance from Navy aircraft located in the Red Sea, that attack was stopped. The 7th Division appears to be at forty percent strength now and the 51st Division is approximately thirty percent strength. The 37th Infantry Division was never committed. It also appears that they're experiencing a fuel shortage as they have almost double the number of tanks associated with an infantry division but have parked them all in this location, as seen on this satellite photo." The photo showed a large number of tanks parked in neat rows.

Looking very happy, the President said, "Damn, those Airborne people are worth their weight in gold. Well, what are we going to do about this tank park?" The President looked at the Joint Chiefs and the SecDef.

"Sir, a flight of B-52s out of Diego Garcia are en route to take care of that tank park. Right about now, they're flying up the Red Sea," Mr. Cheney said.

"Are we sure they're still there?"

"Yes, Mr. President, we have eyes on the target."

"Good," the President said, turning back to Colonel Atwell. "Continue, Colonel."

"In the east, the 1st Republican Guard Corps is continuing to adjust its positions while the 9th Iraqi Corps moves into positions in the UAE. Next slide, please. As you can see, sir, instead of occupying the major cities of Dubai and Abu Dhabi, the 9th Corps commander has moved his forces out along the border region more and is preparing defensive positions across the front."

"Does General Schwarzkopf now feel he has the forces necessary to get the job done?" the President asked.

"Sir, once the 50th Armored Division arrives and the rest of VII Corps closes in along with the III Corps headquarters, he feels he'll have the combat power he needs to take back the UAE. It remains to be seen if he will be able to move on from there or if Saddam commits some of his other available divisions. Remember, sir, Saddam has the fourth-largest army in the world and fifty divisions at his disposal, plus a sizable air force to back up his army," Mr. Cheney interjected. The President just grunted and turned to face Colonel Atwell.

"Colonel, I'm sure you have a nice neat presentation planned for this morning, but I'm pressed today, so let me shoot questions and let's see who's in the know now," the President said with a smile that only Colonel Atwell could see. These shoot-from-the-hip questions made all the generals and secretaries very nervous as Colonel Atwell wasn't expected to have the immediate answers, but they were.

"How's the flow for the VII Corps going? Do I need to call the Prime Minister?" the President asked, looking around the table.

Finally, General Powell spoke up. "The flow is going well, Mr. President. The German and Dutch transportation systems are bending over backwards to move our stuff as quickly as possible to the ports. Priority has been given to our rail moves, and the national police in both countries are guiding and escorting our convoys expeditiously through major cities. We're not having any problems at this time."

"Good. How about ships? Are we getting the right types and enough of them?" the President asked. Powell looked to Admiral Kelso, who looked right back at him. The Army was responsible for obtaining and loading ships, not the Navy, but the Navy owned the ships of the military sealift fleet. Once the ship left the dock, it was the Navy's responsibility, but to shipside and loading was the Army's responsibility.

To terminate the staring contest between them, Mr. Cheney spoke up. "There's a limited number of RoRo ships, Mr. President, and we have contracted for any and all that the shipping companies can provide. They've even cut back on commercial traffic to accommodate our needs."

"What's the status of our four National Guard divisions? How soon will they be deployed?"

"Sir," General Vuono said, "the 50th Armored Division is en route to ports in New Orleans and Beaumont, Texas, for ship loading. The soldiers commence flying over in a week, arriving about a week before their equipment. The 29th Infantry has shipped its equipment from Norfolk, and its people start flying over tomorrow from Richmond. The 28th Infantry Division is en route to the National Training Center for certification and will be followed by the 35th Infantry Division. As each finishes their training, their equipment will be shipped straight over from Oakland. General Schwarzkopf felt that he could start things off without them and would not need them until he started moving up the east side of Saudi and taking Riyadh," General Vuono concluded.

"How are our air assets holding up?" the President asked.

"The air assets are holding, sir," General McPeak said. "We are able to attain air parity in most cases and superiority for short periods. As we receive additional support from the Navy and our allies, I believe we will be able to claim air superiority. We are a bit surprised, however, as to the ability of many of their pilots and the quality of their aircraft. They have the latest Soviet fighters and are flying them extremely well. In addition, they have the Soviet air-defense systems and are employing them en masse. Possibly the folks over at Langley can enlighten us as to where this stuff is coming from," he concluded.

This was General McPeak's first time in the Situation Room with the President. His predecessor had been relieved the previous month because he couldn't keep his mouth shut when being interviewed by the press. He'd divulged that we knew the location of Saddam every day and could take him out very quickly. After that, Saddam had never stayed in the same place two nights in a row.[11]

"Let me ask the million-dollar question. When does General Schwarzkopf think he'll be ready to launch an all-out offensive?" the President asked. The cone of silence descended on the room.

Finally Mr. Cheney spoke up. "Sir, we need to consult with him before we answer that question. A lot of factors are going to come into play before we can give you an accurate date. We have a lot of forces still to move into the area. We have a logistics buildup that needs to take place. There is required training of not only the Guard units but the units from the VII Corps, just to name a few items."

---

[11] Richard Cohen, "Where Gen. Dugan Went Wrong," *Washington Post*, September 18, 1990, https://www.washingtonpost.com/archive/opinions/1990/09/18/where-gen-dugan-went-wrong/a7dee390-8035-4438-9128-f34738c94109/.

"Well, can you give me a ballpark date? Look, I've got Margaret asking, along with the King, the Sultan of Oman and the Emir of Kuwait. I'd like to be able to give them something," the President said.

"Right now, Mr. President, I would hazard a guess that we're looking at a spring offensive," Mr. Cheney said. He could tell that the President wasn't happy with that response but accepted it without comment and stood, indicating the meeting was over.

Chapter 42

Thanksgiving

27 November 1990

Middle East

Thanksgiving dinner was one of two times a year when service cooks went above and beyond the call of duty. It was second only to Christmas dinner. This was the time for the cooks to shine, and they normally did. Fixing Thanksgiving dinner normally took a couple of days, especially for the Army cooks who were working out of field kitchens designed more for T-rations than A-rations.

"Sir, Sarge Jones is here to see you," Lester said, opening the door of Cory's vehicle.

Cory looked up from his writing. "Sergeant Jones, how are things in Jonestown?"

Sergeant First Class Jones was the mess sergeant for the 3rd Battalion, 327th. Cory considered him a lot more than just a mess sergeant. Just after they'd arrived in sector and things had settled down, Jones had insisted on getting a couple of two-and-a-half-ton trucks to run back to Jeddah, no questions asked. Two days later, Cory had stumbled across a camp of five GP medium tents with cots, shower point, and a mess section. It seemed that Sergeant Jones had built a camp for the rifle companies to come back to for a twenty-four-hour rest every five days, situation permitting. The soldiers loved it and dubbed it "Jonestown."

"Sir, things are going just fine. I think the boys like the idea of coming off the line for twenty-four hours and getting a cold shower and sleeping on a cot. We also make sure they have a hot T-rat meal when they come in and a hot breakfast when they leave."

"Well, I can tell you from talking to the kids, Jonestown is a hell of a morale booster. I thank you," Cory said. "What's on the menu for Thanksgiving dinner?"

"This year's Thanksgiving will not only include turkey and ham but, compliments of the Saudi King, quail is also being served. We'll have mashed potatoes, green beans, corn, rolls, apple and pecan pie as well as pumpkin pie, all fresh and no T-rats," Jones said with some pride.

"Oh my God, I'm hungry already. Are we sure we have enough for everyone?"

"Sir, the brigade mess sergeant attempted to short us, but we got our fair share. We good. We also have fresh milk. Been a bitch of a time keeping it cold to stop it from spoiling, but then we discovered that it's that milk that tastes just like regular milk but doesn't need to be refrigerated. Comes from Germany."

"I'll take your word for it. How are we going to feed the guys on the line?"

"Sir, the XO has a plan for that. We have enough Marmite cans that we can truck out food to the line doggies and serve them right there," Jones said.

"OK, but I don't want the cooks exposed. Wherever you set up, I want you behind something so you're not seen from the Iraqi positions. Understood?"

"Yes, sir. I have no intention of exposing my guys."

****

Sergeant Brewer sat on top of his track vehicle overlooking the other track vehicles in the company. He was a member of the 1st British Armoured Division, 4th Brigade, 1st Battalion Royal Scots and proud of the fact that they were the oldest regiment of the Royal Army. They were enjoying a Thanksgiving dinner as well.

"Hey, Sarge, do the Yanks eat like this every day?" Private Harrison asked.

"Harrison, are you daft? These Yanks are celebrating a holiday in their country called Thanksgiving. Supposedly when the first ships arrived in America, the people sat down with the indigenous population and had a great feast. This celebrates that event. The rest of the year they live on them bloody MRE rations," Brewer said.

"Well, it's better than the bullet beef we've been getting. I'm so sick of eating that stuff I enjoy an MRE when we get them. I'm going to see if I can get some more of this food. Should I bring you back another plate?"

"You damn well better not come back here without a plate for me, mate," Brewer said with a smile.

****

As in most homes, Thanksgiving Day in the Hanner household was a day of family, good food and football. That was the way it had always been since Ed was a little boy. Usually there would be a smoked salmon on the table as well if Ed had had a pretty good summer fishing off the Oregon coast during the salmon run. He liked to catch them before they swam up the rivers. Ed's kids, a son, eight, and a daughter, ten, regarded smoked salmon like candy.

"Dad, did we get a letter from Mom yesterday?" Brian, Ed's son, asked as he walked into the kitchen in his pajamas.

"Afraid not. She's really busy in her job over there," Ed tried to explain. Wendy had joined the National Guard unit in Coos Bay when money had gotten tight. Ed had a good job in the Weyerhaeuser plywood mill, but a growing family needed a bit more than Ed was making at the time, so she'd joined for the extra money. Her part-time National Guard duty had turned into full-time work at the armory. When the unit had been called up, she'd had to go too.

"Oh… well, are we going to have a Thanksgiving dinner?" Brian asked.

"You bet, tiger. The turkey has been thawing for three days and I just put it in the oven stuffed with sausage stuffing. You and Sissi can help me make the mashed potatoes and the broccoli."

"Yuck… I don't like broccoli," Brian said with a matching facial expression.

"Well, then, you can help with the smashed sweet potatoes."

"Oh, double yuck. Mashed sweet potatoes look like earwax," Brian complained.

"Well, then, you can do the dishes, because everyone has to pitch in around here," Ed said in a tone of frustration. He was trying, but he was beginning to realize life for a working wife wasn't easy. About then, the doorbell rang.

"Sissi, can you answer the door, please?" Ed yelled, his hands wet as he washed the potatoes.

"I can't. I'm drying my hair. Make Brian do it," a voice from down the hall commanded.

"Brian, go answer the door."

"I can't… I'm still in my PJs."

Oh, hell, who could this be? Ed was thinking, grabbing a towel as the doorbell rang again. He walked across the living room with Brian in tow behind him. Boomer, the dog, continued to enjoy his favorite chair, Ed's chair.

Ed opened the door in a bit of a huff. "Yes, what—oh, hi, Mrs. Esser," he said, quickly changing his attitude. "Come on in. Excuse the mess," he said as he stepped back and held the door open for her. "The kids just got up and haven't gotten to their chores yet. Brian has to get dressed. Boomer, get down." Brian left to get dressed. Boomer didn't move but continued to lie in Ed's chair as Mrs. Esser stepped in.

Mrs. Esser lived across the street with her retired husband. He had been a logger his whole life, working in the forest in southwestern Oregon. Their kids were grown and living in Portland and San Francisco but seldom came and visited.

"Ed, I can't stay, but Bob and I would like you and the kids to join us for dinner. We'll be eating about three o'clock and it's very casual. I have a ham ready to go in the oven and lots of trimmings."

"Gee, I don't know what to say. That's mighty nice of you, but I have a turkey in the oven right now, and—"

"Good, you can bring it over. And I've made a pumpkin pie as well as mincemeat pie. I remember Wendy saying you liked mincemeat pie."

"Dad ... just say yes," a small voice sounded off.

Ed turned to see both the kids in the doorway.

"Mrs. Esser's cooking is way better than yours," Sissi said. She followed up with, "Your cooking isn't bad, Dad, but hers is so much better."

"Nice recovery, kid. You'll be eating Swanson frozen dinners for the next month," Ed replied. He turned back to Mrs. Esser. "I guess I'm overruled... and I'll bring the turkey. Is there anything else we can bring?"

387

Brian and Sissi gave each other a high-five slap.

"No, just dress casual, and we'll see you at two thirty for a cocktail before dinner. See you kids."

"Bye, Mrs. Esser," the kids responded in unison as she departed. Brian turned and noticed the smiles on the kids' faces. It was going to be an OK Thanksgiving after all. Boomer didn't move.

Chapter 43

Time to Get Serious

1 December 1990

CENTCOM Forward HQ

Military Technological College

Muscat, Oman

General Schwarzkopf had called the meeting, and his key leaders were in attendance. When Stormin' Norman walked into the room, everyone stood and stopped talking.

"Sit down, gentlemen," he directed and took a seat at the head of the table. "How is everyone doing today? You all get enough to eat Thursday?" he asked, not expecting a negative answer from anyone. "I've asked you here this afternoon to give you an idea of what I'm thinking about where we go from here. As you know, the 1st Republican Guard Corps switched out with the IX Corps, who is preparing defensive positions close to the border versus sitting back in the cities. The IX Corps has six divisions, of which he left two infantry divisions back in Saudi to secure oil refineries. That leaves only four divisions to face us, but I expect we'll get a strong counterattack from the 1st Republican Guard Corps once we launch our attack. Once the VII Corps closes in and we get the 50th Armored Division settled along with the two Egyptian divisions and what we currently have on the ground, I believe we'll be ready to go on the offensive. The President has been good about not pushing me, but Cheney was asked for a date. I want time to build an overwhelming force that's logistically well stocked and an air campaign that gives us air superiority from day one. What I need from you gentlemen is an idea of when you think you'll be ready to launch the attack," Schwarzkopf explained. "I want to review what we have in-country now and what will arrive within ninety days. Let's start with the Army assets, General Yeosock."

Yeosock, like all the key leaders, had prepared a slide showing the Army assets in-country or arriving in the next ninety days. "Sir, as you can see, we have three Army corps headquarters on the ground at this time with habitual corps-related assets, to include combat support and service support. Those are XVIII Airborne, VII Corps and III Corps. III Corps and VII Corps are located here in Oman, and XVIII is located in Jeddah." Yeosock paused for a moment. "Division-wise, we have the 82nd and 101st Airborne Divisions, and the 24th ID with the 197th attached. 1st Armored Division and 3rd Armored Division will complete closing by the end of next month. 1st Infantry Division is flowing at this time. 1st Cav Division has closed as of yesterday. We have the 3rd and 2nd Armored Cavalry Regiments and the 18th and 12th Aviation Brigades, each with two battalions of attack helicopters. The British 1st Armoured Division is also completely closed and is here in Oman. The 50th Armored Division is in its mobilization station and will ship its first vehicles this week. The 29th Infantry Division is shipping his vehicles out of Norfolk this week and his people fly out tomorrow. The 28th Infantry Division is at the NTC at this time and the 35th Infantry Division is at the Joint Readiness Training Center going through final train-up. All four National Guard divisions will be here by the end of the ninety-day period," Yeosock said, pausing to take a drink of water.

"What are the host nations bringing?" Schwarzkopf asked.

"Sir, they've brought and closed in-country the 3rd Mech and 4th Armoured Egyptian Divisions. They're flowing into Salalah at this time. The Saudis have the 20th, 10th and 8th Mech Brigades, the last two being in Yanbu. They also have the 45th Armoured Brigade, which is in Jeddah, and the 2nd Saudi National Guard brigade. Kuwait has the 35th Mech and 15th Infantry Brigades along with the Al Fatah Brigade. Oman has given us a brigade with a UAE mech battalion attached. That's all for Army right now," Yeosock said.

Schwarzkopf sat for a minute, lost in thought with his eyes cast down, almost as if he was sleeping. Looking up, he asked, "Do you think in ninety days you'll have the ground forces to take the UAE?"

Without hesitation, Yeosock replied, "Yes, sir, we can." Suddenly this meeting had new meaning to those present.

Looking across the table at Vice Admiral Mauz, Schwarzkopf asked, "How are we looking at sea?"

"Sir, currently there are or will be six aircraft carriers on station. *Midway*, *Ranger*, *Kennedy*, *Saratoga*, *America* and *Roosevelt*. *Eisenhower* has already rotated home. Both of our battleships are present, *Missouri* and *Wisconsin*. We have eighteen cruisers, thirteen destroyers, fifteen frigates, one submarine and two hospital ships," the admiral said. Mauz was new to the staff, having only recently been appointed at COMUSNAVCENT. "This doesn't include the British, Canadian or Australian naval forces, which you have already been briefed on."

"What about the Gator Navy?" Schwarzkopf asked, surprising everyone that he knew the nickname for the amphibious fleet.

"Sir, we have eight amphibious assault ships, twenty-eight landing ships and five minesweepers, not counting what our British friends have brought," Mauz replied, nodding to acknowledge the British commander present.

"When's the last time they exercised a major amphibious assault?" Schwarzkopf asked, getting everyone's attention.

"Sir, I'm not sure—I'll have to get back to you on that," Admiral Mauz said.

"General Boomer, do you know when they last exercised a full-blown amphibious assault?" Stormin' Norman asked, looking at the MARCENT commander.

"Sir, a practice exercise wouldn't hurt," Boomer replied, giving the smart answer.

"What Marine Corps assets have we got?" His question was directed right at General Boomer.

"Sir, the 1st and 2nd Marine Divisions with the 1st Marine ashore and the 2nd on the ships. Also the 3rd Marine Air Wing is present for duty," General Boomer replied.

"Mauz, Boomer, how soon can you put together a full-blown amphibious assault training exercise? Give ourselves a good evaluation on how ready we are to conduct such an exercise," Schwarzkopf asked, inwardly smiling. *They didn't expect that I can see*, he was thinking.

Silence held over the room for a moment as the two men looked at each other; then Admiral Mauz spoke up. "Sir, we can do it in thirty days, as it's a training exercise. You give us the beach and the Gator Navy will have the 2nd Marine Division ashore in thirty days."

"After this meeting, see Ops and they'll give you the beachhead. This will be a full-blown live-fire exercise, gentlemen, understood?" Norman ordered.

'Sir, do you want the ships to fire as well?' Mauz asked.

"Admiral, I want everything that's going to participate in an amphibious assault against the Iraqi Army involved and shooting. No make-believe stuff. Blow him up, understood?"

"Loud and clear, sir."

"General Horner, how are we looking as far as our air assets are concerned?" Schwarzkopf asked.

"Sir, currently—not including the Navy's aircraft on the six carriers, which will be integrated into the air campaign—we have the 14th Air Division with an assortment of fighter aircraft; the 15th Air Division with reconnaissance aircraft; the 16th Special Ops Air Division; the 17th Air Division with the refuelers; the 7th Air Division with heavy bombers; and the 7440 Composite Air Wing out of Incirlik, if we can get the Turks to allow us to use them," General Horner reported. As Horner spoke, the tension and anticipation in the room increased.

Turning to the CENTCOM logistics officer, General Pegasus, Schwarzkopf asked, "What is our logistical status?"

General Pegasus was prepared to answer without hesitation. "Sir, we have a hundred-and-eighty-day stockpile of fuel, food and ammunition at this time. We have sufficient medical facilities both ashore and at sea to service our casualties. Between what we've brought and the host nation, we have sufficient transportation to follow the forces and resupply them. Our sea and air flow of logistical supply is functioning and secure."

Having heard from everyone at this point, Schwarzkopf looked around the room at the faces of those that would be responsible for executing future operations. Their faces all portrayed the same picture—confidence. They understood the risk but also understood what was required to drive the Iraqi Army back to Iraq if not completely destroy its army and topple Saddam.

"Gentlemen, in thirty days I will present the operational plan for the invasion of the UAE and the ultimate liberation of Saudi Arabia and Kuwait. Any questions?" He paused. "Good, then let's get to work."

Chapter 44
Planning Guidance

2 December 1990
CENTCOM Forward HQ
Military Technological College
Muscat, Oman

General Yeosock was pleased that some decisions had been made as to when to kick things off, as were the others present in the meeting. Troops sitting for so long in-country with the anticipation of going into combat but not knowing when was taking its toll on morale. A couple of cruise ships had been contracted to take personnel out for three days of rest and relaxation. However, when Yeosock had visited the ships to observe who was getting to spend the three days, everyone appeared to be from the rear-area supply and service support units and no front-line combat soldiers or Marines. *Isn't that the way it's always been?* he thought as he watched the soldiers, Marines and Air Force personnel scamper aboard. Turning to his aide, he said, "Colonel, make a note to look into how we're allocating positions on these cruise ships to the units."

"Yes, sir, I'll get whoever's in charge of this program on your calendar to brief you," the aide said as they walked back to Yeosock's staff car.

As they rode back to the headquarters building, Yeosock was lost in deep thought. His mind was on the upcoming operation, on which he hadn't been asked for input. General Schwarzkopf was playing his cards close to his chest. He'd gone into a closed-door meeting with the CENTCOM operations officer and the Jedi majors right after the last meeting. The Jedi majors were being very secretive about what was being developed for an operational plan, and that bothered Yeosock as well. He wasn't used to being closed out.

****

Major Stube had been summoned to the office of the CENTCOM G-3, his immediate boss. General Schless had spoken with General Schwarzkopf and received some guidance on his view of the upcoming campaign.

"Sit down, Jack," Schless said, pointing at a chair at the small conference table in his office. "I received some guidance from the general today and want to pass it on to you in your planning considerations. First, you have thirty days to come up with an acceptable operational plan that we can brief the commanders on. That will give us another two months to prepare for the start of the operation."

"Sir, we're looking at launching in ninety days, is that right?" Major Stube said, a bit surprised.

"Yes, but that doesn't mean the ground operations will commence. The Old Man sees a vigorous air campaign prior to the ground campaign. One of your assumptions to make is that we have air superiority over the ground campaign. Without that, we're not going to launch a ground campaign," Schless acknowledged.

As he spoke, Major Stube was making notes. His paper was divided in half. On one side he wrote assumptions and on the other directives.

Schless continued, "Besides air superiority, he wants the 1st Republican Guard, the 2nd Iraqi Army Corps and the 2nd Republican Guard Corps pounded into the Stone Age with a vigorous air campaign.

General Horner's team will be getting the tasking later today to concentrate all bombing efforts on those ground forces in addition to airfields and ADA command and control centers."

Again, Major Stube was writing notes, and Schless paused long enough for him to finish. "What else, sir?" the major asked, looking up.

"Second, you are to employ all our assets in this initial push. Nothing is to be held back. He wants to hit the forces in the UAE with overwhelming force. He isn't giving you any more guidance besides that, as he wants to give you free rein in your thinking. Third, once the campaign in the UAE is concluded, he wants to be able to roll right into a campaign to clear out Saudi Arabia. Again, nothing is to be held back."

"Sir, what about the XVIII Airborne Corps in the west?" Stube asked.

"What about them?" Schless countered with a puzzled look.

"Sir, they're out there on the fringe of the fight. Not sure—"

"Yes, they are, and so far they're the only ones that have bloodied the Iraqis' noses aside from the 10th Saudi Mech Brigade. Your plan has got to include them as well. We can't just leave them out there playing with their toes. But we still have to secure Yanbu and Jeddah, so some forces are going to have to remain there, unless of course those Iraqi forces in that area can be cleaned out in the next ninety days. I don't think that will happen."

"So if we figure out or it becomes obvious that the Iraqi threat in the west can be minimized, then we can use the 101st and the 82nd, correct?" Stube asked.

"Like I said, you're free to come up with whatever plan you can and use the forces that we have or will have when we launch the ground phase," Schless said. "Oh, keep in mind we have to be sensitive to Saudi and Muslim feelings. No US forces in Medina or Mecca. Put that down as a directive. They'll have a shit fit if we roll into either of those cities. The Saudi or Arab forces have to go there, but not us. Understood?"

"Yes, sir. We'll consider the 8th and 10th Saudi Brigades for those targets, and Mecca has the 8th sitting there now and no Iraqi forces are even threatening it," Stube said.

"Another thing: we want minimal damage to cities and towns. The Old Man doesn't want to get US forces bogged down in street fighting. Leave that to host nation forces. Look at using our people to overrun and isolate the Iraqi forces. The host nation folks can do the cleaning up," Schless pointed out, another directive Stube noted. "Any other questions?"

"No, sir, I'm sure we'll have some when we get into this," Stube commented.

"Well, the door is open, so just come and ask. I look forward to seeing what you guys come up with," Schless said, closing the discussion.

Chapter 45
Find and Kill

4 December 1990
101st Airborne Division HQ
Yanbu, Saudi Arabia

General Peters had been in command of the 101st Airborne Division for a year. Getting selected to command this division was a lifetime dream for the young general officer. A graduate of VMI versus West Point, he'd believed this to be the crowning achievement of his military career when he had taken command back at Fort Campbell, Kentucky. Not only was he an astute artillery officer, but he could hold his own in the political arena of the top echelons of the Army. His thoughts were interrupted by his aide.

"Sir, Lieutenant Colonel Roe is here," the aide informed him.

"Good, send him in," Peters directed as he stood and moved towards a map board. Colonel Eric Provost, the division G-3, was already in the room.

"Sir, you wanted to see me?" Hawk said, entering the general's office.

"Yeah, Hawk, got a little job for you. Come here." Peters motioned for Hawk to come over to the map board with the locations of friendly forces and known Iraqi forces plotted on the map. "As you know, we done kicked some Iraqi ass last week, but some got away. Well, it's time to find them and kick them again. I want you to take your birds north and find the remnants of the 7th and 51st Divisions and the 37th Division. I'm sending some TACP folks with you in your little birds, and when you find them, call in every air strike you can and pound them into the Stone Age. Any questions?" Peters asked.

"No, sir. I may need a FARRP located further north than the one at Al Ais," Hawk said, thinking out loud.

"Already have one standing by to be inserted here at Bir Jaydah, eighty miles north of Al Ais. It's a well-protected location from any vehicular traffic. An infantry company will be securing it for you. I would suggest that the route from Al Ais to Bir Jaydah should first move northwest to Tawala and then northeast back to Bri Jaydah, but that's up to you. How soon can you launch?" Peters asked.

"Sir, one hour after the FARRP goes in. That'll give them time to get up there and get it set up before we show up. Initially, we'll only need fuel when we get there the first time," Hawk indicated.

"Good, Colonel Provost will call you when they're off and en route. Good hunting, Hawk."
****

As Hawk flew north with two troops, he wondered what he would find up there. He had elected to fly one of the unit's OH-58s with the senior TACP officer with him. He had two Cobra gunships following him. His other troop was screening forward of the 2nd Brigade and harassing the 3rd Regiment of the 51st Mechanized Division.

"We'll refuel in Bir Jaydah and then fly east at NOE towards Maggattyah to see what we can see," he told his passenger, Lieutenant Colonel Jarvis, the Division TACP commander. Jarvis, like all officers in the TACP, was a fighter pilot on a TACP assignment.

"Sounds good, Hawk. Need to drain the bladder about now," Jarvis joked, watching camels meandering as they passed over them. As the refuel point in Bir Jaydah came into view, Hawk commenced a deceleration and the two Cobra gunships did likewise. The rest of the troop was about an hour behind Hawk and would relieve him on station. Jarvis, however, would remain in the area, switching aircraft if they were finding targets.

"I'll get it refueled while you take a piss and then we'll get going," Hawk said as he rolled the throttle back to flight idle and set the friction locks on the flight controls. He was going to hot-refuel the aircraft. Suddenly his door was opened, startling him a bit when he noticed a young American soldier standing in the door.

"Sir, I'll refuel you," the young specialist said with a grin. "We got nothing better to do sitting up here brushing flies off." Hawk gave him a thumbs-up and released the friction locks on the controls. When the bladder on Colonel Jarvis was drained and the bladder on the aircraft full, Hawk increased the throttle and pulled in collective, executing a rapid ascent and departure.

"OK, we're going to head due east in a contour flight mode until we get close, then we'll drop to NOE. The Cobras will keep us in sight. Let's see what we can see," Hawk said with a smile. He loved this part of the mission. Hide-and-go-seek was a favorite childhood game of his. He'd never thought he would be doing it in a helicopter someday. As they flew east, they crested a ridgeline and dropped into a ravine that initially ran north–south. There were no signs of vehicular traffic in the ravine as it was fairly narrow. When Hawk came upon an east–west ravine, he entered it and slowed his speed down to barely a fast hover.

"If my navigation is correct, the town of Fadhia should be on the nose in a minute or so," he said to Jarvis as he looked down at his map strapped to his leg.

"Holy shit," Jarvis said in almost a whisper.

"What?" Hawk responded, almost in a panic, and then he saw it. Laid out in neat rows side by side was a group of fifty T-72 tanks, parked in five rows of ten tanks each. No crews could be seen.

"Do you want to take these out, or are you just along for the ride and I'm doing all the work?" Hawk asked sarcastically, laughing.

"I'm on it." And immediately Jarvis was talking to a flight leader of a flight of eight F-16 jets carrying an assortment of bombs and missiles. As Hawk sat at a hover, his Cobra gunship cover was begging him to allow them to shoot.

"Sabre elements, let's see if we can find an air-defense weapon someplace around this tank farm," Hawk transmitted. It didn't take him long to spot an SA-9 Gaskin missile launcher, and where there was one, there would be three more, which were found equally fast.

Turning to Jarvis, Hawk said, "Let your guys know we've identified four SA-9 positions. We're going to take them out and that'll mark the target for them. Four burning vehicles should be a pretty good marker."

"I know my boys would really appreciate that, Hawk."

Jarvis informed the jets of the enemy situation. As Hawk hovered, his two Cobra gunships moved into position to engage the SA-9 launchers.

"OK, Hawk, they're one minute out," Jarvis said. It was obvious that the SA-9s knew the jets were in the area as their turrets began turning in the likely direction of attack for the jets. Before they could launch, however, all four exploded as four TOW missiles slammed into the launchers. Hardly anyone noticed as almost immediately the tanks began exploding, cluster bombs and five-hundred-pound dumb bombs ripping through the parked vehicles. As the dust settled, Hawk conducted a battlefield damage assessment. That was fifty tanks that wouldn't be engaged in any future fighting. Returning to Bir Jaydah, Hawk briefed the new crew that was there to relieve him and took Colonel Jarvis with them to find more targets. Hawk was satisfied with a good day of hunting.

Chapter 46

Planning Process at Work

5 December 1990
CENTCOM Forward HQ
Military Technological College
Muscat, Oman

General Schless had arranged for Major Stube and the Jedi majors to get the latest intelligence update before they started planning the offensive operation to liberate the UAE. Schless was interested as well and decided to sit in on the briefing.

Once introductions were made and everyone was seated, a lieutenant colonel pulled down the first slide, which showed the task organization for the Iraqi Army.

"Gentlemen, the 1st Republican Guard Corps has withdrawn from the UAE and has been replaced by the 9th Iraqi Corps. If you're not Republican Guard, then you're second-string in the mind of the Iraqi leadership and Saddam. However, they've been upgraded with some of the latest Soviet equipment. The question is, do they really know how to use it? If the Soviet advisors that are with them have anything to say about it, the answer is yes. Currently, the 9th Corps is deployed along the UAE and Omani border with the 10th Armoured Division in the north; the 1st Infantry Division deployed in Al Ain; the 17th Armoured Division deployed south of Al Ain and 49th Infantry Division along the border south of the 17th; the 45th Division on the southern border from Arada to Al Yarya; and the 52nd Armoured Division acting as a corps reserve along the coast south of Abu Dhabi. His logistical support is coming from Iraq over water to Dubai and Abu Dhabi as well as along the coast highway." The briefing officer indicated each position with a laser pointer as he spoke. "Any questions?" he asked.

Stube raised his hand slightly. "Sir, I thought the 49th and 45th were up in Al Jubail and Dammam."

"They were, but they were brought down in the past five days and rejoined the corps," the briefing officer said. "Any other questions?" As there were none, he continued.

"The terrain along the border varies from desert sand dunes in the south to rugged mountainous terrain in the north. In the south, the dunes run northeast to southwest. Dunes are approximately two hundred feet high, with approximately one-eighth to one mile between dunes. This terrain does not favor a defender as there are just too many passages through the dunes to be covered. However, this doesn't favor the attacker either as you'll have difficulty massing forces in the area. That's probably why he positioned the 52nd Armoured Division in this area to counterattack a force coming out of the dunes," he said, pausing for a moment.

"Having said that, you will note he's positioned the 49th Infantry Division in this dune area as the area between the dunes will afford good mobility to an armor force attempting to move through it. He's positioned the 49th to be a trip wire to alert the 52nd and have it counterattack in this area where the dunes stop and the ground offers good maneuver room to mass a force and counterattack.

"The 17th Armoured is also in a dune area, but he has positioned his forces right along the border, taking advantage of the obstacle created by the buildings and houses that occupy this area. In addition, he's emplaced tank ditches and other obstacles. Positioning along the border and the lesser defended area to the south will provide him with an opportunity to strike anyone going against the 49th in the northern flank as the 52nd counterattacks to the front. The 1st Infantry Division is occupying Al Ain and is heavily fortifying the town. They won't wait for an attack but will begin engaging targets that appear.

"From Al Ain north, the border is very rugged mountain terrain, with really only one road that could be used by any sizable force, and that's the road from Fujairah. He has a small garrison in Fujairah to guard the port area. Are there any questions about the disposition of his forces in the UAE?" the briefing officer asked. General Schless looked over at his team of Jedi majors, who all shook their heads.

"I think we're good. Let's move on," General Schless said.

"Yes, sir." The briefer placed another map on the map board. In red, the typical color for enemy forces on a map, the locations of the 2nd Iraqi Corps and the 2nd Republican Guard Corps were depicted. With his laser pointer in hand, the briefer began, "The 2nd Republican Guard Corps is in a defensive posture around the city of Medina. The 7th Adnan Motorized Division was involved in heavy and continuous fighting all the way to Medina and then got into some serious door-to-door fighting in Medina. They haven't been able to hold the city or put down the resistance and are heavily engaged. The 5th Mechanized Division walked into a buzzsaw from the 82nd on Medina Ridge and are now in defensive positions, barely hanging on. Both of these divisions we estimate at fifty percent strength. Questions?" he asked, and there were none.

"The 2nd Iraqi Army Corps has stretched his supply lines as far as he can go. At this time, the 2nd Infantry Division is occupying Tabuk and is at eighty percent strength. The 14th Mechanized Division is just south of Tabuk and is at thirty percent strength, having been hit repeatedly in air strikes. The 51st Infantry Division attempted to swing to the east and link up in Medina but got caught by the 2nd Brigade of the 101st and has been reduced to one regiment that has pulled back to Al Jaharah. The 7th Infantry Division attempted to push through the 101st on the west and was chewed up by the 1st and 3rd Brigades of the division and pulled back to Mughayra. They're about fifty percent strength now. Only the 37th Infantry Division hasn't seen significant combat but has been hit a couple of times by air strikes. They're currently located at Taqah. Any questions about these units?" Again the audience was silent.

Finally General Schless spoke up. "You've said nothing about the 1st Republican Guard Corps."

"I was just coming to them, sir. The 1st Republican Guard Corps swapped places with the 9th Iraqi Corps and the Headquarters for the 1st RG Corps is in Al Hofuf, we believe from what we've determined through signals intercepts. His divisions are positioning themselves along a line from As Salwa on the east coast to Al Hawlyan to Al Kharj on the west. One division is located in Al Hofuf along with the Corps headquarters. We haven't determined yet which division is which, nor have we been able to locate the 4th Al Fao Infantry Division."

"I notice a large goose egg for the 4th and 7th IraqiCorps. Want to enlighten us about them?" Major Stube asked.

"Sure, the 4th Corps had been following the 2nd RG Corps and took over responsibility for Buraydah, Unayzah and the area southeast to Riyadh. Of the eight divisions in that 4th Corps we have identified an armor division at Al Artawiyah and a mechanized division at Ha'il in the west. There are infantry divisions located at Buraydah and Unayzah, as well as two divisions in Riyadh. One division is located around Shaqra and one division is unaccounted for at this time. These divisions form a second defensive belt backing up the 2nd Republican Guard Corps," the briefing officer explained.

"And the 7th Corps?" General Schless asked.

"Sir, that's his second belt for the 1st Republican Guard Corps. The 7th Corps has eight divisions with three of those infantry divisions in Kuwait; an infantry division each in Al Jubail and Dammam; an infantry division at King Khalid International Airport; and an armored division at Ash Shayyit. The corps headquarters is located at Al Khafji. That, gentlemen, concludes the locations of the known Iraqi units," the briefing officer concluded.

"Well, you certainly have given us enough to think about. Major Stube, have you got any questions?" General Schless asked.

"Do you have the locations of any obstacles that he's constructing or minefields that he's put in?" Stube asked.

"At this time I do not expect major obstacles just forward of his positions. He hasn't bothered to put in the million-mine minefields of World War II. You've received a brief on the minefields in the Strait, haven't you?" the briefer asked.

"Yeah, we're good there. What's his airpower like?" Major Rumgay asked.

"He's able to attain air superiority for limited periods of time and air parity most of the time. The Air Force has been hitting his airfields in Saudi pretty hard. At this point the President has restricted us from hitting air bases in Iraq," the briefer stated.

"OK, gentlemen, if there are no more questions for the colonel, then let's get our thinking caps on and start developing some courses of action," General Schless said, standing and signaling that the briefing was concluded.

****

Major Stube and his team returned to their office and began assessing the enemy situation.

"Jack, that's a hell of a lot of bad guys. I'm beginning to think we still don't have the forces to go all the way. We can do the UAE part, but I'm not sure after that," Jim Rumgay said with a look of concern on his face.

"If this is all we have to work with, then we're going to have to somehow whittle down the odds big-time," Bob Peters interjected.

"Let's not get ahead of ourselves before we map the first phase out. Let's look at the liberation of the UAE and see how that finishes up and what assumptions we make before we attempt to eat the whole pie at once," Roy McClain said. Everyone looked up to Roy a bit, as he was usually the farsighted thinker. Fred Thompson, the one Air Force officer in the group, said nothing but just took it all in.

"OK, let's first look at what we have to work with on the day this kicks off," Jack said and began writing on a whiteboard. As he wrote, Roy read off the list of assets.

Available Forces Ground

Corps Headquarters

III Corps Hq

XVIII Corps Hq

VII Corps Hq

Divisions Army

24th, 1st Cav, 1st ID, 3rd Armored, 1st Armored, 101st Abn, 82nd Abn, 50th NG Armored, 28th Infantry (NG), 29th Infantry (NG), 35th Infantry (NG)

Marine

1st Marine Div, 2nd Marine Div

British

1st British Armoured Div

Egyptian

3rd Mech Div, 4th Armoured Div

Host Nation Units

North Omani Brigade (reinforced)

United Arab Emirates Mechanized Battalion

Task Force "Othman"

Kuwaiti "Al Fatah" Brigade

Kuwaiti 2/5 Mechanized Battalion

Bahraini Motorized Infantry Company

Task Force "Abu Bakr"

2nd Brigade, Saudi National Guard

Task Force "Tariq"

Royal Saudi Marine Battalion

Task Force "West"

Royal Saudi 8th Mechanized Brigade

Royal Saudi 10th Mechanized Brigade

Royal Saudi 45th Armour Brigade

Regiments

2nd Armored Cav Regiment

3rd Armored Cav Regiment

Combat Aviation Brigades

12th Combat Aviation Brigade

18th Combat Aviation Brigade

6th Combat Aviation Brigade

When Jack was done writing, everyone stepped back and looked at what they had. Bob was the first to speak up. "So we have three corps headquarters to control eleven US divisions, one British division, two Egyptian divisions, two armored cavalry regiments, three combat aviation brigades, and five host nation task forces, and one Marine headquarters to control two Marine divisions, one being at sea," he pointed out, thinking out loud more than instructing his fellow Jedi majors.

"Let's not forget the air assets," Major Thompson said. "We have five aircraft carriers and another arriving shortly, each with about fifty-eight fighter aircraft and an attack squadron of fourteen aircraft. That's three hundred and forty fighters and eighty-four attack aircraft. Then we have one hundred and thirty-four Air Force fighter squadrons with twenty-four aircraft in each squadron for three thousand two hundred and sixteen aircraft. That's just in the AO, not counting what the heavy bombers from Diego Garcia are bringing. The 3rd Marine Wing has forty Harrier attack aircraft, forty-eight Hornets and ten A-6 Intruders along with support aircraft and Cobra gunships. Those aircraft will primarily be supporting the Marine divisions in the overall air tasking order," Major Fred Thompson said.

"I understand there was a bit of a disagreement between Horner and Boomer over how those aircraft would be used," McClain said.

"Let's say it's been resolved to everyone's satisfaction," Mike Monroe, the token Marine officer on the team, responded. No one bothered to ask how it had been resolved, but it had been. It seemed that General Horner wanted to include the Marine Corps aircraft in the general air tasking order each day and not necessarily in support of the Marine units on the ground. General Boomer wanted those aircraft in support of the Marine units.

Stube regained control of the meeting. "OK, it's obvious we don't have enough forces to commit three divisions against each of their divisions. So we're going to have to look at fixing some in place and penetrating elsewhere with at least a three-to-one ratio. We also should consider a deception plan if possible."

"First thing we need to do is move the 1st Marine Division off Masirah Island and get them on the mainland to be in position to launch an attack. The 2nd Marine is at sea and we only have enough Gator Navy ships for one division to conduct an amphib landing," Monroe pointed out.

"Once we have a plan that's acceptable, I'll get General Schless to cut the order. It's either that or they're going to be left out of the fight and I don't think General Boomer is going to buy into that," Stube said.

"Jack, why don't we break down into three two-man teams and develop three courses of action? We can come back together in the morning and present our courses of action to the group," Major Mike Monroe suggested.

"Sounds good. How about me and Jim, Roy and Fred, and Bob and Mike? We meet back here in the morning and lay it all out," Jack said. With that, everyone broke up into groups and started looking over maps.

****

The next morning, the group assembled back in the office. They hadn't invited anyone to this first session, as this was their time to pick apart the courses of action that had been developed by each group.

"Who wants to go first?" Jack asked.

"We might as well get things started," Bob said and stood to hang his map overlay. "We'll call this course of action one. We envision an amphibious landing in the north on this stretch of beach south of Dubai. It's a forty-seven-kilometer-wide beach with few homes or shops, and the hydrography will support an over-the-beach landing." He indicated

411

an area from Mina Jebel Ali south for forty-seven kilometers. "From there they'll push inland to strike the 10th Armoured Division from the rear while simultaneously the 1st Marine Division attacks north towards the 10th Armoured Division. The host nation forces attack to fix the forces in Al Ain in place. Three divisions attack the 17th Armoured Division while three divisions attack the 49th Division with a reserve division to exploit the penetration. In the south, two divisions attack to fix and destroy the 45th Division. The exploitation division attacks the 52nd Division and fixes in place until additional forces can support. Questions?" Bob asked.

"I like the amphib operation and the actions against the 10th Armoured. I think you're a bit light with the penetration force and their ability to fix and hold the 52nd for any period of time," Roy pointed out.

"Roy, let's see what you have," Jack indicated.

"We see the same amphib op in the north. We didn't commit anyone against the forces in Al Ain as they're infantry and hunkered down in the city. We don't want to be engaging the city with artillery or getting bogged down in street fighting, so we're bypassing it. We have three divisions going against the 17th Armoured Division and four divisions plus the host nation forces going against the 49th Division. The two divisions will go after the 45th Division. The four divisions and host nation forces will continue the attack to the 52nd Division," Roy explained. "Once the 52nd is destroyed, this will position forces well to take on the 1st Republican Guard Corps if they counterattack or position us well to continue the attack against the 1st Republican Guard Corps should they hold in place." No objections were raised.

"OK, let's see what you got, Jack," Roy said.

"We also planned the amphibious landing in the north and the actions against the 10th Armoured Division. We didn't commit anyone to Al Ain as, like you, we don't want to be bogged down in street fighting. We did, however, place the host nation forces against the north flank of the 17th Armoured with one division on the southern flank of the 17th. Another division would go against the northern flank of the 49th Division and one division on the southern side of the 49th. That leaves us five divisions to penetrate over the 45th and take on the 52nd. It gives us flexibility as I visualize one of those five possibly turning north and striking the 49th in the rear, allowing one division to hit and fix the 45th in place and three divisions pass between the 45th and 49th to take out the 52nd," Jack stated. Everyone moved closer to the map and began studying Jack's proposal.

"I like that it puts a much larger force against the 52nd," Roy said.

"The terrain here in the south on the Omani side is better for dispersing a large force, as the terrain isn't as bad, say, in front of the 17th," Peters pointed out. "The sand dunes aren't as bad in the 45th sector as they are in the 49th sector too. I say we present all three courses of action and recommend the third. The other advantage with course of action three is that it positions up to five divisions if the 1st Republican Guard Corps moves against us."

"OK, now what about on the western front? Can't forget about those people," Jack indicated.

Everyone looked over the maps again. Roy was the first to speak up. "Well, for the forces available, we have the 82nd and the 101st in place as well as the 10th and 8th Saudi Brigades, the remnants of the 45th Brigade. We still have the 29th, 28th and 35th National Guard divisions in the process of deploying. Why not weight the XVIII Airborne Corps with those three divisions? That would give Luck five

413

divisions to fight with. With the Saudi units, he could hold the 2nd Iraqi Corps at bay, especially if we keep pounding them with air strikes the way we have been and use the two National Guard divisions and the 82nd and 101st to take out the 2nd Republican Guard Corps. Once that's done, a decision can be made to turn and go after the 2nd Iraqi Corps or to head off towards the 4th Iraqi Corps. Certainly they couldn't take on the 4th Corps, but the threat of them would hold the 4th Corps in position so it couldn't support the 1st Republican Guard Corps."

"I like that," Jim Rumgay said. "It secures their logistics tail. It provides good lines of communications and puts pressure on the center, fixing it in place."

"Let's write them up and call in General Schless for his approval," Jack said, and the meeting broke up to put pen to paper.

Chapter 47
Things Start Moving

15 December 1990

Oman

With the final course of action accepted and approved, positioning the forces could now commence. The first problem was a traffic management plan to reduce confusion as to where units were and where they needed to move to in order to stage for the upcoming offensive. Fortunately, elements of the VII Corps had their ships diverted from Muscat to Salalah and their personnel were flowing into the international airport in Salalah. As soon as planes landed, the soldiers were moved out of the area to staging areas outside of town that the Omani government had erected for them. Tent City, as it would be known, was the most luxury these soldiers would see for some time to come.

"Sir, I tell you this is going to be a nightmare. We have four divisions to move some four hundred miles north and only one major highway and one other paved road to do it. In a lot of areas, our vehicles can get off the roads and travel overland, but it's still going to take a toll on the vehicles," Brigadier General Holt, the VII Corps G-4, said, addressing General Franks.

"Well, we need to push out some MPs and the 2nd ACR to recon some routes that we could use. Get with the G-3 and get a tasking order out to the 2nd ACR. The sooner them boys find us a route and mark it, the quicker we can start pushing people out, starting with those National Guard truck stop units along the routes. Those guys are incredible. Truck pulls in and the driver gets out. Gets a shower and a hot meal. Depending on his hours driving, he gets a cot and some sleep. While he's doing that, they run his truck through an inspection to refuel and repair anything that needs to be repaired. Whoever dreamed this one up deserves a medal," Franks said. "How many of those units do we have, anyway?"

"Sir, I believe we have seven of those units in-country right now, but I'm not sure," Holt admitted.

"Well, we need a few more yesterday. See what you can do about it," Franks directed. "And I think we should have the maintenance units put out some road rangers as well."

"Road rangers, sir?" Holt questioned.

"Yeah, like you see on the interstate in the States. Maintenance trucks running the road to help stranded motorists. Create something like that here. Pick a maintenance battalion and assign that mission to them."

"Yes, sir," Holt said, taking notes and making a reminder to get on the phone with CENTCOM.

****

Out on Highway 31, convoys were almost bumper to bumper moving north. Huge HETs or heavy equipment transporters moved with M-1 tanks and Bradley fighting vehicles loaded on their backs. Between them were five-thousand-gallon fuel trucks, semitrailers, both military and civilian, carrying all the essentials for war. Personnel were being flown north from the airport to an airstrip at Fahud, which would be in the rear of the corps sector. Here they would connect with their respective vehicles.

As the vehicles moved north, Specialist Burger was surprised to see so many US Air Force personnel at the air base at Thumrait, north of Salalah. US and British jets were landing and taking off with thunderous roars from their engines. His assistant driver, Specialist Ford, had been taking a snooze but woke up to the sound of the jet engines.

"Where the hell are we?" Ford asked, not yet awake and reaching for a warm bottled water.

"We're about forty miles out of Salalah and keeping along Highway 31. That's some air base over there and a lot of activity. Looks like F-16s, but there are some in desert colors that I don't recognize. See? There's one taking off now," Burger said, taking his eyes off the road and vehicle to the front.

"Hey, pay attention to your driving. Last thing we need is to get into an accident and be stuck out in this godforsaken desert," Ford said with some disgust in his voice.

"What, don't you think this is so cool being here?" Burger asked.

"I think it's cool being in this operation, but not here. I joined to get the college money and always thought that if I did go into a combat situation, it would be someplace nice, like southern Italy or France, not this desert shithole. I wanted to meet foreign women and drink good wine. This place doesn't have either. They don't drink and the women all have black bags over their heads. Who knows what they look like? No, this isn't what I signed up for. My grandfather was in Italy in World War II and told me how great it was to be driving a truck there. Not this shit," Ford said with disgust in his voice.

As they continued along the route, an occasional truck was passed on the side of the road, undergoing some repairs. Roadside assistance crews from the various motor vehicle maintenance units had been formed and were being kept busy with vehicles that had broken down or run out of gas. Getting off the road was no problem as the land was as flat as could be and the sand was hard-packed and easily supported the weight of any and every vehicle. Off in the distance, they could see dust clouds where some vehicles were running on an alternate route across the desert laid out by the 2nd Armored Cavalry Regiment. Moving the entire VII Corps in one direction would take too long on one road, so alternate routes were necessary to keep things moving in a timely manner.

****

The first element to arrive by C-130 at the Fahud Airport was an ALCE team, followed by heavy forklifts to unload pallets of everything.

"Major, once people start arriving, I'll have a team here to direct where they're to go to get into unit assembly areas. I hope that the vehicles will arrive first, before the troops start coming. Otherwise, they're going to have a hike," said Lieutenant Colonel Billings, the Corps advance party commander.

"Sir, where do you want the pallets moved to? Because this place is going to be covered in pallets when the aircraft flow starts," Major Gains said. She was becoming an old hand at commanding the ALCE team, and this was not her first experience with establishing an airfield.

"Let's put the ammo that comes in over there on the northeast side of the airfield and everything else on the northwest side. I'll have some supply people from the 213 Supply and Services Battalion over here in an hour to start organizing a reception area for the logistics and have them get with you. Do you expect any of that to arrive in the next hour?"

"No, sir. The first couple of loads coming in are my stuff to set up the airfield control party and our accommodations. Your first loads according to the plan won't arrive for another three hours at least. Once I establish comms with Salalah, I can give you more accurate timelines for things arriving and what those are."

"Our first loads should be several heavy forklifts that will move stuff off the airfield once you get it out of the planes. I want to be sure we keep the ammo well away from the airfield, but we won't be able to haul it very far until I get some flatbed trucks in here to move it to a better location," Colonel Billings stated.

"Sir, there's an Air Force engineer element en route to here to help expand this airfield with a turnaround area and maybe extend the runway. The C-130s can handle this runway but would like it a bit longer," Major Gains informed him.

"As long as it doesn't cut down the flow, I have no problem with that. Should have been done days ago, but no one knew we'd be coming here. We'll just have to make do, Major," Billings said as he turned and went looking for someone from the 213 Supply and Service Battalion.

****

"Sir, the first of the launches are arriving and ready to start hauling us off this rock," Colonel Lohman said. "The units have all received movement times for the over-the-beach operations, and there are MP units ready to clear the road all the way to Al Husayfin on the border with the UAE. The launches will be taking us to just south of An Nuqdah, where the supply boats run out from."

"What route are they directing we take to move to Al Husayfin? I don't want this to turn into a goat rope for our division, getting in a traffic jam with another division moving south or crossing paths," Major General Hopkins said.

"Sir, we're to take the E32 highway north to where it intersects Highway 15 and stay on that until we hit the O1 highway, which goes right to our area. The MPs will be at each intersection, controlling traffic and clearing the way for us. Units shifting from up in that area are restricted to Highway 21 and Highway 31 coming south. That keeps the flows away from each other," Colonel Lohman stated.

"OK, Colonel, put your money where your mouth is," General Hopkins said with a smile, digging in his pocket and pulling out a dollar bill. "I'll bet a dollar some Army strays wander over onto our road and foul up the works."

"Sir, I'll take you up on that. And if, just if, one of our units strays into the Army traffic, you owe me a dollar," Lohman said with an equally big smile.

"Colonel, if one of our units strays onto the Army roads, you will get my dollar and the commander's balls for good measure," Hopkins said with a bigger smile.

****

Captain al-Bishi sat at the outdoor café, the Firq Restaurant, on the main intersection in Nizwa, into which Highways 21, 31 and 15 all flowed. He had been seated for over two hours and silently noted and recorded the number and type of vehicles coming south on Highway 21 and continuing down Highway 31. None of this military traffic was moving north on Highway 15. Another member of his Special Forces team was doing the same in Sama, where Highway 21 intersected Highway 15. According to his phone reports, he was seeing military traffic moving north, and it was all US Marines.

As Captain al-Bishi sat peacefully sipping his coffee, he noted the Americans all had numbers on the bumpers of their vehicles. These numbers were very easy to read, and he had learned how to interpret them. On one side of the bumper was the unit designation and on the other side the vehicle number. He was thankful that they provided this information, as it made his job so much easier, allowing him to identify units that were moving. Some vehicles were painted a desert sand color while others were painted green. He realized that the green vehicles were from the VII Corps and the others were from the United States. *Interesting*, he thought.

As he sat concentrating on the military convoys passing his table, he didn't notice the two gentlemen seated a few tables from him, who were not interested in the convoys but in him. A waiter approached al-Bishi. "Sir, can I bring you something to eat? You have been drinking coffee for the past three hours and your stomach must be feeling the caffeine. You will not be sleeping tonight," the waiter said.

Damn, it has been noticed, he thought. "Yes, please bring me a menu. I thought my wife would be here long before now, but she has been delayed. I would like to order," al-Bishi said, smiling up at the waiter, who bowed slightly and left to fetch a menu. As he did so, one of the men that had been watching this exchange got up and followed the waiter.

"Excuse me," he said to the waiter once inside.

"Yes, may I help you?" the waiter asked. His eyes widened when he saw what the gentleman had in his hand, holding it in front of the waiter's face. The Internal Security Service or Jahaz al Amn al Dakhly credentials were seldom seen, and most people would be very happy never to see them.

"How long has that gentleman been sitting there?" the agent asked.

"Sir, he has been drinking coffee for three hours now or close to it," the waiter answered.

"How do you know that?"

"Sir, I make most of my money on tips, so I like to see my tables turn over quickly. The longer he sits there, the more I lose in tips that others would be leaving me. Our rule is one hour, but he has been there for three and now he is about to order food. It will be another hour for sure," the waiter lamented.

"Has he made any phone calls in those three hours?"

"Yes, sir. He has made some and received some as well. I did not hear what was said, but I know he has been on the phone," the waiter answered as small beads of sweat appeared on his forehead.

"Thank you, and say nothing of this. Here is something to make up for his time at your table. See me once he leaves. You can bring a menu to our table as well," the agent said as he stuffed a few bills in the waiter's hand.

"Yes, sir. Very good, sir. I will be right with you," the excited waiter said.

"Calm down. Just act like nothing has happened, and do not be looking at our table unless we wave to you. When you bring him his bill, you will bring ours as well, but just drop it on the table and keep moving. We will leave payment on the table under a plate. Do I make myself clear?" the agent asked.

"Yes, sir, very clear, and thank you," the waiter stammered. He would have an interesting tale to tell tonight at home.

Chapter 48

Countermine Operations

15 December 1990

Salalah, Oman

The USS *Avenger* was the most recent addition to the US Navy minesweeper fleet. Commissioned in 1987, she resided in her home port of Naval Station, Charleston, South Carolina. Her crew of six officers and seventy-five enlisted sailors consisted mostly of the "plank holders," crew that had been aboard when she was commissioned. She was not a big ship in terms of size, being only two hundred and twenty feet long and thirty-nine feet wide with a draft of thirteen feet. Some luxury yachts were bigger. And she was not a fast ship, cruising at fourteen knots. Built of Douglas fir timber coated with fiberglass, she was perfect for the job she had to perform, finding and destroying undersea mines. The last thing you wanted for that job was a metal ship that would set off a magnetic mine. The one drawback for the crew was that in rough weather, she bobbed like a cork on the sea.

To prevent the minesweeper from making the long voyage to the Arabian Sea, the *Avenger*, along with USS *Androit* (MSO-509), USS *Imperious* (MSO 449) and USS *Leader* (MSO 490), was loaded aboard the Dutch heavy lift ship *Super Servant III* and transported to the Gulf of Oman, where they were offloaded and entered service. To say the least, the crews appreciated this as otherwise it would have probably been a long seasick voyage. The USS *Androit*, USS *Imperious* and USS *Leader* were part of the US Navy Reserve fleet, with Naval reservists manning the ships.

The knock on his cabin door startled Commander Jim Keys. He had been in command on the newest minesweeper of the fleet for a year now. He was a Navy ROTC graduate and was following in his father's career footsteps, although his father had been a Navy lawyer. Like many service brats, he liked the military lifestyle, which wasn't for everyone. Of course, it was rough on the married life, and Keys had been divorced from his high school sweetheart.

"Enter," Keys called out. The door opened and his executive officer, Lieutenant Tony Jamison, entered.

"What's up, Tony?" Keys asked. Alone, they were pretty informal with each other.

"Sir, you have a meeting with the squadron commander in one hour. He's sending his launch over to pick you up, as well as the skippers from the other ships. We might be finally getting the word on what we're going to do and when," Jamison said.

"That would be nice. I guess I best change uniforms for this gathering. You say all the skippers are invited to this?" Keys asked as he stood in the small cabin. Luxury wasn't something afforded to captains on minesweepers. A bunk, a desk attached to the wall and a couple of chairs were about it, along with a washbasin and a small shower stall.

"Yes, sir. Even going to have all the British skippers as well and the four Saudi skippers. At least they were all listed on the message traffic," Jamison said.

****

Two hours later, Jim Keys found himself aboard the mine-countermine flagship, USS *Tripoli*. She had been with the amphibious forces, but her flight deck was needed for MH-53 Super Sea Stallion helicopters that served in the countermine operations. All the other skippers were present as well, some familiar to Keys and others not familiar as they were British and Saudi nationals. Regardless, the conversations all revolved around one question: *What are we doing here?*

In the conference room, a petty officer called out "Attention on deck!" as Rear Admiral Blumfield entered. Blumfield was an Academy graduate, class of '70, and had served on surface ships almost his entire naval career, except for the time spent in the five-sided palace, commonly called the Pentagon.

"Gentlemen, take your seats," Blumfield said, moving to the head of the conference room table, where thirteen skippers were seated along with the commander of the Sea Stallion Squadron. In addition, the skipper of the USS *Princeton* was present as the *Princeton*'s role would be revealed shortly, since she was a recently commissioned *Ticonderoga*-class cruiser. Minesweeping operations was not one of her roles. She was equipped to conduct anti-surface, anti-submarine, and anti-air operations.

"Gentlemen, I have asked you here to give you an overview of what we will be doing in the near future and some of the challenges we're facing in accomplishing our mission. First, this is classified as a top secret briefing, so I don't want to hear about it on the mess deck. Understood?" Blumfield said. Everyone, to include the Saudi officers, acknowledged this with a nod.

"In the upcoming operational plan, an amphibious assault is being planned on the coast of the UAE, which as we speak is being reconned by SEAL teams." Murmurs could be heard around the table. "We will be expected to clear the waters leading to those beaches of sea mines. But first we have to clear the Strait of Hormuz of sea mines. That might be a bigger problem as the Iranians consider that to be their waters. They have mined the north side, and the Iraqis mined the south side. We will concentrate on the south side. We have a plot of the existing channel through the Strait at this time and will only clear a portion to widen the channel for our ships. Our real effort will be off the coast of the UAE. The only coastline that the UAE has on the Gulf of Oman is around Fujairah, and although the hydrography is excellent, the city is right up against the water. The decision has been made that we will not destroy the towns, which is in this case what it would take to force an over-the-beach landing. Therefore, we will be clearing the Strait and clearing out a beach on the Persian Gulf side of the UAE," the admiral outlined.

Commander Keys half raised his hand. "Excuse me, sir, but can you tell us where that landing beach will be?"

"At this time, I can't, as I don't know. Several places are being examined and when I find out, you'll find out. Just know that once it is designated, we're going to be going in and clearing out the approaches," Admiral Blumfield said.

"Sir," Captain Hontz, skipper of the USS *Princeton*, called out, gaining the admiral's attention.

"Yes, Captain," the admiral acknowledged

"Sir, why is the *Princeton* participating in this?" Hontz asked. He suspected he knew the answer but wanted confirmation.

"Captain Hontz, the *Princeton* will provide air-defense and anti-ship coverage for the minesweeping operation. Our ships are really not equipped to take on an enemy aircraft or Silkworm missiles. Do you have a problem with that, Captain?" the admiral asked.

"No, sir, I just don't like the idea of taking my ship into mine-infested waters, that's all," Captain Hontz said.

"I can appreciate your concern, but every ship in the United States Navy can be a minesweeper, once. We will do our utmost to see that you don't encounter any mines. Any other questions?" This evoked a chuckle from the attending skippers.

"Sir," the skipper from the HMS *Cattistock* said.

"Yes, sir. Your name, sir?" the admiral asked.

"Commander Lovell, Her Majesty's Ship *Cattistock*, sir."

"And your question, Commander?"

"Sir, do you have an idea of the size and depth of the minefields on the Gulf side of Oman?"

"Good question, Commander. Here we have a problem. No satellite coverage has been devoted to mine operations in the Gulf. What intel we have has been secondhand and sporadic. We believe that the Iraqis have put in a hundred-and-fifty-mile-long field along the coast, approximately twenty miles deep. It appears they have emplaced several rows of mines in that box. Intelligence feels we will encounter somewhere between one thousand and two thousand mines, both contact and influence," the admiral informed them. Low whistles and murmurs could be heard as the fifteen skippers exchanged looks.

"Gentlemen, that's about all I can tell you at this time. When I have more information on our future, I'll contact you. Once we get underway, we won't have an opportunity to get together again. As long as we're at anchor and basing out of Salalah, I'd like to have a weekly meeting to discuss our future. Will that be acceptable?" the admiral asked. Everyone was in agreement.

"In that case, gentlemen, will you all join me in the wardroom and have lunch? My launch is standing by to return you to your ships when you're ready to depart," the admiral offered. Everyone accepted the dinner invitation.

****

Commander Keys stepped off the admiral's launch and was met by his XO at the top of the gangplank. "Tony, let me change and meet me at the Nav station," Keys said, moving quickly to his cabin to change. Jamison moved out to the ladder going up to the Nav station. Keys joined him in less than ten minutes.

"Pull up a chart of the north shore of the UAE," Keys directed. Jamison dug in the map cabinet until he found the map he was looking for.

"What are we looking for, Skipper?" Jamison asked, noting the excitement in Keys's eyes.

"We are looking, my young friend, for a deserted stretch of beach on the north shore with a hydrography that will support over the beach operations," Keys said, spreading his hands over the map to flatten it and then resting on his elbows to study the map. As they studied the map, some things became obvious.

"Up here on the north shore, it's too mountainous right down to the water, and the hydrography is wrong. Moving down the coast, it's too built up or not a wide enough area," Keys said, moving his finger down the coast.

"Sir, what about this area west of Dubai? The hydrography is right. The beach is wide—what, twenty-seven kilometers?—and there's little in the way of buildup," Jamison pointed out.

"Yeah, that looks possible. Going west of there, the coast is a mixture of islands, very shallow waters. Shit, that has to be the beach," Keys said.

"Beach for what, sir?" Jamison asked.

"Beach for an amphibious assault. We're going to be tasked to not only clear the Strait but also clear a minefield off a beach for an amphibious landing," Keys said, standing up straight.

"No shit, sir!" Jamison said. "This will be a first since Inchon in Korea," he exclaimed.

"Yep, and we're going to be part of it. Gives me goose bumps just thinking about it," Keys said as he placed the map back in the map case. "Mum's the word for now, Tony, understood?"

"Aye-aye, Skipper."

Chapter 49

The National Guard Arrives

16 December 1990

115th Infantry Brigade, 29th Division

Yanbu, Saudi Arabia

Stepping out of the air-conditioned charter jet from TWA, Lieutenant Colonel Gooderjohn was overwhelmed with the heat blast that greeted him in Yanbu. As he came down the stairs to the tarmac, a soldier handed him a liter bottle of water. He had already drunk two quarts of water in the last two hours on the flight.

"What is this for?" Gooderjohn asked.

"Sir, you have to drink this to stay hydrated," the young soldier said. "I'm just doing what I was told, sir." Taking the water bottle, Gooderjohn moved off with the other two hundred and fifty members of his battalion that had flown over with him. A female sergeant first class with a bullhorn started speaking when the planeload was assembled in a hangar.

"Everyone, listen up. Welcome to Yanbu, Saudi Arabia. You will be here for approximately seventy-two hours. In that time, you are to drink a liter of water an hour and get yourselves acclimated to the heat. Today it is a pleasant one hundred degrees. Tonight it will be a pleasant seventy degrees and you will be thankful you have a sleeping bag. Nights get downright cold here in the desert. A couple of buses will arrive shortly and take you to the area where you'll be staying until you move out. Your battalion sergeant major was in the advance party and has designated your area. He'll meet you when the buses drop you off. Your rucksacks and baggage will be transported to your battalion area for you to claim. Chow is served twenty-four seven and is located in the vicinity of your temporary quarters. Latrine facilities are also co-located with you, but showers are limited and there is no hot water for showers. Enjoy."

She finished her speech and departed just as four buses pulled up, and the battalion sergeant major was the first off. Without a bullhorn, he made himself heard.

"Listen up, people. Shut up!" he yelled. "Alright, when I call your name, get on one of the buses. When you get to where you're going, someone will point out where your company area is, and your first sergeant will meet you there. Before you leave here, make a sensitive items check. Colonel Gooderjohn, sir, if you will, there's a vehicle behind the buses that will take you over to the battalion area."

"Thank you, Sergeant Major," Gooderjohn said, picking up a small bag and heading to the pickup truck waiting for him. As the truck took him across the airfield, he noted some large craters off the runway and some new asphalt on the runway. Each corner of the airfield, from what he could see, had HAWK missiles positioned. Several partially underground sandbagged bunkers were noted as well. Each had a camouflage net suspended over them. As he headed into the battalion operations center or TOC, he noticed several rows of vehicles lined up behind it. He stopped for a moment and stared at them. They were all painted in desert camouflage. When they'd been put on the train to go to Norfolk, they'd all been OD Green. Somewhere along the way, they'd all gotten a paint job. As he entered the TOC, an NCO came through the door.

"Oh, good day, sir. Glad I found you. You have a meeting at the brigade TOC in thirty minutes," the sergeant said.

"Crap. I wanted to just find a bed for a few hours and sleep. OK, where's the brigade TOC and where are my sleep quarters?" Gooderjohn asked.

"Sir, I'll show you where you're sleeping. It's nothing fancy, mind you. Sergeant Major said it would have to do," the sergeant said as he escorted Gooderjohn over to the sleep area. Gooderjohn found his bed was an Army cot in the middle of the company bay area. He would be sleeping just like the rest of his soldiers, and sleeping was exactly what he wanted to do after the twenty-three-hour plane flight.

"OK, now where's this meeting I'm supposed to be at?" he asked his escort.

"Sir, I'll take you there. It's on the other side of our vehicle park," the sergeant said as Gooderjohn picked up his hat and headed for the exit point in Tent City.

***

"Gooderjohn, nice to see you made it. Good flight?" the Brigade commander asked.

"Yes, sir, if you call sitting for twenty-four hours a good flight. Truthfully, I would love to just get some sleep right about now," Gooderjohn said as he pulled out a folding chair at the conference table. The meeting was being held in the Brigade TOC, which was set up in one half of the departure lounge for deportees. The other battalion commanders were already present.

"Well, you can after this meeting, and this won't be long. We'll be here for a week, and you need to get your troops acclimated to the climate. Let them sleep in the day but train at night. Having them out walking at night with plenty of water. They can work on their vehicles as well, but if the air raid siren goes off, it's lights out immediately and find a bunker. We need to conduct inspections for all the vehicles, and I would recommend you set up an inspection line for the mechanic to go over each vehicle. Those Bradley fighting vehicles have been sitting on those ships and port areas for over a month now. Some seals may need replacing. Fluid levels need to be checked. I would recommend everyone use graphite to lubricate weapons, as using oil will only trap the grit on the weapon. One thing we don't do in training is clean our ammo because we use it right away. Here they may not be using it, and if it's sitting in magazines, it's going to corrode in this salt air and jam the weapons. Every day, ammo has to be taken out of the magazines and cleaned. Be sure your vehicles have additional filters—"

"Sir, excuse me," Warrant Officer Gregory, the battalion motor officer, said.

"Yes, Mr. Gregory?"

"Sorry, sir, but we've already seen a problem with the air intakes on the Hummers. There's an easy fix," Gregory said.

"And what might that be?"

"Sir, if the wives would send us their discarded pantyhose, we can put those over the intakes on the Hummers and that'll cut the dirt getting into the filter by almost half," Mr. Gregory pointed out.

"You're joking, right?" Colonel Warren asked.

"No, sir, I'm as serious as a heart attack," Mr. Gregory said with a straight face.

Colonel Warren studied the man's facial expression, still expecting this to be a joke. Finally, he said, "Alright, gentlemen, you heard the man. Have everyone write and ask their wives and sweethearts to send them their pantyhose. I can just imagine what the reaction is going to be back home when those requests are read," Colonel Warren said with a chuckle. "Anything else, Chief?"

"No, sir."

"OK, moving along. After a week here, we'll be moving out to replace either the 82nd or the 101st, who have been on the line and holding the Iraqi Army at bay for a month now and need to come back in for some downtime. At some point we're going over on the offense, and I don't know what our mission will be, but I don't think we'll be sitting here pulling security on this airfield. The 28th Division is flowing into a city down south, Jeddah, and for the time being their mission is the same as ours," Warren pointed out.

"Sir, do you think we're going to get into it with the Iraqis?" the 2nd Battalion commander asked. His tone in asking the question set off alarm bells in Warren's head.

"Well, I hope we didn't come all this way to just sit on our asses. Yes, I think we're going to get into it, and you need to let your soldiers right now that we are. The Iraqi soldier has been portrayed as being ten feet tall. Do you see any Arabs around here that are ten feet tall or weigh more than a hundred and fifty pounds? No, you don't. Get your soldiers in the right frame of mind. A winning frame of mind. Any questions?" Warren asked. *God don't tell me I have a defeated attitude with a battalion commander*, he was thinking.

"All right, next order of business. Everyone is confined to this airfield. No going into town. We want as small a footprint on the locals as possible. We're here to win the war and not lose the peace. The local customs are so different from back home that we cannot afford to have one of these guys go into town and screw things up. So everyone is confined to the airfield, and that applies not only to this brigade but to all Americans located here. Certain people will be able to go into town to coordinate business, but they're primarily the supply people. If you train hard at night, they'll be too tired to attempt to go to town, and you know someone will do it. If it happens, a summary court-martial at a

434

minimum, no Article 15s. Is that understood?" Warren asked. He wanted to be sure that this did not happen.

"Not since World War II has a National Guard division deployed to a combat zone. This is going to be big news back home, besides the fact that our families want to know what we are doing. The press is going to be all over this place. They must be treated with respect, but remember, they're not here to be your friends but to get a story. Be sure they're getting the right story and not Joe Dope's bitch session. Everything is on the record with these people regardless of what they say. Treat them as if they were O-4 majors. No classified information about our strength, or where we're going or what we're doing. Watch the boys and counsel them about making irresponsible comments. When they're in your AO, have a responsible NCO escort them. If a soldier doesn't want to talk to them, that's the soldier's right, and the press has no right to stop a soldier either. Any questions?"

"Sir, will they be escorted by the public affairs folks?" Gooderjohn asked.

"No telling. Ideally, yes, but they just might be wandering on their own. If they are, report it right away and we'll get someone to escort them to the division public affairs office.

"OK, we have these new navigation devices called SLUGGER. They're about the size of a cigar box and will be issued one per company. They use satellites to pinpoint your location on the ground within ten meters. Learn how to use the damn things. All the fire support officers will also have one. Once we're out in the desert, navigation is going to be a bitch. These will really help, but it's going to take some training to use them right." Colonel Warren paused to check his notes in his little green notebook that every commander carried.

"OK, that's all I have for this evening. Gooderjohn, you managed to stay awake. Congratulations. If there's nothing else, I'll see you all in the morning at 0800. We'll meet each morning at 0800 and each evening at 1800 hours. Any final questions?" There were none, and everyone departed back to their battalion areas.

Chapter 50
Relief in Place

30 December 1990
XVIII Airborne Corps HQ
Jeddah, Saudi Arabia

The two National Guard divisions, the 28th and the 29th, were mostly on the ground and had been for the last two weeks, with some supply and logistic tail still flowing in-country. General Luck had been around and visited both of them and was impressed with what he saw. They weren't up to the level of an active Army mechanized division, but they weren't bad either. He felt assured that with a bit of time they would be ready to take on the Iraqi forces before the corps. The 28th was sitting in Jeddah and the 29th was in Yanbu. It was time to relieve the 101st and the 82nd. Also at his disposal were the 8th Saudi Mechanized Brigade, the 10th Saudi Brigade and the remnants of the Saudi 45th Armoured Brigade.

"Get me General Yeosock on the phone, please," Luck said to his aide as he walked back into the office with the aide in tow.

"Yes, sir."

Entering his office, General Luck began removing his load-bearing equipment, LBE, to include his sidearm. When he left his office, he dressed just like any private in the corps: helmet, LBE, sidearm, gas mask and CPOG, or chemical protective overgarment, which every soldier absolutely hated to have to put on. When done, he grabbed a bottle of water from the small ice chest in his office.

"Sir, General Yeosock will be on the line in a minute," the aide said, sticking his head through the doorway.

"Thanks, Brad. Close the door, please," Luck responded, reaching for the phone as he swallowed another mouthful.

"Hello, John, how is your day?" Luck said as he heard Yeosock come on the line.

"Good, whatcha got?" Yeosock asked.

"John, I have these two Saudi brigades and part of a third here in my AO. Could we get a Saudi general with staff to come over and pull them together into a task force? I have a plan that I could use them better than having three separate brigades running around as they please. It would make the command and control so much easier and more efficient," Luck said.

"How are you thinking about using them?" Yeosock's interest was piqued.

"I'm thinking of having them relieve the 101st in the north and set up a defensive line. The 37th Iraqi Army Division is about the only viable force up on the north with the 2nd Iraqi Army Division sitting in Tabuk. That would free up the 28th Division for me to use along with the 29th in the push through Medina and down to the road towards Buraydah," Luck said.

"Hmm," Yeosock muttered. "Maybe you should reconsider something. Medina is considered one of the holy cities. We should let a Saudi force go in there and clean it out rather than putting Americans in there," Yeosock pointed out.

"Yeah, we can do that. I'll take one of the Saudi brigades and run them into Medina while I have one brigade of the mech divisions take their place on the line. Once Medina is cleaned out, the local Saudi National Guard can control the city and I can swap out the two units. What do you think?" Luck asked.

"I think I need to find you a Saudi general to take charge of those Saudi brigades. I'll get back to you. Anything else?"

"No, that's it. Give my regards to Norm."

****

General Luck approached the Saudi general who had just been shown into his office. MG Abdul Ali Faheem was not what General Luck had been expecting. MG Abdul was tall for an Arab, well built and muscular. Most Saudi generals had expanded waistlines, but not MG Abdul. His V-shaped upper torso indicated a rigorous workout routine. His high cheekbones and cold blue eyes seemed to pierce right through a person. Both men extended their hands.

"Very good to meet you, General Abdul," Luck said with sincerity.

"And I you, General Luck," Abdul said with a British accent.

"Please have a seat," Luck said, pointing at one of the overstuffed chairs in his office.

"Thank you. I want you to know that I am very glad to be assigned to your Corps and be taking command of the Saudi forces under your command," Abdul said.

"Well, I can tell you I'm glad you are here. As you know, the 7th Republican Guard Division is in Medina and the Saudi National Guard forces there have been harassing the daylights out of them. They've been whittled down to about a reinforce brigade now. I want to clean them out but don't want to send American soldiers in there to do it. Suppose we send one of your brigades in and finish the job north and let me deal with the Iraqi 2nd Corps with air support from you?" General Abdul offered.

"General, you appear to be well informed of our current dispositions and plans," Luck said, leaning slightly forward in his chair.

"Soldiers talk and others listen," was all General Abdul would say.

"Very well. You and your forces will take Medina. My operations officer will draw up the plan and get it to your staff. The day of the attack will coincide with the day General Schwarzkopf indicates and not before. However, we need you to do a relief in place with the 82nd Airborne. How about tomorrow, you and I travel up to the 82nd and I introduce you to Major General Ed Ford? He can give you a brief on his disposition and what he's seeing," Luck said.

"I will look forward to that, sir." Abdul stood. "Until tomorrow. My aide will get with yours for the details of our trip tomorrow," he concluded, shaking Luck's hand and departing the office.

****

The helicopter flight out to the main CP for the 82nd was pleasant in the early-morning hours, as the sun had just crested the horizon and the air thermals hadn't started for the day. General Abdul hadn't ridden in a Black Hawk before, as the Saudi Army had just acquired several and they hadn't been seen much outside of Riyadh before it was overrun. He was rather enjoying the flight. He also hadn't served in this region and was enjoying being able to see the terrain from the air. As he did so, he was making mental notes about the landscape. His concentration was broken when the pilot announced they would be landing in two minutes. As the aircraft touched down and the dust settled, the crew chief slid the door open as Major General Ford was approaching the aircraft.

Saluting, Major General Ford said, "Morning, sir," acknowledging Lieutenant General Luck.

"Morning, Ed. I'd like you to meet Major General Abdul. His unit will be conducting a relief in place with some of your units. His unit is going to go in to clean out Medina and hold the remnants of the 2nd Republican Guard Corps," Luck said as the two major generals exchanged handshakes.

"Sir, I'm glad to meet you and give you this ground," General Ford said.

"And I, sir, am happy to take it. It is time to clean these people out," Abdul replied.

"Shall we go into the TOC and give you a brief on how we're deployed and what we've been seeing? We haven't entered the city at all but have remained in overwatch positions and have a good idea of what has been going on and where they're strongest," Ford said as he led everyone to the main TOC.

Inside, the G-3 staff were standing with the G-2 to give the brief. They even had an interpreter with them, as they weren't sure of Major General Abdul's command of the English language. Motioning to a seat in the very front, General Luck sat on one side of General Abdul while General Ford sat on the other.

"Good morning, sir," Colonel Dobbins said, addressing the three general officers. "I'm Colonel Dobbins, the G-3 for the division. This briefing will discuss the current disposition of our division and the disposition of the Republican Guard Forces from what we've learned from observing and from members of the Saudi National Guard forces that stayed behind and are harassing the 7th in Medina. At the conclusion of the brief, Lieutenant Colonel McKenzie and I will be available to answer your questions. If you direct your attention to this map," Dobbins said as he picked up a pointer and pointed at a map of the division sector with an overlay showing the position of the division forces, "here in the northern portion of our sector, we have the 1st Brigade with three battalions opposing the remnants of the 7th Republican Guard Division. The 7th was hit pretty hard in its move towards Medina by naval and Air Force assets and the 45th Saudi Armour Brigade. When it arrived in Medina, we calculated his strength to be seventy percent. He then launched an attack on the few roads through the 1st Brigade sector and paid dearly for that. At the conclusion of that engagement, we calculated his strength to be less than fifty percent. Since then, the Saudi National Guard stay-behind forces have been interrupting his resupply, taking out key leaders and generally creating fear and uncertainty in his forces. We've arranged for a Saudi National Guard member to serve as a liaison to General Abdul prior to you launching your operations.

"The 1st Brigade has one battalion on the left flank with two companies forward and one in depth. The forward two companies have mines and obstacles on the main roads, and I might add about the only roads through their sector. The third company in depth is at the crossroads where those two roads intersect.

"The second battalion in the center has three companies all arrayed in depth along the one road through his sector, which is the major highway coming out of Medina. He has an engagement area that all three companies can cover by fire simultaneously. That engagement area is also ringed with mines.

"On the right flank, the third battalion has two roads through his sector, one of which is a major highway. He has two companies each covering an engagement area along the roads, and one company in

442

depth, positioned so a portion of that company can cover each engagement area.

"Each battalion has a supporting 105 battery in their sector. Initially we didn't have any 155 support, but with the air support we've received, it wasn't necessary.

"We have road obstacles in these locations and we will remove them prior to your attack if you're going to use these roads initially. Minefields are indicated, and most are FASCAM fields that have self-destructed. We've been given a system called MOPMS, Modular Pack Mine System, which is a mine-laying system that's experimental right now, but we've received it and it performed well. One individual can control up to seventeen containers, and each has a mix of antitank and antipersonnel mines. These have been emplaced around the engagement areas in case they attempt another attack. Initially the FASCAM fields were emplaced by helicopters as well as Air Force assets dropping CBU-89/B and CBU-78/B bombs. If there are no questions, I will be followed by Lieutenant Colonel McKenzie, the G-2," Colonel Dobbins concluded, trading places with McKenzie.

"Good morning, sir, I will cover the 7th Republican Guard Division as we currently understand it. As Colonel Dobbins told you, we estimate the 7th's strength to be less than fifty percent at this time. Morale appears to be low from the reports we've received. Resupply has been greatly disrupted due to air strikes on the main road leading from Buraydah in addition to frequent mine-laying operations along the road.

"From what the Saudi National Guard liaison officer can tell us, it appears that the bulk of his forces are holed up in the district of Ad Difa here and down to Khakh in the south. That's about eleven thousand meters. Ash and trash units are occupying the city proper. We—"

"Excuse me, Colonel," Abdul interrupted, "but what is 'ash and trash units'? I am not familiar with this type of unit."

"Sorry, sir. That's American slang for supply and service units," McKenzie confessed.

"Thank you. That sounds very appropriate. Ash and trash... I like that term. Ash and trash...I must remember this," Abdul said with a chuckle. "Please continue," he directed.

"Yes, sir. Currently we have air parity with this air coverage. As you'll be launching your attack at approximately the same time that XVIII Airborne Corps is going to launch against the 5th Republican Guard Division to the south, you may anticipate friendly air superiority over you."

"What about the artillery support that the 7th has? Have they been hitting you very much?" General Abdul asked.

"Sir, most of their artillery was taken out as they advanced towards Medina. We place priority of targets as his air-defense weapons first, artillery second, and tanks third. Once he entered Medina, we shifted the priority to hitting artillery, reinforcements and supply depots in that order. He doesn't have much artillery left and none is getting through to him, nor is he getting much in the way of resupply. Not going to say you're going to have a walk in the park in there, but he won't be anywhere near full strength, or half strength for that matter," General Luck said.

"That is good, General. This will be a good test for my soldiers. It is embarrassing enough that he got this far. It is time we, the armed forces of Saudi Arabia, reclaim what we lost, our country and our dignity," General Abdul said with some pride.

"Sir, I think we'll pause at this point, have some lunch and then come back and discuss the 5th Republican Guard Division and what we've done to them," General Ford said as he stood and pointed to the door.

Chapter 51

New Year Command Brief

2 January 1991
CENTCOM Forward HQ
Military Technological College
Muscat, Oman

New Year's Eve was a rather sober affair, considering that no alcohol was allowed for US forces. New Year's Day was an off day for everyone to enjoy watching football games for those that had TV access. Unfortunately, most games were televised in the early-morning hours as Oman was eight hours ahead. A three-in-the-afternoon kickoff was starting at 11:00 p.m. in Muscat. January 2 was a duty day, but not until noon for the CENTCOM staff. General Schwarzkopf wanted an update on the unit status and locations. Without divulging it to anyone, he was ready to set some dates on the calendar if the staff assessment was good.

"Good afternoon, sir," General Schless said as Schwarzkopf took his seat and everyone settled down.

"Afternoon, everyone. Let's get going," Schwarzkopf said in his usual joyful tone. He was a bear of a man, but you could always tell when he was in a good mood. Today he was in a good mood.

"Sir, we will be covering the latest intel updates, followed by an update on the status of each of the forces, and our overall supply status," Schless said. "Sir, the G-2."

General O'Donnell stepped up to the podium. "Sir, the enemy continues to prepare his positions in the UAE. There have been no additional forces introduced to the UAE theater nor into Saudi Arabia.

446

The forces in the UAE are being resupplied by both ground transportation and over-the-shore resupply coming in at the ports of Al Jazeera and Al Hamriya," O'Donnell said, pointing to each port. "Iraqi naval vessels are using the port of Al Mina in Dubai, which has drydock facilities. The Iraqi Navy captured several vessels when it overran Saudi and Kuwait, and some of those crews switched loyalty. Those vessels are patrolling the Persian Gulf but haven't ventured through the Strait. They've established a radar site on this abandoned oil platform off the coast of the UAE and are capable of looking into a large portion of the Strait. They maintain a couple patrol boats in the vicinity with anti-aircraft missiles. The radar also tracks aircraft as well as ships coming through the Strait."

Looking over at General Schless, Schwarzkopf said, "Something is going to have to be done about that site. Let's talk after this." Schless nodded in acknowledgment and wrote some notes.

O'Donnell went on to explain, "Frogfoot aircraft are staging out of the Abu Dhabi International and Dubai International airports, but all other aircraft are coming out of Saudi Arabia, Kuwait or Iraq. Both of these airports have a mix of air-defense weapons, to include SA-9, SA-6, ZSU-23-4, ZSU-57-2 and SA-7s. In—"

"Excuse my interrupting you, but what do we know about his air-defense systems?" Schwarzkopf asked.

"Sir, the Iraqi air-defense system is a centralized system employing Soviet tactics. The system was built by Thomson-CSF, a French company, but is connected to a British logistics and battle management system. It's a system tailored to the Iran-Iraq conflict and designed to handle twenty to thirty aircraft raids such as Iran was throwing at them. Truthfully, we don't believe it could handle a major surge campaign. A surge day during the Iran-Iraq War was twenty aircraft a day in raids of four aircraft at a time. The best pilots aren't in the air-defense roles but in the ground-attack support roles," General Horner interjected.

"What about SA-2 and SA-3s?" the CENTCOM commander asked.

"We've seen some over Kuwait and northern Saudi but haven't seen any in the southern or western parts of Saudi or the UAE. His western most system is around Riyadh and in the east around Dammam. We've been plotting them and have a good idea where each of the systems is located and they'll be the first to be taken out when the air campaign starts," Horner explained.

Nodding in approval, Schwarzkopf told O'Donnell to continue.

"In the west, the 2nd Iraqi Army Corps is at thirty percent strength, opposing the 101st Airborne, with the 2nd Iraqi Army Division at eighty percent strength and still sitting up in Tabuk. The 2nd Republican Guard Corps is down to less than forty percent strength, with the 7th Republican Guard Division stuck in Medina and under pressure from the Saudi National Guard forces that remained in the city. The 5th Republican Guard Division facing the 82nd Airborne has been on the receiving end of air strikes and is down in strength as well. Reports indicate that resupply to both of these Corps is limited due to distances, a scorched-earth policy exercised by the retreating Saudi forces, and air strikes interdicting the supply lines," O'Donnell said, pausing to reorient this map to the west.

While he did so, Schwarzkopf turned to General Yeosock. "Can General Luck hold them?"

"Sir, the XVIII Airborne Corps has the two National Guard divisions closing in on Jeddah and Yanbu and has now three Saudi brigades, two mechanized and one an armor brigade, plus an armor team from the 24th that arrived in the opening days. Gary Luck intends to turn the Saudi brigades against the 7th Republican Guard Division in Medina and then execute a relief in place with the 101st and send Saudis to Tabuk. He's going to use the rest to take out the 5th Republican Guard and move on to Buraydah. He doesn't want to have American forces in Medina since it's considered a holy city." Yeosock explained.

"I don't know," Schwarzkopf said. "Luck will be fighting in two directions. He'll be looking east with the bulk of his force and north with a tiny force of Saudis. See me after this and let's talk to Luck," Schwarzkopf said. Schless knew Schwarzkopf well enough to see the wheels turning in Stormin' Norman's head.

"What else you have, O'Donnell?"

"Sir, you asked about chemical weapons. We haven't seen any movement of those weapons from his strategic stockpiles in the northern part of Iraq, nor any indication that he's moved any chemical weapons into Saudi or the UAE," O'Donnell explained.

"Good. Keep an eye on those weapons. If you see any indication, I want to know about it immediately. Understood?"

"Yes, sir. Moving along, we have been monitoring his communications and have discovered that there are some Russian personnel operating with the Iraqis and specifically as pilots and air-defense advisors. We don't know if they're official military personnel or a quasi-mercenary force. We suspect a bit of both but will continue to monitor the situation. We're sure that there are a couple of Soviet naval advisors on the patrol craft and we're pretty sure there are a couple of Soviet officers on the oil platform with the sea and air radar. We've identified his primary command frequencies and are prepared to jam them on your orders, especially with the Republican Guard Corps."

"Good, the 1st Republican Guard Corps is the main target, followed by the 9th Iraqi Corps, but I want to hit the 9th when we launch the attack and then monitor and switch to the 1st Republican Guard Corps when the 9th starts crying for help. This should coincide with our air campaign," Schwarzkopf said, and the horse holders began writing notes. Looking back at O'Donnell, he said, "Anything else?"

"Sir, just that we've been monitoring his logistics, and it appears that he has fuel shortages in the west with the 2nd Iraqi Corps as he parked a good number of tanks for lack of fuel and we hit them with air strikes as well as a supply depot. We doubt if he has the supply reserve to continue any kind of attack and may even have trouble attempting to conduct a retrograde operation," O'Donnell concluded. "That's all I have for you today, sir."

"Good rundown. Who's next?" Schwarzkopf asked, already knowing the answer to his question.

Exchanging places with O'Donnell, General Schless took center stage. "Sir, the status of our forces is as follows." He pointed to a highlighted VGT slide with each unit listed and the status of its forces expressed in percentages. One hundred percent equated to all elements in-country and logistics currently sufficient for a 180-day offensive campaign. "As you can see, sir, all elements of the 82nd and 101st Airborne Divisions are one hundred percent. The 29th and 28th Infantry Divisions are fifty percent at this time and within the next ninety days will be one hundred percent. The 24th Infantry Division is one hundred percent as is the 3rd Armored Cav Regiment. The elements of the VII Corps are at seventy-five percent strength with the 50th Armored Division being at fifty percent. It, too, will be one hundred percent in the next ninety days. Our two US Marine divisions are at one hundred percent at this time. The British 1st Armoured

Division is one hundred percent and our host nations' forces are reporting one hundred percent along with the two Egyptian divisions."

"So what I'm hearing is that within ninety days we'll be at one hundred percent strength in our ground forces that have been allocated to us. Is that correct?" Schwarzkopf asked.

"Yes, sir, that is correct," General Schless responded.

Turning his attention to Admiral Muse, Schwarzkopf asked, "And for our naval elements… are we at full strength?"

"Sir, naval forces are at full strength with ninety percent operational aircraft afloat. The *Wisconsin* and *Missouri* are with the amphibious force. The 1st Marine Division is currently moving from their staging area to Al Mirayr. The path through the minefield is plotted and hasn't changed, but we're continuing to monitor it so any changes will be addressed prior to the fleet passing through the Strait. We do have a concern for this abandoned oil platform that has both air and sea radar, however," the admiral stated.

"Don't be. We're going to take care of that," Schwarzkopf informed the group. Several looks were exchanged.

"General Horner, how is the Air Force status at this time?"

"Sir, we have a sufficient number of aircraft across the full spectrum of capabilities. We have ninety percent availability right now, and on day one we can surge to twenty-five hundred sorties a day for a thirty-day period at eighty percent availability[12]. On day one we will have ninety-eight percent availability," Horner explained.

---

[12] A sortie is defined as one aircraft taking off, conducting a mission and returning.

General Schwarzkopf sat for a minute, deep in thought. *Have I covered all the bases?* "General Pegasus, how are our logistics for supporting an operation?" Schwarzkopf asked, knowing that you could have the best fighting systems, but if your logistics failed, you failed.

"Sir, we currently have on hand sufficient logistic stockpiles to conduct a one-hundred-and-eighty-day campaign. Our supply systems and flow are uninterrupted. Our supply depots are heavily guarded both from ground infiltration and from air threats. We now have port security from the US Coast Guard and haven't had any more threats from commandos or underwater divers. Supply ships are being quickly unloaded and supplies cleared from the port areas. Airflow of personnel is on schedule and uninterrupted with escort fighters for each aircraft approaching the Peninsula airspace. In ninety days we will have increased our logistics base to a two-hundred-and-thirty-day level," Pegasus explained, handing him a briefing book outlining everything in the logistics arena.

Before Schwarzkopf reached for the book, he looked at Pegasus. "Sign the book, attesting to its accuracy." There was almost stunned silence at this request, but General Pegasus took out a pen and did so before handing the briefing book over to Schwarzkopf. Finally, Schwarzkopf stood and turned to face the group.

"Gentlemen, we have good intelligence, we have sufficient supplies, and we have sufficient forces for the first phase of this operation. Adjust your plans accordingly as we will commence offensive operations on 1 April. General Schless will have the operational orders to you in thirty days. Are there any questions?" he asked, knowing there probably would be none. The expressions he was seeing were all smiles, as everyone understood they were finally going to get this show moving.

452

Chapter 52
Not-So-Abandoned Oil Platform

5 January 1991
Persian Gulf

Major Uri Aleksenko from the Soviet Air Defense Force did not particularly like being stuck on an old abandoned oil platform. Sergeant Nikolai Dragunov was keeping him company as he was a technical advisor for the radar system that had been installed. Since the winter had settled on the Persian Gulf, the days were comfortable, with the nights becoming cold enough that a jacket was necessary. Both men had developed a taste for Cuban cigars since arriving in the Middle East and could afford to purchase them. On this night they were on the rail looking out over the Strait and the Gulf waters. A single cargo ship coming out of the Strait had passed them, all aglow with lights. The lights from atop of the skyscrapers in Dubai could be faintly seen on the southwestern horizon along with the glow of lights from Ras Al-Khaimah some twenty-five miles to the east-southeast.

Behind and above them were the 1S11 and 1S31 radar systems that had been significantly modified for this location. Both had been taken off their normal vehicle, which was part of the SA-6 Gainfield air-defense system, and modified to be placed on this oil platform. The systems were capable of picking up aircraft coming in from the Strait of Hormuz or anywhere up to two hundred kilometers away. If the operators knew what they were doing, which Major Aleksenko had his doubts, then this jerry-rigged system should prove to be an exceptional early-warning system. The operative word in this equation was *should*. But that was largely dependent on the ability of the operators to know what the hell they were doing. Despite more than a year of training, his partner in crime, Sergeant Dragunov, was harboring the same troubling thoughts about the Iraqi technicians and their ability to use and operate these bastardized radar systems properly.

"Major, whose idea was it for these radar systems to be removed from their vehicles, transported to this oil rig, and reassembled, expecting them to function properly?" Sergeant Dragunov asked. They were alone, so he felt it safe to ask such a question. In the old days or back in the Soviet Union, the proper address would be "Comrade Major" or "Comrade Sergeant," but out here alone, familiarity was being observed.

"Sergeant, enjoy your cigar and do not ask questions. As they say, 'Ours is not to reason why, ours is but to do and die.' Somebody higher up than you and I thought this up and we were tasked with executing it. If the systems do not work, we blame it on the Iraqis, who are about as dumb as the camels they ride," Major Aleksenko explained, showing his disdain for the Iraqis and his current assignment. "Besides, this is not such a bad duty. We have no flies bothering us. We have no smelly sheep crapping everywhere to worry about; we have—"

"No women and no vodka is what we have, Major," the sergeant interrupted. "I am so tired of drinking tea that I even piss tea now," Sergeant Dragunov muttered under his breath.

"Cheer up, Dragunov. Soon we will be posted back to our home base in Kiev and will have a year's pay in our pockets above our normal pay," Aleksenko pointed out.

"I suppose you are right. The bonus pay for coming here does make it worth it. Sure as hell cannot spend it on this oil rig," Dragunov said as he took a last puff on his cigar and tossed it into the water below. "I am going to turn in after I make one more check of the equipment and the night shift operating it."

Major Aleksenko watched as the cigar stub descended like one of the meteors that he'd seen so many times before at night on the platform. What he hadn't noticed was what was located just under the dark water near where the cigar had landed. Instead, he turned and headed back to his own duties for the time being.

****

USS *Florida* SSBN-728
Arabian Gulf

The *Florida* silently followed a Russian cargo ship through the Strait, avoiding the minefields and confirming their locations. Once the sun had set, she slowly and quietly rose to periscope depth.

"Conn, Sonar," Petty Officer Simmons announced.

"Sonar, what you got?" asked Commander Fletcher.

"Conn, the only traffic is Sierra One, the Russian cargo ship we were following. He is twenty-five miles southwest of us on a steady course. The target is two thousand yards on the nose from us," Simmons reported.

"Good," Fletcher said, looking at the chief of the boat, Master Chief Jack Bridges, who was chief of the watch, standing over the ship control party.

"Mr. Kennedy, proceed to periscope depth," the captain directed. Mr. Kennedy was on his first deployment, having graduated from the Submarine Officers Course just prior to the departure. As a new lieutenant aboard, Commander Fletcher was taking note of how he performed.

"Proceed to periscope depth, aye, sir," Kennedy said and turned to the dive officer of the watch. "Dive, make your depth sixty feet."

"Make my depth sixty feet, aye, sir. Full rise, both planes give me ten degrees up. Chief of the Watch, flood auxiliaries," the duty officer on watch ordered.

"Take us to sixty feet, ten degrees up, reduce speed to three knots," the COB said to the planesman and the helmsman/fairweather planesman. The *Florida* responded beautifully, raising her bow ever so gently and gliding to the desired depth.

"Sonar, Conn," Mr.Kennedy called out. "Report all contacts."

"Conn, two contacts. The Sierra One we're following at twenty-five miles and the target at two thousand yards," Petty Officer Simmons reported. Simmons had been with Fletcher for the past year, and his voice gave some reassurance to Fletcher.

"Roger, Sonar," Fletcher responded. As the *Florida* reached periscope depth, the PERVIS system showed those on the Conn what the periscope was seeing on the surface. Two thousand yards away, they spotted their primary objective, the oil platform. It was bathed in lights against a moonless black sky, perfectly silhouetting itself for them.

****

Lieutenant Higgins had just broken the surface along with his team, SEAL Team Two, when two glowing cigars landed fifteen feet away in the dark waters. The thirty men of the team were in the water with him. All of the SEALs turned and looked to make sure they hadn't been spotted and that their stealth was still intact.

They each knew the job they had to execute, the importance of the mission, and how quickly things could go sideways on them if they weren't careful. They'd done their homework, though. Prior to boarding the *Florida*, they'd diagrammed the oil rig onshore and done several walkthroughs. Some of the team members had been a part of the mission back in 1987 to seize an Iranian oil platform. That experience had been invaluable during the walkthroughs. They were all aware of who the prize targets were for capture. This mission wasn't meant to grab and seize the platform. It was a snatch-and-grab mission. The only two people on this platform that mattered were two apparent Russian soldiers.

This was the first oil platform a ship or aircraft would run up against once they exited the Strait, which was what made this particular platform so valuable. The rig itself wasn't anything special. It was supported on six tubular steel legs, ten feet in circumference, with two boat docks connected by gangplanks to the steel legs. The rig was four stories high, with the lowest level being thirty feet above the water. On the topmost level was a helipad with three military MILVANs on the side of the helipad. The two outer MILVANs had radar antennas on top, rotating constantly.

The operators for the system sat inside the air-conditioned center MILVAN and monitored the radar systems. One flight down was the crew quarters, a dining facility and a recreation room with Iranian and Iraqi television. LaserDiscs were also present for the crew's entertainment. Of course they had been censored by the Islamic clerics. A medical clinic was also on this level. The bottom two floors contained the machinery to pump oil, which they'd long since been abandoned as this platform was more of an early-warning system than an oil-producing platform. The generator that serviced the entire facility was located on the bottom level.

Lieutenant Higgins had broken his thirty-man team into three teams. One team for the upper floor and the MILVANs, one team for the second floor and the crew's quarters, and the last team for the generator and a security element. The security element would clear the bottom two floors of any potential guards and secure the exfiltration route. Since they had the bottom two floors, they were the first out of the water and silently moving up the stairs to the bottom two floors.

For this part of the mission, they utilized their MP5s with silencers and subsonic rounds. When it came time to rock and roll in a real gunfight, they'd switch back to their standard ammo, but for right now the subsonic rounds would help ensure their silenced MP5s would stay silent. This first part of the mission required absolute stealth.

When Lieutenant Higgins got the word that the bottom two floors were secured, the rest of his teams approached the flights of stairs near the boat docks. The top-floor team went up one side and the second-floor team went up the other side. Reaching the top floor, the team spread out before crossing the helipad and surrounding the MILVANs.

A pair of SEALs crept up to each of the vans. One operator grabbed the door while the other had his MP5 aimed at it. On the count of three, the operator holding the door yanked it open. The operators had just moments to look at the surprised soldiers and verify they weren't the Russians they were after. Once they did, the operators opened up with their MP5s. In fractions of a second, they had riddled their bodies with bullets before they could sound an alarm or alert their comrades that they were under attack. With the element of surprise still on their side, the operators moved to their next objective, supporting the snatch-and-grab team that was responsible for grabbing the Russian soldiers themselves.

Lieutenant Higgins was on the second floor. Opening the door to the corridor, he saw it was empty. His ears registered some music softly playing from the direction of the mess hall area. As Higgins moved down one side of the corridor, another team member moved down the other side. Coming to a closed door, they bypassed it, letting another team clear it.

Further down the hall, they saw the open door leading to the recreation room and the mess hall. The medical facility was easy to identify from the large red cross and red crescent on the door.

Higgins had a good idea which rooms contained the Iraqi commander and the two Soviet advisors; they were likely in the section of the deck that held six separate rooms. Most of the quarters on the platforms tended to sleep four. But as this platform wasn't functioning as an oil platform, there were fewer people aboard than normal. Most of the quarters only had one or two people utilizing a room. At this hour, very few people were awake.

As Higgins and his partner approached the kitchen, a person suddenly appeared in the hallway. A cook had walked out of the kitchen and practically bumped right into Higgins.

Placing the silenced barrel of his MP5 in the man's face, he whispered in Arabic, "Shut the fuck up."

The cook almost immediately dropped to his knees and softly began speaking. With his weapon in one hand, Higgins held his finger to his lips, giving the universal symbol to be quiet. The cook slowly nodded and hushed up.

Turning to his comrade, Higgins said, "Zip-tie his hands and feet, gag him and let's move."

Higgins's partner pulled the zip ties from his front chest rig and motioned for the cook to follow him back into the kitchen. He told the man in Arabic to lie down on his belly and place his hands behind him. He tied up his hands and then his legs. He then grabbed for a rag and put it partially in the man's mouth and placed a piece of duct tape over it to hold it in place.

Continuing deeper into the facility, Higgins located the three rooms he was looking for. The doors were closed. He wasn't sure who occupied which room, but this wasn't a time to go in guns blazing. Besides Higgins, five other operators lined up against the doors, two SEALs on each door. Higgins noted that none of the doors appeared to have locks, as there were no slots for keys. He tried the doorknob on his door, which turned ever so quietly.

Looking at the other two teams, he saw that each had done the same and each was grinning like Cheshire cats. Holding his left hand up with his teammate poised to rush the door, Higgins held up one finger, then a second finger, and as the third finger was raised, three doors crashed open. The operators rushing into each room were on top of the individuals in the beds before they had a chance to reach for a weapon or alert anyone to what was happening.

"*Privet mayor*," Higgins said in Russian.

The Russian looked surprised as hell. Then he looked angry. Replying in his native tongue, he angrily asked, "What is the meaning of this? I am a Soviet citizen. You cannot treat me like this. Who are you?"

They could hear a string of profanity in Russian coming from Sergeant Dragunov's room.

Higgins smiled as he replied in flawless Russian, "Yes, you are a Soviet citizen and a Soviet major in the air-defense force advising these Iraqi soldiers on the radar systems upstairs. Therefore, Major, you are a combatant and will be treated according to the Geneva Convention. Now, we can do this the easy way or the hard way. It is up to you."

Almost stunned at the accusation, Aleksenko stammered, "Are you Russian?"

"You can walk to where we need to go, or we will hog-tie you and carry you up. I would suggest that you walk. Oh, to answer your question, my grandmother was Russian but managed to defect to the West," Higgins explained. At this point, the major had placed his boots on and stood. One of the operators zip-tied his hands in front of him so he'd be able to walk.

"I will cooperate," the major said in a defeated tone.

"Good, let's move." Higgins said. Pressing his throat mike, he transmitted, "Alpha Team, packages are secured. Move to phase two."

In response he heard four clicks, indicating the team understood and was moving into position. The third click came from the boat team that had departed the *Florida* when the assault had started. They were now speeding across the water to retrieve the SEALs. The fourth click came from the Night Stalkers' Black Hawks, which were now on their way to pick up the Russians, the prized target of the mission.

"Dolphin One, Stalker Two-Six, over," Chief Warrant Officer Bob Witzler transmitted. His copilot for the mission, Chief Warrant Officer Bob Fladry, was flying the aircraft while Mr. Witzler coordinated the mission. Both were under night vision goggles and only two hundred feet above the water, flying at one hundred and twenty knots. In the back, the crew chief, door gunner and two Special Forces soldiers were prepared to take the prizes aboard.

"Stalker Two-Six, Dolphin One, moving to the pad and will be ready in five mikes, over," Higgins broadcast.

"Roger, five mikes," Witzler responded.

****

As the MH-60 approached the well-lit oil platform, both pilots resumed flight without the use of the night vision goggles. The platform was lit up like a Christmas tree, making the NVGs redundant.

As Mr. Fladry made his approach, he could see the ten SEAL members and three other individuals kneeling on the side of the helipad. As the MH-60 gently touched down, six of the SEALs grabbed the three individuals and half ran and half dragged them to the aircraft. The human packages were shoved into the birds before the SEALs moved back to the edges of the platform. Their part of the mission was now over.

The two Special Forces soldiers on the birds got the prisoners situated in their five-point harnesses. Once they were ready, they gave the pilots the thumbs-up. They were ready to get out of Dodge.

Seeing the soldiers in the back giving him a thumbs-up, Mr. Witzler called out to his partner, "I got it."

"You have the aircraft," Fladry responded.

With that, the MH-60 quickly started to move forward and dove off the side of the oil platform. The three passengers were convinced in that moment they were going to die until Mr. Witzler pulled in more power and resumed his two-hundred-foot altitude. He then turned to the darkened coast to the northeast, passing between Fudgha and Bukha, Oman. From that point they would fly southeast to Haffah and out over the Gulf of Oman to a waiting refueling C-130. Their final destination was a secure location outside of Sohar where they would deliver the prizes. It was a long night of flying.

****

As the MH-60 lifted off, the ten SEALs made their way to a set of stairs on the side of the oil platform. As they left, the explosives left behind in the MILVANs and around the radar systems were set to blow in minutes.

"Let's get everyone below and off this thing, Chief," Higgins said to his senior chief and executive officer for this mission. "Be sure we have a good head count. I don't want to somehow miss someone before the explosives blow."

As SEALs loaded into their boats for the ride back to the *Florida*, the explosives they left behind lit up the sky. The enemy's early-warning system was officially down. Mission accomplished.

Chapter 53

We Have Questions

7 January 1991
Camp Justice
Diego Garcia

The interrogator, a man that went only by the name John, watched the Russian major through a one-way mirror. He sat silently in a chair in the center of the room, a single lightbulb dangling directly over his head. It cast ominous shadows about the room and kept the edges bathed in darkness. The man's zip ties had been removed. A new set of ties bound his wrists to the arms of the chair he was seated in, his feet similarly bound as well.

Unable to move much, the Russian just sat there, waiting for what would come next.

"What is it you want me to extract from him?" John asked without taking his eyes off the prisoner.

An aide to General Schwarzkopf answered, "We want to know what he's doing working for the Iraqis. How long has he been working for them? How many other trainers or observers like him are working with the Iraqis? As he gives you some of that information, use your brain as to what would be the next logical thing to ask. We need to know how involved the Soviets really are and what else they might be providing the Iraqis with."

John snorted at the questions, not particularly caring for the tone of the man asking them. It wasn't that they weren't good questions; they were just too simple for a man of his skill.

"Do you want me to find out if the Russians have any soldiers, sailors, or airmen actively fighting with the Iraqis?" John inquired.

"Yes, yes, that would be great. That's the kind of information we're looking for," the aide said.

Without saying anything further, John left the observation room to go greet his Russian guest.

John was a native Russian speaker himself, so he started his conversation with Major Aleksenko in their native tongue. Staying in the shadows so Aleksenko couldn't see him yet, he asked, "What is your name, rank, and serial number?"

The question seemed to have caught the Russian off guard. He hesitated for a moment and then recited the requested information. It was a universal question all prisoners of war were asked no matter what side they were on.

Having gotten the basics out of the way, John began the dance. The dance that involved asking his Russian guest a lot of mundane and innocuous questions while periodically throwing a money question into the mix. For the most part, Aleksenko answered all his questions, but when John would reach a money question, a question he was tasked with getting an answer to, the prisoner hesitated. Then he stopped answering questions altogether.

Rather than getting angry, and still having not revealed himself to the light, John left the room for a brief moment. Before he left, though, he turned on some soft, soothing piano music. He hoped the music would help relax Aleksenko while he prepared for the next phase in his interrogation.

Having left the room, John walked over to his partner, a man with a medical degree who helped him from time to time when it looked like a medical interrogation was going to be required. They talked briefly, going over what kind of drugs might work best on Aleksenko. Ultimately, it was decided the best approach was to give him a happy drug, something that would lower his internal guard and make him chatty and a little loopy at the same time. Once they figured out what they were going to give him, they had to figure out the delivery method, ideally one that wouldn't alert him that he was being given the drug. This way, he wouldn't try to fight it. If they were lucky, he wouldn't even realize he'd been drugged at all.

They came up with the idea of increasing the temperature of the room and placing the drug in a cup of juice. At the same time they'd provide him some buttered bread and a piece of American beef jerky, make it almost like a meal. He'd eat the food, down the juice, and in minutes he'd be spilling his guts. At least that was how they hoped it'd work.

One of the military guards walked into the room. He moved into the light with a small tray of food on a portable TV tray. Placing the TV tray in front of the prisoner, he pulled a pair of wire cutters out.

"Whoa, what are you going to do to me with those?" Aleksenko blurted out in broken English.

The uniformed soldier softly replied, "I'm going to cut your dominant hand free so you can feed yourself. Is it your right or left hand?"

Aleksenko eyed the soldier cautiously, not taking anything for granted. "I am a prisoner of war. There are rules about torture."

"OK, fine, don't tell me which is your dominant hand. I'll go ahead and cut the tie holding your left wrist down." The soldier then moved to cut the tie, but before he could, Aleksenko blurted out, "My right hand is my dominant hand. I would appreciate it if you would free that one."

The soldier smiled and freed that wrist. "We're Americans, we aren't going to torture," the soldier said. His comments were part of the ruse John had designed. He wanted Aleksenko as relaxed and calm as possible. The more they could get him to lower his guard, the better the chances the drugs would have the desired effect.

Having not eaten anything in nearly twenty-four hours, the Russian major proved to be hungry. He scarfed the food down and then emptied the glass of juice. When he'd finished eating, the soldier came back in and removed the TV tray. He then placed a new zip tie on the man's right wrist, but this time, he made it loose and comfortable instead of super tight.

"Would you like me to readjust the tie on your left wrist as well?" the soldier asked.

At this point, Aleksenko was starting to feel the drugs, he smiled a dopey smile and nodded. "*Da*" was all he said.

A minute or so later, the soldier left the room. "His pupils are fully dilated. He's feeling the drugs, big-time."

John and his medical assistant smiled at the report. "I guess it's time to earn our pay," John said with a nod.

Upon entering the room, John still stayed in the shadows. He told Aleksenko that a medical doctor was going to attach some equipment to him to make sure he was medically alright. But while that was happening, he had some questions to ask. Aleksenko just smiled and nodded.

As the doctor attached some electrodes to Aleksenko's chest, he got the polygraph equipment fully hooked up. He then moved to a table that had been set up behind Aleksenko and attached all the wires to the equipment. He gave John a thumbs-up.

467

Still standing in the shadows, John asked, "Aleksenko, why are you in Iraq and not back home? Iraq is a terrible place. No women, no vodka, and god-awful heat."

Aleksenko laughed at the question. It reminded him of his conversation the night before with his sergeant. "The only reason I am here is because of the money."

"The money? You mean the bonus pay? It's not that much more money."

Aleksenko scoffed at John's response. "You are mistaken, comrade. The request was simple. If you volunteered to assist our allies the Iraqis during their time of need, then your pay would be tripled for the duration your services would be needed. Better yet, you would receive an automatic promotion to the next grade and your choice of assignments. Only a fool would turn down this opportunity. Plus we get to shoot at Yankees. What's not to like?"

Laughing, John said that was a good deal. He then grabbed a chair and brought it over and sat in front of Aleksenko. When he sat down, he was wearing the uniform of a KGB officer, a colonel, to be precise. "Aleksenko, do you know what they gave us when they asked that we send volunteers like you to Iraq?"

Aleksenko squirmed a bit in his seat. He was obviously a little concerned about talking with a KGB colonel. "I'm afraid I only know what they offered the military."

"Aleksenko, do not be concerned by my presence. I, like you, am stuck here in Iraq. But unlike you, we didn't get offered any sort of bonus. We got screwed over and told to report here to Iraq to help their internal security forces with the occupation of their newly captured lands. It's a shit duty, Aleksenko. A complete shit duty if you ask me."

"I'm sorry to hear that, Comrade Colonel. That does sound terrible. Look at it this way—at least you are not deployed to the field with these camel riders. I honestly don't know how anyone can drink so much tea. And their constant calls to prayer... I will be glad when I return to Kiev and not have to hear that again."

"Yes, you are right, Comrade Major. At least we do not have to deploy with the Iraqi Army. So, if you had to guess, how many of our comrades do you believe are here in Iraq with us right now?" This was one of the main questions John needed to get answered.

Aleksenko paused for a moment, almost looking like he was thinking about something, "Is this a trick question, Comrade Colonel? Are you trying to trip me up and get me to answer something I'm not supposed to?"

John threw his hands up in the air as he laughed. "Was I that obvious?"

Aleksenko let out a nervous laugh. "Kind of. What am I doing here, comrade? Is this some sort of dream I'm stuck in?"

"Aleksenko, you are stuck here in Iraq like the rest of us until this silly Arab war is done. Here, would you like to have a drink with me? I managed to smuggle some vodka through the embassy."

The major's eyes lit up at that. Like most Russians, he hadn't had a strong drink since arriving in Iraq. The two of them drank a couple of shots together. The alcohol only enhanced the drugs' effects.

"Major, in your professional opinion, do you believe we have enough soldiers here to help these Arabs win this war, or do you believe more should be sent?"

"Ah, Colonel, that is a tough question. We have some twenty thousand soldiers here already. Could we use more? Sure, but to what end? We are all but advisors and trainers, not fighters. I mean, except for the pilots, of course; they actually get to fight."

John lifted an eyebrow at that. "You mean the pilots get to fight? I thought they were just advisors like yourself."

Aleksenko laughed a deep belly laugh. "Comrade Colonel, you can't possibly think these Arabs are that good. *Nyet*, comrade, those are Soviet pilots shooting all those American warplanes down, just like it's Soviet aircraft, not those poorly maintained Iraqi ones. I think if we wanted to ensure a greater Iraqi victory, then they should send more pilots and aircraft. As long as the Americans don't control the skies, I think the Iraqi numbers alone will be sufficient to win."

"Yes, you are probably right," John said as he poured his friend another shot of vodka. "But you need more than just aircraft to dominate the skies."

"True enough. That is why two brigades of S-300s were brought in. The Americans won't know what hit them when they start to encounter those missiles."

John smiled and nodded in agreement. He kept Aleksenko talking for another two hours as they finished off the bottle of vodka. In that time, he'd gotten all the information they needed. They now had proof that the Soviets were providing more than just equipment and advisors—they were providing pilots and aircraft along with their most advanced state-of-the-art air-defense systems. Before John left, he arranged for Aleksenko to be brought to a cell with a bed and its own bathroom. They'd let the Russian sleep off the drugs and alcohol. If they needed anything further from him, they'd circle back. If he became uncooperative, they'd play his previous interrogation back to him. If he still chose not to cooperate, then a copy would make it back to the real KGB, who would be waiting for him when the war ended. In either case, Major Aleksenko was going to be a cooperating source for the CIA for the foreseeable future.

Chapter 54

The Trojan Horse

9 January 1991

XVIII Airborne Corps HQ

Jeddah, Saudi Arabia

General Luck stood in the XVIII Airborne Corps operations center, studying a map of the region. No one said anything, not wishing to break his concentration. Everyone could see the wheels turning in his head.

"Sir, you wanted to see me?" asked General Ford, commander of the 82nd Airborne Division. His face showed how tired he was as he had been in the fight since the beginning, although as things had quieted down a bit, he was getting some sleep. He had also lost some weight, but almost everyone on the front lines had done so. The same could not be said for those in the rear area.

"Yeah, Fred. How're your boys doing?" Luck asked. Luck always asked about the soldiers.

"Sir, they're doing fine. A bit restless, but the Iraqis just barely keep it interesting. A shell here, a shell there. Keeps the boys awake at night, but they make up for it in the day. The Iraqis aren't real eager to come out and play. I think the biggest worry right now is having enough MREs to feed the number of Iraqis that are defecting and coming over, General Ford said."

"I have noticed a few additions to the POW camp. We getting any good intel out of them?"

"Getting some, but not much. Same old stuff. They're Republican Guard soldiers and are running low on food and fuel. Claim if they had fuel and food they could take us," Ford said.

"Yeah, right. How did that work for them last time they tried?" Luck asked.

"Sir, if those attack helicopters from the 101st as well as the Marines hadn't shown up when they did, it might have been a different story," Ford said.

"Well, OK. The reason I got you here is General Schwarzkopf wants to explore a different course of action for us. We were planning on pushing east through the 2nd Republican Guard Corps and attacking towards Buraydah. The old man is thinking strength against weakness. His thoughts are instead of us attacking east, we go north towards Tabuk and then swing east, coming behind all his forces in Saudi, cutting off their supply lines. The only problem I see with this is we'll have the same problem as the 2nd Iraqi Corps with extended supply lines… unless we have a port on the Red Sea farther north where we can resupply from," Luck said as he placed his finger on the map just ten miles south of Al Muwaileh. He picked up an aerial photo, which he handed to General Ford. Ford noticed a well-developed seaport, the only seaport in this part of the country.

"The Iraqis have ignored this seaport. They have no use for it as they can't get any ships there. There's a good road from there to Tabuk. We'll have to clear out some destroyed vehicles from the 14th Division that we nailed in an air strike and do some engineer work on the road, but it'll open a supply line for us. There's only one problem," Luck said.

"And that is, sir?" Ford asked with a sideways look.

"There's no airfield anywhere near it to land troops and it's too far for helicopters," Luck responded, waiting for a suggestion, which he knew was coming.

"Sir, this sounds like the perfect opportunity for an airborne division-size drop," Ford said with a sly smile.

"You read my mind, General. Draw up a plan that I can take to Schwarzkopf and Horner for the C-130s," Luck said.

"Yes, sir," Fred responded, not hiding the enthusiasm in his voice.
****

Back at the 82nd TOC, General Ford was looking over aerial photos and maps of the area that General Luck had indicated was the port that needed to be secured. The lack of an airport in the immediate area, or even close, ruled out an air landing operation.

"Can't believe that there are no airports of any kind in this portion of the region," Colonel Dobbins, the G-3, mumbled under his breath.

"Surprising as hell, considering this is about the only sizable port in this area too," General Ford replied.

"Sir, looking at this terrain, about the only flat area is along the coast, but that would have us dropping very close to the ocean. Not the best of situations. Some of these kids will probably wind up in the water," Dobbins said, looking up from the map with concern.

"Not having anyone going for a swim. Not loaded down with combat gear. No, sir." Ford made it clear.

"Sir, what about dropping along the road? It's certainly flat and wide enough. The aircraft could easily follow it, and it would put us right at the entrance to the port. The straight stretch of road is certainly long enough, being over four thousand meters long from this southern road intersection going north. If we drop at night, there should be no breeze until morning. We could put pathfinders in an hour before the drop and they could mark the DZ, provide security and block any traffic, which shouldn't be much late at night," Dobbins pointed out.

"What about these power lines on the east side?" Ford noted.

"Sir, we cut the power for that one night. Someone may get hung up, but we make sure everyone jumps with a rope to lower themselves if they get tangled. It's not ideal, but it's about all we have to work with," Dobbins said.

"How big of a force do you think we need to drop?" Ford asked.

"At a minimum, sir, it needs to be a full brigade with artillery and a med detachment initially," Dobbins answered.

"For a full brigade, we're going to need… what… how many C-130 aircraft?" Ford pondered and began calculating on a piece of paper. "Let's see, C-130 can hold sixty jumpers, so we need one and a half per rifle company, times three is four and a half aircraft, so five aircraft per battalion, times three battalions is fifteen, and add an additional five for medical, brigade staff, and another for heavy drops—that's twenty-one aircraft. CENTCOM shouldn't bitch too loud, do you think?" Ford asked.

"Sir, you know they're going to bitch. We should ask them for the aircraft to do two turns and really hear them scream bloody murder," Dobbins chuckled.

"We can ask, but I'm sure they're going to say no," Ford responded, leaning back in his chair.

"Sir, what about asking for a flight of C-141s? We can get a full rifle company and a half on one of those birds," Dobbins offered.

"I doubt that would happen. They're considered strategic assets and are wrapped up in priority cargo transport. To hold six or seven of them out of the strategic flow would probably not be tolerated," Ford explained. "But wait one...," he said, suddenly leaning forward in his chair and grabbing an aerial photo. After a minute, "We may not be able to drop another brigade, but we sure as hell can get another brigade in there!"

"Sir?" was all Dobbins had the time to say before General Ford was up and reaching for a phone.

****

General Ford made his way right over to General Luck's office, not waiting for the aide to announce his arrival but going straight in. Luck was seated behind his desk looking over some papers when Ford charged through the door with a shit-eating grin on his face.

"OK, what has you all fired up that you have to charge into my office?" Luck asked, sitting back in his chair. *Oh, this ought to be good*, he was thinking, looking at the expression on Ford's face.

"Sir, I need twenty-one aircraft to get one brigade on the objective... and one cargo ship," Ford announced.

"Ed, I can understand the twenty-one C-130s, but a cargo ship? What the hell for?" Luck asked.

"I can get one brigade in with the twenty-one planes. I can get another brigade in on a cargo ship arriving in the port thirty minutes before the drop," Ford stated.

"OK, run this by me again. The first part I understand, it's the second part that confuses me," Luck said.

"I want to get in a minimum of two brigades. I can get one in by plane. The other I load on a cargo ship here in Jeddah. We sail it north to arrive in the port one hour to thirty minutes before the drop. Once the drop is completed, the guys on the cargo ship disembark and secure the port facilities. We tell no one what the real cargo is aboard the ship, not even the Saudis. Once the gangplank is in place, the soldiers charge off and seal the buildings and port facilities. Hell, sir, the Marines can't do the job. They're all being committed in the east," Ford commented.

"General, you are as nutty as a fruitcake," Luck said as he reached for the phone. "Get me General Yeosock on the line. Yes, I'll hold."

Chapter 55

XVIII Airborne Corps OpPlan

20 January 1991
XVIII Airborne Corps HQ
Jeddah, Saudi Arabia

General Luck had gathered his division commanders to give them an overview of the upcoming operation. The commanders of the 28th and 29th Divisions had arrived in-country, and their divisions were currently in training around Yanbu and Jeddah. Personnel for both divisions were quickly becoming acclimated to the weather, which had dropped to a comfortable eighty-five degrees in the day.

"Morning, everyone," General Luck said as he walked into the briefing room.

"Attention," shouted an NCO that hadn't seen the general walk in.

"Keep your seats," Luck directed as he stepped up to the head of the room. "I wanted to discuss with you the operation we have planned once things kick off. We're not going to be sitting in this defensive posture much longer. I can tell you that the date for D-Day has been set, and the clock is ticking. In the meantime, we continue holding in the defense while the Air Force gains air superiority and our attack helicopters continue locating and chewing up his supply lines. And they have been doing a damn good job at that," he added, acknowledging the 101st and 82nd Attack Battalions as well as the Air Cav troops.

"Thank you, sir," General Peters of the 101st said. "I'll pass that along to my boys."

"Likewise, sir," General Ford said.

"OK, now—CENTCOM's original thought was for us to attack east and go after the IV Corps around Buyaydah. They've reconsidered that move. The IV Corps has eight divisions, with one being mech and one being armored. Us going against that would be almost stupid as it would be putting a much smaller force against a much larger force in prepared positions and it wouldn't take advantage of our mobility. So, CENTCOM went back to the drawing board after I talked to them," Luck said as people exchanged looks.

"Instead we're going to hold the 5th and 7th Republican Guard Divisions right here with our Saudi Task Force and we're going after what's left of the 2nd Iraqi Corps with a follow-on of swinging east and cut off the Iraqi forces supply lines," Luck announced. Right away, he could see the objections coming.

"Sir, that's going to stretch us too much with attempts at resupply. That's the same thing that's gotten the 2nd Iraqi Corps in trouble. Their supplies are so low that they can't do a thing," voiced a logistics staff officer.

"That's very true, Colonel. They've been attempting to resupply all the way from Al Jubail for fuel and from Baghdad for everything else," Luck agreed.

"Yes, sir, and we would be in the same boat attempting to resupply from Jeddah or Yanbu," the colonel stated, very proud of his observation and looking for support.

"Colonel, we aren't going to resupply from Yanbu and Jeddah. We're going to resupply from here," Luck said as he pointed at the port, which was only eighty miles from Tabuk. Everyone leaned forward in their seats to see what he was pointing at.

"This is Objective WET. It's about the only deepwater commercial port in this part of the country, and it will provide for our resupply. Our resupply of essential items will be delivered to this location once we've seized it," Luck pointed out.

"Sir, that's over two hundred and fifty miles from Yanbu," a brigade operations officer stated.

"Yes, it is, Colonel. In fact, it's two hundred and eighty-three miles from Yanbu," Luck confirmed

"Sir, the choppers don't have enough fuel to fly that far, and a ground attack would take four to five days to reach there at best," another brigade operations officer pointed out.

"You are quite right, Colonel, but that's a relatively short distance for an airborne insertion," Luck said, catching everyone's undivided attention.

"Gentlemen, let me give you the overview of the planned operation. At the designated H-hour, one mechanized division will conduct a movement to contact from Yanbu up the coast road to Objective WET. At this time, we anticipate that this would be an unopposed movement, but it would ensure clearing out any reconnaissance forces that may be in the area. This would be a four-day movement if unopposed. Also at H-hour, one division would attack to destroy the 7th Infantry Division and continue to attack towards Mogayra with one brigade of the 101st conducting an air assault insertion to seize the airfield at Mogayra. On order, that division continues the attack to Hegra and be prepared to proceed to Tabuk. On order, 101st will conduct air assault insertions to destroy logistic centers, seize choke points north of Al Buriekah, and conduct passage of lines with the mechanized division. At H plus two, one brigade from the 82nd will conduct an airborne drop to seize and secure this port—Objective WET. Simultaneously, one brigade will arrive by cargo ship in the port and seize the port as part of a deception plan," Luck indicated, which generated several loud murmurs as it had never been done before.

"One brigade of the 82nd will conduct a truck movement to airport vicinity of Al Wajh located here," Luck said as he pointed at the location on the map, "and be prepared to conduct airborne insertion vicinity of Tabuk. Upon linkup of 82nd with ground forces, one brigade of 82nd will be prepared to conduct ground movement to Tabuk, clearing main highway to Tabuk. I cannot stress enough the importance of clearing this highway as this will become the lifeline for the Corps. One brigade will provide security at Objective WET until Corps support assets can assume security mission. This would complete phase one of the operation," Luck concluded. "Alright, sharpshooters, let's have it," he enticed them, knowing that there would be some doubters out there.

"Sir, has an assault off a cargo ship ever been done before? I mean, there's a single-file gangplank normally," one staff officer asked.

"I don't think so, but there was a Trojan Horse a few thousand years ago. This cargo ship will be our Trojan Horse. It'll arrive the evening before the drop and will have some excuse why they have to wait to start unloading. Containers will be on deck and full of troops. The ship will be equipped with its own cranes, as there are no cranes in this port facility. During the night, when there's minimal personnel, and coinciding with the airborne drop, the shipping containers will be lowered over the side at the same time that troops begin down the gangplank. That will put forces on the ground as the drop is commencing. If we can get a cargo ship with three cranes, then three shipping containers will go over the side together. Other questions?" Luck called.

"Sir," General Peters called out.

"Yes, Benny," Luck responded.

"What's the final objective for the 101st at the end of phase one?"

"Good question. There's a military compound in Tabuk, just west of the airport. As it stands right now, I'm going to have the 82nd responsible for seizing the airport and you seizing this military compound. We cannot seize the airport with this compound being left alone. We've got to hit them both at the same time with overwhelming combat power," Luck pointed out.

"Can do, sir."

"Alright, if there are no more questions, I want you all to go back and think through the missions I've outlined. Come see me or the staff if you have concerns or questions. There's no corner on good ideas, so if you have one, let's hear it. I want all the wrinkles straightened out before the orders from 3rd Army come down. Now get out of here."

Chapter 56

Prelude to Air Campaign

1 February 1991
Iraqi Air Force HQ
Baghdad, Iraq

Hamid Raja Shalah al-Tikriti, commander of the Iraqi Air Force, was looking over the latest reports and did not like what he was reading. His deputy and wing commanders, as well as his Soviet advisor, were seated before him.

"Gentlemen, I do not like what I am seeing here in this report. If I am reading this correctly, we are losing Iraqi-flown aircraft at a rate of six-to-one versus the Americans and British. This is unacceptable," he said, looking at the faces of those in front of him. "Would someone care to explain this to me?" No one really wanted to get into this, but they all knew the answer.

"General, I think I can best explain this," General Dimitri Yahontov responded, to the relief of the Iraqi generals present.

"Please, do tell, General," al-Tikriti said.

"Sir, the simple explanation for this is the Americans are better trained. Their pilots have had extensive training at both their Top Gun school for the Navy pilots and at Red Flag in Nevada for their Air Force pilots. In addition, their AWACS planes are providing twenty-four-hour air watch and know as soon as we launch a strike. These planes fly with a heavy fighter cover as well, so trying to go after them is not a simple matter," General Yahontov explained.

"Our pilots fought against the Iranians for what, six, seven years? They should be as trained as the Americans," al-Tikriti pointed out.

"A pilot will only be as good as his adversary trains him. The Iranian pilots were garbage and so our pilots were never really tested like the Americans are at their schools. In those schools, they have extensively studied Soviet air combat tactics and vigorously exercise against them. Your pilots have not had that experience," Yahontov pointed out, being careful not to mention that the Iraqi pilots that had been sent to the Soviet Union for training had not received the same level of training as the Soviet pilots, and now it was showing.

"Tell me, General, how many Soviet pilots have we lost in thus far? We have been playing with the Americans now for seven months. What is your ratio against these vaunted Americans?" al-Tikriti asked. Yahontov could sense the air force commander was coming to a boil.

"Sir, we have lost twelve pilots, giving us a one-to-one kill ratio," Yahontov answered.

"Twelve pilots while maintaining a one-to-one ratio!" the general berated.

He didn't say anything for a moment, his eyes clearly boring into his subordinates. "Listen, putting the training deficiencies aside, we are losing pilots at a rate of six to one. That is unacceptable. Maybe our pilots were not adequately trained when we sent them to your schools. Maybe we should have done a better job preparing them for this conflict. But we have to find a better way of leveraging what we have," al-Tikriti said in a calmer voice. "General, perhaps your pilots could be used in a more aggressive manner. Maybe we engineer some sort of air raid where we marshal more of your pilots together for a large raid instead of having them scattered about the battlespace."

The Soviet general did not like being told how he should employ his limited fighter assets, but even he conceded the point that something needed to be done. He then nodded his head in agreement.

"Listen, all of you. Saddam is not happy with the air campaign. The Americans continue to have an uninterrupted flow of men and supplies coming into Oman. We have got to stop this if we are ever going to have a chance at winning this war. Therefore, for the next week we are going to conduct minimal sorties to rest our pilots and give our ground crews some additional time to prepare the aircraft. I'd also like our Soviet pilots and aircraft consolidated at a few bases closer to the front. In seven days I want ninety percent availability of our fighter and bomber aircraft for one all-out air raid."

The generals all seemed to perk up and smile at this idea—all save the Soviet general.

"In eight days, we are going to launch an air raid and hopefully campaign once we have control of the skies, to cripple the port of Yanbu, Jeddah, Muscat. This must be an all-out effort. This cannot fail, Generals. Do I make myself clear on this?" General al-Tikriti said as he stood up, signaling the end of the meeting and the end of any further debate.

As he left, there was no doubt in anyone's mind what he had meant. After the recent wave of failures, this was the end of the road. Saddam's patience, such as it was, was at an end. Not only were their careers on the line, but their lives were as well.

****

General Ahmad Hussain Khalil, commander of Iraq's rocket forces, was not accustomed to being summoned to General al-Tikriti's office. In his heart he felt that his stature was the same as the commander of the air force, but he also understood that this was not the time to push that.

Arriving a few minutes early, he expected to be waiting, so he was surprised when he was ushered right into al-Tikriti's office.

"General Khalil, so good of you to come over. Please have a seat," al-Tikriti said, extending one hand and pointing at an overstuffed chair with the other.

"Thank you, General," Khalil replied as his guard went up. *This is too friendly.* "To what do I owe the pleasure of this invitation?"

"Right to the point. I like that, so I'll be right to the point as well. In eight days, the air force is going to launch a major assault on the ports of Jeddah, Yanbu and Muscat. We would like the rocket forces to participate in this campaign. Your rockets would add to the confusion to the American Patriot batteries attempting to decide who to engage and may help save some of my pilots as well as further destroying some of the ports with your missiles," al-Tikriti explained.

"Saddam will have to approve this action," Khalil said very matter-of-factly.

"He has been briefed and has agreed that this campaign needs to be undertaken. I told him I wanted your participation, and he agreed if you said you could support such a campaign."

"I will have to move some missiles to be in range of Muscat. I had six in the UAE, but they were destroyed in an air strike. I can move some down to the vicinity of Hof and Riyadh and be within range to support this."

"Excellent. Then please issue the orders. But before you do, what can you tell me about these Patriot missiles I had heard about on the television?"

"Uh, yes, well, my sources tell me the American Patriot system can only track aircraft. They are still struggling with tracking and engaging fast-moving missiles. We believe their PAC-1 missile is what they have deployed right now. From the intelligence reports the KGN have provided about the system, they are attempting to develop a PAC-2 missile that can intercept my Scuds, but it is a year at least from development. At least that is what the KGB has told us. They could, of course, be wrong," Khalil explained, a little taken aback that the head of the air force would actually take the time to ask him about this, but happy he had.

"This is good. Then let us hope the information the Soviets have provided proves to be true. I am glad I can count on the rocket forces supporting us in this campaign."

The two generals stood and headed for the door, but before General Khalil left, he turned, adding, "I will have my executive officer, Colonel al-Jaziri work out the details with your operations people. We will be in place and ready when the launch order is given," Khalil said.

****

2nd Battalion, 43rd Air Defense Artillery Regiment
Muscat, Oman

"Have you ever fired one of these Patriot missiles in anger, ma'am?" the young staff sergeant asked.

Shaking her head, Second Lieutenant Dawn Anders replied, "No, just in training exercises at Fort Bliss and White Sands. We fired at drones and only one missile per class. Have you?"

Anders had graduated from Penn State and received her commission through ROTC. She hadn't volunteered for air-defense artillery as a branch. She was hoping to be a supply officer, something she thought would be more beneficial when she left the Army. Her intention was to stay in to complete her four-year commitment to pay for her college and leave.

Staff Sergeant Harrison shook his head in the negative. "Unfortunately, no, ma'am. When we got here, there weren't any air strikes into Oman, and there still haven't been. I mean, we got hit pretty hard by a bunch of Scuds back in October, before we were operational, but that was about it for aerial threats. Truth be told, it's been pretty damn boring. We sit and test the equipment each day and run through drills, but we still haven't launched a missile to even put those drills into practice."

Staff Sergeant Harrison blew some air past his lips in obvious frustration, adding, "Last week before you arrived, we got a shipment of the new PAC-2 missiles. Right now each launcher has two PAC-1 and two PAC-2 missiles loaded up. The captain said the PAC-1 were still good for knocking down planes and the PAC-2 would be for those Scud missiles should they get a hair up their ass and want to fire 'em at us, but I'm not sold on being able to hit a missile with a missile."

"Hmm, that's a good point you bring up, Staff Sergeant. How many launchers are we playing with besides those in our own battery?" Anders asked. Being new to the unit, she was still learning all this.

"Well, ma'am, we have our four launchers. Then we're tied in with two HAWK batteries that the Oman Army has. Everything is deployed around the city to protect the airport and port here in Muscat. Another two batteries are further out, also providing protection. I guess the port and airport are pretty important, so they largely get all the protection."

"Yeah, the port and airport are the lifeline to this entire effort," was all Anders could say as she studied the batteries' phased-array radar scanning the sky.

"Why are you so concerned, ma'am? Anything that gets in the air, we can see it, which means we can shoot it. Simple, really," Harrison questioned.

"Sergeant, what concerns me, and the CO, is the high mountains surrounding Muscat. They provide some good interference. You saw how hard it was to track the Scuds during that last attack, I'm told. Tracking incoming Scud missiles isn't the problem. The trajectory of the Scud missile to climb to one hundred and sixty thousand feet en route and then drop down on the target gives the tracking radar ample time to acquire, track, and engage the target. What concerns me and the battery commander is the engagement time for low-level aircraft. Those can be tracked by the satellites, but if the attacking aircraft are right down on the deck, we'll have a very limited opportunity to acquire and engage." Lieutenant Anders pointed out.

"But ma'am, there are Vulcan guns around the airport and harbor, aren't there?"

"I believe there are some from the 11th Air Defense Brigade, but I couldn't tell you who they are or where they are. I just hope they're on their toes. Let's get to checking the launchers now and stretch our legs, shall we?" Anders said, moving off to the first launcher's location.
****

XVIII Airborne Corps HQ
Yanbu, Saudi Arabia

"Hey, guys, I got chow here for you in the truck," Sergeant Nelson said to his crew. Sergeant Nelson was the team leader for am M167 Vulcan air-defense gun system (VADS).

"What, another morning of MREs? When are we ever going to get some real food for breakfast?" Private Alexander whined.

"Alexander, quit your bitchin'. This morning I'm serving, eggs, bacon, sausage, pancakes and coffee," Sergeant Nelson declared as he opened the back of the Humvee and pulled out a Marmite can along with a large thermos of coffee.

"Hot damn, Sarge, you the man," Specialist McGee said, jumping up from his sleeping bag and grabbing a paper plate as Sergeant Nelson opened the lid and began spooning out eggs.

Specialist Hammer was climbing out of the weapon system. "Hey, someone grab me a plate. Damn, I can smell it over here."

"Alexander, take a plate over to Hammer, and then you get some for yourself," Nelson directed.

"Ah, come on, why am I always the last one?" Alexander complained.

"You're not. You know I always eat last," Nelson said as he loaded up Hammer's plate.

"Hey, Alexander, when you grow up, you'll see that the leaders always eat last. They make sure there's enough for everyone before they eat. That's what a good leader does—they take care of their people first," McGee said as he loaded his plastic fork with eggs covered in Tabasco sauce.

"Damn if this doesn't taste good. I was really getting tired of eating MREs, Sarge," Hammer said as he crunched down on a piece of bacon. "Hey, Sarge, how much longer do you think we're going to be sitting here in Yanbu watching this airfield?"

"Until the Division commander tells us to move. Ask him when you see him," Nelson directed.

"You know, I'll just do that. I sort of like it here, especially if hot chow is going to be coming regularly," Hammer said, sipping his coffee while sitting in the firing position.

Chapter 57
Flaming Glory

5 February 1991
4th Squadron
United Arab Emirates

Major Nikolai Kamanin was flying his Su-25 so low he felt he could reach down and touch the water. If he flew any higher, though, he'd likely get detected. In the sky high above him was a dogfight the likes of which he'd never seen before. He knew his friend Popkov was likely up there leading his squadron against the Americans.

There you are.

He found his target, the Sultan Qaboos Port. His flight of four Su-25s had slipped past the mountains to the east over the coastal town of Bandar Jissah and flown out to sea. They'd stayed low and hugged the coast so they wouldn't overfly any American warships. They were close and easily in range of their own air-defense weapons.

It hadn't taken Kamanin long to reach the port, placing them in a perfect position to attack it from the sea—an angle of attack the Americans hadn't considered.

As his aircraft grew closer to the port, he went through the arming process as he prepared to unleash his attack. He turned the targeting warhead on for two of his Kh-29 air-to-surface missiles and prepared to fire them. He was targeting the large cranes used to unload the massive cargo ships. Two of his four aircraft would specifically target some of the ships in port, hopefully sinking them next to the piers. The last two aircraft were armed with four B-13L rocket canisters. Each one carried five 122mm unguided rockets. Their job was to strafe the warehouses and depots in and around the port. These locations were stacked high with supplies and munitions, things that would hopefully all go up in smoke.

Once his flight of four had made their initial attack run, they'd circle back and look to unload the rest of their ordnance before heading home. What Major Kamanin hoped for most was that the rest of his squadron attacking the international airport would be able to knock the place out of commission or at least destroy a lot of fighters on the ground. They were the ones with the truly hard mission.

The targeting display told him each missile was locked on and ready. He had designated the base of the cranes for the 320-kilogram or 705-pound warheads. Kamanin wanted to destroy not just the massive shipping cranes but also the base of the pier the large structures were anchored into. When he flew around for his second pass, he planned on plastering the rest of the port with his unguided rockets.

Then his RWR started blaring a warning alarm, letting him know he was being targeted by some sort of radar system.

Depressing the firing button, Kamanin sent his two missiles off, on their way to help take down the port. So did his three other pilots. Moments after they fired their missiles, the surrounding sky filled with tracer fire from some nearby ships and ground base guns near the port.

Kamanin took evasive maneuvers as he saw strings of red tracers crisscross the sky where he'd just been moments ago. Then he saw a brilliant flash. One of his comrades' aircraft had been hit by a missile that had come out of nowhere. It had swooped down from the sky above and slammed into the plane, meaning he and his flightmates had serious problems. One or more fighters, likely a navy fighter, had just gotten the drop of them.

Banking his Su-25 hard to the side, he accelerated quickly while at the same time gaining altitude as he tried to figure out who had just bounced them.

Then he saw it, the contrail of another missile, fired from a dozen or so kilometers away and heading straight for one of his friends. Angling his aircraft in that direction, Kamanin flipped his targeting system from ground to air mode. His R-73 Archer air-to-air missile got an almost immediate lock on the enemy aircraft as it looked to be turning away from them and climbing for altitude. When his missile had a solid lock on the American fighter, he fired.

With his missile on its way to the target, Kamanin turned hard back to the port. He wanted to finish unloading the remainder of his ordnance on the port and would then look to get out of here. Repositioning for another attack run, Kamanin was having a hard time trying to even find a target. The port was covered in thick black smoke everywhere. The two ships his comrades had gone after were ablaze. He wasn't sure if they were sinking, but they were certainly on fire. The warehouses and depots also looked to be ablaze.

Not seeing an immediate target, he gave his aircraft more power and zipped right over top of the port. He continued on past the port. As he did, he spotted a large oil refinery. He RWR then came on again, letting him know he was being locked onto by another radar. This one looked to be a ground unit, likely one of the Patriot systems.

Knowing his plane might get shot down or worse, blown up, he gave his engines all the power he could, going to full throttle to try and get in range of the refinery. He had ten 122mm rockets left, and he planned on using them to try and take that refinery out. If he could, maybe it'd help hurt the coalition war effort.

Warning, warning, warning. The automated system started screaming in his ear, telling him a missile had been fired at him. Craning his neck around to look for the missile, he finally saw it. The damn thing was close. The launcher must have been nearby. The missile had leveled out and was flying right for him.

Kamanin looked at his range to the refinery and knew it'd be tight. He popped some flares, hoping that might buy him some time, and then dove for the deck. He weaved around one canyon, dispensing additional flares as he steered into another canyon. Then he rose back up to two thousand feet and saw he was approaching the refinery. He aimed the plane, making sure his rockets were positioned to land all along a row of storage tanks and a large building. Depressing the trigger, he started sending rockets at a rate of one for every half a second.

Come on, just a few more rockets, just a few more seconds and then I'm ejecting, he thought. He knew the enemy missile, if it was still chasing him, was likely practically on top of him.

Then that sixth sense pilots seemed to have told him he needed to eject. He still had four rockets left, but he trusted his gut and pulled the levers. In a blink of an eye, his canopy was shot off his plane and he was thrown several hundred feet into the air and away from his plane.

His chute hadn't even opened when he saw the Patriot's large missile and warhead slam into his plane. His baby, the aircraft that had seen so many battles with him, that had kept him alive through so many combat missions, was now nothing more than millions of pieces of flaming debris as it was being dispersed across the ground below. When his parachute deployed and his body started to dangle, he took a moment to survey everything around him. What he saw shocked him.

495

The refinery had taken some good hits from his rockets, so he felt good about that. Especially after he saw one of the storage tanks explode. Then a second and third one blew up as well. But that wasn't what shocked him. Everywhere he looked, he caught sight of military encampments. He'd had no idea there were this many enemy soldiers across the border just waiting to be unleashed on his Iraqi partners. In that moment, he knew that no matter what he and his comrades did moving forward, the Iraqis were going to be defeated. It was just a matter of time.

Seeing that he was getting closer to the ground, he started looking for a decent place to land. Unfortunately, the winds had blown him closer to one of the large encampments, and there appeared to be a small group of soldiers running out to greet him.

Damn, who am I kidding? I'm a Caucasian Russian in the Middle East. Like I can hide among the population.

As he got closer to the ground, dozens of what he assumed were American soldiers were standing nearby, waiting for him. When he landed, he saw a number of soldiers with their rifles pointed at him. He moved slowly and took his helmet off. The look on the soldiers' faces when they saw a Caucasian pilot and not an Arab one cause a moment of confusion. They asked him in English what unit he was from. Kamanin knew some English from his time working as a military attaché at their consulate in Los Angeles. There was one specific phrase that he had practiced over and over again when he was alone. He'd always hoped that one day he would be able to use it.

"I am Major Nikolai Kamanin of the Soviet Air Force, and I would like to defect," he replied and then raised his hands in surrender.
****

"*We got incoming!*" Lieutenant Anders practically screamed as the AN/MSQ-104 engagement control console lit up, indicating incoming Scud missiles. Sirens began wailing all over Muscat as early air-defense warning systems began picking up inbound Scuds heading not only to Muscat but also to Yanbu and Jeddah, as well as Salalah.

Sure enough, the mountainous terrain around Muscat was limiting the sight of the AN/MPQ-53 radar from seeing the missile's launch in its early stage. The National Early Warning Satellite Radar System, a grouping of satellites built specifically to detect ballistic missile launches, had detected the launches immediately. That alert had been sent by NORAD, who had then notified the 11th Air Defense Command and then the batteries responsible for engaging the missiles.

Within seconds, the batteries were ready to track and commence engagements. As each Scud came within the sixty-five-mile range of the Patriot batteries, the system automatically launched missiles at the Scuds. In the first three seconds of launch, the PAC-2 missiles had reached their attack speed of Mach 5, closing the distance between each other rapidly. With Scud missiles still approaching, Lieutenant Anders heard a Vulcan cannon open fire. Suddenly the AN/MSQ-104 console showed multiple air targets approaching fast from multiple different attack vectors.

"Damn, we have aircraft inbound," Anders declared, looking over the shoulders of the two young soldiers sitting at the consoles. Both were hunched over, intensely studying the screens and allowing the system to automatically select the most dangerous targets to engage first.

Boom!

The concussion from the blast picked Anders up and tossed her against the wall of the engagement control center van as it knocked the two other soldiers out of the chairs.

"Ma'am, are you all right?" asked one of the soldiers as he staggered to his feet and reached over to help her get up.

"I think so," Anders said, trying to steady herself. "How are you two?"

Anders was seeing double at this point and attempting to refocus her eyes.

"I think we're good," one of the soldiers answered.

Then another bomb landed nearby, peppering their vehicle with shrapnel as it tossed them to the floor again.

"They're trying to take us out with their aircraft," one of the operators said, hoping that no other bombs would hit any closer than that last one.

A Vulcan opened fire again, making a loud ripping sound as the multibarreled gun opened up on something close.

Anders looked at the command console and saw that it was still functioning in automatic mode. They heard another pair of missiles fire from one of the battery pods still operational.

Distant explosions could be heard, but it was hard to tell if they were Scuds hitting or enemy aircraft dropping bombs or missiles hitting something. Whatever it was, sheer terror was happening around them and the best they could hope for was that some of their missiles might knock a few of these Scuds or enemy aircraft down.

****

VADS Vehicle
Jeddah Airport

Saudi Arabia

The soldiers manning the Vulcan truck had one of the most important, yet most boring jobs you could have. They spent their days or nights hanging out in the track, in the sweltering heat, with essentially nothing to do. Unless the base alarms went off, letting them know an inbound attack was heading their way, or they received a call to activate their search radars, they pretty much sat around not doing a lot. That was, until tonight.

Sergeant Nelson was sitting in the rear of the truck reading a book when he heard a Patriot missile launch nearby and the air raid siren blare across the airfield moments later.

His buddy Hammer was in the gunner's seat and went right into action. He activated their search radar and started looking for potential targets headed their way.

Alexander was climbing in the rear hatch of the M167 track, which was a modified M113, when Hammer let loose a burst from their six-barreled 20mm cannon. The roar of the gun was distinctive and loud. It sounded like it was tearing fabric, but in reality, it was a loud tearing noise from the cannon rounds ripping through the sound barrier.

Hammer had spotted the low-flying planes coming straight at the airfield. They'd swooped in around the mountain range near Jeddah, the one blind spot their air-defense systems had to contend with.

McGee had been asleep when the shooting started, but as soon as it did, the kid had jumped to his station, grabbing extra ammo and getting it ready to feed into the gun once it started to run low. If Hammer got careless or too carried away, he could burn through their 2,100-round belt in seconds.

"Hot damn! We got one, Sarge!" Hammer cried out excitedly as he watched the left wing on the Su-25 Frogfoot separate from the aircraft. It went into a violent series of rolls until it hit the ground, exploding in a massive fireball.

"Hammer, two o'clock low, another Frogfoot," Nelson called out urgently.

"Got it, two thousand meters," Hammer replied, glancing at his range radar.

"Engage," Nelson ordered.

The six barrels spun up and fired off nearly two thousand rounds at the fighter angling in for an attack. The plane managed to fire two missiles, both taking aim at the ground radar systems around the airfield. Seconds after the missiles left the plane, Hammer's barrage of rounds connected with the Frogfoot, ripping the front of the aircraft apart. It tumbled and splattered itself across the ground.

"Splash two!" Hammer yelled as Alexander began reloading the ammo boxes.

The Vulcans around the airfield were also engaging the incoming aircraft. There were more coming from the north along the coast and out of the mountains. Then one of the Vulcan trucks blew up, an antiradiation missile having slammed into it.

"Oh shit, they just blew up Ducey's track!" Hammer declared in shock and disbelief.

Now the Patriot missiles and HAWK missiles started scoring some hits of their own. The air defense missiles had been engaging some of the aircraft well above and outside the range of the Vulcans.

"I think they're trying to knock out our airfield and the port area. There's a lot of fire over to the west in the vicinity of the port," McGee said, taking a quick glance in that direction.

"Stay focused on what's in front of us. Concentrate on our piece and protect this airfield." Suddenly Sergeant Nelson's tone changed as he looked right at Hammer. "I'm tracking two bandits, eleven o'clock low and coming in fast right for us!" he practically screamed as he watched the two aircraft in his binoculars get larger and larger.

"Got them, one thousand meters."

"Engage," Nelson yelled, hoping like hell they didn't fire an antiradiation missile at them. They had their search radar going.

The six-barrel rotary gun opened up, spitting a stream of red tracers out. The stream briefly touched the front of the first aircraft and tracked down its body until it exploded right in front of the second aircraft.

By now, the other Vulcan tracks were engaging the second aircraft. The Frogfoot had managed to overfly the parking ramp of the airport and proceeded to release a stick of bombs that started exploding and ripping through the parked helicopters, causing numerous secondary explosions.

As the Su-25 tried to accelerate up and away, it was ripped apart by two streams of red tracers.

Moments later, the guns around the airfield fell silent. No more missiles were firing and no more roaring engines of aircraft. As quickly as the air attack had started, it was over. Burning wreckage littered the parking ramp. Dozens of helicopters were on fire, and a couple of hangar buildings also looked to have taken some damage. Two radar trucks had been taken out, and it looked like one of the Vulcan tracks was also a burning wreck. The enemy had succeeded in part, wrecking the airfield temporarily, but it had come at a high cost.

Chapter 58
Press Corps

6 February 1991
XVIII Airborne Corps HQ
Jeddah, Saudi Arabia

Colonel Beckworth had been the public affairs officer for the 29th Division for almost a year when the division received its deployment order. In the civilian world, his job was news anchorman for one of Baltimore's largest television stations, WMAR Channel 2, ABC.

He knew someday he would move up into the CEO position and then to the national level. As a key player in the Baltimore television scene, he had the connections he had developed over the years. While covering the Spiro Agnew story in the early 1970s, he'd met the governor, who had encouraged him to join the Maryland National Guard and work in the Public Affairs Office. Promotions and rank had come quickly, and some suspected that Beckworth might be holding all the cards when it came to dealings with the governor.

"General Steinhauer, sir, Ms. Laura Ambrose from CBS's *60 Minutes* would like to sit with you tomorrow for an hour. She has questions about our deployment and readiness," Beckworth said, standing in front of Steinhauer's desk.

"I don't have time to waste talking to some woman that is going to write and edit whatever she wants to hear. No, dump her off on some other stiff," Steinhauer decreed.

"But, sir, she insists on talking to you," Beckworth almost pleaded. Getting this interview for Ambrose would be a huge feather in his cap from moving up in the hierarchy of television. "The governor really wants our story told." He didn't lie, but he did stretch the story a bit.

Tired of being badgered over this issue, the general relented against his better judgment. "Alright, if it's so damn important to the governor, I'll give her fifteen minutes."

"Sir, we're going to need at least thirty minutes. It takes time to set up the cameras, the lights, makeup," Beckworth attempted to explain.

"What is this, a damn Hollywood production?" Steinhauer fumed.

"Sir, please," Beckworth said, hoping he wouldn't have to beg to make this happen.

"Alright, but I'm not doing makeup. I'll find something important to do before so they can use my office to set up. But thirty minutes is it. Understood?"

"Yes, sir, and thank you," Beckworth said, knowing this conversation was over. He'd gotten what he wanted. *You asked for thirty minutes, but we're going to take an hour, General. You just can't get up and walk out in the middle of an interview*, Beckworth thought privately.

****

Following Day

The petite, shapely woman with auburn hair held out her hand as she approached General Steinhauer. She was in a formfitting tan outfit, trying to imitate the combat fatigues the soldiers around her wore. It might have looked nice stateside, but it looked out of place amongst the troops. It was likely custom-made for her by a tailor in the New York fashion district for interviews just like this. Naturally, she left the top

503

three buttons open to give her bosom some air in the extreme heat of Saudi Arabia.

"Sir, may I introduce Ms. Laura Ambrose from *60 Minutes*. Ms. Ambrose, this is Major General Joshua Steinhauer, commander of the 29th Infantry Division," Beckworth introduced them.

"How do you do, General? Thank you for giving your time to do this interview. I understand we have an hour, which will result in a twenty-minute presentation after the editors get done editing it down to the final product, but I assure you this is going to be a glowing piece about the 29th Infantry Division and the National Guard soldiers that it comprises."

One hour? When did this thirty-minute sit-down turn into an hour? Steinhauer fumed internally while maintaining his poker face.

"If you're ready, General," she said as she took charge of the meeting.

General Steinhauer smiled. "Of course, Ms. Ambrose," he said and then shot a dirty look at Beckworth for having ambushed him like this.

Beckworth just shrugged, playing it off like this wasn't his fault.

"General, if you'll sit there, I'll take this chair and we can begin as soon as we have you wired up," Ambrose explained as a technician approached the general with a small microphone that he clipped to the general's fatigue shirt.

"Before we get started, Ms. Ambrose, and in keeping with the local culture, please button your blouse to the top. We're guests in a foreign country and we're doing our best to honor their local customs as best we can," General Steinhauer requested.

"Oh my. Certainly, yes. I wouldn't want to offend the Saudi King. I'm interviewing him for this piece later in the week," she replied as she buttoned her blouse up.

"I'm sorry about that, Ms. Ambrose. Colonel Beckworth should have helped you out by informing you of the local customs. You had no way of knowing," he said as he stared daggers at his public affairs rep. He was really growing to dislike the prima donna media whore of a colonel.

"Thank you, General. Am I appropriate now? Can we get started?"

"Absolutely. Your show, ma'am," Steinhauer said with a smile.

Steinhauer one, Ambrose nothing.

"I'm here with General Josh Steinhauer, commander of the 29th National Guard Division. The Division is made up of units within the Maryland National Guard—"

"Excuse me for interrupting you, but I have to correct something. My unit is the 29th Infantry Division and is comprised of units from Maryland, Virginia, Kentucky, North and South Carolina, as well as West Virginia. Please continue," Steinhauer said with a smile.

Steinhauer two, Ambrose none.

"Sorry about that. Let's continue, shall we?" Ambrose said. "I am here with General Josh Steinhauer, commander of the 29th Infantry Division, made up of units from Maryland, Virginia, Kentucky, North and South Carolina and West Virginia. The 29th Division has a long history in the defense of our nation from the First World War to right now, here in the Middle East. In the Second World War, the 29th Infantry Division was the division that was in the first wave on the beaches of Normandy. The—"

"As much as we would like to take credit for being the first on the Normandy beaches, I'm afraid we cannot take sole credit. The 116th Infantry Regiment, part of the 29th Infantry Division, was in that first wave and they were under the command of the 1st Infantry Division. The rest of the division didn't come ashore until much later in the operation. I like to give credit where credit is due. Colonel Beckworth should have provided that to you on background," Steinhauer clarified, again with a smile.

Steinhauer three, Ambrose zero.

Visibly flustered, Ambrose checked her notes and regained her composure. "Oh yes, of course, General. Let's talk about the current operation here in Saudi Arabia. Has all of the 29th Infantry Division been deployed now?" Ambrose asked, feeling that was a safe question.

"That is a great question, Ms. Ambrose. For security purposes, especially since we know the Iraqis are trying to gather intelligence via our own news media, who is really just trying to reassure a nation, as much as I'd like to disclose that, I'm afraid I cannot answer the question directly. But our division is ready to execute the President's orders," General Steinhauer replied with a reassuring smile.

Steinhauer four, Ambrose zero.

Steinhauer glanced at Beckworth. The look on his face said he was dying a slow and painful death.

"Well, General, we wouldn't want to endanger your men. Perhaps we can talk about the host nation support that you have received?" Ambrose asked, leaning forward in her chair slightly.

"Sure, we can talk about that. The Saudi people have been outstanding in supporting us. We haven't had much interaction with the local people due to operational security, but what we have had has been excellent."

Ambrose smiled at finally getting at least one of her questions answered. "And would you say that the soldiers of the 29th Infantry Division have had an opportunity to experience the culture of the country?"

"Absolutely not. The towns are off-limits to almost everyone. Our soldiers' lifestyle does not fit with the Arab and Muslim cultures, and so it's best that our soldiers aren't intermingling with the locals," General Steinhauer explained.

"That's an interesting assessment. So, General, you don't feel that the Arab or Muslim culture is appropriate for our soldiers?" Ambrose asked.

"Quite the contrary, Ms. Ambrose. If a soldier wishes to embrace the Muslim religion, he has as much right to do so as a Catholic or Protestant. But as you know or should be aware of, in this nation, they don't allow the commingling of religions and don't allow the Christian or Jewish faiths. It's not a case of command policy not allowing intermingling with the locals but a Saudi policy that deters that, and General Schwarzkopf was correct when he said that we didn't want to win the battles against the Iraqis only to lose the war because we upset our hosts. We must honor the local customs and traditions. Surely you can understand that, can't you? A perfect example of this was when you first walked into my office. Not knowing the local customs, you had the first three buttons on your blouse open. Back home, that wouldn't have been a problem. But that kind of apparel choice is not appropriate here. Again, I want to apologize on behalf of my public affairs group for not having informed you of that earlier. That's my fault for my people having failed you," General Steinhauer explained and then accepted responsibility for a mess-up that had likely embarrassed her.

Steinhauer scores number five, game, match, set. Ambrose none.

"As much as I appreciate your taking the time to speak with me, I really must be going. I have to carry out an important inspection of my soldiers prior to a potential combat order. Now if you will excuse me," Steinhauer said as he began to remove the microphone. "I made it clear to Colonel Beckworth that you had thirty minutes, and I believe that time is about up. You have a good day, and Colonel Beckworth will assist you in anything else you want to see around the division."

He then stood and handed the microphone to one of the technicians before heading for the door.

"But, General, I'm not done," Ambrose protested.

"I understand that, ma'am, I really do. But I command this division, and I have to see to the welfare of my men and their preparations before battle. Good day."

As he left the room, Ambrose gathered her stuff and turned towards Beckworth. From the look she gave him, he knew any hope he had of moving to the big leagues was not going through her.

Chapter 59
Return to the Fold

8 February 1991
Tm D/3-4 Armor
Medina Ridge

Sitting in the lawn chair that his driver had somehow "liberated," Lieutenant Bagel, was fairly comfortable, reading a copy of *Chickenhawk* and enjoying the shade offered by the large canvas tent that they had made into a sunshade. Captain Poggi, Delta/3/4 Armor company commander, had been gone for two days back to Jeddah. Things had been fairly quiet over the past couple of months since the battle back in August when they'd first arrived.

"Hey, Jason," Lieutenant Kincade called out as he approached Bagel. "Did the old man say when he'd be back? I'll bet he has a comfortable room back there in Jeddah and hot chow with flush toilets and hot showers," Kincade said as he placed his beat-up lawn chair next to Bagel's. "Want a Coke? It's warm," Kincade offered as he sat down and handed the can to Bagel.

"Yeah, thanks. What have you planned for today?" Bagel asked, popping the top of the Coke can. It wasn't a real Coke but something made in Saudi or the Middle East that sort of looked like Coke and sort of tasted like Coke but wasn't a real Coke.

"Today is general maintenance on the weapons systems. Damn dust gets into everything over here. Seems we can't keep anything clean unless we do it daily—hell, hourly on some days. This worthless sand gets into everything. Did you know that Saudi imports sand to make concrete? That's how worthless this sand is. Imagine all this sand

and it's worthless," Kincade said, picking up a handful and letting it flow through his fingers.

"Yeah, but what's under it isn't worthless. That's why we are here, I'm sure. Hell, if Saddam would have guaranteed the flow and price of oil and we were sure he meant it, I doubt if we would have come running to help Kuwait and the Saudis. We just can't let one guy control over half the oil in the world," Bagel said, taking a sip of his warm Coke.

"Hey, Lieutenant Bagel," Staff Sergeant Hernandez called out from the top of the M-1 Abrams tank.

"Yes, Sergeant," Bagel replied, half turning in his chair to face the noncommissioned officer.

"Sir, you're wanted on the horn. Captain Poggi is calling you," Hernandez called out. Bagel immediately stood and began walking towards the tank. *Wonder what he wants now?* Bagel was thinking as he climbed up on the tank and reached into the turret to retrieve his helmet and mike.

"Panther Six, Panther One-Six, over," Bagel replied, using the new call sign that the powers that be had assigned. The call signs changed each month.

"Panther One-Six, Panther Six. You are to load up and proceed to my location. Need you to be here by 1400 the day after tomorrow. Call me when you depart your current location. Understood? Over."

"Panther Six, Panther One-Six, roger, understood to load up and proceed to your location immediately. What is your location? Over."

"Panther One-Six, the lead vehicle will take you to the rendezvous point and I will meet you there. HETs should be arriving at your location by 1800 this evening. Panther Six out."

Wonder what this is all about, Bagel was thinking as he removed his helmet and called to Kincade. Staff Sergeant Hernandez was looking up from inside the turret with a shaving brush, doing some light housekeeping. Kincade came over, and Bagel motioned for Hernandez to come topside.

"OK, the old man just called and said we're to move out and proceed to his location. Let's get everything packed up. He's sending the HETs and they'll be here by 1800 tonight. It'll be a night move and we'll ride in our vehicles. No one is to be riding on top. Understood? Make sure all the vehicles are topped off and weapons loaded up, full load. Order of march will be two tanks up front, three Bradleys in the middle, two tanks rear, followed by you"—he pointed at Kincade— "bringing up the rear. I'll be in the second tank. Any questions? And, no, I have no idea why he wants us back there. I'll get with the first sergeant so he can get the headquarters elements loaded up. Kincade, I want them positioned between you and the last tank, OK? So let's get things ready," Bagel concluded. All instructions were a matter of following the standard operating procedures that they had been executing for the entire time they had been in-country and the procedures that they had developed over the years at the National Training Center in California.

****

Where the hell are the HETs? Lieutenant Bagel was wondering. Everything was ready to load on the massive trucks that would transport the tanks, Bradleys and M-113s back to Jeddah. Loading up on the HETs meant that paved roads could be used without tearing them up, which would happen if the armor vehicles were driving on the paved highways. The other advantage of using the HETs was that the trip would be much faster, with less wear and tear on the fighting vehicles. It was now 1900 hours and still no sign of the HETs. Bagel was getting a bit worried.

"First Sergeant, how about you take a Humvee and see if you can find these guys along the road towards Jeddah? Drive out about an hour, and if you find them, bring them in. If you don't, just come on back and I'll call back to Jeddah to see what's what," Bagel asked the first sergeant without making it an order.

"You got it, sir. Beats sitting here waiting. If I have comms with you, I'll call as soon as I find them. Just save me some coffee for when I get back," the first sergeant asked, also without making it an order.

"You got it, Top," Bagel replied as he had great respect for this noncommissioned officer.

As the first sergeant climbed into his vehicle, headlights lit up his vehicle. The HETs had finally arrived. "You have that coffee for me, sir?" the first sergeant asked, getting back out of his vehicle.

"Damn, that was a quick trip, First Sergeant. I should have asked you to do that an hour ago," Bagel joked.

The first sergeant was already talking to the head of the HET convoy, a young sergeant who could speak some Arabic and give directions to the drivers. He was positioned in the lead vehicle, all of which were owned by a private Saudi company being paid by the King. As the HETs lined up, each lowered the ramps on the rear. Bagel, with a green chemical stick in his hand, raised his arm and in a circular motion gave the universal sign for "crank your vehicles." Once all the vehicles were cranked, Bagel switched to two red chemical sticks and individually signaled each vehicle forward to an HET and assisted in guiding the driver onto the ramps and loading. Once all vehicles were uploaded, Bagel climbed up on his already loaded vehicle and gave a

512

thumbs-up to the young sergeant to move out. Only thing left now was for everyone to get comfortable in their vehicles and leave the driving to the HETs. It would be a six-hour drive, at least.

****

Arriving at the outskirts of Jeddah, the convoy began to slow and pull off to the side of the road as the sun crested the eastern horizon. As soon as it did, the temperatures in the vehicles quickly rose, waking up most that were asleep although some were getting used to sleeping in the warm temperatures. Most of the troops could sleep about anywhere under about any conditions.

As Jason raised up in the turret, he could hear his company commander's voice. "Bagel, where the hell are you?"

"Hey, sir, right here," Bagel responded as he cleared the turret hatch and was on the back deck of the Abrams tank. "What's up, sir?" he asked.

"We're going to join up with the rest of our battalion. These HETs will follow me to the port, where an LST is waiting to take us aboard and move us to join the battalion in Oman. It's about a fifteen-hundred-mile trip and should take us about three days to get there. The quicker we load up, the better. When we get in the port, we come off the HETs and drive right on to the ship," the company commander explained.

"Sir, I thought the Navy had done away with all the LSTs in favor of the new LCACs that they were replacing the LSTs with," Bagel asked, a bit perplexed.

"Yeah, they are, but they have some Newport LSTs that they've been using as fuel carriers. What we're getting, I understand, is not a Newport but a Boxer-class LST. The Boxer class were built in World War II. The thing we're getting is a relic that was a floating museum

513

and has been recommissioned and sent over. She just happened to be empty and is coming through the Suez Canal, so the powers that be decided to put us on board. So for three days, you get to enjoy a cruise on the USS *Memorial*, LST-325... now follow me," the captain ordered as he walked back to his vehicle.

The USS *Memorial*, LST-325, could easily handle the eight fighting vehicles of the team and the M-113s as well. Since she was capable of holding over four hundred soldiers, the team pretty much had the run of the ship since they were the only ones on board except the crew, who all appeared to be the age of the soldiers' grandfathers. Loading went fast as the crew quickly guided them aboard and had them secured to the belly of the ship to prevent any rolling in heavy seas. The hot chow, air-conditioned sleeping quarters and flush toilets as well as hot and cold running water made some wonder why they hadn't joined the Navy instead of the Army, but they kept those treasonous thoughts to themselves and certainly didn't express them to the first sergeant.

Chapter 60
Move to the Front

15 February 1991
Tm D/3-4 Armor
Vicinity Salalah

Offloading the World War II LST was a piece of cake as it pulled up to a beach and dropped its ramp. Standing on the beach were a couple of goat herders, simply amazed that a ship could crawl out of the water and put its nose on the beach. Disgorging the four tanks, four Bradleys and their M113 armored vehicles made it even more amazing. This stretch of white-sand beach was twenty-one miles east of Salalah with a dirt road that led from the beach to the four-lane highway into Salalah.

"Bagel, when you get to the main road, a convoy of HETs should be waiting for us. If not, then we'll wait there until some show up. You lead and I'll bring up the rear," Captain Poggi directed.

"Roger, sir. As soon as I get an up from everyone we'll move out," Bagel replied, appreciating the fact that he wasn't going to be eating anyone else's dust. When the last vehicle rolled off the ship, the entire ship's crew was standing on the bow, waving to the soldiers. The crew was swelling with pride that they had contributed to the war effort. They would now proceed to Masirah Island to pick up some wheeled vehicles for the 1st Marine Division.

"Panther Six-One, Panther Six, move out," came the order from Captain Poggi.

"Panther Six-One, on the go," Bagel responded and told his driver to follow the dirt road. The road was well marked and only a short ride to the main highway, where twelve HETs waited to load the track vehicles. An NCO in a Humvee was with the HETs. Bagel recognized him right away.

Staff Sergeant Reynolds from the service platoon had brought the HETs to the linkup point and would lead them all back to the battalion's location.

"We got far to go Staff Sergeant?" Bagel asked.

"Sir, you have about four hundred miles to go on the back of this thing," Reynolds replied, pointing at the HET.

"Damn. Wasn't there another port closer than this?" Bagel asked, a bit surprised.

"Yes, sir, but this has been designated the port for VII Corps assets and that means you. We're part of VII Corps now. I know it doesn't make sense to bring you in here when Muscat is a lot closer, but I just run convoys so I got no say how we run this here man's Army. Now if I was in charge—"

"I got the picture, Sergeant. Let's just get the vehicles loaded," Bagel said, calculating that they had about a ten-hour ride to get to the battalion area. *At least with the hatches open, it'll be relatively cool and we can catch up on some sleep, something we haven't done in the last three days*, Bagel was thinking.

****

The ten-hour trip was uneventful, which was not a bad thing for soldiers traveling on the back of HETs. For those ten hours, the highway was almost bumper-to-bumper military vehicles heading in both directions. Those traveling in the same direction as the HETs were loaded with supplies from the port or buses with soldiers arriving at the airport. Those heading in the opposite direction were generally empty and returning to the port or airport. Bagel figured they were close to their destination when the HETs rolled into Fahud and he saw all the Corps support elements.

As the vehicles came to a stop, a Humvee approached and Captain Poggi dismounted from his track and went to talk to the individual in the passenger seat. After a ten-minute discussion, Poggi came back to Bagel's tank, which had been unloaded from the HET along with all the other vehicles.

"OK, we're in the corps and division rear. That's the battalion S-3 Air and he's going to lead us up to where the battalion is located. It's about seventy miles from here but all dirt roads, so be prepared to eat dust. Since the sun is about to set, be sure your night vision goggles on the drivers are good to go. We drive with blackout lights from here on. Any questions?" Poggi asked.

"Sir, can you show me on the map where we're going in case we get separated?" Bagel asked as he pulled out his map and spread it out on the front of the tank. Poggi stepped up and studied the map for a moment to orient himself on it.

"We're here in Fahud and will be going up this route to here." Poggi indicated with his finger. Bagel made a mark on the map for his destination. Lieutenant Kincade had joined the discussion and was also plotting locations on his map. The maps of the AO had been issued to them when they'd offloaded the ship so they had time to study them and become oriented on the maps.

"Lieutenant Kincade, you will return to your company when we get to the battalion area. I'm going to ask the old man to leave your platoon with me for the duration," Poggi said as he had come to have a good rapport with Kincade after being together for the past six or seven months.

517

"OK, when the last vehicle is offloaded, I'll take the lead and you follow. First Sergeant will take the last position in case we have a breakdown. First thing we're going to do when we get to battalion is have maintenance give these vehicles a good going-over. If you can have a list of everything that needs to be fixed or addressed on the maintenance list. I want—"

"Excuse me, sir," the first sergeant yelled, "we're ready to roll."

"OK, First Sergeant, let's load up," Poggi yelled back. "Load up, gentlemen," he said in a quieter voice, addressing Bagel and Kincade. Already the sound of heavy diesel engines could be heard as the soldiers were anxious to get moving. They didn't need a second invitation to start their engines. Poggi walked back to his tank and climbed up and into the turret, taking the tank commander or TC position.

Rolling past Bagel's tank, Poggi took the lead and everyone else fell in behind for the seventy-mile trip. Seventy miles of eating dust.

Chapter 61
Final Brief

1 March 1991
CENTCOM Forward HQ
Military Technological College
Muscat, Oman

Everyone was assembled in the large auditorium that CENTCOM had secured for this brief. Military police guards were posted at each door, inside and out. Several Omani police cars surrounded the outer perimeter of the compound, along with some armored cars with heavy weapons mounted. Anyone that wasn't supposed to be here wouldn't dare attempt to enter. Inside, all the division commanders, separate regimental commanders, and separate brigade commanders as well as all ships' captains were assembled. The Air Force was well represented as well with each of the wing commanders present. When General Schwarzkopf walked into the room, everyone immediately came to attention.

"Keep your seats, gentlemen," Schwarzkopf ordered. He waited for everyone to settle down before he spoke again.

"Enough of this sitting on our asses. It's time to start kicking butts," he started off with. Low murmurs could be heard, and he waited for them to quiet down. "I'm going to give you an overview of the upcoming operation. As with every battle plan ever written, this plan will last for as long as the Iraqi Army lets it play out and then the winging it will commence. I'm confident that we have a good plan and will get the job done. First things first," he indicated and picked up a long pointer. Two soldiers removed the canvas cover from a large map on the stage. The map was well lit, so it was easy for everyone to see as it was almost fifteen feet tall and covered all the Arabian Peninsula.

"First overlay, please," the general requested, and an acetate sheet dropped from the top. It was covered in red with the known positions of the Iraqi forces in the UAE, Saudi Arabia and Kuwait.

"This is the Iraqi forces facing us as they're currently deployed. In the UAE, we have the 9th Iraqi Corps with the 10th, 17th, and 52nd Armoured Divisions and the 1st, 45th and 49th Infantry Divisions," he stated, pointing out the location of each. "Over here on the west, XVIII Airborne Corps has done a good job of stopping the 2nd Republican Guard Corps with the 5th Mechanized Division and the 7th Motorized Division. The 7th is bogged down in Medina and the Saudi National Guard forces there are wreaking havoc with them. The 5th is at less than fifty percent strength and our Air Force has cut off most of their resupply. They're dying on the vine. The XVIII also took on the 2nd Iraqi Corps with the 2nd, 7th, 37th, and 51st Iraqi Infantry Divisions, as well as the 14th Mechanized Division. With the help of the naval air assets in the Red Sea, they caught the 14th in the mountains and ate their lunch. They're sitting at twenty percent effective now. The 2nd Iraqi Infantry Division is sitting at Tabuk and never came south. The 7th walked into a buzzsaw, as did the 51st, and they're down to thirty percent strength, and the 37th is trying to get back to Tabuk, but our air assets keep hitting him," General Schwarzkopf outlined, pausing for all that to seep in.

After a moment, he continued, "His second line of defense stretches across Saudi from Buraydah on the west to Al Hofuf in the east. Across this belt he has the 1st Republican Guard Corps with five divisions stretching from the coast west to Haradh and connected to the 4th Iraqi Corps with eight divisions stretching from Haradh to

Buraydah. Only the 1st Republican Guard Corps are the elites, the rest being Iraqi Army forces and not up to par in training and equipment with the Republican Guard divisions. Lastly, the 7th Iraqi Corps is sitting in Kuwait with eight divisions, doing nothing." Pausing again, Schwarzkopf opened a water bottle and took a long pull.

"He initially enjoyed air superiority but has been whittled down in size. Our pilots are better trained and have better aircraft and a logistic maintenance program to keep them in the air. We're pretty sure that some of their aircraft are being flown by Soviet pilots that have turned mercenary. We know there are some Soviet advisors with their air-defense forces as well as with naval forces. They'll be treated like any other prisoners of war. I can say with certainty that we have air parity at a minimum and superiority in most cases. This air campaign that he just attempted hurt a bit but didn't cripple us in logistics or combat power. We will, on the other hand, show him what an air campaign looks like.

"His naval forces at present control the Gulf only because he has, along with the Iranians, mined the Strait. We have determined the path through those minefields and will shortly commence clearing a wider path through those minefields. In conclusion, gentlemen, we know his disposition of forces, we know his status of logistics, and we know the combat power of each of his divisions and air force." Schwarzkopf paused to take another drink of water.

"Next slide," the general called, and another acetate sheet dropped down with blue markings indicating friendly forces maneuver. "Gentlemen, our mission is to eject Iraqi forces from the UAE, Saudi Arabia and Kuwait. Phase one of this mission will eject Iraqi forces from the UAE and inflict heavy damage on the second defensive belt prior to the arrival of ground forces. We will continue to destroy the Iraqi Air Force and sweep the Iraqi Navy from the Gulf. On D-Day, we

521

are launching our air campaign, concentrating on his command and control facilities with cruise missiles, his logistic centers with heavy bombers, and his airfields with our fighter aircraft. At D plus three, naval forces will clear the Strait of Hormuz and move into the Gulf, isolating the coast of the UAE and destroying any Iraqi naval vessels found. Prior to commencing our ground attack, the Air Force will concentrate our heavy bombers on these front-line forces in the UAE. When we're sufficiently satisfied that we have rendered him ineffective, we'll launch our ground assault. When the ground attack kicks off, our air campaign shifts to the second line of defense: the 1st Republican Guard Corps. Close-air support aircraft will support the ground assault and hit the front-line troop positions.

PHASE 1

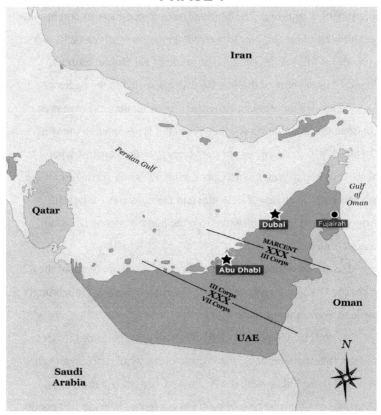

We launch our ground assault with the 1st Marine Division in the north to seize the airport at Fujairah and attacking along the Fujairah to Malha road. We expect light resistance around Fujairah. This will put them against the 10th Iraqi Armoured Division. III Corps makes a supporting attack with TF Host Nations attacking south of Al Ain to fix enemy forces there while the 3rd and 4th Egyptian divisions attack the 17th Iraqi Division. The 50th Armored Division and the 1st British Division attack to destroy the 49th Iraqi Infantry Division. The main effort is VII Corps in the south, who attacks through the 45th Iraqi

Infantry Division and destroys the 52nd Armoured Division. On the morning of D plus one, 2nd Marine Division conducts an amphibious assault west of Dubai, blocks westward movement and attacks to join up with 1st Marine Division," Schwarzkopf said to the sound of "oorah!" from some of the Marine officers seated in the audience.

"Once we have crushed the Iraqi forces in the UAE, we prepare to continue the attack north towards Kuwait." He pointed to the west. "On D-Day, XVIII Airborne Corps continues to defend against what's left of the 2nd Republican Guard Corps, with TF Saudi consisting of the 8th and 10th Mechanized Brigades and the remnants of the 45th Armored Brigade. One brigade from the 82nd Airborne Division conducts an airborne drop—"

He was interrupted by a loud "hooah!" from members of the 82nd Airborne Division in response to the Marines' "oorah!" This brought a smile to Schwarzkopf's face.

"—to seize the port located here. This must be seized intact to support future operations. One brigade of the 82nd will conduct an over-the-shore linkup with the Airborne force while a third brigade clears the coastal road to said port. On order, one brigade will conduct an airborne assault to seize the airport in Tabuk. Simultaneously the XVIII Airborne Corps attacks to destroy forces in sector and seize Tabuk with the 29th and 28th Mechanized Divisions. 101st Airborne will air-assault to establish forward operating bases to supply fuel to the advancing mechanized divisions, clear choke points and destroy enemy forces in sectors terminating in an air assault to sieze the military compound in Tabuk. The end of phase one is complete with the seizure of Tabuk and the destruction of enemy forces in the UAE," Schwarzkopf concluded and placed the pointer against the map board.

"Gentlemen, I don't have to tell you this will be a long road back to the Iraqi border. We will rely heavily on our air and naval forces to clear the skies and support the attack. I have no doubt that we will be victorious in our endeavor, but I also want to accomplish this with minimal US casualties. In addition, let's be cognizant of the civilian populations and inflict a minimal amount of pain on them. We're here to liberate them, not hurt them. Attempt to avoid damaging infrastructure as best you can. I do not want to win the battles but lose the war.

"Alright, gentlemen, you have the overview for this campaign. More detailed instructions will be coming down in the weeks to come. Tomorrow I fly back to the States to brief the President and the Joint Chiefs. For right now, keep doing what you are doing. Oh, and one last thing—this is classified top secret, so I best not be hearing about it in the chow line. Am I clear?"

"*Yes, sir!*"

Chapter 62
Presidential Approval

5 March 1991
Situation Room, White House
Washington, D.C.

Everyone in the Situation Room listened in silence. There were no comments made by anyone. Occasionally the President would interrupt with a question, but generally the question required a short answer. Powell and the rest of the Joint Chiefs remained stoic and quiet. This was serious business and not time for grandstanding. That time had long passed, and they all knew it. Most had received a condensed version of the brief already, and questions had been asked and answered.

"Mr. President, if you have no questions, that concludes this brief," Schwarzkopf said, pulling his notes together.

"Thank you, General, for making this presentation yourself. Let me ask, on a scale of one to ten, how confident are you about this plan?"

"Nine," Schwarzkopf said without hesitation.

"Why not a ten?" the President asked with a puzzled look.

"Because the enemy has a vote, Mr. President. They always do, and we believe we have considered all his votes. I'm confident we will drive him out of the UAE and Saudi as well as Kuwait. My goal is not only to do that but to render his army incapable of coming back and doing it again in six months," Schwarzkopf explained.

"Do you believe you have the ground forces to do that?" the President asked.

"Enough ground forces, no, Mr. President," Schwarzkopf replied but quickly added, "but we don't fight just as an army of soldiers but as a combined armed force comprised of ground, sea and air forces capable of overwhelming and destroying his forces. Ground power alone will not do it. It takes a combined armed force to do it, and we have that with the combination of all three. Are you asking if I would like to have more ground forces? The answer is yes. Are you asking if I need more ground forces? The answer is no. Our plan relies on our Air Force and Navy assets to clear the skies. With Marine aviation and some air and naval ground attack fighters, we'll be able to wipe the Iraqi ground forces out as our own ground forces advance to contact. Just prior to our invasion, we're going to launch an aerial campaign like nothing seen since World War II and we're going to pound his troops into the Stone Age while destroying his logistics needed to support those troops."

The general paused for a moment as he surveyed the room before adding, "From what we've seen, we have a better trained, better educated, and better equipped as well as better supplied and highly motivated ground force that can and will overwhelm the opposing forces. Iraq's recent combat experience was against the human waves of Iranian soldiers. His next experience will be against the armor and mechanized wave of our coalition forces," Schwarzkopf concluded.

Turning in his chair, the President looked to an adjacent screen where Mrs. Margaret Thatcher was seated. "Madam Prime Minister, your thoughts, please," the President asked.

"I believe our forces are in very capable hands at this time, and General Schwarzkopf has my full confidence and support in this endeavor. Thank you, General Schwarzkopf," the Prime Minister said graciously.

527

"Thank you, Madam Prime Minister," the general responded.

Turning back to face General Schwarzkopf, the President stood and approached with his right hand extended. "General, execute the plan, and may God be with you."

Invitation to Continue the Action

We hope you have enjoyed reading *Desert Shield*. If you are hungry for more, you are in luck. The next book of the Crisis in the Desert series, titled *Desert Storm*, will be released December 14, 2021, and is currently available for preorder.

About the Authors

Matt Jackson enlisted in the US Army in 1968 and served on active duty until 1993, when he retired as a colonel. In the course of his career, he commanded two infantry companies, one being an airborne company in Alaska. He also commanded an air assault infantry battalion during Operation Desert Shield/Storm with the 101st Airborne Division. Staff assignments with troops included operations officer in an air cavalry squadron, operations officer in a light infantry battalion, and executive officer of an air assault infantry brigade. When not with troop assignments, Matt Jackson was generally found teaching tactics at the United States Army Infantry Center or the United States Army Command and General Staff College, with a follow-on assignment as an exchange instructor at the German Army Tactics Center. His last assignment was Director, Readiness and Mobilization, J-5, Forces Command, and Special Advisor, Vice President of the United States. Upon retiring from the US Army, he went into private business. He and his wife of fifty years have two sons, both Army officers.

Matt Jackson has written three other books in the *Undaunted Valor* series: *An Assault Helicopter Unit in Vietnam, Medal of Honor*, and *Lam Son 719*. His next book will be *Undaunted Valor: Easter Offensive*, which will be released in 2022.

****

James Rosone started his military career in 1996 as a communications specialist with a self-propelled 155mm howitzer unit. He was later crossedtrained into becoming a forward observer for the artillery guns. James then transitioned from the Army to the US Air Force in 2004, where he went on to serve as a human intelligence collector. In this job, he worked as an interrogator throughout Operation Iraqi Freedom, interrogating senior-level Al Qaeda members and other terrorists, insurgents, and former regime members.

James would go on to work as a government contractor in intelligence for the Department of State and Defense in the Middle East, Eurasia, and Europe, continuing the hunt for Islamic extremists, transnational terrorists, and criminal organizations. In 2015, James began writing as a form of PTSD therapy, publishing his debut novel in 2016. He has since gone on to publish more than twenty highly successful books in the thriller and science fiction genres. James's most current military thriller series is *The Monroe Doctrine*, which explores what would happen if China were to encroach on countries in the Western Hemisphere.

James now works to mentor other veterans struggling with PTSD through writing therapy, teaching them how to become successful authors so that they can write to support their families. You can learn more about James at his website, www.frontlinepublishinginc.com or join his mailing list to stay up-to-date on new releases or sales.

Acknowledgements

I would like to thank all the great leaders and soldiers I served with during Desert Shield and Desert Storm. There were so many, but I'd especially like to acknowledge the soldiers and noncommissioned officers of the 3rd Battalion, 327th Infantry. The Army authorized me to command the battalion, but they gave me the privilege of command. Great leaders provided guidance and mentorship throughout my time, and I am forever grateful to General Binford Peay, CG, 101st Airborne Division (Air Assault), and General Hugh Shelton, Assistant Division

Commander for Operations, 101st Airborne Division (Air Assault). I would be remiss if I did not thank General Mike Oates, who was a major during Operation Desert Shield/Storm in the division. All are retired now, but still provide guidance and mentorship to today's leaders. Lastly, I would like to thank my wife who held up the homefront for the past fifty years, and my two fine sons that carried on the family tradition.

--Matt Jackson

CPSIA information can be obtained
at www.ICGtesting.com
Printed in the USA
LVHW021539010322
712307LV00013B/856